JUSTICE FOR ABBY

BOOK SIX IN THE *BODYGUARDS OF L.A. COUNTY* SERIES

CATE BEAUMAN

Justice For Abby

Visit Cate at www.catebeauman.com
Follow Cate on Twitter: @CateBeauman
Or visit her Facebook page:
www.facebook.com/CateBeauman

First Print Edition: April 2014

ISBN-13: 978-1496094254
ISBN-10: 1496094255

Editor: Invisible Ink Editing, Liam Carnahan
Cover: Demonza
Formatting: Rachelle Ayala

DEDICATION

To Dave and Karen. It's a lucky woman who can say she not only likes but loves her in-laws.

Chapter One

May 2014

"Abby, wake up. We're stopping in a second."

Abby stirred as Alexa's voice floated through her dreams. She blinked several times, yawning huge and stretching in the passenger's seat as the warm winds blew through her sister's open window. "Where are we?"

"About sixty miles from Hagerstown."

"Thank god." She sat up further, glancing out at lush green trees and the endless stretch of farmland, eager to be home. "It feels like we've been in the car for *hours*."

Alexa rolled her eyes, chuckling. "Ab, we've been driving for less than four, and you've slept almost the whole time."

She smiled. "Some of us require plenty of beauty sleep."

Scoffing, Alexa slid her a glance. "I've gotta make a pit stop. My eyeballs are practically floating. See?" She quickly turned her head, widening her huge, lake-blue eyes, illustrating her point. "Can you wake Livy?"

Abby peered in the back, her heart melting as sweet little Livy slept with her mouth hanging open, clutching her favorite stuffed frog while her blond pigtails danced in the breeze. "Let's let her sleep. She wore herself out. I'll stay with her while you do your thing."

Alexa looked in her rearview mirror and put on her turn signal, preparing to take the exit. “It’s getting dark. There aren’t many cars in the lot.”

Abby studied the mostly empty rest stop and thick tree cover blocking her view of the interstate, unfazed by Alexa’s perceived sense of danger. She was too used to her sister’s overly precautious nature to do more than glance Lex’s way and blurt out, "worry wart alert, worry wart alert,” in her teasing robot voice, grinning when her sister tossed her a baleful look. “Just go pee, Lex. Livy and I’ll wait here with the windows up and doors locked. Nothing’s going to happen in the five minutes you’ll be gone.” She shook her head, rolling her eyes, and reached in her purse, grabbing her phone. “I’ll even punch nine-one-one into my cell. I’ll keep my thumb hovered over ‘send’ the entire time.” She held up her cell phone with her thumb above the button in demonstration as Alexa pulled into a spot close to the bathrooms.

“I’m sorry, did you say you wanted to walk back?” Alexa smiled as she unfastened her seatbelt. “You sure you don’t want to come?”

“Pee already, Lex,” Abby said with an exasperated laugh. Lex was already wound tight, and their mini-vacation was barely over.

“Okay, be right back.” She rolled up her window and secured the locks as she got out, gently shutting the door.

Wincing, Abby glanced at Olivia, making certain the quiet slam didn’t wake her niece, and turned, huffing out a breath as Alexa hesitated, looking toward the car. “Oh, Lex, *go*.” She made an exaggerated go-ahead motion with her hands. If her big sister wasn’t worrying about something, she wasn’t breathing.

Sighing, she watched Alexa pull open the door to the pretty brick building. Then she turned her focus to her cell phone, her thumbs flying over the keys, adding 'to-dos' to her growing list. The week away had been fun, but now she had a million things to take care of before her long-awaited flight to LA. Two more weeks and she was outta here, off to nail down her dream job with Lily Brand. Her college diploma was hot off the press, but she'd been preparing for this interview since she sewed her first stitch with Gran's old Singer years ago.

Lily Brand wanted her, and she was more than thrilled to work for one of the world's hottest designers and philanthropists...for the time being, but in three years everyone would be wearing Abby Harris designs. She would be a household name. Now she just needed to convince Lex to put her money pit on the market and move herself and Livy out to Los Angeles so they could all be together. Life would officially be—

Something tapped against the backseat window, interrupting her thoughts.

Frowning, she turned, gasping as she stared at the gun pointing at Livy through the glass. "Oh my god," she trembled as her phone fell from numb fingers. Her gaze darted from the mean eyes behind the black mask to the weapon.

"...door."

His mouth moved, yet she heard nothing but the rapid pounding of her heart as she struggled to think. Was this really happening? Yes, of course it was. Livy needed help. They *all* needed help. The police would—

The muscled man smacked the pistol against the glass, making her jump. "Open the door," he said in a thick Russian accent.

She was going to refuse, but then she spotted another hulking man skirting around the gray van parked in the next row, coming their way.

The masked stranger at the window struck the glass harder, settling his finger on the trigger.

"Okay. Don't hurt her," she shuddered out, groping for the handle, too afraid to take her eyes off the weapon mere inches from Livy's head. "Don't hurt her," she repeated, remembering to release the lock, and opened her door.

"Unfasten your seatbelt slowly. Don't try anything funny."

Swallowing, she complied as she darted a look at the keys in the ignition. If she could somehow get in the driver's seat... But the gun aimed at her niece left her no choice but to comply with his demands.

"Auntie Ab?" Olivia stirred in the backseat.

She didn't dare look at the groggy angel calling her name. "It's okay, Livy. Go back to sleep."

"Where are we, Auntie Ab?"

"Livy, go back to sleep," she struggled to say over the terror and tears clogging her throat. "Shut your eyes—" Before she could say more the man grabbed her arm, yanking her from her seat. "Let me *go*!" She fought to free herself from his biting, meaty grip.

"Auntie Ab!" Olivia started to cry. "Auntie Ab, come back!"

Both men took hold, one gripping her shoulders, the other her ankles, whisking her away from Alexa's car. "Help! Help me!" she screamed uselessly, kicking her feet, twisting and turning, trying desperately to free herself.

"Shut up, bitch!"

She ignored the nasty demand and wretched

stench of cigarette breath, fighting for her life as the restroom door opened and Alexa stepped from the building.

"Help me, Lex! Help me!"

Alexa stopped dead, blinked, then ran forward. "Stop it! Leave her alone! Abby! Abby, no!"

"Alexa!" She fought harder as the men moved closer to the open doors at the rear of the van. "No! Please, no!" she begged, trying to claw, bite, anything as they stepped up into the vehicle.

The man at her feet dropped her legs with a jarring thud and shut them in the dark, stuffy vehicle, silencing Alexa's terrified shouts.

"Let me *go*." Abby squirmed in her captor's vise-like grip while the other man hustled to the cabin, driving off with a screech of tires. "Let me go," she repeated, fighting to breathe as her abductor increased the crushing pressure of his arms around her chest, restricting her movements further.

"Shut up."

"Who are you? Why are you doing this? Please let me go. I won't say anything. I'll pretend this never happened."

"Shut *up*!" He squeezed her until she gasped, certain he would crack her ribs. He gave her a violent shake and shoved her to the hard, unforgiving floor.

Heated tingles surged through her elbow, numbing her entire arm. She cried out in unspeakable agony, clutching at the bone, holding her body tense against the pain and a strong bought of nausea. Taking several deep breaths, she gingerly bent the tender joint, finding a glimmer of relief when she realized it wasn't broken. All of her limbs needed to be in working order if she had any hope of getting away.

She glanced up as the man pulled off his mask, revealing short black hair and clean-shaven olive skin. He might have been handsome before the broken nose and jagged scar along his right cheekbone, but as he stopped his movements and stared at her through glaring brown eyes all she saw was a monster.

"You like what you see?" He sent her a cruel smile.

"Why are you doing this?" she whispered as she scooted further back against the side of the vehicle, wanting to put as much space between herself and the vile stranger as she could. "You have the wrong person," she struggled to say, fighting to school her rapid breathing in the stuffy confines.

"Don't talk."

"What are you going to do to me?"

He reached over and grabbed her jaw, squeezing. "I said shut *up*."

She did her best not to whimper as his fingers bit into her skin with punishing pressure.

"You listen to the things I tell you." He pulled his hand away.

Her face pulsed where he'd undoubtedly left bruises, but she didn't dare rub at the ache as he studied her in the shadows

The driver said something in Russian and the van slowed. The man at her side answered in his foreign tongue, still staring at her. Seconds later the vehicle bumped down what could only be a dirt road, jostling Abby about. She sat up, glancing at the back double doors, trying to spot the release latch. There had to be one. There had to be a way out of this nightmare.

"You think you will escape?"

Her eyes darted to the vile creature close by.

"You will never get away. You should get used to this."

She *would* get away, or die trying. Surely she was dead if she did nothing at all. She looked back to the door as the van slowed, then stopped. A fresh wave of dread sent her heart on another race when the driver got out. What were they going to do to her, rape and kill her? Would they bury her so Alexa never found her body? Her sister's terrified eyes flashed through her mind, and she resolved right then and there to fight until they robbed her of her last breath.

She scrutinized the door again, finally making out the latch as she devised her plan. If she could just get the door open, she would run for her life. Her five-four frame was trim and compact. She could *move* if she had to, and she definitely had to.

Her captor at her side turned, reaching into the cabin, and she saw her chance. It was now or never. She scooted toward the doors and reached for the handle just as the back opened.

"Going somewhere?" Dark brown eyes smiled into hers. The driver's face was handsome but his eyes cruel—just like his partner's. "Dimitri, I believe we have a flight risk."

"*Nyet*. She will behave or she will be punished. She will never get away, because I will always find her." He bent low as he walked to the doors, eyeing Abby the entire way. He stopped in front of her, and his big hand shot out, slapping her.

The metallic taste of blood filled her mouth as she jerked back, crying out from the shocking sting on her cheek.

Dimitri gripped her face, pulling them nose-to-nose. "Do you understand, little bitch?"

She blinked as tears fell, breathing in stale cigarettes.

He squeezed harder. "I asked if you understand?"

"Yes," she choked out, sure her jaw would disintegrate if he didn't release her from his hold.

"Good." He nodded. "Now get in the car, or I will discipline you again."

She was afraid he would knock her unconscious if she didn't obey, so she walked along the rutted road, staring at the roof of a beautiful old farmhouse peeking over the trees less than a quarter mile away. Safety was so close, yet so far away as she moved closer to the black Honda with tinted windows, noting the Maryland plates.

Dimitri opened the back door, giving her a violent shove to her seat as he slid in next to her. She inched her way over to her side and slowly reached for the handle, ready to make her escape.

"It's locked, but this is a nice try."

Abby glanced at Dimitri as her hopes of running withered. With nothing else to do, she moved closer to her window, watching the sun vanish along the horizon, wondering if she would be alive when it rose again tomorrow.

"We are late." The driver got in, started the car, and drove away.

Late for what? Where were they taking her now?

Dimitri said something in Russian, and Abby strained to listen, catching the words 'Victor' and 'Hartwell' in his rapid speak.

The driver grunted, tossing something over the seat.

"Put this on your head," Dimitri demanded.

Abby stared at the poorly sewn black fabric he held up. How would she see where they were going? How would she get help, which was exactly the point she supposed.

"You do not listen well. They said you were

beautiful and smart, but I'm thinking this might be wrong. Your mind does not seem as good as your looks."

She didn't know what he was talking about. Who were 'they'? "You have the wrong person," she tried again even though it was useless. She had seen their faces. For that alone she would die.

"You are the right one. Trust me. Now put it on."

She hesitated, hating the idea of losing her ability to see where they were taking her.

He grabbed a handful of her waist-long black hair, yanking her face to his. "I said put it on."

She stifled her yelp, took the bag, and covered her head, blinking in the darkness. She gripped her clammy hands in her lap as the pitch black left her more vulnerable than she already was. Goosebumps puckered her skin as she moved closer to her door, not wanting Dimitri's large frame touching her exposed arms in her tank top or her legs in her denim short shorts. She was suddenly aware of how much of her was uncovered. A rush of panic tightened her throat, making it impossible to swallow in the stifling confines, so she breathed deep, concentrating on the bold, berry scent of her shampoo, finding comfort in the familiar.

"We will work on your listening." His big hand cuffed the side of her head.

She flinched and held herself rigid, ready, waiting for the next blow she couldn't see coming while the car remained quiet and time stretched out endlessly. An hour passed, or maybe two, her mind racing the entire time, trying to comprehend what was happening. Where did these men come from? Were Alexa and Olivia okay? Would she see her family again?

The vehicle slowed, turned right, and came to a stop.

"Keep the bag on your head and do what Victor and I tell you," Dimitri said close to her ear.

Her heart ramped up to slamming, and her eyes darted about as the driver—Victor, apparently—got out. Seconds later her door opened. "Out." Victor grabbed her arm and yanked her from her seat, pulling her forward. "Walk."

Abby tripped several times as she hurried along the uneven surface, listening to the crickets singing and children playing far in the distance. A car wooshed by somewhere beyond. The sounds reminded her of a quiet neighborhood on an early summer evening.

"Go up steps." Victor yanked on her arm.

She used her free hand to catch herself on the concrete before she fell.

"You idiot. Go up three."

She counted three steps and was brought inside, catching glimpses of glossy pine floors and gorgeous oriental rugs through the opening at the bottom of her makeshift mask. The soles of her sandals slapped against the solid wood as she kept her free hand out in front of her, afraid she would crash into something as she struggled to keep up with Victor's pace. Another door opened, and musty air wafted into the bag.

"Go down steps. Twelve."

She pressed her palm to the cool stone at her left, steadying herself as she was pulled down the stairs, counting as she went.

The black bag was ripped from her head, along with several strands of her hair. Abby blinked against the bold light of the naked bulbs hanging from the low ceiling. She glanced around the dingy space in shock as her gaze traveled from girl to girl—six young teens, dirty, bruised, and malnourished, staring up at her through bland eyes while they sat or lay on filthy mattresses on the dirt floor. "What—"

"In." Victor shoved Abby into a small, windowless room, slamming the door, locking her in with a rusty scrape of something sliding against the heavy metal barrier.

She walked on shaky legs to the wooden chair in the corner and collapsed to the uncomfortable seat, clutching her arms around her waist, shivering as she bit hard on her bottom lip while tears rained down her cheeks. Where *was* she? What was this place? She shuddered, remembering six sets of listless eyes holding hers. Nothing good was happening here.

She covered her face with trembling hands and gave into her sobs, relieving the worst of her dread, wishing for nothing more than to be home with Lex and Livy. Thinking of her sister and niece, she forced away her tears, taking several deep breaths of stale air. If she wanted to see her family again she needed to pull herself together. She couldn't get herself out of this—whatever *this* was—if she didn't think. There had to be a way out. Her eyes darted around the barely lit space, searching for a weapon, another exit, anything.

The door opened, and she rushed to her feet as a tall, well-built man stood haloed in the beam of light from the room beyond. Abby blinked as he stepped forward. "Renzo?" She bolted from the corner and fell against her friend's firm chest as a wave or relief flooded her. "Oh, thank god."

His strong arms wrapped around her.

"I'm so glad you're here. I don't know what's going on. I need help. Can you help me?"

"What happened?" He eased her back some, but she refused to release him from her grip.

"My family—we were on our way home from Virginia Beach. We stopped at a rest area, and two men grabbed me and brought me here."

"You were with your sister and niece?"

"Yes, Alexa and Olivia. I think they're okay, but I need to call and make sure. Will you get me out of here?"

"Of course."

She could hardly believe she was leaving. "Thank you. Thank you." She hugged Renzo again as tears of gratitude flowed free. "I knew this had to be some sort of mistake."

"Come on, let's get you home." He wrapped his arm around her waist and walked with her to the door. "Oh, wait." He stopped.

"What?"

"I can't let you go."

"What—what do you mean?" She freed herself from his grip, studying Renzo's handsome Italian features and dark brown eyes laughing into hers as they had many times while they'd talked and joked at numerous fashion events. But something was different. Renzo was suddenly altogether different.

"You'll be staying here until we send you somewhere else." He shrugged, as if what he said was no big deal.

"Renzo, what are you talking about? I can't stay here. I don't want to stay here. My sister will be worried sick." Her voice started to rise, as did her fear.

He gripped her shoulders and yanked her forward. "Watch your tone."

"I'm stuck in some basement against my will with several girls who look like they're a breath away from death. Don't tell me to watch my tone."

He grabbed her hair close to the scalp, jerking her head back. "Speak to me like that again. I dare you."

She sucked in a shuddering breath through her teeth. Who was this man? Who was this stranger? "Renzo, I have to go. I have job interviews—"

"You have a new career. You can thank me later." He leaned forward, closing several inches of distance, pressing his lips to hers.

She moved back as far as his hand in her hair would allow. "Renzo, stop."

"Don't play shy, Abby. I've been waiting for a taste of you for the last five months." He released and pulled her closer as he slid his hand down her back and over her ass. "*Fuck*, yeah. You feel just like I thought you would—tight, firm. You're fucking hot, Abby. Those dark blue eyes, all that long black hair, your body." He ground himself against her as he backed her to the wall. "Do you know what hot girls want?"

She pushed at his chest as he held her in place. "Stop, Renzo."

"You didn't answer the question, so I will." He caught her full bottom lip between his teeth. "You want to be fucked." He pulled her magenta top from her shorts and slipped his hand down the front of her denim bottoms, groaning. "Lace underwear."

She gulped air into her lungs as she attempted to squirm away, her terror growing as she stood pinned and helpless. "Don't. Don't. I thought we were friends."

He stopped his exploration just shy of invading her with his greedy fingers, laughing. "You thought we were friends?" He shook his head. "No, we're definitely not friends. You're a bitch, and that's how you'll be treated." He brought his mouth to her neck, sucking hard, making her gasp with the sharp pain. "I've been waiting for the right moment to bring you aboard. The first time I saw you at the Christmas show, strutting around the runway in those hot little clothes you designed, I knew you would be perfect."

She stared up at the person who'd fascinated her with his adventures as a fashion photographer, at the "friend" who had made her laugh and taken her to dinner, fully understanding that this man lording over her was the epitome of evil. "What are you going to do to me?"

He grinned. "So many things, but that's personal. Let's get down to business." He molded his palms to her small, firm breasts, squeezing.

"You're hurting me." She tried to pull his painfully probing hands away.

"You'll learn to like it rough." He squeezed again as he smiled.

She shoved at his shoulder. "Renzo—"

"You're going to be my personal assistant—take care of the books, dole out the girls to customers, make them dresses and costumes when we send them off to our high-paying clientele."

She froze, her stomach churning, as she digested the details of her new 'job.' "You want me to help you prostitute women?"

He shook his head. "Our clients don't like women."

She thought of the sickly teens in the room beyond, utterly disgusted. "No. No, I won't do this."

"You absolutely will." He slammed her against the rough concrete, scraping the skin of her back as his hands found their way under her tank top, shoving up her bra, holding her in place with his hips as she attempted to evade him. "You'll dance too and show off these magnificent titties." He pinched her nipples until she clenched her jaw. "You're mine. You'll do exactly what I say, when I say it." He yanked her away from the concrete blocks. "Because if you don't, we'll grab your sister and that brat you talk about all the fucking time."

Her fear magnified as she thought of Alexa and sweet little Livy alone and vulnerable in the tiny house tucked among the woods. "Leave—leave them alone."

"You remember the rules, do what I say, and they'll be fine. You've got yourself a great career with the ring. You even get a room upstairs if you behave. And no one else will touch you but me." He leaned forward and kissed her again, snaking his tongue into her mouth.

She cringed, turning her head.

"Kiss me."

She stood still, too terrified to move.

"You just don't learn, do you?" He slapped her and shoved her to the ground. "You *will* do what I say."

Abby held her throbbing jaw, quietly crying as she sat in the firmly packed dirt.

Renzo opened the door. "Better get some sleep. Tomorrow you'll be learning the ropes in the office and at the club." He locked her in the small, stuffy space with a slide of something against the door and shut off the light, leaving her huddled on the floor in the dark.

Chapter Two

Los Angeles
December 2014

Abby set her glass on the waiter's tray as he walked by. She returned his polite smile, inching her way closer to the flashing lights of Ethan's vintage arcade games—the only empty corner in the bustling game room. The Cooke's massive home busted at the seams with everyone waiting to ring in 2015. Bodies bumped and brushed, filling every square inch. Everywhere Abby turned there was another face—thankfully most were familiar.

She made it to her destination, sliding into the spot by the Pac-Man and Donkey Kong machines, smoothing her clinging, short black dress with its plunging backline. Grinning, she watched Olivia weave through the crowds and grab Kylee's hand. Kylee turned and hugged her best friend before the two ran off—pretty, energetic little blonds, laughing on their way to the playroom in matching party dresses she had surprised the girls with.

Abby continued to scan of the noisy masses in search of her sister, pausing when she spotted Wren and Tucker snuggled up, smiling and flirting in their own little world as Tucker boxed his soon-to-be wife against the wall. Morgan walked by with Hunter in-tow, and they stopped to chat with Ethan and Sarah—

so many stunning people in a gorgeous home. Abby treasured the snapshot of normalcy, hugging the moment of utter contentment close as she stood among family and friends, knowing she would never take such simplicities for granted again.

"Here, I brought you a glass of champagne." Alexa sidled up next to her in a dark blue maternity dress, showcasing her growing baby bump. Her flawless skin glowed, as did her bright blue eyes. Her sister was finally happy.

"Thanks." Abby took a small sip as she stepped from her spot, rejoining the chaos. "Where's your glass of juice to ring in the New Year?"

"Hailey's grabbing me one."

Someone bumped Abby, sending her into Alexa's side. She tensed her shoulders, trying to ignore the skittering of unease, and smiled at her sister. "Sorry about that."

"It's really crowded in here. Are you okay?"

Personal space and small spaces in general had been an issue over the last several months, but she could handle this. If she struggled not to bolt from the room, no one needed to know that but her. None of the guests among the walls of the Cooke Fortress were here to harm her. "Yeah, I'm fine. This is fun. Sarah and Ethan know how to throw a party."

"They certainly do." Alexa twisted her waist-length black hair up and off her neck. "Whew, it's hot."

Abby swiped at her own hair she'd chopped to her shoulders hours after her rescue. "Definitely."

"Juice for my lady." Jackson swooped in with a flute of orange juice in one hand and Olivia in his opposite arm.

"Look, Auntie Ab, I have Ginger Ale for the

celebration." Livy held up her plastic cup triumphantly. "Do you want some? I'm sharing. Sharing is a nice thing to do." She beamed her smile, Jackson's smile. She was his mirror image.

Abby helped herself to a small sip of soda. "Thanks, pretty princess." She brushed a finger down her niece's nose. "I thought you were playing with Kylee."

"Hailey's getting Kylee Ginger Ale too."

"I see."

Olivia gasped. "There's Kylee." She squirmed to get down. "I need to *go*, Daddy."

Jackson set Livy on her feet, and she was off.

"How is she still *awake*?" Jackson's blue eyes followed his daughter as he wrapped his arm around Alexa's waist. "I hate to say it, but we may have a future party animal on our hands."

Alexa leaned against Jackson's side. "Hopefully that trait lived and died with you. Maybe you should've napped with Livy before we came over."

He nuzzled her neck. "I guess so."

Abby studied her beautiful sister, at peace and relaxed, and her gorgeous brother-in-law, unmistakably happy—college sweethearts back together after so long.

"The ball's about to drop," someone shouted over the music, conversation, and laughter.

"Ten, nine, eight..." Abby chimed in, grinning at Alexa, taking her hand as the famous Times Square lighted ball made it's descent on the movie-sized screen occupying the back wall. "...seven, six, five, four, three, two, one! Happy New Year!"

Jackson kissed Alexa enthusiastically, then turned to Abby, planting one on her cheek. "Happy New Year, Abby."

She gave him a peck in return and a huge hug, holding on, always grateful to Jackson and Alexa for bringing her home. If they hadn't found her... "Happy New Year."

She hugged Alexa next. "I love you, Lex."

"I love you too."

She eased back, staring into her sister's face, which was almost identical to her own, grinning again, and caught Jerrod looking her way across the room. Her roommate took a sip of water—never alcohol when he was on duty, which was always—and gave her a nod. Abby waved and returned her attention to Alexa. "Here's to a new year."

"It's going to be good, Ab." Alexa gave Abby's arm a gentle squeeze.

"I think you're right." But there were obstacles to face yet.

"I know I am." She kissed her cheek. "I'm going to go find Livy."

"Of course. Send her my way when you track her down."

"Okay." Alexa and Jackson wandered off hand-in-hand.

Abby took another sip of champagne and set her glass on a tray.

"Hey."

She turned as someone tapped her shoulder.

A heavyset man with beer breath grabbed her up in a tight hug, lifting her off her feet. "Happy New Year."

Her heart kicked into high gear, and she automatically shoved at his shoulders. "Don't touch me."

The man released her and shrugged, moving on to Austin and Hailey several steps away. "Happy New

Year, Mamma," he said to Hailey as he patted her ever growing baby belly. "When're you gonna have that kid anyway?"

Hailey laughed. "In March."

"How much have you had to drink tonight, buddy?" Austin asked, winking at Hailey as he slung his arm around her shoulders.

Abby's breath rushed in and out, and she trembled, even as she realized the grabby stranger was harmless. Air. She needed air. "Excuse me. Excuse me," she murmured, fighting her way through the crowds to the open sliding glass doors by the pool. Finally she freed herself from the masses and bee-lined her way to the rail overlooking the cliffs and endless Pacific below, gulping in the cool, biting breeze while the winds tossed her hair around her naked shoulders. The pounding surf soothed with each deep breath in and slow exhalation—a coping strategy she'd mastered. Relaxing her grip on the chilly metal, she rolled her eyes to the stars, seething with frustration. Why did she have to break out in a damn cold sweat every time someone looked at her the wrong way or touched her? Why couldn't she just shrug the moment off the way Hailey did? A year ago she would have. A year ago she would have hugged the guy back.

"Abby?"

She whirled, her guard still up, as Jerrod walked her way. Pasting on a smile, she swallowed the defeat of her latest setback. "Hi."

He stopped in front of her, holding out a bottled water. "I thought you might want a drink."

She took the bottle. "Thanks."

"It's cold out here." He rubbed his hands over the arms of his white button-down. "You've gotta be freezing."

"I think it feels good." Goosebumps covered her skin, but the chilly air was better than the hot, crowded house.

"You're shivering."

"I'm fine." She wasn't ready to go in and deal with the people and noise yet.

"I'll be right back." He walked off, returning moments later with one of Emma's pale pink blankets, settling it around her shoulders.

She pulled the soft, warm fleece tighter against her. "Thank you."

"You're welcome." He skirted around her and leaned his powerful frame against the rail, crossing his muscled arms at his chest as the wind ruffled his short, dirty-blond hair. "Nice night. The stars are bright."

She looked up again at the flecks and twinkles high above. "Mmm. Perfect for ringing in the New Year." She twisted the cap on her bottle. "Happy New Year, by the way."

"Happy New Year." He gave her a rare wink.

She smiled, treasuring the small gesture. Jerrod was friendly and kind but a constant professional. They'd lived together for months, yet she'd never seen him fully relaxed. Sipping her drink, she studied his strong jaw and firm lips complementing a spectacular face, eyeing him as he watched her.

"So, that guy, Darren, he's pretty harmless. He does PI work for Ethan."

Jerrod had seen her shove the PI away. Great. She wrinkled her nose, barely suppressing the need to close her eyes in humiliation. Jerrod had seen her at her worst, but every display of her inner turmoil was a step in the wrong direction. "He surprised me, that's all."

He nodded. "Just thought I'd let you know."

She sipped again and looked down. "Thanks."

"So," he reversed his arms, still resting against his chest, "have you changed our plans for tomorrow yet, or are you going surprise me at the last minute like usual?"

She grinned. "You can relax, big guy. No changes. I'm working from home until two, just like we planned. You can lay around in your boxers and watch football." Not that he would. He would appear from his room clean-shaven and properly dressed in slacks or jeans as he did everyday. In the five months they'd shared her downtown condo, she'd never seen him any other way—except for the rare occasion he wore gym shorts and a t-shirt to the breakfast table. "Is there something else you need to do?"

"Nothing that can't wait."

Relaxed again, she rested against the railing, her arm brushing his.

"Are you ready to head home?"

"Yeah. I need to say goodbye to Lex and Sarah, who didn't drink a drop of champagne tonight, in case you didn't notice." She wiggled her brows.

"I can't say I did."

She raised her brow at him. Jerrod had eyes like a hawk. He saw everything, watched constantly. She pushed herself closer to the man who easily had six inches on her short frame, even when she was in heels, absorbing the warmth of his body, staring into his eyes. "I think Sarah's pregnant."

He blinked, unfazed. "Cool."

She sighed. "Do you ever gossip, speculate, have *any* fun?"

He shrugged. "I guess it depends on what your

definition of 'fun' is. Wondering about things that are none of my business doesn't top my list."

A bouncy pop song played through the outdoor speakers. "What about dancing? Is dancing fun?" She wiggled her shoulders and hips in time with the catchy beat, enjoying herself immensely as she pulled him away from the railing. Teasing Mr. Serious was definitely fun.

He stood still. "Abigail, you know I don't dance. And I'm on duty."

"Uh oh, he's breaking out the 'formal.'" She raised his hand above her head and spun. "Why do I always feel like I'm in trouble when you call me Abigail?" She continued her dance, grinning when he did. "Loosen up. We're at a party."

"*You're* at a party. I'm working."

She shimmied to the left of his solid chest, then to the right. "We're at Fort Cooke. I don't see any evildoers scaling the cliffs." She moved in and bumped her hip to his, looking up into his pretty baby blues, batting her lashes and was rewarded with a chuckle. "Oh. Oh. There it is." She poked him dead center in his firm stomach. "You make me work too hard for those." She tugged on his hand. "Come on, bodyguard. Let's go home."

~~~~

"Abby."

She opened her eyes as Jerrod's voice penetrated her foggy brain. "Hmm?"

"We're here."

She glanced toward the bluish glow on the dashboard, surprised Jerrod was turning into the entrance of the underground garage. "It's already
~~~~

two?"

"We made good time. Traffic wasn't bad."

She sat up in her seat, fixing the cashmere wrap around her shoulders. "I didn't realize I fell asleep."

"You were out before we made it to the highway."

"Huh." She yawned. "It must've been the two glasses of champagne." Stretching, she watched Jerrod scan the shadows in the dimly lit area, as he did every time he pulled his Audi into their reserved spot. He killed the ignition and unsnapped the strap on his holster.

"Ready?"

"Yeah."

He gave her a nod and got out.

She unfastened her seatbelt, waiting for Jerrod to come around to her side. He opened her door, and she stood, blocked by his body, moving just to his right as they walked to the garage-level entrance—a well-choreographed dance they perfected months ago.

She slid her plastic card in the slot, waiting for the door to release. Jerrod pulled on the handle, letting her in ahead of him, covering his holster with a quick slide of his jacket as they stepped into the warmth and comfort of their swank surroundings. Abby's heels clicked against glossy marble as they passed potted palms and bold, modern paintings decorating the walls on their way to the elevators.

"Happy New Year, Mr. and Mrs. T."

"Happy New Year, Moses," Abby smiled, never bothering to correct the night guard's assumptions that she and Jerrod were married or that their last names started with a 'T.' Lily Thomas Brand's name was on the lease, not hers or Jerrod's—just one of the numerous precautions Ethan Cooke Security had set in place.

The elevator doors slid open, and they both stepped in.

"Good night," Jerrod said as the doors shut. He gave her a small smile and pressed the button for the nineteenth floor.

"Ugh, I have to take these *off*." Abby balanced herself with a hand on Jerrod's arm while she slid her feet from her ice pick heels and wiggled her aching toes. "Better," she sighed, standing straight, looking at their distorted side-by-side images in the gold plated metal. "So, do you think you'll ever get sick of being Mr. Thomas? I'm pretty sure Lily doesn't mind, but..." She shrugged, sending a gentle elbow to his ribs.

"I have no problem being the man behind the woman."

She laughed. "Why, Jerrod, you made a joke. Twenty-fifteen is just beginning, and you're already a changed man."

He smiled, flashing her his slightly crooked right incisor.

She smiled back, wanting another one of those grins. There was something about that imperfect tooth among the straight rows of whites that made her melt. "By February you might start loosening your tie." She gave the black silk a tug. "Then I won't know what to do with you."

He chuckled.

"By March you could be walking around the apartment in your pajamas." She gasped and pressed her fingers to her mouth.

The door opened, and he stepped out first. "Who says I wear pajamas?"

She stopped mid-step, pleasantly surprised by his willingness to play. "Mr. Quinn, I do believe I might swoon," she said in her best southern drawl. "I feel the vapors coming on." She fluttered her hand in front of her face.

"We should hurry and get inside then. Dead weight's a bitch to carry, even with someone your size." He slid the key in the lock, opening the door to the well-lit entryway.

Abby walked in before him, passing the wall of glass showcasing the city beyond, tossing her shoes to the floor and her wrap over the closet doorknob. She turned, really looking at the man she shared such a huge part of her life with, suddenly, oddly, and powerfully attracted. Jerrod was hot, there was no doubt about it with his irresistible baby blues, long lashes most women would kill for, and amazing ass in a pair of Levis, but she'd never seen him as anything more than her good friend and bodyguard. Jerrod was just too serious. He wore his professional mask twenty-four seven, which was a major turnoff. But this guy—the one who indulged her pithy comments and laughed, he was irresistible. She'd seen Mr. Funny on occasion, but tonight his grins and rare show of humor sent tingles of lust shooting through her belly—a first in more months than she could remember.

"I'll...be right back," she murmured, surprised, confused, frowning as she headed to the kitchen for a drink and a moment of clarity. She grabbed a glass from the cupboard, opened the refrigerator for the pitcher of filtered water, and poured, shaking her head. The champagne must have packed a bigger punch than she realized.

Shoving the pitcher back in the fridge, forgetting her glass entirely, she started toward the hall, curious to see if her stomach flip-flopped again or if she had fallen victim to a moment of alcohol-induced madness. "You know, I think I might be a little drunk."

He turned as he hung his coat in the closet, shaking his head. "You're not drunk, Abby. You're not even half in the bag."

She studied Jerrod's well-muscled build and sexy face, relieved when her belly remained flopless and she only saw her hunky pal instead of a potential love interest. No madness here, thank goodness, just a silly moment of...whatever that was. "Yeah, I guess."

"I want to show you something." He closed the closet and turned toward the entrance, reaching for a thin bar, sliding it across the dark, glossy wood of their front door, locking it in place with a click.

The slight scrape of metal made her flinch. "What—what is that?"

"A security bar. I installed it today while you were with Jackson and Alexa."

She stared at the white metal trapping her in her own home, swallowing the familiar tang of fear as she stepped back. "Why did you do that?"

"Jackson and I thought we should take a couple of extra measures with the trial getting closer. It's easy to use and unobtrusive." Jerrod pulled the bar up and sent it home effortlessly.

The piece clicked, scraped and clicked again. Abby stepped further away as past and present blurred. *Get in the closet, little bitch. You want to try to run away, you can sleep in here.* The slam of the door and slide of metal trapping her in the dark echoed in her head.

"...wrong?"

Her eyes darted to Jerrod's as sweat dribbled down her back, and she clutched clammy hands together, fighting to keep her breathing steady.

"Abigail." He walked to her. "What's..."

His mouth moved, but she couldn't hear what he was saying over the pounding in her skull.

He touched her arm.

"Don't!" She cringed, crashing into the table behind her, knocking chunky blue candles to the floor as she shoved at his chest. "Don't touch me!"

He held his hands palm up and took a step back. "Take it easy, Abigail. I'm not going to hurt you."

The wave of terror ebbed as the concern in Jerrod's steady eyes registered, and she was immediately ashamed. Jerrod would no more harm her than Jackson. "I'm—I'm sorry."

He slowly lowered his hands. "You don't have to apologize."

"I'm sorry," she repeated and turned, hurrying to her room, closing the door as far as she was able. She sat on her bed and switched on her bedside lamp. Why was this *happening*? Twice in one night she'd freaked. She covered her face with her hands and rocked, fighting back tears of mortification. Not only had she lost it, but she'd shoved Jerrod. Why did she *do* that? With a shake of her head, she let loose a groan of misery. Jerrod had witnessed several of her panic attacks; he'd helped her through many, and she'd *never* lashed out the way she did moments ago.

Sniffling, she dropped her hands and stared out at the city through her enormous windows, rushing to her feet as another thought frightened her. What if she was losing ground? Surely she was. Weighty tension settled along her neck and shoulders as she started pacing. What if Dr. Tate was wrong and she wasn't doing exceptionally well? She'd had her last session with her psychologist just before Thanksgiving. Weeks, only weeks and she was regressing. Dr. Tate had warned of triggers and temporary setbacks, but this had to be more. She'd gone an entire month without a glimmer of panic, and before that a month again. Now in less than two hours she'd had a double-whammy.

She clenched her fists and walked to the window, pressing her head to the cool glass. What if this new pattern wasn't temporary? What if she was finally heading toward the breakdown she'd barely avoided? She slammed her eyes shut as she slipped further into the depths of her fear, thinking of her mother. Maybe this was how everything started for the woman she hardly remembered—the panic attacks and confusion. Would the alcohol abuse come next, and then the stays at the mental health clinic until she decided life was too much to handle and gave up?

At moments like this she understood her mother's decision to end it all, which frightened her further. The idea of being helpless and afraid left her as terrified as the damn bar across the door in the other room. She didn't want to feel weak again or continually fight memories better left buried. She wasn't sure she would be able to find her way out of the hellish pits she'd freed herself from a second time.

"Stop," she whispered on a shaky breath, squeezing her eyes tighter as she visualized her mental stop sign. This type of thinking wasn't productive. With great effort, she emptied her mind, imagining all of her negative thoughts rolling away. Steadier, she turned from the view she loved and moved to the antique cherry writing desk Gran left her—one of the few nice pieces of furniture they'd had in their tiny apartment in Hagerstown—searching for a sketchpad. Drawing new designs for the runway always soothed when she was troubled. Hopefully by the time she finished sketching the flirty skirt she hadn't been able to get out of her mind she would be ready for bed.

With her book in hand she lifted a stack of fabric orders she had yet to sign off on. As she searched for a pencil, she bumped the edge of the small calendar still turned to December on her pegboard. Pausing, she flipped up the page to January and stabbed the pin home, determined to put 2015's rocky start behind her. This year was going to be a hell of a lot better than the last. She was finally going to have her life back. No more working from home or black caps and nondescript jackets every time she and Jerrod wanted to go out. No more babysitters watching her every move or paychecks being transferred from the Lily Brand financial offices to Ethan Cooke Security for her safety or the hundreds of other precautions she and Jerrod took to keep her alive.

Eventually she would be able to walk down the runways again and talk to the press instead of hide in the back, leaving before the showstoppers took their marks for each finale. Hopefully she would be able to join the Lily Brand team at Fashion Week in late February instead of wait from the safety of her condo for everyone's return, like she did in the fall. And maybe this would be the year she finally convinced Lily to help her start the line she'd been obsessed with ever since she wrapped Lex's sprained ankle with their dresses on Zachary Hartwell's roof.

She just had to make it through the trial early next month...unless Renzo's attorneys found another way to stall, which the Federal Prosecutor assured her wouldn't happen, but she would wait and see. The United States versus Lorenzo Cruz and Zachary Hartwell should have come and gone in late

September, then in early October, and again in November, but Zachary's brutal prison-cell slaying left both the prosecution and defense scrambling, and the trial had once again been delayed.

Flipping to the next page on her calendar she stared at the dark black circle highlighting February eleventh and pressed a hand to her jittery stomach as she thought of coming face-to-face with her captor.

She stepped back from her desk, no longer interested in her sketches as she walked to her bed, unzipping her black dress, letting it slide to the floor. She unclasped her strapless bra and replaced her evening clothes with the maroon camisole she'd designed and sewed herself one afternoon while she was bored.

Sliding the covers back, she lay down, resting her head on the pillow, closing her eyes, willing thoughts of Lorenzo from her mind. There would be no more fear tonight. Every night she fell asleep afraid, Lorenzo Cruz won.

Chapter Three

Jerrod stared after Abby as she rushed to her room, trying to figure out what the hell just happened. Abby had gone from fire-eater to terrified so quickly he didn't realize something was up until it was too late. He looked from her partially opened door to the security bar resting in its place, clenching his jaw, recognizing that the latest safety feature must have triggered some sort of flashback. "Way to go, Quinn," he muttered, pissed at himself for putting that wild fear in her big blue eyes. If he'd been paying attention to Abby instead of clicking the bar in and out of place, he would've seen that something was wrong.

"Damn." He shook his head as he picked up the candles and set them back in place. First her encounter with Darren and now this—definitely not what she needed. Abby was doing a lot better, but she was still fragile. Two emotional jolts in one night didn't help, especially when she would see them as setbacks.

Don't! Don't touch me!

Her words echoed through his head, as did her frantic shove to his chest. He'd witnessed some of Abby's worst moments, but this was the first time she'd ever directed her fears toward him.

Swearing again, he shoved his hands in his pockets and stared out at the dozens of partygoers still roaming the streets far below. He should've mentioned his plans to add the bar instead of springing it on her the way he did. He knew better, but Adam's e-mail this afternoon left him more concerned about Abby's safety than her horrific memories.

His old roommate and Fugitive Task Force team member sent word that authorities in Las Vegas were investigating a possible sighting of Victor Bobco. Potential dangers threatened Abby every day. She was a walking target no matter where they went, yet Adam's latest heads-up had him more on edge than usual. Credible tips had come in before, but this threat was different. Vegas was too damn close, and Abby's schedule was ramping up with the trial date moving closer and Fashion Week only six weeks away.

Keeping Abby out of the spotlight was more important than ever. Zachary Hartwell was dead, and Lorenzo Cruz was set to take the fall as the primary leader of the most prolific and powerful sex ring the Mid-Atlantic authorities had ever seen. The Federal Prosecution had been unsuccessful in convincing Blondie Williams, Eric Stevens, or the hordes of other bastards on the ring's payroll to turn state's witness and testify, which left Abby in the hot seat. She alone had toppled the ring with the access she'd had to financial records and the organization's inner workings, which she shared minutes after her rescue.

Brothels and stash houses throughout Baltimore, DC, Philly, and into Jersey had been raided and shut down. Dozens of victims had gone home and several more arrests were made, but two key players remained at large, and they had everything to lose if Abby survived to testify. Victor Bobco and Dimitri Dubov would hunt for her until they silenced the ring's most damaging witness. And Victor was potentially no more than an hour and a half away by plane.

Jerrod pulled a hand from his pocket and rubbed at the back of his neck in an attempt to ease the painful knots of tension. He and Abby had managed to live off the radar after their return from Maryland in July. The Ethan Cooke Security team had taken every precaution Jerrod adhered to during his three-year stint with the US Marshals' WITSEC program after Abby refused witness protection and only agreed to testify if her sister was left out of the entire mess. Even with his extensive experience in witness relocation and re-identification he often wondered if the endless measures taken to keep Abby safe were enough. Her career posed a huge threat no matter how behind-the-scenes she stayed. One reporter or photographer in the wrong place at the wrong time had the potential to end in disaster, but he could hardly expect Abby to hide behind the walls of their condo indefinitely. She couldn't heal if she wasn't allowed to live her life.

Sighing, he glanced toward Abby's room again and started down the hall, wanting to be sure she was okay. He raised his hand to knock and dropped it, watching her pull back her covers in her pretty little nighty designed to make a man *want*. His gaze traveled over well-toned calves and smooth thighs, along her tiny waist, pausing on small, firm breast straining against filmy fabric. He tightened his stomach against the sucker punch of longing, studying her goddess-like face—big blue eyes, flawless skin, her small nose and pouty lips that haunted his dreams. She was hands-down the most beautiful woman he'd ever seen.

He stepped back as she lay in her bed, fighting the need to call her name. She'd come such a long way in the months they'd lived together, but she still struggled, as she had tonight. Abby would bite off her tongue before she let anyone know, but he did. It was impossible to spend twenty-four hours a day, seven days a week with someone and not learn everything about her.

In his almost seven years on the job, whether as Marshal or Close Protection Agent, this was the first time he'd struggled with friendly yet professional boundaries. There was something about Abby that demanded tenderness. Over the last six months he'd tried his best to give her what she needed while fighting to keep his guard up in the name of self-preservation. Abby was his principal. She could only ever be his principal. Her safety and his philosophies demanded it be so.

He looked at Abby once more as she settled against her pillow. Turning, he walked to the next room over and closed his door. He loosened his tie and unbuttoned his shirt as he stared out the massive wall of windows, wondering how long she would fill his thoughts before he was finally able to sleep.

~~~~

The blasting techno beat pulsed in Victor's chest and feet as he descended Club Tronic's stairs to the basement. Luka followed close behind.

"You're sure it is her?" he asked.

"Yes. The tip was good. She was working at the department store in Boulder City. Anton grabbed her on her way home."

Victor stepped into the crowded room, walking past boxes of assorted liquors stacked to the ceiling. He smiled, savoring the rush of relief, eager to exact
~~~~

his revenge as he studied the woman they'd been looking for. She sat in the metal folding chair in a white blouse and navy trousers, quietly sobbing, visibly shaking with her hands bound behind her back and her long black hair cascading from the bag covering her head.

He stopped in front of her, lording over the bitch who had ruined everything. "You hid well." Gritting his teeth, he let his hand fly across her face. He nodded his satisfaction as she yelped her surprise and fell from her chair, landing with a nasty thump on the dirty concrete. He crouched down next to her, close to her ear. "Dimitri told you we would always find you, and I'm now here."

She breathed out primal grunts of pure terror, and he laughed, pulling the burlap from her head. He blinked, surprised by the black eye and her swollen, bloodied mouth.

"She fought me," Anton supplied.

He frowned, grabbing her chin, yanking her face up for closer inspection as his momentary relief vanished into disbelief. "You idiots! This is not Abigail Harris!" He rushed to standing, blinded by a wave of pure fury. "How do you make such stupid mistakes?"

"I followed the tip!" Anton shouted.

Victor pulled his gun free, firing twice into Anton's chest, making the woman scream. "This is what you get for being dumb."

Anton clutched at his wounds, gasping and gurgling, falling back into the stacks of boxes, creating a cascade of broken glass as he collapsed to the floor.

"Idiot!" Victor shouted, directing his temper toward Aleksey. "You know what she looks like. And you." He pointed the gun at Luka. "She was in your brothel!"

"Victor, it has been months. We are working off our memories."

"And pictures!"

"She looks much like her." He gestured to the woman. "She is badly beaten."

Victor glanced down at her raw face in disgust. "But it is *not* her."

"It is hard to see through the blood and bruises."

"I could tell right away." He shoved his weapon into the holster. "Dumb shits. No more excuses! I wear disguises and fly here. I risk getting caught because you say you are sure. We cannot make such mistakes. We must find her, or she will send us all to hell!"

"We will find her, Victor," Aleksey assured.

"There is only me and Dimitri left to put this organization back together. Now I have to call and say we do not have her. Get rid of his body."

"And her?" Aleksey gestured to the woman.

Victor stared at the trembling woman curled in a self-protective ball. "I will take care of her." He kicked her leg. "Get up."

"Please don't hurt me," she sobbed.

"Stand."

She struggled to sit up with her hands still bound. "Please don't hurt me."

He knelt down, his patience thin, slapping her. "Stand *up*! You will make this useless trip worth my time."

Tears poured down her cheeks as she got to her knees, then stood on trembling legs.

He grabbed her hair and yanked her head sideways as he pushed her backwards, slamming her into the boxes.

"Please," she whispered.

He gripped her white blouse, ripping the silky

fabric, exposing her breasts in a simple cotton bra. "Your tits are disgraceful." Shaking his head, he tore her clothing for the second time. "Pitiful." He stared at small swells, twisting her nipples as she sobbed. "Shut up. I don't want to hear this. I cannot get hard when you whine."

"I want to go home."

"You will not go home." He unfastened her trousers and pushed his fingers inside her. "Like a desert."

She moved her hips in her attempt to dislodge him. "You're—you're hurting me."

He bunched his fist and plowed it into her stomach, smirking as she crumbled forward on a sharp expel of breath. "That hurts more."

She coughed violently, gasping, and vomited, spewing bile on his shoes.

His breathing grew ragged in his rage, and he fisted his hand again, landing a blow across her face. "Bitch!"

Her head lolled back as she groaned, half conscious.

"Stay awake while I punish you."

"I—"

"Useless whore!" He grabbed her by the neck and shoved her to the floor.

She cried out as her elbow smacked against the concrete.

"Make another sound and I will punish you more." He yanked on her pants and underwear, pulling off her clothing.

"No," she murmured but did nothing to fight as she stared at the ceiling through her battered eyes.

He worked his way into her dryness, finally moving when blood covered him, and he took her in violent thrusts. He gave an unsatisfied grunt as he came. "You are a bad fuck and no use to me."

"Please let me go."

He gripped her face in his hands, staring into her terrified blue eyes, wrenching her neck, causing a quick snap. Standing, he spit on her lifeless body, giving the bitch a kick, and turned. "Get rid of this one too." He zipped and fastened his pants. "We are running out of time." He lit a cigarette, sucking hard, waiting for the rush of nicotine as he glanced from Aleksey to Luka. "The next time my phone rings, you better have the right one, or you two are next." He pulled his phone from his pocket and dialed Dimitri as he climbed the stairs, leaving the remains of his distasteful night behind him.

Chapter Four

Abby stood in her dining room workspace, humming along with Sarah McLachlan's smooth voice crooning through the speakers. She grabbed one of the half dozen pins she held pressed between her lips and secured the clinging, one-sleeved black top above the short denim skirt riding low on her mannequin's hips.

With a tilt of her head she eyed the fit of her sample outfit, making certain her visions on the sketchpad translated well in 'real life.' She stepped back, continuing her scrutiny of the simple yet flirty design. "Perfect," she muttered, smiling, knowing she would see this look, *her* look, gracing the catwalk during one of the industry's biggest weeks. Most of her creations made up Lily's spring and summer collection—a huge step in the right direction and a dream come true, or one of them anyway. Eventually Lily would see that she was ready to take on her own line—the *Escape* line—but first she had to help the team get the upcoming season off the ground.

She unpinned the figure-hugging fabric and walked back to her worktable, marking the small adjustments she'd noted with her model's slim build in mind. She sat in front of Gran's old Singer she'd used since she was a teenager and altered her hems, occasionally glancing up at the bold, waxing moon outside the window. Lifting the lever, she turned the garment and continued with her work, stifling a yawn.

She had yet to sleep—except for the thirty

minutes or so she'd dozed off and dreamt of Margret. She'd woken with a start, her heart aching, her spirit bogged down with the heavy weight of guilt. Somewhere out there, the sweet-faced fifteen-year-old, her favorite of all the victims passing through the raunchy stash house in DC, was still waiting to be found.

I want to go home, Abby. I just want to go home. The words echoed through her mind, and she closed her eyes against the haunting memories of Margret's teary, desperate whispers. How many times had she soothed Margret, promising her that everything would be okay? How many times had she hugged the thin girl, reassuring her that she would find a way to set them free?

But she hadn't.

Dozens of girls had been rescued during the raids in July, but not the one she yearned to save most. Six months had passed without a lead, despite Abby's weekly check-ins with Special Agent Terron through the dummy e-mail account Jerrod had set up. She had little trust for the taskforce and its agents who'd willingly let her rot while they waited for their big break, hoping to bring down Zachary Hartwell, but she needed to do whatever she could to return Margret to her family safe and sound.

I just want to go home. She heard the words again and shook her head, willing Margret's tortured voice away, fully aware that her best efforts might never be enough to bring back Margret.

Sighing, she forced away her troublesome thoughts and focused on her work, sending the needle through fabric, creating her final seam when she heard something clatter down the hall by the bedrooms. Startled, she flinched and glanced at the funky wall clock Wren had helped her pick out for the modern space—six a.m., which meant Jerrod was up working out. He bench-pressed and arm curled, jump roped and squatted, keeping that gorgeous body of his sinfully delicious. Rain or shine, holiday or not, he was up at five forty-five starting his day.

She looked out the window, taking in the endless city lights and stood, needing to get on with her own. She took the skirt off the mannequin and walked with the new top and bottom to the small privacy screen, stripping from her robe and nighty. She fastened on the strapless bra she kept handy and pulled on the new clothes she would dress Monique in for a final fitting once her model finally kicked the flu bug plaguing her.

Sliding on black heels, she made her way to the center of the room, staring into the three-way mirror, studying the way the lines lay on her body. She backed up several steps and moved forward—head and back straight, arms at her sides, one foot crossing in front of the other, strolling down the improvised catwalk, constantly scrutinizing the black fabric clinging to her curves and the short denim slung low over her slim hips, stopping mid-thigh. The 2015 spring/summer line demanded fun and flirty. This number delivered both in spades.

Turning, she stood hipshot, studying her profile from the side, checking for flow. The snug, black fabric stopped just above her belly button, exposing a sexy inch and a half of toned tummy, with dark denim and three-inch heels completing the look. The top would pair well with skinny jeans as well as numerous other options. Versatility was key. She turned again, walked back, and repeated her process, catching Jerrod's eye in the mirror as he stood in charcoal-colored gym shorts and a white t-shirt, drinking a tall glass of water. She averted her gaze with a wince and glanced at the smooth oak floor, struggling with the embers of embarrassment after the way she'd behaved. She met his eyes in the mirror again, trying to gauge him as he took another long guzzle. "Good morning," she tried.

"Morning."

She cleared her throat in the heavy silence. "I thought you might sleep in since we're not going anywhere until this afternoon."

He shrugged. "I slept plenty."

Nodding, she licked her lips, desperate to move past the awkwardness. "Jerrod, I'm sorry about last night...this morning..." She shook her head. "Whenever it was." She turned from the mirror, facing him. "I'm really sorry for everything."

"You don't have to apologize." He set his glass on the white granite countertop. "I already told you that."

"Yes I do." She walked to him, stopping almost toe-to-toe, taking his hand. "I trust you. I feel safe with you." She wrapped her arms around him and rested her head on his chest, finding comfort nestled against his powerful body.

He returned her embrace, hesitantly—like always—holding her to him gently. "Abigail, you don't always have to be strong. You've been through hell. We both know it's going to take some time to work through that."

"But I pushed you." She eased back enough to look him in the eyes. "I shouldn't have done that. You're nothing like the others. I know that. I want you to know that I know that."

"I do." He rubbed rough palms up and down her arms in a rare gesture then stepped away, reaching for his glass.

Warmth hummed along her skin, and she took her own step in retreat, brushing her palms along the path his hands had just taken, attempting to banish the newly familiar sensations. She studied his steady blue eyes and the sexy scruff along his jaw, struggling to ignore the accompanying flutters in her belly.

Jerrod paused with his glass halfway to his mouth. "What?"

"What do you mean, 'what'?"

"You're frowning."

She blinked, standing ramrod straight, realizing she was not only frowning but staring. "Oh. Huh. I don't know." She shook her head and took another step back, dismissing the whole thing as foolishness...or distracted thinking. She brightened as she realized that's exactly what this was. If she was picking apart silly, made up sensations, she wasn't focusing on Margret's heartbreaking situation. Relaxed again, she uncrossed her arms.

He shrugged and drained the last of his drink. "I think I should be the one apologizing. I didn't realize installing the bar would be a trigger. We should've talked about it first."

"No. It's not that big a deal. It's just—I was..." She almost shared her horrors of being trapped in the hot, dark closet for days. She almost admitted that one experience alone was the reason she still couldn't bear to close herself behind her bedroom or bathroom door, but she didn't. Her scars, her problem. Jerrod knew plenty about her situation, but he didn't have to know everything. She could hardly expect him or anyone else to believe she was normal if she bombarded him with another one of her one hundred and one neuroses. "It doesn't matter."

"I can take it off."

She shook her head. "If we didn't need it, it wouldn't be there."

"Abigail—"

No more. "I want to make you breakfast. How about an egg white omelet with spinach, tomato, and a sprinkle of feta?"

He raised his brow. "Do you think I'm foolish enough to turn that down?"

She smiled, relieved that the air was clear and he was going to let the bar issue go. "Give me a minute to change out of one of two thousand-fifteen's hottest summer looks, and I'll get to it."

"Isn't Monique supposed to be wearing that?"

"Yes, but she's sick, and we wear the same size. I wanted to check the fit and make sure I didn't need to make more in-depth alterations."

He looked her up and down. "It's kinda skimpy. And tight."

She beamed. "I know. It's perfect."

"It doesn't exactly scream 'casual day at the office.'"

She laughed, delighted with his critique. "I certainly hope not. This is for the woman who's a little more daring. She would wear this for a night out with the girls or maybe that special guy. It's casual, fun, flirty." She gave him a playful wink and poke to the stomach.

He grinned.

"The sundresses, slacks, and other office attire are hanging with Lily until the show."

"I'll leave the fashion to you."

"And the omelets. Give me just a minute."

"I'm gonna catch a quick shower."

"Let the washing commence. I'll begin my

culinary masterpiece in twenty minutes or less." She walked to the privacy screen, gathered up her nighty and robe, and made her way to her room for a shower of her own.

Thirty minutes later Abby stood in the kitchen in her red tank top and snug black workout pants, singing along with 2014's Top 100 Countdown while she whisked a bowl full of egg whites and one yolk for color. She dumped the eggs in the hot pan and gave her hips a wiggle as she grabbed three slices of bread from the whole grain loaf and popped them into the toaster. She broke into a series of kick-ball-changes, spun, and slid backwards in socks, pulling off a decent moonwalk, whirling when she collided with the solid mass in the center of the kitchen. Smiling, she continued her dance, breathing in Jerrod's fresh, soapy scent, eyeing his still damp hair and freshly shaven face, his Levis and light blue Polo shirt. "I love this song. It screams girl power, ya know?"

"I guess."

"I know it's not all gritty and electric guitar like the stuff you listen to." She rolled her eyes. "No wonder you never smile. You wanna dance?"

"No."

"Aw, come on, big guy." She moved in closer, taking his hands, placing them on her shoulders. "We're perfectly safe here, bodyguard, so let's *mambo*." She settled her hands at his waist and moved backwards with several jerks of her hips, pulling him with her as she broke into the dance. "It's quick, quick, together like this." She stepped forward, crashing into his chest when he made no attempt to reverse his position. Pursing her lips, she shook her head mournfully. "Bump on a log." She turned away to save the eggs from burning. "One of these days I will succeed in teaching you the dance," she said in a thick Spanish accent.

He chuckled as he grabbed two glasses. "Do you want orange juice?"

"Mmm, just a little." She added chopped spinach, tomato, and a sprinkle of feta to the pan and folded the eggs over, well used to omelet preparations. The cheap meal had been a staple in Gran's house. "We're about two minutes away from a five-star breakfast."

"I'm going to get the paper."

"Okie-dokie." She cut off a fourth of the enormous omelet for herself, placing two perfectly cooked pieces on plates, then plucked the toast from the toaster. She brought the dishes with her to the small table instead of the bar where they typically ate. Today was their day off—or mostly. She wanted them to enjoy it.

The door closed, and Jerrod walked to the table, settling in the seat next to her. "Smells good."

She breathed deep. "Mmm."

He cut in and took a bite. "Delicious as always. Thanks."

She savored the fluffy eggs, feta, and veggies on her tongue. "You're welcome."

Jerrod unfolded the paper as she stared out the windows, glancing toward the lights already on in Ethan Cooke Security's thirty-fourth-floor offices five blocks away. She smiled, watching Los Angeles awaken for the day. She loved the city, was fascinated by the people, the buildings, the *energy*. Hagerstown had been a safe, quiet place to grow up, but she'd yearned for the excitement of urban living for as long as she could remember. Life moved faster here. She could watch the hustle and bustle from her windows high above or take the elevator down nineteen floors to the bottom and be a part of the action—with a dozen safety precautions in place, but that was a temporary problem. She picked up her glass of juice, enjoying the sweet bite of orange. "So, what's happened in the world since yesterday?"

Jerrod turned the page. "Well, rumor has it we rang in a new year."

"You don't say."

"There was a water main break over in West Hollywood. Guess it's a damn mess."

She sipped again. "Fascinating."

"Looks like the cops finally made an arrest in the 'Pirate Bandit' case."

"Good. Another bank robber off the streets."

He frowned, grunting as his eyes tracked along the next page. "They found that woman who was abducted in the Las Vegas area Wednesday night."

"That's great."

He shook his head. "She's dead."

"Oh." She scooted closer to Jerrod's side, glancing at the picture of the beautiful raven-haired victim, reading the story of the newlywed found badly beaten, raped, and stuffed in a dumpster behind some nightclub. "That's so sad. I hate stories like this. I was hoping they would find her alive."

"It's unfortunate. Hopefully they'll catch the bastard who did it."

"Yeah." She played with the remaining bites of her breakfast. The story hit too close to home. How many times had she witnessed a beating in the stash house or in the filthy dressing room at Lady Pink? And rape... She'd been powerless to stop the violence. She set her fork down and picked up her juice, sipping, relieving her dry throat as Jerrod turned to the next page and brought the paper closer to his face.

"What the fuck?"

Abby's eyes popped wide, and she barely kept the juice from dribbling out of her mouth as she stared at Jerrod. Never ever had he raised his voice. And she'd rarely heard him utter the f-bomb. "Easy there, big guy. The Lakers aren't doing that bad." She expected a smile, but didn't get one.

"Abby, this story's about Lily."

"What?" She set her glass down with the first stirrings of unease and scooted close to Jerrod again, looking over his shoulder.

LILY THOMAS BRAND EXPLOITING THE EXPLOITED read the headline. Below it were pictures of Monique, Tera, and Trista walking the catwalk at last month's show. "What *is* this?"

"A big goddamn problem. Who's Toni Terrell?"

"Uh, she's only one of the biggest fashion reporters in LA." She glanced at the byline, noting Toni's name.

"Damn." Jerrod stood and grabbed his phone from its holder against his hip, texting something, as she pulled the full-page article in front of her.

...Lily Thomas, known for her philanthropic acts...former prostitutes walking the runways in the fashion queen's wears...paid below standard wage...damage to an industry already under scrutiny for exploitation...

"No." She pushed back from the table and stood, afraid she would lose her breakfast. "No. This is wrong. I didn't—I would never take advantage. They're going to school. The money they earn is giving them an education and a shot at something better."

"Abby, this isn't your fault."

Her eyes flew to his. "Yes. Of course it is. I asked

Lily to hire them." Her cell phone rang on her worktable. She hurried forward, her breath tearing in and out, and snatched it up, glancing at the readout before she answered. "Lily?"

"Did you see *The Times*?" Lily's raspy smoker's voice barked into the phone.

"Yes," she struggled to answer as unshed tears tightened her throat. "Why did Toni do this?"

"Because she's a bitch and she can. Rumor has it she's feeling slighted by the lack of backstage access before and after the shows."

"Because of me. This is all because of me."

"Abby, that's bullshit," she paused, sucking on her cigarette no doubt. "Toni probably got word that I granted Harold Burgis exclusive, behind-the-scenes coverage for our upcoming Fashion Week preparations."

She slid a strand of hair behind her ear. "So this is payback, humiliating three women?"

"My attorneys are already on it. I'll have her ass for this. I won't have my name dragged through the mud because her panties are in a twist. God knows we pay more than standard rates for our models. And prostitutes..."

"I don't know how she found out." Abby paced to the window and back. "No one was supposed to know." She plunked herself in her chair, her forehead resting in her hand.

"How she found out about what?"

"Trista, Monique, and Tera."

"What about them?"

"Lily, they *are* former prostitutes, 'former' being the key word here."

"Oh for Christ's *sake*, Abby. Do you have any idea what kind of firestorm this is going to create? Already has created? Why the hell didn't you *tell* me?"

"No one needed to know."

"I did."

"No." She shook her head. "I promised them no one would ever know."

"Abby..." Lily sighed.

She rushed to her feet again. Her job was on the line, but worse, she'd broken her word. "They're beautiful women who fit the modeling bill. What they did before they walked the runway is no one else's business. They're out of the halfway house, sharing an apartment. They've all passed their GEDs and are enrolled at USC changing their lives. Lily Brand is helping them accomplish this with a decent paycheck."

Lily muttered something and laughed. "Hot damn. You're fucking brilliant, Abigail Harris. Tell Jerrod I'm coming by at four."

"I'm supposed to meet Monique for the fittings if she's feeling well enough." If Monique would even talk to her again.

"Cancel."

"Lily—"

"Just let me work my magic. I'll see you at four."

"Okay. Bye." She ended the call, staring at her phone, struggling with the confusing ending of their conversation. Lily seemed surprisingly fine with Toni's article, but she wasn't. Trust had been broken, a vital component between the women who attended her support group.

"Here." Jerrod tapped her juice glass against her arm.

"No thanks." She sniffled as she blinked, looking at him. "This isn't how it was supposed to be. They had a right to move on with their lives without anyone knowing what they did to survive."

Jerrod set down the glass and shoved his hands in his pockets. "What did Lily say?"

"That she's going to work her magic." She pressed her lips firm as they trembled. "What if she can't? This could seriously damage everything Lily's worked so hard for. And Trista, Monique, Tera... This is awful. I feel awful."

"Everything will work out."

She wiped at her face as a tear fell. "I need to call them. I need to find a way to make all of this okay."

"You didn't do this, Abigail."

"No, but they trusted me to give them a chance. I wanted them to have what I could offer without strings attached." She shook her head. "I need to make some calls."

Jerrod nodded and stepped back, letting her pass.

~~~~

Jerrod leaned on the edge of his desk, wiggling a pen between his index and middle fingers while he, Jackson, and Ethan dissected the latest threats to Abby via conference call. New Year's Day had quickly turned into any other workday the moment he laid eyes on Toni Torrell's shitty article.

The team dealt with frequent complications. Curveballs and tactical issues were expected in their line of work, but this was an angle they hadn't seen coming. Jerrod spent the last six months shielding Abby from photographers and other prying members of the media only to watch their situation turn critical at the hands of some bitchy reporter seeking her revenge. Abby's quiet, off-the-radar life was in jeopardy. Every precaution they'd taken would be for
~~~~

naught if she was somehow connected to Lily Brand's PR-crisis.

From the beginning, Abby's main concern had been Lily and the models. Her heart was so big she naturally thought of everyone else first, but Jerrod thought only of his principal.

"The risks are certainly there," Ethan said. "Lily will be under more scrutiny than usual, and she contends with plenty when things are good. The press will be up her ass until this dies down."

"Yup." What more did he need to say? Jerrod tossed the pen on the small stack of paperwork he had yet to get to and rubbed at his jaw. Abby's current situation was one he'd never dealt with in WITSEC. The men, women, and families he relocated were assigned low-profile, simple lives where the likelihood of discovery was almost nonexistent. This, however, was a ticking time bomb waiting to explode.

"Abby's going to have to lay low until this thing blows over," Jackson said. "She'll hate the hell out of it, but I don't see anyway to avoid it."

Jerrod grunted his agreement as he moved his hand, kneading at the ache along his neck and shoulders. "We'll steer clear of Lily Brand's corporate offices for awhile or anywhere else the bastards might be waiting to grab a picture of her."

"She and Lily may need to sever ties for the time being," Jackson added.

Jerrod stood and walked to the window, looking toward the skyscraper housing the Ethan Cooke Security offices. "Abby won't go for it."

"She may not have a choice," Jackson replied.

Abby had gone along with every precaution they'd asked of her since the beginning, but she wouldn't accept this one. Breaking ties with Lily, even temporarily, meant risking her spot on the Fashion Week Team. She wouldn't give that up for anything. "I don't know, man. Abby's always cooperative, but she'll fight this."

"I'll talk to her," Jackson said.

"Be my guest. You two are family, but I'm telling you it won't fly. She's worked too damn hard to earn her spot."

"Then what's the solution?" Ethan asked.

Jerrod shrugged and shook his head. If there was an answer, he needed to figure it out. Abby's healing was going better than even her therapist had expected; working for Lily Brand was a huge part of that. Her career gave her purpose. Her passion gave her the fire she needed to make it through the rough patches. "Honestly, I'm not sure, but I know she still has a shit-ton of stuff to do before the team heads to New York next month. She's mentioned fittings with Monique and the rest of Lily's models several times." He glanced toward the offices again as an idea began to take shape. "We can set it up so they meet us at Ethan Cooke Security. We'll have someone bring them and take them home, which will keep the press at bay. Abby can use one of the conference rooms."

"And Abby can keep in touch with Lily via conference calls for the time being," Jackson added. "We'll have her use Ethan Cooke Security phone lines. If someone decides to get nosy we don't have to worry about e-mails being traced back to Abby."

"Yeah. Okay." Ethan gave his approval. "Sounds like a solution for now."

"What about the models?" Jackson asked. "Abby talks about them a lot, but should we be worrying about backlash? Do you think they'll offer Abby up to the press?"

Jerrod sighed, hating the idea. Abby had done nothing but good things for all three young women. “The thought’s crossed my mind, and we’ll monitor the situation, but I don’t think so. They’re really close to her. She’s given them opportunities they wouldn’t have had without her help.”

“Well that’s something at least,” Jackson said. “Hopefully Lily can turn this thing around before it goes any further.”

“Supposedly she’s working on something. I’ll get the details when she swings by at four.”

“She’s coming to the condo?” Ethan asked.

Jerrod walked to his king-sized bed and lay back against the chocolate- and cream-colored comforter Wren had insisted on for his room. “She and Abby planned it, but this will be our last visitor that hasn’t been cleared by me first. I’ll need someone to pick up Lily and drive her over. I don’t want to worry about a tail.”

“Stone can get her,” Ethan supplied. “I’ll have Mia give Lily a call and set it up.”

“Good. Thanks.”

“So, what’s the plan with that high school fashion show Abby was telling Alexa about, and the one next weekend?” Jackson wondered.

Abby told him on more than one occasion how much she was looking forward to the upcoming events, but she was going to have to be willing to give and take for the foreseeable future. Scheduling fittings at Ethan Cooke Security was one thing; fashion shows in the middle of a media firestorm was entirely different. “She’s going to have to bow out. Her world’s about to get real small, but there’s nothing I can do to change that. No risks.”

“Sounds like we have things under control for

now," Jackson said.

"As much as they can be."

"We'll keep our ears open. Evacuation plans are ready to roll should the shit hit the fan," Ethan added.

"Let's hope the hell not."

"Hear, hear," Jackson said. "Give us a call if you need anything else."

"Will do." Jerrod hung up, letting the phone drop to his side as he closed his eyes, weary after a mostly sleepless night and completely shitty start to the day. Things weren't looking to improve anytime soon. Eventually he and Abby would have to talk.

Opening his eyes, he tilted his head in the direction of Abby's voice as it filtered through the wall, trying to figure out how he should tell her that her life was about to change yet again, that even more safety measures were officially in effect, and the upcoming fashion shows were out of the question. She wasn't going to like it, and he hated the idea of putting the sad, wounded look back in her big blue eyes. She ripped him to pieces when she cried, but what the hell else was he supposed to do? He'd done everything he could think of to make Abby's situation better. He was trying to meet her halfway.

He sat up and jammed a hand through his hair, catching the ridiculous direction his thoughts were taking. Why was he worrying so much about Abby's feelings? Since when did he make security decisions based on emotion? He didn't. He stood and walked to his desk, plunking his ass in the chair to focus on the work he needed to finish up. His job was to keep Abby alive at all costs. Her feelings and emotions were not the priority. Safety always took precedence; that was exactly the way it was going to stay.

CHAPTER FIVE

JERROD STACKED THE PILE OF PAPERWORK HE'D SIGNED OFF on and glanced at his watch—one-fifteen. He'd spent the last few hours catching up on the work Abby's busy schedule hadn't allowed him to get to. Now that he'd answered the dozens of e-mails and submitted January's projected budget, he needed to talk to her. He stood with a reluctant sigh and walked to the next room, knocking on her partially opened door.

"Yeah."

He peeked in, breathing in Abby's subtle flowery scent as she sat at her desk in front of her own mound of paperwork. "Looks like you're busy."

"No. Come on in." She set her pen down and unfolded her legs out from under her. "You're the perfect excuse for a breather. Have a seat."

He glanced at the bold blue comforter and layers of plush yellow pillows on her queen-sized mattress, flashing back to the nighty she'd worn only hours ago, and slid his hands in his pockets. This wasn't where he wanted to have their conversation. "Have you had lunch?"

She shook her head. "I'm not really hungry."

Abby's appetite was the first thing to go when she was upset. Her small frame couldn't afford to miss many meals. "I am. What do you say we split a sandwich?"

"I should probably have something."

That's exactly what he'd been counting on. If he

could plop a few chips and a piece of fruit on her plate, she might eat that too. He smiled at her as they walked to the kitchen, and she immediately grabbed the loaf of whole grain bread.

He stepped in front of the refrigerator, opening the door before she had a chance. "I'll make lunch." It was the least he could do before he ruined the rest of her day.

"You don't have to."

"I want to." He snagged the loaf from her hand and reached for the package of deli-sliced cold cuts. "Let me guess, turkey breast and avocado."

"Mr. Quinn, you know me so well."

"It's almost like we live together or something." He glanced over his shoulder, smiling at her, and brought the various sandwich fixings to the counter.

"I guess I'll get the fruit and make a salad—with extra cantaloupe—because I kind of know you too." She gave him a gentle jab to his side on her way by.

"Who can say no to extra cantaloupe?"

"Not you."

They worked side-by-side, as they often did, Jerrod pulling bread from the plastic packaging and Abby prepping fruit. "How did things go with your friends?"

"Good. Better than I expected, actually." She stopped slicing the bold red strawberries. "They're pretty upset with the situation, but they're still in for the show next weekend. All three have assured me this isn't my fault."

"It's not."

"I feel like it is."

"Nope. You aren't responsible for some bullshit article." He spread a healthy glob of Dijon around the slice of soft multi-grain and layered several slices of meat on top, deciding that now was as good a time as any to move the conversation along. "So I had a chance to talk with Jackson and Ethan a while ago."

"Oh?" She paused, glancing at him, then added grapes to the bowl.

"We're going to have to make a few changes—mix things up a little."

She stopped, her hand resting on the container of cut cantaloupe. "Like what?"

He hated the guarded look that came into her eyes, but he couldn't blame her for preparing herself for the latest round of changes. Every time they had this conversation, Abby lost another piece of her independence. "Well, we won't be able to go into the Lily Brand offices for awhile."

She nodded, her shoulders visibly relaxing as she got back to work. "I figured as much."

"And after today we'll probably keep contact with Lily limited to phone conferences."

Her brows furrowed. "What does that mean exactly?"

"She can't come to the condo for a while—her or any of your friends."

"Jerrod—"

"We can't risk it, Abby. We can't risk the press following one of them and getting a picture of you. We're going to move all of the remaining fittings to Ethan Cooke Security. We'll give you one of the conference rooms to use."

She stared at him, frustration radiating in her eyes before she looked away and reached for the cling wrap in the drawer to her right.

He digested her stony, pissed off silence and clenched his jaw. Might as well finish it off and give her the rest. "And the upcoming fashion shows are out."

Her eyes flew to his. "*What*?"

"They're out, Abigail."

"No." She yanked plastic wrap from the roll and covered the small salad she'd prepared. "No," she repeated, shoving the box back in the drawer and slamming it closed. "There has to be another—"

His phone rang, cutting her off. He glanced at the readout. "It's Stone. I need to take this." He pressed 'talk,' looking at Abby as she stared daggers at him. "Quinn."

"Hey, it's Stone. Lily popped up at the office. She wants to come over now."

"Now?" His gaze followed Abby around the small kitchen as she shoved Tupperware containers back in the fridge and yanked a plate from the cupboard.

"I can be there in ten maybe twenty minutes, depending on who's following me."

"Yeah, come on over." He rubbed at his jaw, cursing Lily's crappy timing. There was no way he and Abby were going to sort this out in the next hour, let alone ten to twenty minutes. She was as mad as he'd ever seen her. "We'll see you soon." He hung up. "Lily's on her way."

"Fine," she said coolly as she started toward the bedrooms.

He followed. "Where're you going?"

She stopped and turned. "I have to change, but don't think this conversation is over. Not by a long shot."

"This is where we're at, Abby."

"No discussions, just this is the way it is."

"Yeah." He shrugged. "Pretty much."

Her nostrils flared with her exhale, and she whirled, leaving him staring as she walked away.

~~~~

Abby sat across from Lily at the dining room table, picking at the Chinese food Lily had insisted they order. She caught another whiff of her boss's garlicky chicken dish and shuddered, pressing a hand to her nauseas stomach. The idea of eating was more than she could handle after the long day of troubling events. First Toni Torrell's article, then Jerrod's lunchtime bomb. No visitors to the house. No fashion shows. More changes she couldn't control.

Sighing, she glanced at Jerrod as he sat on the couch, watching football, chowing down on eggrolls. He looked over his shoulder, and their eyes met before she stared down at the shrimp and sautéed veggies on her plate. This entire situation wasn't his fault. Somewhere deep down she understood that, yet she couldn't banish her anger. Every time Jerrod, Jackson, and Ethan 'changed things up,' she lost more freedom. Luckily, Lily was amazing and willing to go along with the latest round of precautions Jerrod had laid out while they waited for their food to arrive, but she herself wasn't. At the rate these new measures kept falling into place, she would be confined to her bedroom by the end of January, which would ultimately make her as much a prisoner here as she had been in the stash house.

"...that's taken care of. I've talked to them as well, so we'll move forward as planned."

Abby set down her fork, shaking her head as she realized Lily was talking. "I'm sorry, what?"

Lily smoothed back her sleek cap of silver hair as she huffed out an impatient breath. "Abby, you're all over the place this afternoon."
~~~~

She winced. "I know. I apologize."

"I said we should plan to move forward since the girls are all set. This is actually a great opportunity for them to make a statement."

Abby nodded. "I agree. Toni's article is crap. She doesn't get to make them feel like they're worthless."

"Certainly not. And she won't, especially by the time I'm finished with this." Lily stabbed a peapod and popped it in her mouth with a smirking smile.

"I hate that I can't be there. I hate that I have to sit back while the four of you take the heat alone."

Lily snagged her hand and squeezed. "I've dealt with bigger problems than this. Your safety is more important than giving that bitch the finger."

"I *want* to give her the finger." Abby squeezed back, returning the gesture of support. How could she put into words the desperate need to do *something*? She stood, no longer able to sit. "I want to strut down the runway with my friends and tell Toni to go to hell. I'm so sick of living in this *bubble*." She gestured to her surroundings. "I hate that I'm always a step removed."

"Which is a huge fucking improvement, Abigail." Lily gave her a firm nod. "Not all that long ago you were more than happy to hide out in the background."

"No." Abby shook her head. "Not happy too, just afraid to do otherwise."

"As you had every right to be."

"But I'm not so afraid anymore."

"Damn right you're not."

Abby returned Lily's smile. Her fifty-something boss, with all her Botox and collagen injections, trademark stylish black-framed glasses, and top-notch wardrobe, was one of the strongest women she knew. She couldn't help but feel more powerful in Lily's commanding presence.

"This whole thing will be over soon, and you'll have your spotlight back, my dear. I have plans for you—very big plans. In fact, I want you at my party tomorrow night in San Francisco."

Abby's eyes grew wide with the idea. How long had it been since she'd been to a real function? Parties had been limited to gatherings at Ethan and Sarah's. "Yes—"

"Uh, Lily." The TV switched off as Jerrod got to his feet and walked to the table. "That's not going to work."

"Sure it will. It's a very low-key deal—just a few of my good friends at the penthouse for dinner."

"I'm guessing there will be some big names among those good friends."

"Well, yes of course, but this isn't a media event. I would never invite Abby if I didn't think she would be perfectly safe. You can use the private jet, and I'll have a car pick you up at the airport."

He shoved his hands in his pockets as he gave Lily a shake of his head. "That sounds good, but we're going to have to pass. There's a little more involved with a security detail than that."

Abby glanced from Lily to Jerrod, then stared at the floor, balling her hands into fists as she listened to him make more decisions regarding her life without asking or considering what she wanted or needed. "I'm going."

The room fell silent.

"I'm going," she repeated as she looked up, locking eyes with Jerrod's.

"I need to use the restroom." Lily scooted her chair back. "If you'll excuse me."

"Sure," Jerrod said, never taking his calm, steady eyes from hers.

Abby waited for Lily to close the door to the half bath. "What are you doing?"

"My job."

"What about mine? I have a job to do too." On a frustrated huff, she skirted the bar and walked into the kitchen, grabbing several Tupperware pieces from the cupboard, needing something to do as she grew angrier.

He followed. "I'm sorry, Abby, but the party's out."

His calm apologies stoked her irritation higher. "No," she mumbled on her way back to the table.

He stopped at her side, leaning his head closer to hers. "What?"

She set the plastic down with a weighty snap. "I said no."

"I wasn't giving you an option. As head of your security I'm telling you you're not going."

Her hands shook with the rush of adrenaline coursing through her veins—part fury, part fear—as she dumped the contents of the take-out box into the container. This was her first confrontation with a man since her early days in the stash house. Even so, she continued on, trying to remember that Jerrod would never hurt her. "And I'm telling you I am."

"Abigail—"

"Don't 'Abigail' me in that school teacher tone of yours." She smashed the lid on top. "Two hours ago you told me I can't have my boss and friends over for the foreseeable future. If I want to finish my alterations for Fashion Week, I have to cart my stuff over to Ethan Cooke Security and inconvenience the models. Now you're telling me I can't attend a simple dinner party? What else, Jerrod? What else are you going to ask of me?"

"Whatever I have to," he said with a hint of apology.

She dismissed the tone of regret. "I've gone along with everything you've asked. *Everything* since day one."

"I know."

"Don't you get it? Don't you understand that every time we take a step back he wins? Renzo never gets to win again."

"I don't—"

"I didn't ask for what I got." She walked to the fridge and shoved the leftovers away. "I didn't ask to be thrown into the back of a van and have everything change. I'm trying to pick up the pieces of my life."

"They're trying to *end* your life, Abigail. Their goal is to see you dead."

She swallowed, knowing he was right. "If I spend the rest of my life hiding, I might as well be dead. I'll meet the models at the office. I'll even miss Saturday's show, but I'm going to Lily's party tomorrow night and to the mentoring event Wednesday afternoon. If I have to attend on my own I will." She shoved passed him and walked to the windows across the room, staring out at the sun starting its decent, trying to find the reins on the temper she hadn't set free in so long. Spewing her frustrations had been somewhat liberating, but even more, it had been wrong. "I'm sorry," she said, turning, but Jerrod was gone.

Lily's heels echoed on the flooring as she joined Abby. "Feel better now?"

She shook her head. "No."

"You look a little lighter without all of that on your chest."

"I don't like being unkind. I know he's doing this for me..." She closed her eyes, again on the verge of tears.

“He’s a big, strong man. He can take a little heat from time to time.”

“But he doesn’t deserve it.” She crossed her arms at her chest, attempting to rub away the chills she felt despite her navy blue sweater. “I’m so done with this. All of it. I’m a survivor, yet everyone still sees me as the poor, fragile woman who was abducted into the sex trade.”

“Bullshit. Since when do you let other people define you? You and me, we define the world. You remember that.” Lily kissed her cheek. “Maybe I’ll see you tomorrow night if Jerrod thinks it’s safe enough after all.”

“Yeah. Okay.” She nodded as Jerrod stepped into the room, shoving his phone back in its holder.

“Ready, Lily?” He looked at Abby as he spoke.

“I am.” Lily put on her coat and Jerrod walked her to the door.

Abby slipped away to her room, too raw to do anything more than lie on her bed and close her eyes against her throbbing headache.

Chapter Six

Abby sat among fashion's biggest names in Lily's luxurious dining room, certain she was having some sort of over-the-top, awesome dream. For surely that's what tonight was—a step onto the pages of one of Livy's enchanted storybooks.

Dashing princes and princesses laughed and chatted while feasting on the land's top fares. White roses in simple crystal vases and dozens of creamy tapers decorated the long table, adding to the magic of the fairytale-like atmosphere. And here she was among the gentry, feeling like the queen in the golden hewed halter dress Lily surprised her with earlier in the afternoon.

Ethan brought by a Lily Brand box containing the stunning, barely there dress with its short silky skirt, cinched waist, and ornately beaded top that plunged deep in the front and left her back bare. She'd matched it with three-inch heels and dangling earrings, and had curled her hair, twisting the shoulder-length black up in a loose updo. The end result was jaw-dropping.

Abby glanced to her right, still struggling to believe she was seated next to Tyler Maxfield, one of her biggest idols. She wasn't a stranger to fashion's elite. She'd posed for pictures and had shaken hands on her trips to New York City, Paris, and Milan during her college days, but it had never been like this. She'd been too busy surviving in the stash house, then hiding in her condo to enjoy the fruits of Lily's thirty years in the industry.

Jerrod chuckled, and she looked to her left, smiling, relieved that he was having a good time while he finished his thick cut of prime rib and spoke with Lina Brovera, Spain's fashion darling. He was gorgeous in his tux, his tough build accentuated by the tailored fit of his jacket. And he meshed well with Lily's A-list guests. The evening couldn't be any more perfect.

"Are you finished, madam?" the waiter asked as he stopped at her side.

"Yes, thank you."

He reached down and took her plate of barely touched salmon.

"Thank you," she said again as he moved to take Jerrod's dish and walked away.

Jerrod leaned in close, his arm brushing hers. "You hardly ate anything."

The heat of his breath feathered her ear, sending a rush of goose bumps along her skin. She turned her head in defense, her face mere inches from his as they held each other's gaze. "I know." She bit her lip and smiled. "I'm too excited. I've actually been talking to Tyler Maxfield. I used to imitate his designs, now I'm having in-depth conversations as if we're on the same playing field."

"Aren't you?"

She chuckled at the idea. "I wish."

"Don't sell yourself short. You definitely held your own."

"Aw, thanks, big guy." She smoothed his lapel, relieved that they seemed to be okay after yesterday's disagreement, even though she had yet to apologize. She'd tried more than once, but he'd been on the phone late into last night and all day today, setting up the details for their evening in San Francisco.

"Excuse me, sir, madam. Your desserts—a chocolate tower with vanilla buttercream drizzle." The waiter set two tall slices of cake in front of them.

"Holy cow, this looks *amazing*." Abby eyed the mousse-like frosting stacked between four layers of dark chocolate. "Excuse me, is that ganache?"

"Yes, a truffle ganache, madam." He stepped away to present two more desserts.

"Is this heaven?"

Jerrod grinned. "We should probably dig in." He picked up his fork and took a bite. "Wow," he said with his mouth full.

"That good?"

"Definitely."

"Is it so delicious you're glad we came even though getting here was kind of a pain?"

He flashed her another smile. "Pretty close." He cut another bite, surprising her when he held the fork to her lips. "Try it."

She sampled his offering, closing her eyes as creamy chocolate melted on her tongue. "Oh my god. This has to be illegal."

"It's a possibility."

She laughed as she picked up her own silverware and enjoyed another taste of pure heaven.

"Excuse me." Lily stood at the head of the table, pretty in her fitted off-the-shoulder black dress, tapping her knife against her glass. "May I have everyone's attention please?"

The crowd of thirty quieted.

"Thank you." She picked up her wine glass and sipped. "I thought I should take a moment to thank you all for coming. It's rare that so many of us are in the same place at the same time, so I love that we've had this chance to get together and catch up."

Everyone clapped.

Lily smiled, giving a small nod, commanding the room to settle again. "At times like this, having close friends at my side is a comfort. As you know, Lily Brand has faced a couple of rough days in the media."

Troubled murmurs carried through the dining room as Abby glanced around, struggling not to squirm with the rush of guilt swamping her.

"*The Times* and Toni Torrell have quite brazenly spewed very serious accusations at the expense of three talented models."

Abby picked up her water, swallowing a long, cool sip, certain everyone somehow knew that she was at the root of Lily's problems.

"Since I've never been one to fold, I'm going to do what I do best and use this latest development to my advantage."

A few people laughed while others cheered their encouragement.

"I thought you might approve." Lily grinned. "I've decided it's time to work on a new cause very dear to my heart. It's here among my friends that I announce the launch of Lily Brand's latest line, the *Escape* line."

Abby set down her glass among the raucous applause, afraid she would drop it as Lily's gaze met hers across the room, and her words sunk in.

"I'll be handing over this endeavor to one of my very best and brightest. She, along with our new product, will make their debut at Fashion Week."

"Who, Lily?" Jeremiah Jacobson asked. "Who's your new designer?"

She shrugged. "I guess we'll all find out next month."

Abby's heart pounded as she looked from Lily to

Jerrod. "Did she just—I can't—Jerrod." She shook her head in utter disbelief, reaching for his hand.

He laced their fingers, holding tight, while the room buzzed with speculation.

"Do you know who?" Tyler asked Abby.

She shook her head again. "I'm—I'm not sure."

"This is news to us," Jerrod added.

"I've never been more excited for Fashion Week. This should certainly kill Toni's buzz." Tyler laughed. "Leave it to Lily to use this entire situation..."

"Yeah," Abby replied with a small smile, still in the throws of shock.

"How about some air," Jerrod said into her ear. "We have about twenty minutes before we have to head to the airport."

She nodded.

Jerrod helped her push back her chair, and they started toward the double-pocketed doors of the balcony, but Lily stopped them. "Heading out?"

Abby's eyes filled as she stared at the amazing woman before her. "Oh, Lily." She moved in to hug her.

Jerrod stopped her with a hand to the shoulder. "If you hug her now, you'll kill the mystery."

"You're right." She took Lily's hands instead. "How do I thank you for everything? How do I thank you for making my dreams come true?"

"You kick ass, kid."

"Oh, I'll kick ass...after the shock wears off."

Lily laughed. "And I want you walking the runway again as soon as the general here says it's safe." Lily stepped back, looking Abby up and down. "Damn, Abigail Harris, there's not much height to you, but you sure as hell know how to make my designs come alive. Doesn't she, General?"

Jerrod nodded. "She looks lovely."

Lily snorted. "Lovely's a little g-rated, but we'll go with it." She winked at Jerrod. "You could make a potato sack look like something everyone wants to wear."

She grinned. "Only if it's designed well."

"Ha. We'll go with that too."

Abby's smile vanished as reality snuck back to amaze her. "Thank you, Lily."

Lily waved the gratitude away. "I've wanted to do this for a while now. Do you still have those clothes you wowed me with at your interview?"

"Yes, of course. They're hanging in my closet."

"Good. You'll need to bring them with you to the shoot."

"What shoot," she and Jerrod asked at the same time.

"Connie Withers wants you for the March issue of *Trendy*."

Abby's eyes popped wide as she absorbed the next surprise. "Nuh uh."

"She wants an interview and photo shoot showcasing the new line—or what we have of it so far."

Abby pressed a hand to her forehead, laughing in amazement. "You're making this up."

"I'm sure as shit not. Nine a.m. Friday at the Trendy studios."

"I can't *believe* this."

"They want to use you for several photos. Are you up for whatever they throw your way?"

"Yeah. Yes. Definitely."

"Lily, Abby can't do this." Jerrod stepped closer to Abby. "Abby, you can't do this."

Abby opened her mouth to object, but Lily cut her

off.

"Of course she can. The mystery behind the designer along with rumors of the shoot will give the brand more exposure. It's brilliant marketing. Everyone will want a copy of the magazine."

"That may be, but we can't take these risks."

Abby opened her mouth again and quickly closed it when Lily jumped in for the second time.

"We're going to use Jackie and Marco for hair and makeup. You know them. You've cleared them both. And I assure you Zenn MacGreggor and Connie are no danger to Abby. I've made sure this is safe, Jerrod. We won't leak the rumored shoot until after it has already happened."

"And the trial will be over by the time the magazine hits the shelves," Abby finally added, frustrated that her new adventure was just beginning and precautions were already ruining everything. "Prosecutor Bitner said there shouldn't be anymore delays."

Jerrod's calm eyes held her gaze. "Just because the trial's over doesn't mean you'll be in the clear."

She pressed her lips firm, well aware that he was right. "I'm doing this. I need to do this."

He shook his head. "It's a bad idea."

It probably was, but she couldn't live in the shadows forever, unless she planned to give up her career, which she didn't. "This is my dream."

"Tell you what, General. I'll talk to Connie about a contingency plan. We'll make sure there's a Plan B if things aren't going the way we want them to in regards to Abby's safety."

Jerrod sighed. "Send me your ideas, and we'll go from there."

"Fine. Done." Lily turned her attention back to

Abby. "Connie wants to discuss the new line and our plans to donate one hundred percent of the profits to the safe houses we're starting here in LA and Baltimore."

"Lily," Abby whispered as her eyes filled again, but this time they overflowed. "Oh, Lily." The clothing line *and* the safe houses. This was everything she'd been wanting—a way to change lives while doing what she loved most. "I don't even know what to say."

"I'll scan over the main points I want you to hit during the interview. Of course you'll have input after we've had more of a chance to talk, but this should get us started."

"Thank you." She sniffled and wiped at her cheeks.

"Shit, Abby, thank *you*. My profit margins are about to go through the roof, *and* there's a good cause behind it. We both get what we want." She glanced around. "I should mingle."

"Okay."

"I'll see you Wednesday."

She nodded, her voice too tight with emotion to do more as Lily walked away.

"Come on." Jerrod took her arm. "Let's get your wrap, and I'll call Austin. We can head to the airport a couple minutes early."

"All right," she murmured, suddenly overwhelmed by the daunting evening. "I'm going to use the bathroom."

"Okay." Jerrod veered toward the hall closet.

Abby continued down the hall, pausing outside Lily's master suite when she spotted another balcony. Craving fresh air, she stepped in and unlocked the slider, pulling it open, bracing herself against the rushing winds and shock of cold as she walked to the railing. Her teeth chattered, and she gripped her arms tightly around herself as she stared out at the city, relishing the freedom and endless views, afraid she might have somehow imagined the entire evening. How often did a person actually get everything they'd ever dreamed of?

"I thought you had to go to the bathroom."

She whirled with a hand to her heart. "I just needed a minute."

Jerrod stepped up next to her, placing her wrap around her shoulders.

"Thank you." She held the white cashmere tight.

"Damn it's cold out here." He shoved his hands in his pockets as he hunched against the harsh rush of wind.

She tilted her chin to the air. "I like the breeze. It's real." She turned, facing him. "Is this—the private jets and limo rides, dinner and conversation with my idols, my own *clothing* line?" She laughed. "Am I going to wake up in my bed, or worse, in the stash house only to realize my subconscious was playing nasty tricks on me?"

His jacket blew about with the next unforgiving gust. "It's too damn cold out here to be anything but reality. Although if we are dreaming, I want more of that cake."

She smiled. "I can't believe this is happening. I wish Gran were here. She would be so proud. And Lex... I don't know what to think or feel."

"Is this what you want?"

"Oh, yeah." She smiled again. "I've wanted this since I sewed my own prom dress. I've wanted the *Escape* line since the night Lex and I were stuck on Zachary Hartwell's roof."

"You've got it. What are you going to do with it,

Abigail?"

"I'm going to take it and run...after I stop being terrified." She laughed again and threw her arms around him, holding on to the warmth and comfort that was Jerrod.

He returned her embrace, his rough hands sliding along the bare, sensitive skin of her back as her wrap flew about like a cape. "Abigail, you're freezing."

She drew away, still holding him, unwilling to let go. "I'd say I'm more afraid than anything." She planted a noisy kiss to his cheek, then looked in his eyes. "And really, really happy."

He wrapped his arms tighter around her without his typical hesitation and turned, taking the brunt of the unforgiving winds. "Congratulations, Abby. Your vision's going to help a lot of people."

"Thank you." She grinned as he did, savoring this perfect moment. Then she remembered yesterday. "I'm sorry."

His smile turned into a frown. "For what?"

"For yesterday."

He shook his head. "It's over. We're here. You're safe. That's all that matters."

"But I—"

"Water under the bridge, Abby."

"Okay."

"Now can we go inside?"

She smiled. "Yes."

"Thank god." He winked.

She laughed and took his hand, walking back into Lily's bedroom as his cell phone started ringing.

He stopped and pulled his phone free, glancing at the readout. "It's Austin. We should go." He pressed 'talk.' "Quinn. Yeah. We're ready." He grabbed her hand and they moved down the hall as he continued his conversation.

Abby gave Lily a wave on the way out, listening to Jerrod spew his jargon, watching him move his jacket so his weapon was at the ready. The magic of the evening quickly vanished when he opened the door, keeping her close, and Austin met them. There were no more princes and princesses or pretty roses and candlelight. She still had her clothing line, but she also had her grim reality.

Chapter Seven

Jerrod stood close to the stage, scanning the small group of parents and faculty members scattered among the first few rows of auditorium seating. For two hours he'd watched the double doors and stage exits closely, making certain everyone entering or exiting wore a red badge identifying them as a member of South Central High's Day of Fashion. He checked his watch in the dim lighting, counting down the minutes until he could get Abby out of here, tensing when the auditorium doors opened for the umpteenth time. His gaze flew to the woman stepping in, and he automatically searched for a tag on her shirt, relaxing—sort of—when he spotted it.

Today should have been a cakewalk. Abby had helped Lily host a similar event with the same group of kids earlier in the fall. The aspiring designers were supposed to share their sketches and the outfits they'd created, get a few critiques, then eat a catered lunch in the faculty lounge down the hall. That was it, end of story, gravy, but nothing was as simple as it had been in October. Instead of enjoying an easy morning of watching Abby interact with a great group of teenagers, he was on high alert, waiting for something to go wrong. He was expecting it.

Lily's plan to turn the media in her favor had worked in spades. The newspapers and entertainment rags no longer focused on underpaid models and prostitution; instead, they filled the headlines with misinformation—from the practical to the absurd—speculating on the identity of Lily's new mystery designer. Abby remained in the clear for now; her name had yet to be mentioned, but she was going to have to throttle back—all the way back before their luck ran out and she was discovered. And today could be that day.

Although Lily kept her at-risk youth program discreet, it was only a matter of time before someone caught wind that Lily was spending the morning at the university. Locked doors and the rent-a-cop stationed outside the building wouldn't keep reporters hunting for the next Lily Brand story away for long.

He glanced at his watch again as Abby's laughter carried through the huge space, accompanied by chuckles from her captive audience crowded around her on the stage floor. She sat with Lily among their 'apprentice team' of ten young men and women, relaxed with her hair up in a pony tail, wearing a red button down sweater with a snug black shirt beneath, dark blue jeans and black boots. Lily was certainly the money behind today's event, but Abby was the star. The kids adored her, hanging on her every word as she answered their endless questions and offered hints and suggestions when she held up each students' sketch one by one.

She loved being here. Her enthusiasm was genuine, her passion infectious. He hated that he had to worry more about door duty, red stickers, and exit plans than the good Abby was doing, but that's the way it was.

She glanced up, meeting his eyes for a tense moment, then gave her attention back to her group. They'd argued again this morning. Despite every logical reason he'd given her for canceling her appearance, she'd refused. *They need me, Jerrod. This might be their only shot at something better.* Her heated words echoed in his head as he scanned the crowd.

A month ago, he would have been all for her participation; hell, even a week ago this wouldn't have been a big deal, but that was before the media circus unknowingly joined in the hunt for Abigail Harris.

"Latisha," Abby got to her feet, smiling at the pretty girl. "Why don't you show us your sample?"

"Sure." Latisha hopped to her feet and stood next to Abby in front of the group.

"All right, let's see what you have this time around." Abby rubbed her hands together greedily, earning another round of chuckles.

Latisha hesitated. "I don't think it's very good."

"Why don't you let me be the judge?"

"Okay." She unfolded a solid black dress with a vivid, multi-colored flower sewn on the side and a tank top matching the bright bloom.

Abby blinked. "Latisha, this is great."

The girl beamed. "Really?"

"Yes. Really. Lily, do you agree?"

"Absolutely."

"Thanks."

Abby took the dress from Latisha. "Your design has great cohesion, not to mention amazing flow. This is very summery. I would wear it."

Latisha eyed her skeptically.

"I'll put it on right now. We'll use this as one of our examples of clean lines and excellent movement. Jeremiah, why don't I take your top too? I think your shirt and Latisha's skirt will pair well."

Latisha's eyes filled with guarded excitement as Abby started toward the small dressing space and a camera flashed. Jerrod focused on the heavyset woman snapping picture after picture in the front row—Latisha's mother no doubt—and walked toward her.

"Excuse me, ma'am." He smiled. "I'm afraid this is a non-photographed event."

"I'm taking a picture of my baby girl. Ms. Abby says she makes great stuff."

"You must be very proud. The dress is beautiful," he added, still going with tact before he was forced to take the camera away, which more than likely wouldn't go over well. "We're trying hard to protect Lily's privacy right now with all of the media buzz. She wants to be able to do this for the kids without drawing attention. It keeps the day special. Lily will take pictures with everyone during the lunch break."

Latisha's mother eyed him, then huffed. "All right. If that's the way you want it." She shoved the camera in her enormous purse.

"For Lily and the kids," he reminded her as he let out a quiet sigh. The last thing the needed was a Lily Brand brawl adding to the headlines.

Latisha's mother grumbled as she took her seat.

"I appreciate it, as does Lily."

The kids clapped, and Jerrod turned, smiling as Abby stepped from the small dressing space, strutting around the stage in the snug, roughly sewn tank top created by Jeremiah and the pretty skirt Latisha made.

"So, what do you think? Constructive thoughts only." She stood hipshot, then turned, walking as she had hundreds of times in their dining room. Even with the shoddy tailoring, she made the outfit look great. "Let's start with what we like, then we'll move on to what our designers could do to improve their techniques. Tamara, your hand is up."

"The pattern is off on the shirt, but the fabric is a nice choice."

Abby nodded. "I absolutely agree. A design is only as good as the fabric. The sketch might be great, but if the actual piece doesn't translate well, your back to the drawing board. Jeremiah, I like the fit, but something fell apart during assembly right here around my arms." She pointed to the lopsided sewing by her armpits. "Let your mannequin be your guide. If it doesn't look right on her, it won't look right on me."

Jeremiah nodded. "Thank you, Ms. Abby, but I don't have a mannequin."

"Oh." Abby looked from Jeremiah to Lily. "Okay, well, there are ways to get around that."

"Abby, I think we can help Jeremiah out." Lily stood and walked to the draped platform crowding the right side of the stage. "Actually, I think we can help all of our designers out. Abby, can you grab the other end."

"Sure." Abby moved to the opposite side taking hold of the huge sheet.

Lily gave a nod, and they pulled the cover back, revealing mannequins, sewing machines, laptops, sketching paper, scissors, and the dozens of other items similar to the ones Abby had scattered about her bedroom and the dining room.

A gasp went up from the students and crowd.

"Lily Brand is happy to share these items with South Central's fashion classroom," Lily said.

The kids jumped up, laughing and screaming, running forward to hug Lily and Abby.

Abby embraced each student, kissing cheeks before she would let them step away. Several minutes passed before the room quieted again.

"All right, guys. Park your butts so we can keep

this session on track." Lily pointed to the stage floor.

"But, Lily, don't you have something else?" Abby asked.

"You know what? I do. Go ahead and tell them."

Grinning, Abby clasped her hands, all but vibrating with the anticipation of sharing good news. "Lily Brand not only has sewing suites for the classroom; she also has one for each of you to take home."

Stunned silence filled the room, and Jerrod braced himself, ready for the next round of excitement as the auditorium erupted with screams. Latisha's mother grabbed him up in a death grip hug as she jumped about. He laughed, hugging her back, unable to remain unmoved by Lily's amazing gesture and what it meant to these struggling families. He caught Abby's eye as she smiled at him, and he winked.

"We'll also include a ten-thousand-dollar fabric allowance for the classroom," Lily hollered, "and you'll each be given a one-thousand-dollar stipend to use as well."

"Oh, Lord, I think I'm going to pass out," Latisha's mother sobbed.

Jerrod guided her to her seat, patting her shoulder, crouching next to her, afraid she would fall to the floor. "Take some deep breaths."

"I'm trying." She breathed deep, fanning her hands in front of her face.

"That's it. Just like that." He stood.

"Practice makes perfect," Lily continued. "You're all good, but when we meet again this spring, I want great. Everyone is welcome to come over for a closer look at your new stuff. We'll gather in the faculty lounge in twenty minutes for lunch."

Everyone moved passed Abby as she descended

the four stairs to the main floor, stopping next to Jerrod's side. "I—"

"Can you believe our luck?" Tamara rushed up to Abby, giving her another huge hug.

Abby eased back, taking Tamara's hands. "Lily sees *a lot* of potential. So do I. You guys keep this up and maybe we'll see you on the Lily Brand team in a few years."

Tamara nodded and stepped away, smiling up at Jerrod from under her long lashes. "Hi, Mr. Jerrod."

He smiled. She was always so friendly. "Hey, Tamara."

"Did you like the shirt I made?"

He had no idea who made what other than Jeremiah and Latisha, and that was only because Abby was still wearing their clothes. "Yeah. It was great," he said anyway.

She smiled again. "Great. Okay. Thanks. See ya."

"Bye." He watched Tamara run off and faced Abby as she grinned at him. "What?"

"She's got a crush on you, big guy."

He frowned as he looked at Latisha's mother on stage. "Who?"

She rolled her eyes. "Why are men so dense?"

He opened his mouth to respond as Jeremiah stopped next to Abby this time.

"Ms. Abby, can I interview you for the school paper?"

"Yes, of course. Just let me change first. I'm freezing."

"Thanks. I'll get my notebook."

"Give me five minutes, and I'll meet you back here."

"Awesome." Jeremiah hurried off, and Abby turned to leave.

Jerrod grabbed her arm before she could walk off. "Abby, what are you doing?"

"I'm getting changed."

He shook his head. "No, the article. You're taking too many risks."

She pulled free of his grip as any remnants of the peaceful moment they shared vanished. "I'm just trying to do my job, Jerrod, and today that's helping these kids stay on the right path."

It annoyed him that she kept painting him as the bad guy. "I get the purpose of the program, Abby. If the situation wasn't what it is, I'd be all for your interviews and guest appearances."

"This is for a high school in the projects. I doubt Dimitri or Victor obtained a teaching license in the past six months, and I'm pretty sure Jeremiah's story won't be picked up by the AP wire anytime soon."

He clenched his jaw as his irritation grew with her haughty tone. "You're making it really damn hard for me to do what I have to for *your* protection."

She sighed as she closed her eyes. "I know." She placed her hand on his arm. "I'm sorry. I'll keep it short and vague. They're counting on me."

"Abby," he trailed off as the woman wearing a black cap in back of the auditorium caught his attention. He searched for her red tag in the crappy lighting, but she turned, heading toward the double doors, before he had a chance to spot it. "Do you know who that is?"

She studied their mystery guest. "No, I don't think so."

He was going to find out. "Don't leave the auditorium," he called behind him as he started up the aisle. "Excuse me, ma'am."

The stranger looked over her shoulder and moved

faster.

There was something familiar about her. Frowning, Jerrod picked up his pace. "Hey."

She pushed through the double doors, and the bright sunlight washed over her pale blond hair and sun-kissed skin.

Toni Torrell. "Damn it." He broke into a run, following her to the hall as she sprinted for the elevator door, sliding closed behind the group that just exited. She made it inside, jamming on the buttons, disappearing behind the shiny metal.

"Fuck." He could do nothing but wait for the panel above the doors to display her destination. A bright red eight filled the small screen, and he rushed to the stairwell, hustling up the four stories, well aware that the likelihood of finding her was slim. The building was huge, and there were too many exits. Keeping Abby close was more important than a fruitless chase.

Turning, he started back down and stopped by the grouping of windows as he caught sight of the pain-in-the-ass reporter running to her car with something in her hand—a camera no doubt. "Fuck," he said again as he yanked his phone from the holder and dialed Ethan.

"Cooke."

"It's Quinn," he said, still catching his breath as he continued on his way. "We have a potential breech. Toni Torrell was in the auditorium. I don't know if she got pictures of Lily or Abby or both."

"Damn. Hunter and I are in the area—on our way back from the meeting with Imagine Entertainment. We can be there in ten."

"We'll meet you outside the west entrance. Goddamn. I knew this was going to happen." He hung up and yanked open the door, moving quickly but calmly toward Abby as she finished her interview.

"Thanks, Ms. Abby," Jeremiah said.

"I'm happy to help. Now, let's eat lunch." She looked at Jerrod as he continued her way. "Go ahead, Jeremiah. I'll be right there."

"Okay."

Jerrod waited for Jeremiah to follow the rest of the group to the faculty lounge. "We need to leave."

She shook her head. "No. We haven't—"

"We have to go, Abigail." He grabbed her favorite black cashmere jacket from the chair, struggling to keep the frustration out of his voice. This entire situation could have been avoided if everyone had followed the team's original plan.

Fear replaced the mutiny in her eyes. "What's wrong? What—"

"That woman I chased—it was Toni Torrell. I think she had a camera."

"She wanted pictures of Lily and the kids."

"I hope you're right." He held out her jacket.

"No one knows who I am." Fear flooded her voice as she put it on. "She doesn't know who I am."

"Let's hope not." He gave Lily a quick wave across the room and walked with Abby down the hall and into the elevator, wondering if their luck had finally run out.

~~~~

Abby slid Jerrod a glance, noting his calm eyes and rigid posture as the elevator doors closed them in for the four-story descent. She looked his way again, clasping her hands tight, waiting for his powerful shoulders to relax, but they didn't. Jerrod was always
~~~~

watchful; he constantly planned for the worst; that was part of his job, but this was the first time she'd ever detected a ruffle in his unshakeable composure. Was he angry with her, or worried? Or both?

He'd warned her this could happen, and she'd taken the risks anyway. She and Jerrod had been careful to avoid cameras over the last six months. For the most part she'd lived her life as if she'd ceased to exist, until Saturday when she'd wined and dined with fashion's best and brightest. For one night she'd indulged herself with a bit of normalcy. San Francisco had been for her, she could admit that, but not today; today had been for the kids. How would Toni's possible pictures change the bubble she and Jerrod had built? "What are we going to do?"

"Get out of here and lay low until we've figured out what we're dealing with."

"She's not interested in me," she reassured herself as much as Jerrod. "She wants the next Lily story, just like the rest of the reporters in this town."

"Abby, you *are* the next story." He shoved his hands in his pockets with more force than usual.

She shook her head. "I'm not. Not yet. Not until Fashion Week."

He eyed her as the doors opened, and they headed down the hall.

"I know you're mad at me—"

"I'm not mad at you, Abigail."

"You're definitely not happy."

"No, I'm not. This scenario right here is exactly what I've been trying to avoid. Your situation is complicated enough without adding Toni Torrell to the picture. "

"I wish I could make you understand how important this was."

"I do."

"No, you don't. I had to do this. I had to do it for the kids."

"Abby—"

"I *was* these kids, Jerrod." She pulled on his arm, stopping him, desperate to make him understand. "Lex had the ambitions and responsibilities while I floated down the road to nowhere. Ms. Beesley helped me make my prom dress. She helped me find my spark. My whole life changed after that. I can do that for them. Did you see Latisha's eyes, and Jeremiah's? They're hungry to learn, and they have potential. They can make it in this industry. They just need guidance and the advantages Lily can offer."

He sighed. "I get it."

She stared into his eyes, realizing he did truly get it, and took his hand, squeezing. "*Thank* you."

He squeezed back. "You're welcome. We have to go." He pulled her closer to him as they walked from the side entrance, and Hunter and Ethan pulled up in one of Ethan Cooke Security's black Suburbans.

"Why are they here? I thought you were going to call a cab."

"They were in the area."

Ethan got out of the passenger's side in slacks and a polo shirt and opened the back door.

Abby slid in the backseat, pushing over as Jerrod got in next to her. Within moments they were through the parking lot and back among the flow of traffic. She waited for the conversation to start or for Hunter to tell one of his jokes, but no one spoke as one mile turned into two, then three.

She stared through the windshield, bopping her leg up and down, absorbing the tension choking the silent car. Restless, she glanced from Hunter to Ethan to Jerrod, then out the window into the thick city traffic, trying desperately to keep her shoulders relaxed as her unease grew. She and Jerrod had never been picked up like this before. Typically they did their own thing. Austin had accompanied them on their trip to San Francisco, but this was different. Everything was suddenly different, and she realized her world was about to shrink again.

She'd attended Lily's dinner party and the event today. Tomorrow she would do her shoot with *Trendy*, then she would more or less be confined to the condo unless plans were cleared through Jerrod first. Her friends would stop coming over; her every move would be watched as closely as it had been in the stash house.

She squirmed at the idea of being imprisoned in her own home, much like she had been in the hot, tiny closet. *You like the closet, yes? Maybe you will stay in here forever.* Dimitri's laugh and the door closing, locking her back in the airless space, echoed through her head. Abby swallowed as her throat constricted and cold sweat beaded along her forehead. She pressed a hand to her chest as her heart began to race. The Suburban didn't have enough air. "I need—I need to roll down the window. It's too hot in here."

"We're almost there," Jerrod said.

She yanked at the buttons on her coat and ripped it off, certain she was on the verge of passing out. "I can't breathe," she gasped, too overcome with fear to be embarrassed when Ethan looked back at her. "I have to get out right now." She scooted toward the door, reaching for the handle, even as Hunter continued driving.

Jerrod snagged her arm in a firm grip and pulled her back to his side. "Abigail. We're almost home," he repeated firmly.

"No." She clawed at his hand holding her in place. "I'm going to faint. I can't catch my breath."

He held her chin between his fingers. "Abby, deep breaths—in for two, out for four." He rolled his window down, and cool, smoggy air blew against her cheeks, carrying the scent of Jerrod's soap with it.

She squeezed his hand like a lifeline and breathed deep, wiping at her face with her forearm as the clutches of terror released her and a rush of humiliation took its place. Dropping her head, she closed her eyes, perilously close to tears. "I'm sorry. I'm sorry I just lost it."

"Panic attacks are a bitch," Hunter piped up. "I have them from time to time. Fucking PTSD."

She sent him a small smile in the rearview mirror, grateful for his understanding. "They really suck."

"You're not kidding. They're pretty tough on a guy's ego."

"I bet."

They both grinned.

"You good?" Jerrod asked as they approached South Grand Avenue.

She was still shaky, but it would pass. "Yeah. Thanks."

He let go of her hand as Hunter took the turn, heading into the parking garage. Hunter pulled up to the lobby entrance, and Ethan got out. He came around and opened her door, shielding her exit as Jerrod hugged his arm around her waist, stepping out just after she did. "I'll call you later," Jerrod said to Ethan.

"We'll keep our eyes on the headlines and see where this thing goes."

Jerrod nodded as Abby slid her card in the slot

and they went inside.

"Afternoon, Mrs. T, Mr. T," Moses said as he pressed the "up" button on the elevator.

"Good afternoon, Moses," she and Jerrod said at the same time as they stepped in.

"Enjoy your day."

"You too," Abby replied as the doors slid closed and she glanced from their side-by-side reflection to Jerrod.

He turned his head, meeting her stare. "You okay?"

"Yeah. No. I don't know." She shrugged, shaking her head. "I don't know what I am."

The elevator dinged, sliding open. Jerrod stepped out first. "We're good."

She followed as he unlocked the door, stepping in before him, happy to be home as she sagged against the wall and pulled off her boots. "How bad is this, Jerrod?"

"I don't know yet. We'll have to keep our eyes on the papers and see what Toni's up to."

She walked to the living room and plunked herself on the couch, pulling the elastic from her hair, massaging her scalp, trying to banish the tension.

Jerrod poured a glass of water and settled himself on the opposite cushion.

She stared out the window as she continued kneading at the ache along the base of her skull. "Tomorrow's it. After tomorrow I'm finished. No more unnecessary risks."

"You need to be."

She looked at him. "What if it's too late?"

"We'll monitor the situation and go from there."

"What's the worst-case scenario?"

"Worst-case scenario is always evacuation, but

let's take this in steps."

She nodded, hating the idea of picking up and leaving everything behind. “I’m sorry again for freaking out.”

He shrugged. “It’s no big deal.”

“Yes, it is. Every panic attack is a step in the wrong direction. Have you ever had one?”

“No.” He set his glass on a coaster on the coffee table.

“I never did either until all of this happened." She stood, overwhelmed by the day, by her entire life. "Not all that long ago I was any other normal woman making her way in the world." And she wanted that back, desperately.

"You still are."

She laughed, refusing to give in to the bitterness of her reality. Her mother let anger and misery eat her whole until eventually she'd given up—a path she never wanted to go down. "No. Not even close." She shook her head. "I'm going to get to work." Right now her sketchpad and fabric felt like the only ‘normal’ she had.

CHAPTER EIGHT

ABBY WORE HER SOFT WHITE ROBE AND SAT IN THE MAKEUP chair, closing her eyes as Jackie lined her lids and Marco curled the ends of her hair. She savored the familiar sensations of brushes gliding along her skin and gentle fingers moving through her black locks in lulling strokes. It had been *months* since she'd taken her place in front of the blinding bulbs of the vanity mirrors. She missed playing dress up; she yearned to strut down the runway as she'd done hundreds of times before.

"So, what's *Escape* all about?" Connie Withers, *Trendy*'s Fashion Editor, asked as she sat in the next chair over, typing away on her laptop.

"*Escape* is a high-quality fashion line that not only looks great but has a purpose. Our goal at Lily Brand is to give every endangered woman caught in a bad situation the opportunity to get away and start over. Everyone deserves a chance to begin again."

"Open your eyes, Abby," Jackie murmured.

She did, just as Jackie came at her with a thick mascara wand.

"And how does *Escape* and Lily Brand plan to accomplish this?"

"We'll open safe houses in the Baltimore and Los Angeles areas to start. We hope to have our first two locations up and running by mid-March. One hundred percent of *Escape*'s profits will go to emergency housing for those in need of a safe place to stay. Counselors will be on hand. Outreach and job training will also be available."

"This sounds great, Abby—and lofty."

She shrugged her shoulders as Jackie applied blusher and Marco pulled the last of her hair needing curls from the small twist he'd created with a clip. "It sounds like the right thing to do."

"The *Escape* line is your baby. You came up with the idea after surviving quite an ordeal of your own."

"Yes." She relaxed her tensing shoulders as she met Jerrod's eyes in the mirror. He sat on the couch behind her, watching her closely.

There was no way to avoid the conversation. The topic of her abduction would come up again and again while she promoted the new line. It was time to get used to that. "I definitely saw the darker side of humanity, but I also had a chance to see the strength we all posses to survive and overcome."

"Is that what you're doing? Surviving, overcoming?"

She uncurled her hands hidden below the black smock. "No. I did survive, now I'm picking up the pieces and moving on. My goal is to leave the past behind and continue looking ahead. I have a lot of amazing things coming my way."

Connie gave her a nod of approval.

"So, what did you think of *The Times* article accusing Lily Brand of not only hiring prostitutes but paying them below the standard wage?"

She swallowed the rush of anger as she thought of Toni Torrell. "I would say her accusations are irresponsible journalism. Our goal at Lily Brand is empowerment, no matter an individual's background. All of our models are paid above union wage. The men and women on our teams do their jobs well. Their past has little to do with their rate of compensation."

"Well said."

She smiled. "Thanks."

"And what about today's headlines? Lily's Youth Program has been a well kept secret."

And she thanked her lucky stars she was still in the clear. Fate had been on her side when Toni's camera captured Lily and the kids crowded around their new equipment while she had been on the main floor speaking with Jerrod. By some miracle she'd dodged the headlines for another day. "Lily's focus is always on helping others—"

The studio door slammed, and Abby jumped as Zenn MacGreggor walked in the room, followed by his harried assistant. "I'm ready to begin." Zenn clapped twice for everyone's attention, as if his three-inch, bleached blond spikes and funky, checkered black and white top weren't enough to draw the eye.

"Oh, we better wrap this up," Connie said with a roll of her eyes. Zenn MacGreggor was well known for his brilliant photography and impossible demands. "Thanks for sitting down with me, Abby." Connie held out her hand.

Abby returned her handshake. "Thank you for giving *Escape* great publicity."

"I'm happy to help." Connie stood, gathering her tape recorder and laptop. "I wish I could say enjoy your shoot, but I won't bother."

Abby laughed.

"Where's my model?" Zenn barked.

"Oh dear," Jackie mumbled as she slid a final brush of powder along Abby's temples.

"Let's make this *happen*, people." Zenn clapped again.

Abby met Jerrod's eyes in the mirror for the

second time, and she shrugged.

He smiled and went back to reading his paper.

“Ms. Harris.” A tiny woman with bright red streaks in her black hair hurried her way. “I'm Leah, Zenn's assistant. If there's anything you need, just let me know. Come with me and we'll get you set up for the first shots.” She grabbed Abby's arm, pulling her to the changing area before Jackie could remove the long black smock. “We have several series we'll run through. Your image will be used throughout the magazine.” She closed them in the dressing room.

Abby eyed the doorknob. “Uh, I need that open.”

“Huh? Excuse me?” Leah turned back with the first outfit in hand, one of Lily's long red dresses that would leave little to the imagination.

She swallowed, loosening the tight ball in her throat. “The door. Please open the door.”

“Oh, sorry. All the way?”

“No. Just a couple of inches is fine.”

Leah opened the door.

“Thank you.”

“Where is my *model*?” Zenn hollered.

“Ugh. Here, turn.” Leah yanked Abby around and pulled off the smock. “Get this on before he throws a tantrum.”

"*Before* he throws a tantrum?"

"This is nothing."

Abby disrobed in front of Leah, too accustomed to being half naked to feel shy. There was little room for modesty in this business. She secured the strapless, backless bra in place and slid the slinky dress over her head, careful not to mess up Marco and Jackie's hard work. She examined herself in the mirror as Leah pulled up the zipper, stopping an inch above her butt, and tied the two strings at the back of her neck. The long dress clung to every curve, exposing most of her right leg, a healthy peek at her cleavage, and left her entire back naked—elegant and extremely sexy.

“Perfect,” Leah smiled. “You look incredible. Let’s go make Zenn happy. I like it so much better when he’s happy.”

Abby chuckled. “I’ll do my best to make him delirious.”

“I wouldn’t hate that.”

They stepped out, and Marco slid two bracelets on her wrist as she walked by. She noted that Jerrod was no longer sitting on the couch.

“Yes! Yes!” Zenn clapped again. “You were almost worth the wait. Come to me.” The man was skinny as a rail and no more than five-foot seven, yet he terrified everyone.

She searched for Jerrod among the cluster of light poles and meters, the makeup space and opened bathroom door. Where was he? Jerrod never left her when they were out. Her brows furrowed with concern as he stepped from the studio's kitchenette, pausing as he put his phone away. Their eyes met.

“I think you might have to knock this guy out,” she said out of the corner of her mouth as Leah dragged her past him. She glanced over her shoulder, waiting for Jerrod's smile, but he only stared at her. Was everything okay? She stopped, pulling away from Leah. "Hold on." She walked to Jerrod. "What's wrong?"

"Nothing."

She studied his calm eyes. "Are you sure?"

"Yeah. I was checking in with Ethan. You'll be the first to know if something's up. Go take your pictures."

"Okay."

"Come *on*, model," Zenn huffed with his hands on

his hips.

Abby rolled her eyes and turned.

“Stand over there.” Zenn pointed to the ‘x’ taped on the floor. "Music!"

Leah hustled across the room. Seconds later music blasted into the room.

"Test shots," he said as he pulled the camera up in front of his face. “Yes! Yes! The camera *loves* you. Leah, fans.”

Leah played with the flow of cool wind blowing Abby's way while Zenn fiddled with his light meters.

Abby looked at Jerrod as he took his seat on the couch, grabbing a magazine this time, searching for any hints of tension. He seemed relaxed.

“Over here, model! Over here! Give me some movement.”

She focused on Zenn and moved her arms and hips, dancing for the lens, jutting her right leg out as she played with the hem of the dress.

“Fabulous. I'm in love! Good. Good. Perfect. But I want more. Give me more."

And she gave it, turning, bending, strutting, consumed by the euphoria of doing one of the things she loved best while Zenn followed her around. The worry of headlines and precautions vanished as she got lost in the glory of posing. How could she have forgotten the rush of working the camera?

"Yes! Yes!" Zenn lifted his head, breathless. "Go change."

Four wardrobe changes and two hairstyles later, Abby stopped for a sip of water as she sat by Jerrod on the arm of the couch in a simple pink tank top, denim shorts, and strappy leather sandals.

“Fix her hair, Marco. I want her ready for spring. Leah, where’s my male model?" He glanced at his watch. "Where the hell *is* he?"

"I don't—I don't know, Zenn," Leah answered.

"He's late," he spat. "I don't have time for late. My flight leaves in six hours."

Marco hustled over with a kit of hairbrushes, ties and spray, immediately pulling Abby's hair up in a ponytail.

"Abby, are you all right if I step out for a couple minutes?" Leah asked, rolling her eyes.

"Definitely." Poor Leah couldn't possibly make enough to put up with the man talking to his cameras. He was *insane*. With a small shake of her head, Abby slapped her hand on Jerrod's shoulder while Jackie freshened her makeup. "How you holding up, big guy?"

"If I had some earplugs I'd be fine. That guy's obnoxious." He tossed a look toward Zenn.

"He's very passionate about his art," she tried.

His brow rose. "I'm feeling passionate about a right hook."

She laughed, and Jackie chuckled.

Leah came back in and muttered something to Zenn, which sent him into another tirade.

"Oh, shit. I'm outta here." Jackie grabbed her brushes on the table and abandoned ship.

"I'm coming with you." Marco hurried after her.

"How can I create a masterpiece when I'm missing a *subject*? I need a model." Zenn whirled. "You." He pointed to Jerrod. "Take off your shirt."

Jerrod set down his fitness magazine. "Huh?"

"Lose the shirt, socks and shoes, and put this on." Zenn threw a sage green button down his way. "You've got good bones and excellent muscles. The camera will like you well enough."

Abby rushed up from her makeshift seat, trying to

stop a disaster in the making. "Uh, he's not a model, Zenn."

"He is today. I have to have these shots *now*. I'm leaving for Europe this evening."

"Yes, but—"

"If you want this exposure for your line, we need these pictures. No exceptions. I have a vision. No model and I scrap the whole thing." He crossed his arms like a spoiled child.

"Oh." What else could she say? She looked at Jerrod, trying to find a way to make this work for everyone. "How do you feel about having a couple of pictures taken?"

"I feel like it's not going to happen."

"Okay." She nibbled her lip as her stomach sank. *Escape* needed this; it was national exposure. "Um, how about we change things around," she suggested to Zenn.

"Change things around? Why, yes, what an idea. Let's change things around. Why didn't I think of that?" He slapped his hand against the table, and Abby flinched.

"All right already." Jerrod rushed to his feet. "I'll take the damn picture." He toed off his sneakers, yanked his navy blue polo from his jeans, pulling it over his head, throwing it to the couch.

Holy *wowza*. Abby tracked her eyes up every glorious inch of Jerrod's cut body, surrendering to the rages of lust rushing through her belly. She could count on one hand the number of times she'd seen him without his shirt on. Four. Four measly opportunities to ogle all of that yumminess. He was *magnificent*—broad shoulders, great pecs, a washboard stomach she wanted to brush her fingers down. And that tattoo, the criss-crossy band encircling an inch of his amazing right bicep.

"See, you'll do just fine," Zenn said.

Jerrod put on the green shirt and started buttoning.

"No, leave it undone. Now come." Zenn left the room with Leah following quickly behind.

Abby hooked her arm through Jerrod's as they walked down the hall. "I'm sorry about this. I don't know what else to do."

Jerrod grunted as they turned into the third room on the left, stepping into a space that looked like a country backyard; fake flowers, bushes, and a wraparound porch included. A swing hung tied to a fake, thick tree branch sprouting from the wall.

"Sit on the swing," Zenn demanded as he read his light meters.

Abby started toward the wooden swing.

"No, him."

"Zenn, this is Jerrod," Abby tried.

"Yes. Fine. Whatever. Sit."

Jerrod took his seat, and Leah rushed over to fix his shirt, rolling the sleeves halfway up his forearms, pulling at the sides so that his stomach was exposed.

"Look at me, Jerrod."

Jerrod looked at Zenn, clenching his jaw.

"Son of a bitch, you're brilliant. The camera *wants* you. Abby, hop on the swing."

Jerrod moved to stand.

"No, stay. Abby, on his lap, facing him. I want you to swing. It's a warm spring day. You're a couple laughing, enjoying each other's company. Make it happen."

Jerrod scooted back, eyeing Abby as she climbed on awkwardly and hooked her legs behind him, placing her hands above his on the rope. "I'm *so* sorry.

You have no idea."

"You owe me big time."

"I know." She smiled apologetically.

Leah swooped in and fussed with both of their outfits, pulling here, tugging there, taking the hip holster from Jerrod's belt, holding it gingerly between two fingers. "I'll just hold this for you."

"The weapon's secure and the safety's on."

"Mmm." She walked over by Zenn.

"Now *swing*," Zenn commanded.

"Demanding bastard," Jerrod muttered as he pushed off, sending them soaring.

Abby's stomach plunged with the movement and settled as she stared into Jerrod's miserable eyes. "This will be over before you know it, big guy."

"Relax, Jerrod," Zenn barked. "The camera sees everything."

"It'll help if you smile." She crossed her eyes and stuck out her tongue, giving him a cheesy grin.

He showed her his teeth in his worst fake smile, and Zenn swore.

She threw her head back, laughing, and Jerrod chuckled, moving one arm to her back, keeping her from falling off the swing.

Zenn took shot after shot. "Yes! Yes! *Perfect*! I got it. Wardrobe change for a wrap. Abigail, go with Leah. Jerrod, come with me."

"Can you handle one more picture?" Abby asked as she freed herself from his lap.

"If it's as painless as this one."

"I'm sure it will be." She leaned in close to his face, grabbing his chin between her fingers. "You're a peach, Mr. Quinn." She kissed his cheek, relieved that everything was working out.

"Come on, Abby." Leah handed Jerrod the holster

and grabbed her arm. "We need to get you changed and have Marco fix your hair."

"Duty calls, soldier. I'll be back in less than five." She gave Jerrod a salute.

He smiled as he followed behind them.

~~~~

Jerrod rubbed at his chin as he sat in his black boxers on crisp white sheets, waiting for Abby to appear from the dressing room, trying to figure out how the hell he'd gotten himself roped into this mess. Just an hour ago he'd been minding his own business, reading the latest issue of Men's Health, thinking about what he would have for a late lunch when they finished here; now he was half naked on some fake bedroom set crowded with cameras, umbrella-things, and fans. He was a Close Protection Agent, not a damn supermodel.

The studio door slammed behind him, and he grit his teeth as Zenn marched back in the room. If he'd ever met a more obnoxious man, he wasn't coming to mind.

"Where's my model?"

If Zenn hollered one more time...

Leah poked her head out of the half-opened door. "We're coming. Marco just needs one more minute with Abby's hair."

"Hurry *up*." He walked over to Jerrod, eyeing him, nodding. "Yes, I like this." He opened his mouth to yell again, no doubt, and closed it when Abby stepped from the dressing room in the white cotton robe she'd been wearing off and on all day. Marco followed behind, toying with loose, glossy ringlets he'd curled in her hair. Abby's makeup was different. It was as if
~~~~

she wore none at all, yet her eyes appeared sooty and impossibly huge.

"Good," Zenn said as he marched back to his camera. "Abby, lose the robe so we can finish this up."

She pulled the tie and set her robe aside, walking to the bed in nothing more than flossy black panties riding high and a matching bra, plunging low, leaving little to the imagination.

Goddamn. Jerrod's gaze trailed over swells of creamy breasts, down her smooth toned tummy, slim hips, and incredibly *hot* legs. He looked up quickly, giving Abby a small smile, struggling to keep his eyes above her neckline. This is *not* what he'd been expecting for the last wardrobe change. What happened to the beautiful, sweet woman he laughed with on the swing? How would he ever look at her again and not see the naughty siren walking his way?

"Go ahead and get on the bed." Zenn told her.

She crawled toward Jerrod.

"Stop," Zenn demanded. "I need a test shot. Head down, Abby. Look up from under your lashes. Son of a bitch, you're perfect. Pout."

She pursed her lips slightly on Zenn's cue.

"Now smile for me—slow, sexy. Bedroom smile, Abby."

A slow smile spread over her lips, and Jerrod struggled to swallow as the camera snapped rapidly. She was killing him.

Zenn lowered the camera, grabbing another lens, playing with his lights and meters.

Abby sat next to Jerrod, legs crossed, completely at ease as if she weren't lounging around in barely there underwear. "This should be it."

"Thank *god*."

"Jerrod, I want you to lay back against the pillows,

knees up, one leg free of the sheets. Abby, I want you on top of him. Go ahead and sit on his stomach. I want light, sexual, playful. Your fun on the swing continued to the bedroom. We're telling a story here. You two have a natural chemistry. Let me see it."

"I'm *so* sorry, Jerrod. *So* incredibly sorry," she repeated as she straddled him, sitting back.

He clenched his jaw as her firm ass pressed against his skin, sending his libido raging.

She looked down. "Have I mentioned how much I appreciate this?"

He grunted.

"You do realize I plan to make you breakfast for the rest of your life."

"And lunch and dinner," he added.

"We should probably throw in dessert for good measure." She smiled, wiggling against him, settling herself.

"Jerrod, put your hands on her hips, and keep talking like you are right now, but try not to look like you're pissed."

"I *am* pissed."

She laughed. "You're such a good sport."

He eyed her again and couldn't help but grin at the foolishness of the entire situation. "I'm never going to hear the end of this at work."

"Yeah, but you get dessert for life."

He chuckled as the camera snapped.

"Good. Better," Zenn said. "Now Jerrod, clasp your hands with Abby's. Abby lean forward. Look in his eyes."

He hesitated, then twined his fingers with hers as she leaned forward, her breasts pressing against his chest, their faces inches from each other, hands resting at the sides of his head.

"I'm thinking this definitely warrants chocolate chip cookies as soon as we get home."

They grinned at each other.

"Make it brownies and this *might* be forgivable—until I go into the office in a couple month and find a blown up shot of you and me hanging around in our underwear."

She laughed as he did. "So, double chunk brownies, then?"

"Now you're talking."

"Excellent," Zenn said, bursting Jerrod's bubble of contentment. For a moment he'd forgotten where they were, that some pain-in-the-ass photographer was capturing every second of this with a camera.

"Now, I want you both under the covers, facing each other. Abby, get rid of the top."

Jerrod opened his mouth to object, but closed it as Abby climbed off him and slid beneath the sheets, unclasping her bra, throwing it to the floor. He turned on his side, hoping he appeared as indifferent as everyone else. No one seemed bothered by the fact that he was laying with a mostly naked woman, his *principal*—including Abby.

"Abby, I want you curled up some, your knees touching Jerrod's stomach, your hand on his waist."

They moved closer, following Zenn's instructions.

He tensed as Abby's knees brushed his stomach and her cool hand rested against his waist.

"Jerrod, arm out. And Abby, I want you laying on it—right on his bicep. Look in each other's eyes. No smiles this time. Serious."

Abby lay her head on his bicep, and they stared in each other's eyes while Leah hustled around, pulling the sheet from Abby, fixing the cover so it appeared rumpled, only covering Jerrod's calves.

"Jerrod, I want your free hand in her hair, swiping it back from her face. Put your arm here." Zenn came over and positioned Jerrod's arm against Abby's soft skin, hiding most of her breast from view. "Now, I want passion. Intimacy. Give it to me."

Jerrod did as he was told, sliding his fingers through soft strands, gently brushing the hair away from her smooth, flawless cheek. The camera clicked continuously as he stared into the depths of dark blue. Here was kindness. Here was the sweet woman he couldn't shake from his brain. He breathed in her scent as he touched her, suddenly, desperately wanting this, but in *their* home, in *his* bed.

"Thank you," she murmured as she moved her thumb along his skin and Zenn hopped up on the mattress, bringing the lens in closer to their faces.

"You're welcome."

"Hot. Smokin' hot. I've got what I need." Zenn jumped down from the bed. "That's a wrap."

~~~~

His cell phone rang as he stepped into the hotel room. He set his bag on the queen-sized bed and answered. "What?"

"I found her."

Dimitri pulled the pack of Marlboros from his pocket as he stared out at Phoenix's skyline and mountains in the distance. "Where?"

"She's in LA working for Lily Brand."

He lit his cigarette, sucking in a deep drag of smoke. "Where does she live?"

"I don't know."

He sighed as he shook his head. Victor was running out of chances to get this right. "How do you
~~~~

not *know* if you've found her? You said this before and it was a mistake."

"*Anton* said this before, and he was wrong. I see her on the internet while I'm sitting down to eat my hamburger and look at sports page and know I am right. Look at *The Times*. See for yourself. The story is breaking news in the afternoon addition. It just popped up."

Dimitri pulled his laptop from his case and connected to the free WiFi.

"She is the new mystery designer," Victor added. "I'm in Long Beach now waiting for our new shipment."

Dimitri typed in *The Times* URL and grinned as her face—the face he'd been searching for—filled his screen. Abigail Harris, former sex slave, was the new top story. "I've got you now, little bitch. I'm on first flight I can get to Los Angeles."

"Call when you arrive and I will pick you up. I'm thirty minutes from the airport."

"Find her address, but do nothing until I come. We will take care of this situation by night's end." He hung up and studied the picture of the beautiful blue-eyed angel who'd been a devil in disguise. "You're mine now," he whispered as he shut the lid and packed up, heading for the door.

CHAPTER NINE

ABBY STARED INTO THE DISMAL GRAY SKY AS THE CAB inched its way through late-afternoon traffic. The wipers swiped at the windshield in a rapid rhythm as rain pounded the roof with deafening drops. The cool afternoon and demanding day should have left her contentedly tired; instead, she was restless and eager to be home and away from Jerrod for a while.

The last couple of hours in her roommate's strong, sexy arms had churned her up, leaving her more confused than ever. She and Jerrod were friends. Their easy relationship was a comfort she'd counted on since her rescue; now everything was different. Something had changed while they lay among the sheets, staring into each other's eyes.

It had been a long time since a man touched her the way Jerrod did. She'd worried some about flashbacks and panic attacks as she crawled across the bed toward him, but then his gaze held hers and everything was okay. Dredges of anxiety returned when she lay mostly naked below the sheets, until his fingers slid through her hair and his arm brushed her breast, soothing as much as setting her aflame. She'd simply melted, yearning for more as she fell under his rhythmic spell. Jerrod had awoken a piece of her she'd feared might never return. For the first time since the rape, the idea of an intimate physical connection wasn't scary. She wanted Jerrod's hands on her again—and hers on him. She suddenly and desperately craved a piece of Jerrod Quinn.

Shocked by her own thoughts, she darted him a glance, giving him a small smile when she realized he was looking her way. “It’s really pouring,” she tried, attempting normal conversation when *nothing* felt normal at all.

“Yeah. It hasn’t rained like this for a while.”

The cabbie took the left on South Grand Ave, pulling up to the curb.

"Thanks." Jerrod handed the man a fifty. "Ready?" he said to her.

“Yes.” She slid closer to his side.

“Out at the same time. Me to the right as usual. Hurry to the doors.”

She nodded and they stepped into the pouring rain, one right after the other, running with Jerrod directly next to her, his arm around her waist as they hurried to the door.

“Afternoon, Ms. T." Moses smiled, handing Abby a towel from the small stack by his station.

“Good afternoon, and thanks.” She blotted her face with the soft cotton and stepped into the elevator, running her hands through her soaked hair as Jerrod sent the car up. “Ugh, I feel like a wet dog.”

“Well, you look a lot better.”

“Aww, you’re so sweet.” She bumped Jerrod in the side, trying to put the foolishness in the cab behind her. *Friends*. She and Jerrod were *friends*.

He smiled and looked out when the door opened. “We’re good.” He let them into their place, and she walked in first.

“Thanks.” She took off her wet jacket. “Here, let me have your coat.”

He slid off the black jacket, handing it over.

She draped the soggy clothes on hangers and

hung them on opposite sides of the closet door, shivering as her hair dripped cold trails down her arms. She wiped at the drops with the towel, stepping closer to Jerrod. “Here, bend over some. You’re dripping all over your shirt.”

He bent forward, and she rubbed the towel over his dark blond hair.

“Thanks.” He looked up, his hair standing in spiky tufts.

She chuckled. “Don’t thank me yet.” She tugged on his shoulder, bringing him closer. “Right now you look like a more conservative, buffer version of Zenn.”

He winced. “Anything but that.”

She laughed, standing on her tiptoes, brushing her fingers through his hair to smooth it back in place. “Thank you again for today. I don’t know what I would’ve done without your help.”

He shrugged. “It wasn’t so bad, I guess.”

“Zenn definitely loved your face." She gave his jaw a gentle pat and continued with her work, more relaxed now that they were home and everything seemed back on track. "You’ll have agents beating down our door in no time.”

He smiled. “I don’t know about that.”

“Oh, I do.” She wiped a stray drop from his cheek. “You’ll be strutting your way down the catwalk in no time. I’ll be able to say I was your first modeling partner,” she sighed wistfully.

They smiled at each other.

She brushed at his sides one last time and settled flat on her feet. “*Voila*. You’re officially put back together.”

“I appreciate it.” He held her gaze.

“Least I can do.” She licked her lips, suddenly nervous as electricity snapped and hummed between them like it had in the studio. Maybe they weren't back on track after all. "So, I guess I'll get started on those brownies."

"Can't wait." He slid his hands in his pockets. "I'm going to make a few calls."

"Okay."

Neither of them moved.

What *was* this? What was going on? The surge of lust rushed back to her stomach as her heart pounded. "Today—" she swallowed the ball of nerves, looked down, clearing her throat, meeting his gaze again. "Did you feel..." What? How could she put into words the intensity passing between them while they lay in the bed, while they stared at each other right now? "I—" Taking a chance, she reached up, touching his chin with the tips of her fingers.

His jaw clenched as he grabbed her wrist, clutching, his eyes burning into hers.

She regained her stance on her tiptoes, needing to see what this was, and pressed her lips to the warmth of his, slowly, gently, easing back, watching him.

He released her arm and gripped her waist, letting go as if she'd burned him, then grabbed hold again, his hands sliding to her hips as she moved in for a second taste. Closing her eyes, she absorbed a hint of his potent flavor as his mouth gave against hers. She stepped closer, her chest brushing his as silky tongues met, and he pushed her back.

"Abigail, don't. Don't," he repeated on a shaky breath as he shoved his fingers through his hair, messing up what she'd just fixed.

Heat rushed to her cheeks as the sting of humiliation coursed through her veins. What did she just *do*? "I'm—I don't know what I was thinking."

He jammed his hands in his pockets. "Don't worry

about it."

She would do more than worry about it. How would she ever look at him again? "I—" She shook her head, turned and hurried toward her room.

"Abigail."

Ignoring him, she kept walking, closing her door most of the way, and leaned against the wall, pressing her hands to her face, shaking her head. "I can't believe I *did* that." She rarely made the first move with a man, and now she remembered why. Never had she gauged a moment so wrong. She'd gotten caught up in an afternoon, which was nothing more than the product of a photographer's direction. Not once had Jerrod *ever* hinted at any sort of romantic interest, and she'd gone and kissed him.

She dropped her hands, cringing, and slid down the wall, sitting on the plush carpet as another wave of mortification rocked through her, making her sick. She and Jerrod *lived* together. He provided her protection. And now a perfectly good thing would be incredibly awkward.

His footsteps started her way, and she grimaced, wishing for a redo. "Please no. Please no," she whispered when he paused next to her door. "*Please* no." She clenched her fists and relaxed when he turned into his own room and shut himself in. "Thank *god*." She didn't want to rehash her major mishap—not with him, anyway. She grabbed her phone from her back jean pocket and dialed her sister's number.

"Hello?"

"Lex—"

"What's wrong?"

"Oh, *everything*." She rolled her eyes, replaying the horrifying moment.

"What's going on?"

"I'm an idiot." She stared at the drops sliding down the huge panes of glass across her room.

"Of course you're not."

"Oh yes I am. I kissed Jerrod."

"*What*?"

She wrinkled her nose and rested her forehead in her hand. "Don't say 'what' like that."

"Ab, what on earth happened?"

"I did the whole photo shoot thing today. The male model never showed up, so the photographer roped Jerrod into posing with me for a few shots."

"Wow. I'm impressed."

She grinned despite the situation. "Zenn can be pretty persuasive, but Jerrod did it to help me out and shut him up." Her smile vanished as she plucked at the soft beige carpet fibers with jerky movements. "So we did this swing shot where I had to sit on his lap—no big deal. Then we had to do this set where I was in panties and a bra, and he was in his boxers. Zenn made me straddle him. I'm sitting on his sexy six-pack, holding his hands, and he's flashing me these killer grins. That crooked incisor gets me, Lex. I like to make him smile just so I can see it."

"There is something about that tooth and those reluctant smiles."

"I know, right?" She shook her head. "Anyway, one direction leads to another, and I'm topless. It was kind of steamy. He was touching me and staring into my eyes. For the first time in a long time I *wanted* someone to touch me. Jerrod. I always thought we were just friends, but lately, I don't know. I think I have feelings for him, Lex."

"Are you sure you aren't confusing emotion with lust?"

"No. Not one hundred percent, but I think it's

more than that. He's such a good guy. He's kind and steady and let's not forget *hot*. He's got the whole package."

"Jerrod's a wonderful man."

"But he's not interested in me." She groaned. "Oh, god, Lex. I kissed him and he only sort of kissed me back."

"What does that mean?"

"It means we did the whole stare into each other's eyes thing, and I touched his chin. He grabbed my wrist and held it, which to me was the signal to go ahead. I kissed him, kind of eased away and went back for more. He seemed like he was into it. His hands were on my hips, then he pushed me back and said 'don't.'" She groaned louder, reliving the embarrassment for the millionth time.

"Hmm. Maybe not all is lost. I mean he didn't flat-out shut you down."

"But he *did* shut me down eventually." She leaned against the wall, and her eyes grew wide. "Oh crap. What if he's seeing someone? The thought never even crossed my mind."

"I don't think he's seeing anyone."

"He's not exactly an open book. I can write down what I know about his personal life on a Post-It note—you know the tiny ones?"

"But he's always with you."

"Not always. Mostly, but I do come and stay with you guys sometimes."

"I'm pretty positive he's not, Ab. Jack said something about him having a serious thing with some woman awhile back, but I'm fairly certain he's a free agent."

"I guess that's something." She sighed and touched her lips, still able to feel his if she let herself.

"What am I going to do?"

"Come have lunch with me tomorrow."

Her phone beeped, alerting her to another call. She quickly glanced at the readout. Lily. She was not in the mood to rehash the shoot. Ignoring the second beep, she focused on her sister. "I don't think that's a good idea right now, Lex. I'm pretty much on house arrest for the foreseeable future until all of this stupid press crap dies down. I was lucky enough to dodge the headlines this morning. The last thing we need is a picture of you and me somehow popping up in the news."

"Abby."

"Stranger things have happened. I want to see you—desperately. I need you, but I need you safe even more. We'll see each other Saturday for Wren's bridal shower at Fort Cooke. I think I can survive that long, especially if I don't leave my room. I can live without food for two days. I have a faucet in my bathroom."

Alexa laughed. "I think you should clear the air. You'll both feel better for it."

"Yeah, maybe, but the faucet idea isn't half bad. So, enough about me and my latest disaster. How did the doctor's appointment go today?"

"Great. Looks like we're having a boy."

Abby grinned as her eyes filled. "Oh, Lex, that's awesome. Why did you let me go on and on when you actually had something cool to talk about? I can't wait to meet him. Any names yet?"

"Owen Michael."

"I love it. Owen Michael Matthews. I'm completely in love, and I haven't even seen his little face yet."

"Four more months to go."

"Mommy!" Olivia called in the background.

"Oh, Livy's up from her nap. I'll be right there!" she called to her daughter.

"I'll let you go."

"Jack's got her. He's working from home since we had the appointment. What are you going to do with the rest of your day?"

"Sulk and make brownies—double fudge, then I'll put something together for dinner. I promised Jerrod three square meals a day plus dessert for the rest of his life as payment for the shoot today."

"Talk to him, Ab. Give me a call if you need anything, and I'll see you Saturday."

"Okay. Thanks. I love you."

"I love you too. Bye."

"Bye." She hung up and sighed. Lex was right; she needed to clear the air. She stood, shoving her phone back in her pocket, and changed out of her still soggy top, replacing it with a navy-blue, spaghetti-strap scoop neck and sweater. She walked to Jerrod's door, raised her hand to knock, and dropped it. What was she supposed to say? *Sorry I planted one on you; let's forget the whole thing!*

Brownies. She would make brownies, figure out exactly how to broach this incredibly awkward situation, then she would talk to him. She stepped back and went to the kitchen, gathering the ingredients for double chunk brownies as her phone rang again. She ignored Lily for the second time as she cranked up the radio and got to work.

~~~~

Jerrod forced the weighted bar above his chest, blowing out with the exertion, still trying to pull himself together. He'd pushed his body to the limits
~~~~

with a strenuous series of pushups, power squats, dumbbell curls, and anything else he could think of in an attempt to banish Abby from his mind, but the physical pain of his workout wasn't doing what he'd hoped. He was coming to the conclusion he would sweat to death before he rid himself of this *want* for Abigail Harris.

He kept flashing back to her amazing body pressed to his in her barely there underwear and the flower-petal softness of her firm breast against his arm as he slid his fingers through her hair. How was he supposed to stop thinking about her smile and those eyes or the way her full lips captured his, giving him a teasing sample of her addicting flavor?

He never should have let that happen. Allowing Abby to kiss him had been an incredibly stupid mistake. He'd tried to fight his needs while her teasing fingers moved along his jaw and he breathed her in, but he hadn't fought hard enough. He'd often wondered what her sexy mouth would feel like against his, what she tasted like, how it could be between them. Now he knew and wished he didn't. It had taken every ounce of willpower he possessed to push her away instead of pull her to him and devour her whole the way he'd wanted.

He glanced at his door, contemplating the idea of rushing to the kitchen, carrying her back to his room, and putting them both out of their misery, so he lowered the heavy bar three inches above his chest, holding his form with fatigued arms, trembling, blowing out rapid puffs, punishing himself for the latest wave of staggering lust. Using the last of his reserves, he settled the bar back in its place and sat up, scrubbing his hands over his drenched face. “Son of a bitch.” How the hell was he supposed to have known one damn photo shoot would change everything?

He'd been attracted to Abby from the first moment he saw her. She was a stunning woman, but he'd handled it. Now he wasn't sure he could. Their entire situation was suddenly different. The professional lines he never crossed were blurring—had been blurring for some time. Abby was the first person he'd ever allowed past his rigid boundaries. Her free spirit was infectious, her spontaneity easy to roll with. She was incredibly sweet and affectionate and touchy-feely with it. He'd grown accustomed to her singing and dancing and constant desire to include him in it. She was a hugger, and god knew why, he missed it when he went too long without one. But now they were walking a dangerous road, and that had to end. It was time to put them back on the right track. No more hugs. Definitely no more kisses. And the dancing had to stop. He was her bodyguard, nothing more.

He grabbed the towel on the floor and mopped up the sweat rolling down his forehead and chest as he walked to the bathroom, dropped his shorts, turned on the shower, and stepped in. He reached for the shampoo bottle, squirted a glob in his hand and massaged his scalp, immediately dismissing the memory of Abby's fingers sliding through his hair.

Rinsing away the lather, he grabbed the bar of soap next, giving himself a quick wash, shut off the water and reached for his towel, going still when the alarm on his cell phone activated with several loud, rapid beeps. "Fuck. Abigail!" He snatched the towel off the bar, wrapping it around his waist as he sprinted toward the scent of freshly baked brownies and blaring music in the kitchen. "Abigail!"

She didn't respond as she belted out the song's refrain, using a wooden spoon as her microphone, and danced around the room with her back to him.

"Abigail." He grabbed her arm, yanking her around, and she screamed.

The spoon fell from her hand, landing with a clatter as she glared. "What are you *doing*? You know I don't like to be grabbed."

"Let's go." He pulled her with him to his bedroom, keeping her as close to the interior walls and as far away from the panes of glass as possible.

"What's wrong?" They stepped in the room as his phone continued its piercing beep. "Oh—oh my god. They found me."

"Stay against the wall over there." Modesty was the least of his worries as he dropped his towel and yanked on jeans and the first shirt he pulled from his dresser. Socks and sneakers came next. "We need to go. Just like we've practiced before."

She nodded as her breathing came in rapid puffs.

He grabbed the cell phone and wallet from his side table, slid his gun in its holster, and left everything else behind. "Come on." Taking her hand, they ran down the hall. He reached in the closet for two black jackets and caps, handing a set to her, putting on his as she did. He pressed Ethan's number on speed dial, listening to it ring once, twice.

"Evacuation in progress. Five minutes or less," Ethan said.

"What the hell's going on?"

"Abby's cover's blown. Her face is all over the front page of *The Times* afternoon edition. Somehow Toni Torrell found out she's Lily's new 'it girl.'"

"Fuck. How long?"

"The story broke about an hour ago. Lily's been

calling the office but Mia's replacement put her messages through to my voicemail. She said she tried Abby and got her voicemail as well. She tried you and didn't get anything."

"My phone hasn't rung."

"I don't know. I've been in meetings. They're already looking for her, Jerrod. The tech at Lily Brand just gave me a call letting me know their computers alerted to a breech in the firewall. There was a search for Abby's address."

"Damn it." This was the worst-case scenario they'd prepared for, but he'd hoped would never happen.

"Austin just got the call. Your team's pulling in. Let me know when you get to the safe house and we'll go from there."

"All right." He hung up, slid his phone in his jean pocket, and peered out the peephole, opening the door and pointing his gun into the empty hall. "Let's go." He moved sideways, constantly glancing from left to right as they made their way to the service elevator. He punched in the code he'd been given months ago, keeping Abby behind him, aiming his weapon at the door as it slid open. *Clear*. They stepped in and descended to the ground floor, neither talking as he'd instructed the three or four times they'd run through this very drill. The elevator dinged and he pushed her into the corner, blocking her body with his as the doors slid open again. He readied his pistol, resting his finger on the trigger, aiming at the two men standing in the hall of the side entrance, holding their badges up for him to see.

"This way," one of the men said.

Jerrod pulled Abby against him, wrapping his arm around her waist despite several men surrounding them. They kept a hurried pace as they walked through the dim garage to the two identical green and white vans with cleaning company logos painted on the sides. The back doors opened on the left hand vehicle, and he lifted Abby in with him. The doors immediately shut behind them, closing them in the dark. Two taps hit the side, and the van took off.

"Jerrod." Abby's clammy hand clutched his wrist as they sat on the bench along the wall, her rapid breathing growing increasingly unsteady. "I—I can't be in here. I can't stay in here."

He studied Abby, already in all-out panic mode. "Just until we get to where we're going."

"I can't," she whispered, her eyes huge, her whole body trembling as she tried to stand.

He tightened his hold around her waist, keeping her at his side. "Abigail."

"I can't breathe." She gasped, pressing her hands to her chest.

He took her chin in his hand. "Yes you can."

"No. It's just like the one—it's just like the one they put me in."

He'd seen her scared before and witnessed several panic attacks, but this was true, stark terror. "Abigail."

She gripped his shirt, yanking him closer. "Get me out of here."

"Abigail," he snapped, grabbing her wrists, feeling the rapid beat of her pulse. "Look at me. Deep breaths."

Tears flooded her pasty white cheeks. "I'm going to pass out. I'm going to—" Her eyes rolled back in her head, and she collapsed against him.

"Son of a bitch." He laid her on the floor, pulling off her cap. "Abigail." He gently slapped at her cheek. "Abigail. Come on."

Her eyes fluttered open.

He relaxed his jaw and fanned her face with the hat. “Welcome back.”

“Jerrod.” She took his hand.

“I’m right here.” He smiled down at her, wanting to keep her calm.

“They put me in a van. Dimitri and Victor put me in a van, and I couldn't get away.”

He stroked her cheek, drying her tears, wishing he could banish her horrible memories. “I know.”

“I hate small spaces. I tried to escape and they locked me in the closet for days.”

He kept his touch light despite the rage boiling his blood. She rarely spoke of the worst parts of her captivity. On the rare occasion she did, he ached for her, understanding she’d lived through two months of pure hell. “No one’s going to hurt you again.”

“Are we almost there?”

“I think so.” They more than likely had a good thirty-five to forty minutes to go in this traffic.

“I’m sorry.”

“Don’t be.”

“I think I’m okay to get up.”

She was so small and defenseless; her cheeks were still sheet white. He lifted her in his arms and sat on the bench, cocooning her against him. “Go ahead and relax until we get there.”

She clung to him, trembling as she looked toward the cabin. “Who are these people?"

"Ethan uses them from time to time. They're used to getting people out of places quickly."

"What’s going to happen now?”

“We'll call Ethan when we get to the safe house and figure things out from there."

“Is Lex okay?”

He nodded. “Everyone involved is being taken

care of. This is precautionary at this point."

"I'm worried about her and the baby. And Livy."

"They'll be fine. Jackson wouldn't have it any other way."

"That's true." She sighed, and her body finally relaxed against his. "I'm tired. I think I wore myself out."

"Why don't you catch a nap?" They would both be better off if she turned it off for a while.

"I can't sleep at a time like this." She settled her head on his shoulder and was out in less than five minutes.

~~~~

"It's over now," Abby soothed, hugging the pretty brown-haired stranger against her as the terrified girl shuddered and cried on the edge of the bed. "What's your name?"

"They told me I have to be Jena, but I'm Margret." She looked up as tears rained from her blue eyes. "I'm Margret Stowers."

"They call me Fawn, but I'm Abby." She wiped Margret's cheeks with a tissue. "Everything's going to be all right." It wasn't, but how could she tell Margret that? The pixie-faced girl couldn't be more than fourteen or fifteen, and she'd just been raped. It wouldn't be the last time. "Can you stand?"

"Yes, I think so. I'm sore. I think I'm bleeding."

Her heart broke as she nodded, brushing soft long locks behind Margret's ears. "We should get you cleaned up." As if that changed anything. She hated that the small gesture was all she could offer. There was so much more she wanted to do, but she was as trapped and powerless as the girl at her side. "Come
~~~~

on." She took Margret's hand, walking with her through the pretty suite reserved for DC's wealthier clients, and brought her to the bathroom, where she ran a washcloth under cold water. "I'll make you a cool cloth. You can wipe yourself up. Did the man use a condom?"

She nodded and wept again. "I want to go home."

Abby's eyes filled, and she swallowed her grief, wanting to be strong for the child quaking at her side. She shut off the tap and pulled Margret close for another hug. "I know you do, honey." She kissed her cheek. "I know."

"They threw me in a van and now I'm here," she sobbed, gripping her arms around Abby. "I'm so scared."

"I'm going to help you anyway I can," she murmured as she rested her cheek on Margret's hair, staring out the painted-shut windows. Outside the sun shined and flowers grew while children rode their bikes along the sidewalks. Freedom. But escape was impossible; she'd tried and spent days in the closet as punishment. She eased Margret back, wiping at her stream of tears. "You should clean up. It'll help with some of the—"

The door burst open, and she cringed as Renzo stepped in. He hadn't been by the house in two weeks. She'd hoped he wouldn't come back. "What the fuck is going on in here?"

"Nothing." Abby pulled away from Margret, already realizing Renzo would make his newest victim pay. "We're just washing up."

His eyes grew hot, angry, crazy, and he smiled as he rushed forward, grabbing Margret's arm. "You crying, little girl?"

Margret's sobbing grew louder, and Abby silently begged her to stop. Crying only made it worse. Renzo fed on their misery.

"Shut up!" he shouted in Margret's face.

Abby pressed her lips together, fisting her hands at her side as her stomach clutched with dread. "Renzo—"

"Keep your mouth shut, Fawn."

Abby instantly quieted. If she said anything more Margret would be punished. She stared at the heavy silver lamp on the nightstand, craving to pick it up and bash the sick bastard over the head. She wanted to grab Margret's hand and run, but there was nowhere to go. Dozens of men stood guard throughout the house ready and waiting to stop her.

"This is your new life, bitch." He slapped Margret, sending her crashing to the floor on a shocked cry. "You better get used to it." He whirled, facing Abby. "And you."

She shrunk back as he rushed forward, grabbing both her arms with painful pressure, yanking them nose-to-nose.

"You need to stop mothering these worthless whores. This is a fucking brothel. Men come here to get fucked." He gave her several violent shakes. "That's what happens here, bitch."

No one knew better what happened here than her. It was her job to keep track of who was forced to perform sexual acts and how often. She struggled to hold back the trembling as he stared her down. Renzo liked it when she was afraid.

"What, don't you have anything to say?"

She knew to keep quiet as she looked into his evil brown eyes.

"Bitch." He slapped her.

She pressed her hand to the sharp sting, muffling a cry as the force of the blow knocked her back a step.

He pulled her to him and ground his crotch against

her. "You and me, we're going to show this new cunt the ropes and maybe, finally, teach you a lesson." He grabbed at her breasts and threw her to the bed.

"No." Her fear grew to terror as she fought him, trying to push him away as he pulled her free of her jeans. "Stop. No. Please, Renzo."

"Oh, yeah." He unzipped his fly, exposing himself. "Oh hell fucking yeah."

Tears raced down her cheeks as she struggled to get away. She'd avoided this fate over the last few weeks by hiding in her tiny room and doing what she'd been asked.

He held her down with a hand to her chest and reached in a drawer, grabbing a condom from the pile. "Stop fighting me, bitch, or I'll make this so much worse." He tossed the package on her stomach and smiled. "Open it."

"No," she shuddered out.

He grabbed her throat, cutting off her air. "I said fucking open it!"

Gasping, fighting for a breath, she ripped at the package.

"Better." He grinned as he rolled on the rubber. "Let's show her how to be a dirty whore."

"Renzo please," she begged, weeping as he pulled her forward, understanding that there was no way to escape the inevitable.

Gasping, Abby's eyes flew open as Renzo's primal grunts echoed in her head. Her heart beat wildly in her heaving chest as she blinked, focusing on the faded rose wallpaper in the dimly lit room. Rolling over, she swiped at her sweat-soaked face and rushed off the twin bed, hurrying to the door. They had her again. Renzo found her and they'd taken her again.

She yanked the door open and slammed into Jerrod.

“Whoa,” he grabbed her arms.

"Don't." She cringed, stepping back. “Don’t touch me.”

He held his hands up, studying her with his calm blue eyes. "Easy, Abby."

She wiped at another drop of sweat tickling her temples as she darted glances around the unfamiliar space. “Where am I?”

“We’re at the safe house.”

The deep rumble of a plane taking off shook the mirror on the wall, and she took another step back, clutching her arms at her chest, trying to think past the dredges of sleep and horrifying memories still crowding her brain. “Where?”

“About five minutes from LAX.”

She inched closer to the window, desperate to yank the shade up and get her bearings.

“Don’t open that.”

Swallowing, she eyed Jerrod, still trying to get a read on the man blocking her only way out. He was her friend, yet she couldn't shake her sudden distrust as Renzo's cruel laughter filled her head. “I need to see outside.”

He shook his head. “You can’t.”

She moved further away, bumping into a rough-looking rocking chair as the walls started closing in around her. "I want to go home."

"We can't, Abby."

A fresh wave of fear sent her heart into overdrive as she flashed back to her arrival at the stash house. This was the same. Everything was exactly the same. Renzo told her she couldn't go home either. He was supposed to have helped her; he was supposed to have saved her and taken her away, but he didn't. "Get out," she whispered, gripping the arm of the ancient rocker in trembling hands.

"Abigail." Jerrod took a step toward her.

"No," she shuddered.

"Abigail, what the hell's going on?" He advanced again.

"Get away! Get away from me!" She shoved him and booked it from the room, rushing down the hall toward the stairs. A man she'd never seen before ran up the steps, his gun drawn, as footsteps rushed up behind her and she screamed. "No!"

Jerrod hooked his arm around her waist, lifting her off her feet. "Abigail, stop it."

She fought him, kicking her legs, swinging her arms.

"It's okay." He braced his other arm around her shoulders, trapping her body against his chest. "It's okay, Abby," he whispered gruffly next to her ear.

His familiar scent crowded her nose, comforting her, as did his arms wrapped tightly around her. The fight left her, and she went limp in his grip, realizing Jerrod wasn't going to hurt her. She burst into tears.

"Everything's all right," he said as he scooped her up and walked back to the bedroom, shutting the door partially. He sat them on the bed, settling her at his side as she sobbed. "Hey." He cupped her face in his hands. "Hey," he said again gently. "Abigail." He slid his thumbs along her cheeks. "What's going on here?"

"I don't know." She cried harder, gripping his forearms, trembling. "I don't know. We were in the van, then we weren't. I think I had a nightmare. I thought they had me again. I couldn't remember if you were like Renzo. He didn't help me," she wept.

"He didn't help me," she repeated as Jerrod pulled her closer.

"Shh." He slid his hand down her hair. "It's over now. It's over, Abigail."

She rested her head on his shoulder, holding on tight as his hand continued its soothing path through her hair. "Why is this happening?" Her breath shuddered in and out as she tried to get herself under control. "Why do I keep doing this?"

"Because you're healing. You can't move forward until you deal with the past."

"I don't want to do this." She eased back, looking into his eyes. "I don't want to be like this."

"You're doing fine, Abby, just fine."

"No. I think..." She looked down at his strong thighs in dark denim, stopping short of confessing her biggest fear."

He slid a finger under her chin, easing her face up until their gazes met. "What?"

"I think—I think I might be mentally ill, like my mother was."

He shook his head. "I'm promising you you're not. You had a scare. I shouldn't have left you in here by yourself."

She took another deep, calming breath as his reassurances bolstered her. "You didn't know."

"I should have." He pressed his forehead to hers. "I sure as hell should have."

"It's okay." She rested her hands on his cheeks, holding him against her, giving him a small smile of reassurance. "No permanent damage done."

"Exactly. No permanent damage done. Remember that."

She nodded.

He untangled himself from their embrace and

stood. “Let me get you some water.”

“I could use a drink.” She needed time to steady all the way out. Jerrod was here. She was safe with him.

He left the room and came back a couple minutes later with a bottled water and a small box in his hand. “Here you go.”

“Thanks.” She took the bottle, twisted the cap, and swallowed several refreshing gulps. “Better.”

“Good.” He smiled.

She frowned, noticing the blood on his bottom lip. "Come here." She patted the spot next to her and pulled a tissue from the box by the bed, folding it in half several times.

He sat down.

“I think I gave you a fat lip.”

He licked his lip. “Guess so.” He smiled again. “Way to go, champ.”

She dampened the tissue and blotted his mouth. “I wish I could say thanks.”

“Abby.” He grabbed her wrist, halting her movements. “I would never hurt you. Ever.”

Guilt consumed her as she stared at the kind man before her. “Oh, Jerrod, I know that. I do.”

“I needed to say it anyway.”

She dabbed at his lip again, absorbing the small dot of blood.

He pulled his head away from her probing fingers. “I think I'll be okay.”

“It’ll be a little puffy for a couple days.” She wrinkled her nose. “Sorry.”

“I’ll live.”

Another jet soared over the house, the low rumble echoing in her feet. “So, why are we here exactly? What’s going on?”

"Somehow Toni Torrell found out you're Lily's new designer."

"*What*? How?"

He shrugged. "I don't know, but you've made the front page of *The Times*. It looks like Toni snapped a few pictures of you yesterday after all."

She shook her head in disbelief. "What does the article say? Can I see it?"

"She did some digging, Abby. The article doesn't just talk about Lily and Fashion Week."

She pressed her lips firm as she absorbed the violation to her privacy. "Sex slaves and abductions sell more papers."

"Abby." He sighed. "I'm sorry."

"It was going to come out eventually, but I wanted to be the one to share my story."

"Understandably."

She steamed out a breath, knowing there was nothing she could do to change what was. "So, now what?"

"We're going to Nebraska."

She raised her brow. "Nebraska?"

"My family has a farm. We'll stay there until Ethan sends a team to meet us in Baltimore for the trial."

"What about Lex?"

"They're going to stay with Ethan and Sarah until things settle down."

"I have to talk to her. I need to make sure she's all right."

"You can't."

"I have to."

"You can't talk to anyone. Not to Alexa, Lily, no one."

"For how long?"

“Indefinitely.”

Indefinitely was a long damn time. She stood, needing to pace away the latest wave of unease. “But what about Margret? How will I know what’s going on with her case if I can’t talk to Agent Terron?”

“I’ll find a way to get you updates.”

"And my job? What about that?" She turned, facing him as she walked his way again.

"Ethan will get Lily the stuff you've been working on so someone can get it finished up."

"But *Escape*. How can I launch a new line if I'm hiding on a farm in Nebraska?"

He shook his head as he shrugged. "I don't know what you want me to say. We're about to vanish. No one knows where we're going other than Ethan and Jackson. There will be no further contact with anyone on either side. We can't risk it."

She turned away, staring at the wall, realizing that the life she'd worked so hard to rebuild was crumbling down around her for the second time.

“I have a new credit card for you—not that you’ll really need it—and clothes.”

She glanced over her shoulder. “What kind of clothes?”

He grinned. “I don’t know. Clothes. Someone from the evacuation team put a few things together for you from the stash they keep down at their office. There’s enough to get you started. We can get more stuff once we’re home, but I doubt we’ll be leaving the farm very often. The idea is to stay low."

"Do I have to stay in the house?"

"No, but we'll stay on the grounds. You’ll have a somewhat new identity. You’ll still be Abigail, but we’ll keep your last name out of things. You work with me at Ethan Cooke Security as an office manager.

You've never been out of California and you love animals, so I offered to bring you home with me for a visit."

Her brow shot in the air as she sat next to him. "Who's going to buy that?"

"Everyone, because it's not all that far from the truth."

"Why would you bring me home if we aren't involved?"

He shrugged. "People will probably assume there's something going on between us. We'll let them think whatever they want."

She immediately thought of their kiss and winced. "Jerrod, I'm sorry about earlier. I shouldn't have kissed you. The photo shoot..." She closed her eyes and shook her head with the rush of humiliation. "I'm sorry."

"Don't worry about it." He took her hand, squeezing gently. "But it can't happen again."

She nodded, absorbing yet another wave of embarrassment.

"You're a beautiful woman, Abigail, but I'm your bodyguard. A romance with the person I'm protecting absolutely cannot happen. My attention has to stay focused on your safety and *only* your safety."

He was letting her down easy with the whole 'it's not you, it's my job' thing. It should've lessened the sting some, but it didn't.

"I understand." She wanted to, but deep down she didn't, because she *wanted* him. She told Alexa she wasn't sure if her feelings were true emotion or lust. As she looked in his calm, steady eyes, she was absolutely certain lust played a very minor role in what she felt for Jerrod.

"So, we're good here?"

"Yes."

"Good, because I have something for you." He handed her the jeweler's box he'd been holding.

"What is this?"

"Open it up and take a look."

"Okay." She smiled and pulled off the lid, staring at a beautiful gold and silver watch. "Jerrod." She glanced from him back to the jewelry. "This is gorgeous."

"I picked it out for you while you were with Jackson and Alexa on New Year's Eve."

A stirring of hope swelled in her heart, despite the conversation they just had. "You did?"

"Yeah." He took the box from her hand and pulled the timepiece free. "I had Malcom swing by the office and pick it up when he dropped off your new clothes. Ethan had it fitted with a transmitter."

Any hints of romance vanished with the practical gesture. "Oh."

"Here, let's put it on and make sure it fits." He fastened the watch in place. "It looks nice."

She examined the dainty twists of gold and silver. "It really is beautiful."

"I thought this would work. It kind of reminded me of you—delicate and pretty, but it has sparkle."

He was killing her with his sweet words. If she were a fool, she might let herself believe there was more here, but she wasn't. Jerrod wasn't interested. "Thank you."

"I can find you anywhere with this. It's peace of mind for both of us."

"Yeah. Definitely." She hugged him. "Thanks again."

"You're welcome. I'm going to check in with Ethan one last time. We'll head out in about half an hour."

"Okay."

He stood and walked off.

She stared after him, then looked at the watch, wishing the token meant more than another safety precaution.

Chapter Ten

Jerrod exited Interstate 80 and took a left toward town. He stopped at the first of three traffic lights along Commerce Way—the only three lights in the entire 'city' of fifteen thousand. He sat idle, shaking his head at the stoplight, waiting for the change to green despite the empty streets around him. Cabs didn't swerve around him in search of their next fare, nor did pedestrians pass in front of the car as they would have in LA. It was two thirty-three in the morning. Parker, Nebraska had tucked itself in hours ago.

The light changed and he accelerated, passing the supermarket his mother had shopped at for as long as he could remember; Parker High, his alma matter; and the police station he'd pulled duty at for the longest damn year of his life, then took another left, rolling over several sets of railroad tracks on his way to the farm.

He turned to glance at Abby, asleep in the passenger's seat. She'd tossed and turned for most of the three and a half hour drive from Denver—the closest airport to his hometown tucked among endless miles of cornfields—and slept on his shoulder during the flight from LA, her defense against her paralyzing claustrophobia. He'd held her hand the entire way, worrying some that she would wake from another nightmare and panic, as she had at the safe house.

Her screams echoed in his head, and he tightened

his grip on the steering wheel, clenching his jaw, admonishing himself again for leaving her the way he did. She'd been terrified, nearly hysterical when she opened the bedroom door and slammed into him in her rush to escape. He should have anticipated flashbacks and nightmares after her reaction to their unexpected exit in the back of the van. He knew better; he knew *her*, but he hadn't been thinking of Abby's triggers when he went across the hall to make his phone calls. His top priority had been finding a way to get her out of Los Angeles after he saw the sad state of the tired safe house they were supposed to have hunkered down in until they left for the trial.

There was no way in hell Abby could have handled being stuck behind the drawn shades and dim rooms of the depressing old house. She needed to be someplace open, somewhere that allowed her plenty of freedom and peace to continue her healing. She'd worked so hard and come too far to go backwards; he'd be damned if her obligations to Prosecutor Bitner and the state of Maryland would set her back. So here they were, in Parker, Nebraska, the one place he'd fought to escape most of his life.

He let loose a humorless chuckle and sighed as the barns and silos of the Quinn Family Farm came into view a mile off the highway. Home sweet home—sort of. He slowed as he approached the old mailbox and turned down the dirt road, bumping along the path, finally stopping in front of the large two-story farmhouse with its pretty wraparound porch so much like the prop used for the *Trendy* photo shoot.

He killed the engine, taking it all in—the denuded sugar maples planted when his great grandfather had been a boy; the huge red barns full of animals and feed for the long winter months; mom's greenhouses where fresh fruits and vegetables grew year round; massive silver silos accentuated in the moonlight; Uncle Jimmy's small house tucked half a mile back; and the porch light glowing bright, welcoming him.

He'd been gone nine months—almost as long as he'd stayed after dad's unexpected death. He'd tried to make a life here; he'd tried to be what his father had wanted, but in the end he'd had to go. Shelby's unrelenting demands and the tedium of small town living had suffocated him, so he left, accepting the job Ethan offered, never looking back...until now. Somehow irony's cruel hand brought him back to the one place he'd never wanted with the one person he desperately did. How the hell was he supposed to handle that?

Unfastening his seatbelt, he turned, looking at Abby, blowing out a breath in defense against the punch of longing. She was so damn beautiful. Her flawless skin and shiny black hair glowed in the beams of moonlight, reminding him of the enchanted princesses she often read about with Olivia.

"Abby." He reached out, hesitating, then slid his knuckles along her jaw, promising himself this would be the last time he touched her this way. She was off limits; he'd made her so when he told her there would never be anything between them. He couldn't remember regretting anything more, but reestablishing their boundaries was the right thing to do. It was the *only* thing to do. Her safety came first. "Abigail," he said again gently, eager to be out of the car and away from her until he found some semblance of balance in their once easy relationship.

She opened her eyes, and he dropped his hand.

"We're here."

"We are?" She sat up and gasped, her eyes

drinking everything in. “Oh, Jerrod, l*ook* at this place.” She beamed at him. “Your home is beautiful.”

He stared at the huge white house with black shutters, the big picture windows and roof he’d shingled with his father and brother one hot summer, trying to see what Abby did. All he saw was a place he’d been bound to for too long. “It’s been the Quinns’ for five generations.”

“It’s perfect.”

“You wanna go in?”

“Yes.” She unfastened her belt and opened her door, stepping out into the frigid night. “Holy *crap*. It’s cold.”

He grinned, white puffs pluming from his mouth with every breath as he absorbed the icy temperatures. “Welcome to Nebraska in January.” He grabbed the carryon full of clothes and toiletries for Abby from the back. “Let’s go.”

She took several steps and stopped. “Look at all of these stars. You can’t see them like this in Los Angeles.” She grabbed his hand in her excitement. “I *love* it here.”

“You’ve been here for five minutes.”

She smiled. “So? It’s love at first sight.”

“They say it exists.”

She laughed. “I think I just proved it.” She squeezed his fingers. “Thank you.”

“For what?”

“For bringing me. For sharing your home.”

“I’m happy to.”

The front door opened, and Jerrod smiled as his mother stepped forward. She was wrapped in her thick, plaid bathrobe, and her blond hair was pulled back in a ponytail. “Mom.”

“Jerrod. You’re home.”

He took the stairs in twos, rushing up, grabbing her in a hug. The tall, strong woman in his arms had always been the backbone of the Quinn men, and she was the person who knew and understood him best.

"I've missed you, honey."

"I've missed you too." He hugged her tight once more, breathing in whatever shampoo she'd found on sale, and kissed her cheek, then stepped back. He glanced at Abby standing in the shadows, huddled in her thin jacket, struggling to keep her teeth from chattering. "Mom, this popsicle over here is Abby."

"Gracious sakes, where are my manners? Come in, come in." She ushered Abby inside. "And you call me Mary."

He closed the door behind them, locking up, absorbing the warmth and lemony scent in the familiar surroundings.

"It's nice to meet you, Mary." Abby stepped forward, giving her a hug.

"Oh." Mom's eyes grew wide as she returned the embrace.

Jerrod grinned. The Quinn's weren't big huggers. Everyone was in for a surprise now that Abby was here.

"Thank you so much for having me." Abby drew away.

"We're always happy to welcome friends." Mom looked Abby up and down, taking in her skinny jeans and jacket they'd pulled from the closet in their hurry to leave the condo. Despite her simple outfit, Abby screamed 'city chick.' "Good heavens, you're tiny, honey. One good gust of Nebraska wind will blow you away. How about a plate?"

Abby smiled. "No thank you."

"Mom's used to burly men."

"Garbage disposals are what you are. How about you, son? Can I offer you a plate?"

He shook his head. "Just a bed."

"You know where they are. Go ahead and settle in. Abby, make yourself at home. I'm sure Jerrod will be happy to show you to your room. I'll see you in a couple hours." She hugged him again. "Good night."

"Good night," Jerrod and Abby said at the same time.

"You ready to go up?" He yawned, exhausted now that he could finally relax.

"Mmm."

"Let's go." He signaled with his head, climbing the stairs with her at his side, stopping at the third door on the left down the long hall. He flipped on the light, and Abby gasped.

"Oh, Jerrod." She walked around the roomy space, touching the dark polished wood of the ornate antique footboard and the matching dressers.

"Does this work for you?"

"It's perfect. I love it. I have my own fireplace."

"All the rooms do. We have central heating now, but they still work if you want to use it."

"I feel like we've stepped back in time. All of these antiques." She smiled, brushing her fingers over his great grandmother's cranberry glass vase on the side table. "Everything's so pretty."

Her delight for the simple things always fascinated him. Her excitement was infectious. "Do you think you'll be okay in here?"

"Definitely." She took off her jacket, pulled back the covers, and hopped on the bed.

Her screams echoed in his head, and he tensed despite her apparent ease. "I'll be right across the hall if you need me."

"Okay." She kicked off one sneaker, then the next.

"I'll leave my door open."

"You don't have to. It's so peaceful." She lay back against the pillow and sighed. "I'm already as comfortable here as I am in our own home."

Their home. Somehow over the last few months the condo had become theirs. They'd lived as any other couple did, sharing meals, cleaning duties, bills. "I'll see you in a few hours."

"Okay. Good night."

He turned, drowning in fatigue.

"Jerrod."

He stopped, turning back to face her. "Yeah?"

She stood, taking a hesitant step toward him, and stopped. "I'm not really sure about our boundaries, because this has never come up before, so I don't know..." She nibbled her lip and looked down. "I know we're just friends and you're my bodyguard..." She shook her head and huffed out a breath as she met his gaze again. "I got your message loud and clear, but I was wondering if it would be okay..."

This was the first time he'd ever seen her so uncomfortable around him. He didn't want things to be this way between them. "Do you want a hug, Abigail?"

She smiled her relief. "You're a mind reader, Mr. Quinn."

"Maybe." He opened his arms, full well knowing he shouldn't. "Well, come on already."

She grinned and stepped into his embrace, wrapping herself tightly around him, resting her head on his chest.

He closed his eyes, holding her close, sliding his hand down her soft black hair. "Night, Abby."

"Good night, Jerrod." She stared into his gaze. "I'm

glad things aren't weird between us."

Things weren't weird per se, but they were definitely different. The photo shoot had changed their status quo. "Me too," he said and eased back, walking into the hall.

She closed her door three quarters of the way and shut off her light, sending the upstairs into darkness.

~~~~

Abby opened her eyes, well rested and warm, snuggled beneath layers of soft blankets. She stretched her arms, locking them under her head as she smiled, staring up at the beautifully coffered ceiling. She'd slept like a rock cloaked in the deep country silence and homey comfort of the old farmhouse. Not even twenty-four hours ago she and Jerrod had been through hell, and now she was on a farm in the middle of nowhere. She strained her ears, listening closely, amazed by the lack of muffled horns blaring or emergency vehicles rushing by. She'd never been this far removed from civilization. Even Hagerstown had its fair share of creature comforts and amenities a short drive away.

Smiling again, she let loose a contented sigh despite her disastrous life. Dimitri and Victor wanted her dead, her career and dreams were officially in limbo, and contact with Lex was out of the question, yet she couldn't help but relax, sensing the freedoms that came with this latest round of precautions. For once her world had opened up instead of gotten smaller. No one would look for her here. For the first time in months she was truly safe, and she planned to take full advantage.

The deep low of a cow somewhere in the distance
~~~~

penetrated her thoughts, and she shoved herself up to sitting, scrambling from the covers in her flossy white bra and panties, looking out the window to the left of the bed. She stared out at snow-covered fields as far as the eye could see, leaning closer to the glass, when she spotted a gray-bearded man bundled in a thick orange jacket and black Elmer Fudd hat walking toward the huge red barn. Hurrying off the mattress, she tossed her bedding back in place, anxious to get dressed and explore. She wanted in that barn. She'd seen a farm animal or two growing up in Maryland but had never actually touched one. Now was her chance. Jerrod told her his family raised chickens and pigs and tons and tons of cows on their small organic farm. Maybe he would teach her how to milk them. She wanted to gather eggs and sheer stuff and do whatever else it was they did around here. Eager to begin, she hurried over to the small suitcase Jerrod left by the dresser and unzipped the bag, pulling free a pair of pink polyester pants. Her smile faded as she held them up. "What on earth is this?" She reached in again, grabbing a pair of underwear big enough for three.

"Abby?" Jerrod tapped on the door and stepped in dressed in jeans and a Huskers sweatshirt. "Oh, shit, sorry." He walked out.

"No. Come back here."

"You're not dressed."

"Come in here, Jerrod. Please."

He came back, muttering something under his breath, averting his gaze. "God. Put something *on*."

"I can't."

His eyes met hers. "What do you mean you can't?"

She held up the beige granny panties. "What *is* this?" She held up the pants next. "And this. My *Gran* wore stuff like this."

"Huh." He scratched his chin.

"Huh? That's all you have to say? How am I supposed to milk cows and fetch eggs in these?"

He covered his mouth with a slide of his hand, attempting to disguise a chuckle.

She dropped her 'outfit' to her side. "Are you laughing?"

"No." He coughed.

"Jerrod." She reached down and pulled a bright blue and pink flowered shirt from the bag and a bra big enough to wrap around them both. "Are you *serious*?"

His cough turned into a full-fledged burst of laughter. "Jesus, Abby, I'm sorry." He struggled to shore himself up and laughed again. "I'm sorry," he repeated.

"This is not funny." She grinned, delighted to hear that deep roar. "It's absolutely not." She pulled the other outfit out, the sizes no better, the shirt and pants no less atrocious. "I mean, come on." She started laughing herself. "Who picked this stuff out?"

He shook his head, snorting out another chuckle. "I don't know, but it looks like we need to go into town. Put your jeans on and come with me. We'll find you something to wear for now."

She pulled on her pants and dashed across the hall, covering her scantily clad chest with her arm.

He opened his closet. "Everything's going to be huge and about nine years out of fashion."

"As long as I don't look like a geriatric Easter egg, I won't complain."

They both grinned.

"Go at it." He stepped out of the way.

There were a couple of sweaters, heavy work jackets, a pair of slacks, a polo or two, and several

Huskers options. "Mmm, I think I'll take this." She pulled the dark red sweatshirt from the hanger. "It looks nice and warm."

"Be my guest."

"Do you have any t-shirts?"

He walked to a drawer. "Take your pick."

She pulled a simple white undershirt from the selection and slid it on, followed by the sweater. "Perfect. Warm and comfy."

"That's the name of the game around here. You want something to eat?"

She shook her head, rolling the sleeves past her wrists, studying him. She'd never seen him dressed for the day so casually. He looked good enough to eat in his relaxed attire, like someone she could relate to on a non-bodyguard-to-principal level. "I want in that barn. Will you give me a tour?"

"After I grab a cup of coffee."

"Can I touch the animals?"

He raised his brows. "If you want."

"I've never felt a cow before or a pig or a chicken. I can't wait." She flashed him a huge grin.

He smiled. "The cows will be busy with the milking, the chickens will more than likely peck at you, and the sows would rather eat that hand of yours than have you petting them."

She grimaced. "Pigs eat people?"

He chuckled. "They can."

She swallowed. Maybe going to the barn wasn't such a good idea after all. "I thought that was some kind of urban legend."

He shook his head. "These aren't pets, Abby."

"What about the piglets? There must be a Wilbur out there for me to love."

"I guess we should go find out."

They walked down the stairs, and she moaned, breathing in something doughy and delicious. "Oh my god, what is that?"

"Fresh bread."

She moaned again. "Your mom makes fresh bread?"

"Every morning."

"Wow." She followed him past the formal dining room with its long antique table and cabinetry and into the kitchen. She gaped. The space was huge and not what she'd expected. Major renovations had taken place. Dark wood, stainless steel, and yards of chocolate-colored granite were everywhere she turned. "Now *this* is a kitchen."

"Good morning." Mary smiled, stirring a large bowl of some sort of batter.

"Morning, Mom."

"Good morning," Abby returned, studying Jerrod's mother. She was young, no more than fifty—tops, with the same dark blond hair and calm blue eyes as Jerrod. Her high cheekbones begged for blusher, and her full, firm lips a bit of gloss. She was tall and sturdy in her jeans and plaid button down, emanating an inner strength Abby envied.

"Can I get you a cup of coffee, Abby?"

"Oh, no thanks."

"Abby doesn't drink coffee." Jerrod handed her a steaming mug of tea.

"Thank you." She smiled, examining the gorgeous bold red pottery. "I love your crockery, Mary. It's beautiful. Your whole home is beautiful."

"Thank you."

"Mom's a hell of a potter."

"Mary, you made this?"

"I did."

Abby sipped her tea, scrutinizing the excellent craftsmanship closer, in awe. "I've never made pottery before."

"You're welcome to join me in the studio any time you like."

"I would love to." She smiled, wiggling her brows at Jerrod, earning a grin and shake of his head.

Mary glanced from Abby to Jerrod. "Like I said, any time."

The side door opened, and in walked a tall man in jeans and a thick, dark Parker Police Department jacket.

"Well if it isn't Little Timmy." Jerrod smiled and walked over, giving Not-So-Little Timmy a guy hug. Timmy was an inch shorter than Jerrod and not as powerfully built, but he wasn't small by any stretch of the imagination.

"Welcome back, big brother," Little Timmy said with a grin.

Abby smiled up at the man who looked very much like Jerrod. Tim's chin was softer, his hair more brown than dirty blond, and his teeth completely straight when he flashed his grin. "Hi. I'm Tim, this lug's little brother." He gave a jerk of his head in Jerrod's direction.

"Hi." She held out her hand, instantly comfortable in Tim's friendly presence. "I'm Abby, this lug's friend." She copied Tim's gesture.

He smiled again and gave her hand a firm shake. "Nice to meet you. So how are you handling farm life?"

"I don't know. I haven't handled it yet. Jerrod's going to show me around and teach me how to milk a cow."

Jerrod paused with his mug halfway to his mouth.

"I missed the discussion about that part."

She shrugged, smiling. "I want to know how."

"We have machines for that." The radio belched on the waistband of Tim's jeans. "Sorry." He turned it down. "My work is never done."

"Tim's the Chief of Police," Jerrod supplied before he sipped at his coffee again.

"Impressive."

"It's not all that glamorous." He scrubbed at his face. "In fact I haven't slept in a solid twenty-four. Bar fight at The Wrangler kept things hopping."

"The more things change the more they stay the same," Jerrod said as he leaned against the counter.

Can I fix you a plate, Tim?" Mary asked as she set strips of bacon into a hot, sizzling skillet.

"I just ate, but thanks, Mom. Tammy fixed me up at the diner."

Mary nodded. "Abby, Jerrod, are you ready for a plate?"

"Abby wants a tour of the barn first."

"Bundle up. It's cold out there."

Jerrod set his mug down and left the kitchen, coming back moments later in his black jacket, carrying hers, handing it over. "We're going to have to do better than this." He swiped a wool hat from the rack as she zipped and pulled it on her head.

She smiled, her shoulders light, reveling in the sensation of complete relaxation. Jerrod seemed at ease as well. "Thanks."

"We'll go into town after breakfast. You can pick out some new clothes." He grinned and winked.

She chuckled, understanding he was thinking of the horrid clothing she'd pulled from the carryon. "Sounds good."

Tim stood in the doorway, watching them. "Mind

if I join you for the tour?"

"Not at all."

Tim stepped out first, then Abby and Jerrod at the same time. She blinked back tears, sucking in a sharp breath from the shocking sting of the brutal winds. "Yikes." She crossed her arms at her chest. "It'll be a while before I get used to this."

"We'll thicken up that California blood," Tim said as they hurried toward the barn.

She spotted a white Honda Civic barreling up the drive.

"Oh shit," Tim said as Jerrod muttered something under his breath and closed his eyes.

Abby light mood vanished as she sensed Jerrod's tension. "What is it? Who—" The screech of tires cut her off as a tall, beautiful redhead got out of the driver's seat and ran toward them in black tailored slacks and a fitted white blouse.

"I knew you would come home." She rushed up, throwing her arms around Jerrod, kissing him. "I knew you would come back to me." She kissed him again and pressed her hands to his cheeks, staring in his eyes. "God, I've missed you."

The pretty redhead's spicy perfume tickled Abby's nose, and her stomach sank as she struggled not to stare at the cozy picture of love reunited. The woman twined around Jerrod had to be the "serious girlfriend" Alexa had spoken of. Despite her sister's best guesses it was clear Jerrod was definitely not a free agent. She glanced up, meeting his eyes, and looked down just as quickly as he untangled himself from his lover's hold.

"I'm back for a few weeks, Shelby, but I'm not staying."

Abby peeked up from under her lashes, swallowing the bitter taste of yesterday's conversation in the safe house as Shelby leaned against his solid chest. Jerrod told her he couldn't be with her for her own safety, but the truth was he couldn't be with her because he was already with someone else.

Shelby's eyes filled as she clung to him. "But Jerrod—"

"Will you excuse us for a minute? Timmy, keep an eye on things." Jerrod took Shelby's hand and started toward the house.

Tim looked at Abby, giving her a small smile. "So, should we go check out the barn?" He held out his arm.

The barn and animals inside lost their appeal as Jerrod and Shelby's voices echoed behind her, but she looped her arm through Tim's, struggling to find her enthusiasm anyway. "I'd like that."

"Right this way, madam."

CHAPTER ELEVEN

JERROD LEANED AGAINST THE FRAME OF THE LIVING ROOM window, staring out at the barn, watching for Abby as the sun began its evening descent. She'd been out all afternoon with Tim at her side, doing whatever chores Uncle Jimmy would allow. He didn't have to stand here and wait; Tim was more than capable of keeping Abby safe on the short walk back to the house, but he was restless and edgy with it—as he always was when he stayed here too long.

He'd only been back a week, and already he itched for the noise and chaos of the city. Mucking stalls, milking cows, and inoculating piglets didn't fascinate him the way it seemed to Abby. He pulled his weight, helping with repairs and whatever else he could, but he'd worked his ass off to get away from the stench of manure and endless worries over crop yield reports.

Nothing's ever good enough for you, son. That's your problem. You always want more. His father's bitter words played through his head, as they did every time he came home, reminding him of why he didn't come often. Dad had been gone almost two years, but the raw memories still lingered.

Clenching his jaw, he braced his hands against the wooden frame as Tim opened the barn door and stepped out. Abby was at his side in her designer jeans, work boots, and one of mom's thick, plaid coats. Her cheeks were rosy and her face unframed with her hair tucked beneath her hat, accentuating her breathtaking beauty as she said something to his little brother, smiling as she spoke.

Jerrod cleared his throat and shifted his stance as he tried to ignore the uncomfortable twist of envy. It had been days since Abby aimed one of her killer grins his way. Other than the uncustomarily quiet trip into town last week for clothes, shoes, makeup, and whatever else she'd needed, he hardly saw her. Abby had fully immersed herself in their temporary new life, spending her days with Uncle Jimmy in the barn or with mom in the studio throwing clay and her nights in her room sketching and sewing, avoiding him.

They still spoke at breakfast and dinner or in the evenings when they watched a movie from time to time, but something was different; Abby was different. She didn't joke with him anymore or dance and sing or pull him to her room to show off her latest fashion ideas. She was perfectly polite...and stiff—at least with him. Abby hadn't been the same since Shelby entered the picture their first day here. His ex's daily drop-ins had changed their relationship yet again.

Uncle Jimmy pulled up in his old F-150 and got out, handing off a wrench to Tim from the bed of his beat-up truck. He turned to leave and Abby stopped him, wrapping her arms around the big, burly old man. Jerrod winced, blinking his surprise when Uncle Jimmy hugged her back and kissed her cheek. He smiled, chuckling, shaking his head. There was something about her that no one could resist. In a week's time she'd charmed the hell out of everyone she'd met, including his mother, and Marry Quinn was a hard sell.

Uncle Jimmy got in his tired vehicle and drove off

with a wave. Abby and Tim waved back and started down the path at a casual stroll, arms linked, smiling, talking. They both stopped, bopping their heads as Abby grabbed the tool from Tim, bringing her impromptu microphone to her lips, then to Tim's as their mouths moved in sync. Tim broke into an awkward dance, pulling Abby along with him. Her hips swayed as she moved her arms above her head. Tim grabbed her hand, tugging her forward, sending her crashing into his chest. They gripped each other close as she tipped her head back, laughing, and Jerrod looked away. How long had it been since he'd heard that sound?

He stepped away from the window as the front door shut and high heels echoed on the hardwood floor.

"Honey, I'm home," Shelby said as she walked into the room in gray slacks and a low-cut black blouse, smiling. "Did you miss me?"

He shoved his hands in his pockets as he stared at the woman he grew up with, then dated and eventually lived with for almost a year of his life. She was beautiful, coolly so. Beneath her pretty Amazon-like package lay a nasty, manipulative viper ready to strike without mercy. Despite their long history, he and Shelby hadn't ended well, yet he hesitated to tell her to go away. "Not so much."

"Don't be a jerk, Jerrod. I'm trying to play nice." She set her purse on the coffee table, pausing as she looked out the window he'd stepped away from. "Well, well, well, there's a cozy picture. Looks like Timmy snagged himself a city girl."

Jerrod breathed in deep, rubbing at the back of his neck. "They're friends."

She pursed her lips and smiled. "Struck a nerve,

did I?"

She did; they both knew it, but he'd be damned if he would admit it. "Why are you here, Shelby?"

"I just got off work." She stepped closer, stopping almost toe-to-toe. "But I've been wondering the same thing about you. Why are you here, Jerrod? You clearly didn't come back for me." She slid her finger down the front of his shirt. "Right?"

He gripped her wrist, halting her movement, refusing to rise to her bait. "I'm back for a visit. That's all."

"What about her?" She gestured toward the window with a toss of her head. "Why did you bring her?"

He shrugged. "She's a friend. We work together. We both had some vacation time, so she came with me."

Her green eyes sharpened. "I'm not buying it."

He was afraid of that. Shelby worked the news in a small town, but her mind was as sharp as any big-time reporters. "I don't know what to tell you."

"How about the truth."

He wanted to tell her to go to hell, but sending Shelby away mad and curious was asking for trouble. She had the potential to be as detrimental to Abby's safety as Toni Torrell had been if he didn't stay cool and keep her close. "Look—"

The back door opened, and Abby's smooth soprano voice melded with the off-key notes of his brother's singing while they belted out Katy Perry's *Roar*. Jerrod adjusted his stance, watching as Tim and Abby turned by the coat hook in the hall, shaking their asses at each other, laughing, while they pulled off jackets and boots. Tim plucked the dark red hat mom had knitted Abby from her head.

"Thanks." She shoved the hat and her gloves in her coat pocket.

"No problem." Tim blew on his hands and rubbed them together. "I'm going to have a cup of coffee. Do you want tea or something?"

"I'll never turn down tea," she said as they started toward the living room.

"Dollop of honey, honey?"

"You know how I like my drink, Timothy. I feel so...special." She batted her lashes, grinning, stopping abruptly and almost crashed into Jerrod as they stepped into the room. "Oh." Her smile faded as she looked from Jerrod to Shelby. "I didn't see you. Hello." She nodded politely to Shelby.

"Hi. How are the pigs?" Shelby asked.

"Growing."

"Dream vacation, huh?"

"Give it a rest," Jerrod warned as he glanced from Abby to Tim. "Slow day at the office, Timmy?"

"Not much going on. Everyone seems to be behaving."

"You've been lucky all week." He shoved his hands back in his pockets, eyeing his brother as the tension in the room grew unbearable.

Abby cleared her throat. "You know what? I'm going to take a rain check on the tea, Tim." Abby took his hand. "Sorry about the milk in the eye." She and Tim grinned at each other.

He shrugged. "Happens to the best of us."

"I'm going to go clean up for dinner and hopefully give your mother a hand if she'll actually let me. Are you staying?"

"Wouldn't miss it."

She nodded and turned for the stairs.

"Abigail," Jerrod called, stepping toward her, not

wanting her to go. "Ethan spoke with Mr. Terron today. He wasn't able to find what you were looking for." This wasn't the time to give her an update on Margret, but he wasn't sure when he would find a moment to speak to her.

She nodded again.

"Time for dinner, everyone," Mom said as she peeked her head in from the kitchen. "Shelby, I didn't know you were here."

"I was on my way out." She smirked as she stared at Abby.

"You're not staying?" Jerrod asked, thinking fast, recognizing the rabid look in her eyes. A look that could only lead to trouble.

Her gaze flew from Abby to him. "Do you want me to?"

"That's up to you."

"Of course I will." She sent him a sultry wink and started toward the kitchen.

He stared into Abby's eyes, catching the hint of hurt, understanding that he was pushing her further away by welcoming Shelby back into his life, but he didn't see much of a choice. Her safety had to come before her feelings. He would dance with the devil to keep her alive.

~~~~

Jerrod kept his pace slow as he and Abby wandered the rows of cows, making certain all was well before they closed up the barn for the night. He was in no rush to head back to the house now that he finally had her alone. Mom and Uncle Jimmy were off to Bingo, Timmy was stuck in town on duty, and Shelby was...who knows where? He could have easily
~~~~

checked on the animals by himself, but he wanted this time with Abby. They needed it after the rocky past few days and tense dinner last night.

She'd met his eyes once during the torturous meal, then stared at the table, playing with the roast beef and vegetables on her plate while Shelby shared stories from their long-ago trip to Bermuda. He'd wanted to clear the air after Shelby and Tim left, but her bedroom light had gone out almost immediately after she went upstairs. He tried again this morning before breakfast, but she'd gone to the barn early, staying out all day until mom forced her in for a quiet, uncomfortable supper.

He stopped next to Abby as she peeked into the second to last stall. "I guess everything's good."

He nodded. "Everyone's officially tucked in for the night." He tried a smile, hoping to keep the conversation going. Abby had barely looked at him, let alone spoken during the last half hour.

She gave him a small smile in return. "Looks like."

He rubbed his fingers over his chin, trying to figure out how to break through this awkwardness between them. He hated that she had her guard up as she met his eyes. He glanced at his watch. "You know, it's still pretty early. Do you want to see if there's a movie on?"

"Oh, I can't." She swiped at the loose strands falling free from her ponytail and crossed her arms in mom's work coat. "I really need to finish up the sketches I'm working on."

He wanted to push, but nodded again instead. If she didn't want to watch a movie, he would find a reason to knock on her bedroom door. One way or the other they were going to move past this. "We should probably head back then."

"Yeah." She started walking away.

He steamed out a breath of frustration as he tossed a glance into the last stall, stopping when he spotted the heifer lying on the hay. "Hold up."

She stopped. "What?"

He opened the pen and stepped in, noting the glob of amniotic fluid and two hooves well on their way into the world. "It looks like we have a calving going on."

"A calving?" She dashed back, stopping at his side. "Oh my gosh. Do we need to call the vet?"

He grinned as she stared down at the cow. He'd watched hundreds of heifers drop their calves, but he'd never done so with Abby. "Nah, I've handled a few of these."

She looked at him, her eyes full of worry as she nibbled her lip. "What should we do?"

"Wait it out. Maybe give Mama here a little hand. Baby's looking pretty big." He took off his jacket, tossing it away, and pushed up the sleeves of his sweatshirt as he knelt down at the cow's back end.

Abby did the same with her jacket and black long sleeves and knelt next to him. "How do we do that?"

"When she has a contraction, we'll give the calf a little pull." The heifer's stomach bunched into a hard ball. "Like right now."

Mama pushed and Jerrod grabbed hold of the slippery, spindly legs, tugging.

"Oh, look." Abby grinned as her dark blue eyes widened with excitement. "I think the head's coming."

He smiled, sitting on his haunches, while mama rested. "Baby's coming along just fine. You wanna try with the next one?"

"Yes," she replied without hesitation.

He scooted back. "Come on over."

Abby knee-walked her way to the spot he'd just occupied.

Mama started pushing again.

"You're on."

She licked her lips looking from Mama to him. "What—what do I do?"

"Hands above the hooves and pull."

Abby hesitated. "I don't want to hurt them."

"You won't."

She put her hands on the calf's legs as he had and pulled. "She's so slippery."

He moved in behind Abby, breathing in her shampoo as he pressed his chest to her back, surrounding her with his body as he wrapped his hands above hers on the calf. "I don't think this is a she. I think we've got a bull on the way. This baby's a big one. Just a little harder." He gave a strong tug.

"It's working."

Jerrod grunted his assent as Mama's contraction ebbed. They were making progress, but they should've had a head with that last round. "I'll be right back." He hurried off to the supply cabinet, grabbing towels, the iodine solution they would eventually need, and gloves, pulling the rubber up to his shoulders as he walked into the stall, dropping the extra supplies by their jackets. "When she contracts again I'm going to help with the head. I want you to pull on the legs like we just did."

She nodded. "Okay."

"Here we go." He reached in the heifer, wincing, his arm aching with the squeezing power of the contraction as he fought to advance the head while Abby went to work on the legs. "Good. Good. Here he comes." The calf's muzzle emerged, and Jerrod tore off his gloves as he hurried behind Abby, resting on his haunches, surrounding her with his body, grabbing hold of the hooves as he did before. "One more good pull," he said, his voice strained with his efforts. "We don't want to rip Mama up, but we don't want to lose the momentum either. We need to get him out."

Mama mooed her protest as the head was finally born.

"Keep going," he urged. "Use what's left of this contraction." They both gave another solid tug, falling back in the hay as the calf's body slipped free.

Jerrod sat up as Abby rested against his chest.

"We did it." She turned her head, looking up at him, slightly breathless, then gave her attention to the cow. "Oh, he's gorgeous." She got to her knees next to the bull as he lay in the hay, a soggy mess, blinking. "He's so sweet."

Jerrod smiled as she hovered over the newborn. "He's pretty cute now, but one day he'll be a mean bastard." He reached for one of the towels behind him. "Here." He tossed the old, ratty cotton her way. "Go ahead and give his nostrils a wipe and dry him off. We'll give him a good rub to get his circulation going since it's pretty chilly."

He grabbed the second towel, and they both rubbed at the sleepy new calf.

"I have a hard time imagining such an adorable baby being mean."

"He will be. Trust me on this one." He grabbed the iodine solution. "Do you want to treat his umbilical cord?"

"Yes."

He handed over the spray bottled. "You'll want to tent the membrane open like this." He pulled the remaining cord open. "Then squirt two shots in and slide it down toward his stomach."

"Will it hurt him?"

He shook his head. "It helps keep him healthy. If we don't do this he can get an infection."

She did as he'd showed her, spraying the solution, sliding it down the length of the cord.

"Good." He nodded is approval. "Now give a spray to the outside as well and he's all set."

She coated the membrane, setting down the bottle with a smile. "This is so cool."

"I'm glad you think so."

"Definitely."

He looked at Mama again still lying down. "We need to get her up." He got to his feet, walking over to the new mother. "Ha. Ha," he shouted, giving her a forceful shove with the side of his leg. "Come on. Ha."

"She needs to rest."

"Ha. Ha." He shoved again, and Mama finally got up.

"She needed to rest, Jerrod," Abby scolded. "She had a hard delivery."

He shook his head. "She needs to get right up or she'll birth her own uterus. We don't want to mess around with that."

She wrinkled her nose and laughed as the bull tried to gain his feet while mama licked him.

He chuckled, enjoying Abby's pleasure at seeing something he'd witnessed countless times in a new light. "What do you say we lay down a clean bed then go in and wash up?" He grabbed the soiled gloves in one hand and held out the other for her to grab. She took it, and he pulled her up.

"What about the animals?"

"They kind of take care of things from here. Uncle Jimmy will give him his inoculations when it's time, but otherwise Mama handles the rest."

"Okay then." She grabbed their jackets, put hers on, and draped his over his shoulders as he held the filthy gloves.

"Thanks."

"You're welcome." She picked up the towels and spray bottle, and they walked out, taking care of the trash, swapping out soiled hay for fresh. Twenty minutes later, they stepped into the cold night, their breath pluming as Jerrod closed the barn up behind them.

"I'm so glad we were there for that."

"I'm sure Mama was too." He smiled as they started down the short path back to the house, relieved that she seemed more relaxed around him. "How about a cup of tea after we clean up?" Now that she was finally talking to him again, he wasn't ready for her to go upstairs and disappear for the rest of the evening.

"Sure."

He opened the back door, letting her in before him. "Why don't I take your coat? I'll stick it in the wash." He peeled his off and grabbed hers.

"Thanks. I guess I'll go up and shower off."

"See you in a few." He walked to the laundry room, stripping off his clothes, making use of the small shower dad had installed years ago. He rinsed off quickly and grabbed the clean pair of jeans and t-shirt folded on the drier. The water shut off upstairs as he headed to the kitchen, flipping on the dim light above the range, turning on the back left burner on the stove.

Abby came down in yoga pants and a long-sleeved cotton top, her wet hair in a ponytail.

"Just in time." He added boiling water to her mug and handed over her cup.

"Mmm." She wrapped her hands around the dark red crockery. "Warm. Thanks."

"It's the least I can do for our resident obstetrician."

Leaning against the counter, she grinned. "I still can't believe we helped birth a calf."

"You're a regular old farmer in the dell."

She rewarded him with another smile. "*You're* the farmer in the dell. How did you know Mama needed help?"

He shrugged, walking to the table, taking a seat, hoping she would follow. "I've been birthing calves for as long as I can remember. My dad started Timmy and me in on the action when we were pretty young."

She pulled out the chair next to his. "He taught you well."

"Yeah, I guess he did." He sipped his tea, not wanting to talk about his father.

"You don't mention him much. You have his chin."

He held her gaze in the shadowy light, subconsciously brushing at his jaw. "We didn't see eye to eye on much of anything."

Sympathy filled her eyes. "That must've been hard."

"It wasn't always easy." He shifted uncomfortably in his chair. This wasn't something he talked about—ever.

"I'm sure he's proud of you."

He chuckled humorlessly. "Yeah, I don't know about that."

She paused with her mug halfway to her mouth. "Of course he is. How could he not be?"

He crossed his ankles and leaned back in his chair. "My father stopped being proud of me a long time ago. Five generations of Quinn men were cops and farmers in this town, including him. He fully expected Tim and me to follow in his footsteps. I had every intention of doing so until I got my own ideas."

"What changed?"

"I was thirteen and fell in love."

She frowned. "Oh."

"With Denver, Colorado."

"Oh," she said again.

He smiled. "My best friend, Nathaniel, brought me along on his family's summer vacation, and changed my life. My parents took me to Lincoln a couple of times as a kid, but other than that I'd never left Parker. I piled into the Sturgis's minivan, staring out at cornfields and wheat for hours—the only scenery I'd ever known, then out of nowhere we're in Denver, surrounded by massive buildings and noise and traffic." He chuckled, still remembering the awe of his first city experience. "I spent seven days and six nights visiting museums and fancy restaurants, sleeping in hotels, taking everything in. I can't remember ever being more fascinated." Until Abigail walked into his life. He looked at her, smiling again. "From then on I didn't want the farm or this moth-eaten town. I still wanted to be a cop, but somewhere important. I told my dad that when I got home, and it pissed him off. Things went south from there."

"Your dreams weren't your father's."

He shook his head. "He assured me I would change my mind, but I didn't. By the time I was fourteen I was more determined than ever to leave. We never had much to say after that. I did my part around here, but we rubbed each other wrong all the damn time. It got to the point where we almost came to blows on a regular basis, so I busted my ass in school, graduated a year early, and got the hell out of here."

"Driven." She swallowed more tea.

"Desperate, I think, to prove him wrong. He always accused me of being greedy, of wanting too much, but that wasn't it. I just wanted—"

"Something different," Abby finished, taking his hand.

"*Yes.*" He squeezed her fingers, relieved that she understood. Shelby never did, or Tim. Mom tried to. "Exactly."

"So you became a cop?"

"In Omaha for a year after college, then I applied for the U.S. Marshals and got in. They shipped me off to LA where I did witness relocation for three years, then they sent me to Manhattan to work Fugitive Task Force. I met my friends Gavin, Shane, and Andy there. Andy's ICE—Immigration and Customs Enforcement, but the different organizations team up on Task Force a lot. We all roomed together and worked on the same cases for the two years I stayed. One night we had an apprehension go wrong and Gavin got shot in the back." He clenched his jaw. "He's paralyzed from the waist down."

"That's terrible. I'm sorry."

"It sucked pretty bad, but he's doing all right." He shrugged even as the memories of his friend bleeding and lying on the dingy floor flooded his mind. "Gavin was pretty touch and go for awhile, so Shane, Andy, and I took turns staying at the hospital. I was walking to the ICU a couple days after Gavin's accident when I got a call from Tim. Dad had just died of a massive heart attack down at the station." He blew out a long, slow breath, remembering the frantic conversation as if it happened yesterday.

She clutched his hand in both of hers, pressing his palm to her cheek. "I'm so sorry, Jerrod."

He closed his eyes, clenching his free hand at his side, accepting the comfort she offered, which no one else had. He opened his eyes, staring into hers. "Me too. We never did patch things up. Maybe we never would have." He shrugged. "I don't know, but I had to try to make it right the only way I knew how. I quit the Marshalls after his funeral. I came home and picked up a badge here in Parker. I met up with Shelby again and tried to make a life."

She removed her hands from his and sipped her tea.

He studied her as she stared at her drink, realizing that this was the perfect opportunity to make her understand. "We had a thing in high school for a while—off and on my sophomore and junior year. We picked things up when I got back, which we never should have. Shelby and I don't work. We never did. I was raw and miserable, maybe a little self-destructive." He shook his head. "I'm still not sure what I was thinking. Long story short, I felt trapped in this town, in a crappy relationship, so I put in for the job with Ethan, and got it. I loved LA and wanted to go back. I tried to be what dad wanted. I tried to be what Shelby wanted. In the end, it was never enough."

"It's a shame they didn't want you to be who you are. You're pretty great, Mr. Quinn."

He gave her a small smile, soothed by the compassion in her eyes. "Has anyone ever told you you're pretty damn amazing?"

"Mirror Abby tells me so all the time."

He frowned. "Mirror Abby?"

"You know, that gorgeous chick who stares back at me whenever I walk by mirrors or windows." She gave him a teasing wink.

He chuckled as she grinned, realizing they had weathered the storm. "You ready to call it a night?"

"In a minute." She leaned in. "I have gossip."

He rolled his eyes. "Oh, goodie."

"I haven't been able to tell anyone."

"Not even Timmy?"

She shook her head. "Not even Timmy."

The idea of her confiding only in him lifted his spirits considerably. "Okay, spill it."

She scooted her chair closer. "I think Caleb has the hots for your mother."

His brow shot up. "Who the hell's Caleb?"

"You know, the milk guy? The one who comes to pick up the supply?"

"Caleb Conroy?" He didn't know how he felt about anyone having the "hots" for his mother. "He's been friends with my family for...forever."

"He's very sweet. I can't tell if Mary's interested or not. I think they should go out on a date." She wiggled her brows.

"I don't know."

"She's wonderful, Jerrod. She should be happy."

"I want her to be happy. My father wasn't an easy man. They loved each other I guess, but..."

"It's weird," she finished.

"Yeah."

She nodded her understanding as she swiped stray strands of hair behind her ear.

He frowned as he noticed the red marks on her upper palm. "Whoa, what's this?" He took her hand, examining. "Those are some blisters, champ. I don't know how I missed these before."

"Uncle Jimmy says I need to toughen up my city hands."

"Uncle Jimmy needs to take it easy." He gently slid his thumb over the raw wounds. "I like your city hands. They're soft."

She tried to pull away as they held each other's gaze. "I think a callous or two builds character."

He let her go. "Looks like you're well on your way."

"I can take it. I'm having so much fun here—all of these new experiences."

"How are things going in the studio?"

She wrinkled her nose. "Clay is definitely not my medium, but I'm determined to create something that doesn't look like Olivia made it."

He laughed. "We have a few weeks for you to master your craft."

"Exactly." She stood with her empty mug. "And I will."

He got to his feet, taking their mugs to the sink, rinsing them and setting them in the dishwasher.

She moved to the counter, leaning against it. "This was fun."

"Yeah."

She yawned. "I guess I should head to bed. I'll see you in the morning."

Tonight had turned out exactly the way he'd hoped, but he didn't want her to go yet. "Good night."

"Night." She turned to walk away.

"Oh, hey, thanks for the help in the barn," he said, stalling for more time.

She turned back. "You're welcome."

He walked to where she stood, shoving his hands in his pockets. "We'll have to tell Uncle Jimmy you've officially been indoctrinated into the world of calf delivery."

She chuckled. "I can't wait to share the story.

You're a great teacher."

"Thanks."

The room fell silent.

Abby cleared her throat. "Well, I guess—"

"I've missed this," he blurted out.

"What?"

"Spending time with you." He rocked back on his heels, suddenly uncomfortable now that his confession was out. "You've been hard to track down the last few days."

She shrugged. "Yeah, I guess."

He took another step closer. "There's nothing going on between me and Shelby, Abigail. I know she comes by a lot, but what we had has come and gone."

She took a step back, her eyes weary. "Why are you telling me this?"

Why was he? It was better that she thought what she did, but he couldn't stand the idea of Shelby getting in the way of what he wanted most. "I don't know. I guess I didn't want you getting the wrong impression."

"I don't have any impressions one way or the other. I'm going to bed." She turned to leave.

"Abby." He snagged her wrist, turning her back to face him, knowing he should let her go. "Wait."

She swallowed as he held her gaze. "What?"

"I don't—I don't know." He moved closer, sliding his thumb along the soft skin of her inner arm, fighting to remember the rules—his rules.

She pressed her hand to his chest, pushing him away, then curled her fingers into his shirt, closing the last of the distance between them as her breath trembled from her lips. "Jerrod, what—"

"I don't know, Abigail," he whispered, only certain that he needed her as he cradled her face, capturing her lips with fevered pressure.

She whimpered as she gripped the back of his neck, pulling him closer. He took her deeper, his tongue diving, enticing hers into a frenzied dance, groaning as her sweet flavor and throaty purrs tempted him to take more. She slid her palms along his back as his fingers wandered into her hair, tugging at the elastic, sending a cascade of cold, damp locks to her shoulders. He tilted her chin up, pressing moist, searing kisses along her neck as her hands found their way beneath his shirt, clutching, teasing, trailing up his stomach and over his pecs.

"Jerrod. Jerrod," she panted, gripping his hips, staring at him with slumberous, desire-filled eyes, moaning as he walked her backwards, reaching into her pants, clutching her ass in skimpy panties, kneading, pressing her to the wall, finally touching her the way he'd longed to for months. He nibbled at her soft, full lips, tugging with his teeth and plundering, starving for another taste of her, certain he would never get enough.

She unfastened his snap, gasping for air as their lips parted and met once more. He lifted her shirt, unclasping her bra, reveling in the feel of hot, smooth skin as he cupped her breasts. She moaned again, arching, urging him on as headlights cut across the windows, sending him crashing back to reality. He blinked, coming to his senses at the sound of the truck door slamming.

"Come upstairs," she whispered out of breath, clinging to him.

What in the hell was he *doing*? "Abby," he shuddered out, resting his forehead against hers. "Abigail, I can't do this." He held her face, looking her in the eyes. "I *can't*," he said desperately, reminding himself more than her that this could never and should never have happened.

Her breathing slowed as they continued to hold each other's gaze, her eyes full of questions.

"Abby, I just can't." But he wanted nothing more than to take her to his bed. He stared at her cheeks pink with passion and her lips swollen from his hungry mouth. "I'm sorry."

She nodded, averting her gaze, pulling away, and went upstairs.

He listened to her hurried steps, scrubbing his hands over his face. "*Damn* it!" He'd started that and ended it in a supremely bastard-like way. Why didn't he let her walk away when she'd tried? What was he going to do about this *want* for the woman he couldn't have?

Sighing, he bent down, picking up the hair tie both had forgotten about. He sniffed at the elastic, breathing in her scent, starting up the stairs as his mother let herself in. He and Abigail needed to talk. He needed to clear the air yet again. He stopped outside Abby's mostly closed door, raising his hand to knock, but dropped it. What the hell was he supposed to say? If he tried to fix this now he would only make everything worse, especially when he wasn't certain he would be able to walk away. Turning, he went into his own room instead. He had all night to lay awake and figure out how to repair his latest mistake.

~~~~

"There is nothing here but furnishings." Aleksey wandered from the dining area to the kitchen, systematically opening cupboards, glancing at glasses and plates, pots and pans and shut them. "There are
~~~~

no personal papers or photos. I only know this is her place because Victor says the computer tells him so."

"Bullshit. There must be *something*, some clue to tell us for sure," Dimitri shouted.

Aleksey pulled the phone from his ear as he wandered back to the bedrooms, stopping in the doorway of the room with brown bedding. "If this is her condo, she lives with a man. I'm looking at weights too big for a woman her size."

"See? This is useful. Open your eyes, Aleksey, and find more."

Aleksey grit his teeth, sick of Dimitri's condescending tone. "My eyes see just fine while I search and you sit back in the safety of a hotel."

"Mind your tone," Dimitri warned. "What have you found on her sister?"

"Nothing." He winced, knowing he wouldn't live much longer if this continued to be his answer.

"This is no good," Dimitri's voice vibrated with frustration. "The little bitch and her family did not just *vanish*. We must find her before it's too late."

Aleksey went back to the room with blue and yellow bedding, sniffing at the hint of perfume lingering in the air. He walked to the closet, opening it, closing it, growing more frantic that the answers Dimitri wanted weren't here. He moved to the empty desk he'd already searched, yanking the drawers free, sliding his hands along the top, catching the edge of a crumpled piece of paper, pulling it loose. He stared at the wrinkled sketch, smiling. "This is her place."

"What?"

"This condo is hers."

"How do you know this for sure?"

"I've found a drawing of the girl she liked to baby in Baltimore. The little mouse you liked to fuck."

Dimitri chuckled. "Which one?"

"You ask me to remember names? The last one you and Victor took."

"Ah, *that* little mouse. We still have her. Track her down. We have lessons to teach."

"It will take a few days." He put the drawers back. "I don't know where they have taken her."

"A point is hard to make when one must wait," Dimitri snapped.

"I'll work quickly."

"I look forward to seeing my little mouse. Perhaps little mouse will bring the bitch out of her hidey-hole."

He hoped for all their sakes Dimitri was right. "I'm sure this will work."

Dimitri hung up without another word.

Aleksey looked at the sketch again, wiping at the sweat along his brow. Dimitri's mouse just bought him more time. She would be on the chopping block now instead of him. He dialed Luka's number, waiting.

"What did you find?"

"Good news. Victor is right; this is her place. We need to find Dimitri's mouse he liked so much in Baltimore. She will lead us to the bitch."

"I will make calls and find her."

"Do it quickly. We must find them both before Dimitri kills us." He hung up, covering his head with his dark hoodie as he walked down the hall and rearmed the security system, messing with the wires and chips until he knew they would never know he had been here. Glancing around one last time, he closed the door behind him, planning to make the most of his second chance.

Chapter Twelve

Abby stepped from the nesting house, closing the door behind her as she blew out a quick breath, shuddering as she absorbed the unforgiving cold. "Holy crap," she muttered, clutching her coat to her throat, hunching against the strong winds as she hurried down the path with her basketful of eggs. Tim had assured her she would get used to the unbearable temperatures, but she wasn't so sure. The wind alone chilled her bones, making outside chores a misery, but the animals needed attention no matter what the thermometer read.

Despite her goose bumps and chattering teeth she grinned, flushed with the successes of her day. Mary officially turned over the hen house duties, dubbing Abby the Quinn Family Farm's new egg gatherer, and Uncle Jimmy finally let her hook one of the cows up to the milking machine. Sighing her contentment, she stared at the big, beautiful house, watching the smoke plume from the living room chimney into dull, gray skies. She shivered, blinking her tired eyes, and laughed, twirling once, careful not to damage the eggs as she continued down the frozen path, reveling in her happiness.

Life was so *simple* here, the pace so slow and easy. The townspeople were kind and the stores small and charming. She could actually think without the familiar burden of fear. The constant nightmares she'd experienced in LA had yet to make an appearance, and the ceaseless need to look over her shoulder was gone. She was *free* and safe. She laughed again with the heady power of liberation, silently thanking Jerrod for giving her this opportunity.

She glanced toward the kitchen windows, smiling, shuddering as delicious tingles rocketed through her core, remembering the way he'd kissed her breathless and surprised her with his hungry demands. Last night opened her eyes to the real Jerrod Quinn. Not only was he a bodyguard and former US Marshall but also a reluctant farmer who helped mama cows birth their calves. He'd shared his story over a mug of tea, finally letting her in, then he'd *ravaged* her, his mouth feeding on hers like he'd been starving; his hands touching everywhere, stoking fires that were still burning. His calm, laidback façade would never fool her again. Beneath the recesses of those steady baby blues lay an inferno of toe-curling sexy she'd never experienced until now.

So why did she walk away so easily when he unexpectedly slammed on the brakes? She cursed herself again as she had a hundred times while she lay awake in the dark, staring at the shadows dancing on the ceiling, tossing and turning like a top ready to blow. Jerrod said he "couldn't" as he'd held her cheeks in his strong hands, staring into her eyes, but Jerrod most certainly could, and she planned to enjoy the ride.

Another slow smile crossed her lips with an anticipation she hadn't felt in a very long time. The cool Mr. Quinn had officially stirred her libido back to roiling. Now that she knew how it could be, she wanted more; she planned to have all of him very soon, but how?

She nibbled her lip as fragrant baths, sexy

nighties, and a midnight visit to Jerrod's room came to mind, but she needed to purchase her tools of seduction first. She swallowed the small lump of guilt, thinking her underhanded thoughts, and shook it away. Sometimes a woman had to take charge, and she was ready. Jerrod definitely wouldn't be sorry, but first she needed to wash the eggs, then she would track him down—not that he was ever hard to find—and they would be off to the town's one department store for something spectacular and lacy.

She pressed her hand to her stomach, calming her jitters as she climbed the steps and twisted the knob, walking into the blessed warmth. She pulled off her hat, stopping short, staring in disbelief as Shelby and Jerrod stood by the counter, his hands gripping her shoulders, Shelby cupping his cheeks, in a full-on lip lock.

Jerrod broke free, pushing Shelby away as the beautiful redhead smirked. "Damn it, Shelby." He glanced over his shoulder, his eyes going wide before he closed them. "Abigail."

Her heart sank as she set down the basket, afraid she would drop it from her trembling fingers. "Excuse me," she mumbled, walking up the stairs blindly, forgetting Mary's rules about boots in the house in her hurry to get to her room as Jerrod called after her. She stepped inside and closed the door, clutching the knob as her breath came too quickly. She wished she had the strength to lock herself in, but she opened the door a crack and sat on her bed, gripping her arms across her chest in the heavy wool coat, despite the heat flooding through the vents.

Shaking her head, she rested her forehead in her hands. Did she actually just *see* that? She closed her eyes and puffed out a breath as her stomach churned with nausea. Jerrod had assured her there was nothing left between him and Shelby, and she'd believed him. He'd never given her a reason not to.

Abigail, I can't do this. I can't. His voice echoed through her head like a nightmare. He could, just not with her.

And to think she'd been ready to try her hand at seduction. She laughed, her eyes filling as she stood, walking to the window, staring out at the snow-covered fields. Jerrod may have left Shelby behind, but he certainly wasn't over her as he'd claimed. Her breath shuddered out as she rolled her eyes to the ceiling. How could she have been so *stupid*?

She unzipped her coat and took it off, laying it on the chair by the fireplace as she glanced at the phone on the side table, yearning to call Lex. Alexa would know what to do; she would know what to say to make all of this make sense, but she couldn't put her family at risk just because she was having a Jerrod crisis.

She nibbled her nail as she paced in small circles, well aware that she would have to deal with this problem on her own. She'd been certain pursuing a relationship with Jerrod was the next healthy step in her road to healing. Dr. Tate had assured her she would know when she found the right partner, and she thought she had. Now nothing was clear.

She walked back toward the window and stopped as a whole new thought occurred to her. What if her abduction was part of the problem? What if Jerrod was attracted to her but realized he couldn't be with someone who'd lived as she did for two hellish months? She'd hardly endured what the other girls did, but she'd done several things she wasn't proud of—lap dances, stripping her body bare in seedy clubs, poll dances to catcalls. What if somewhere below the recesses of Jerrod's compassion he thought her dirty? She'd thought *herself* dirty until several sessions into her therapy and numerous meetings with her support group.

Jerrod had been supportive from the beginning, but dealing with panic attacks and offering comfort after her dreaded nightmares was easy when he could take a step back. A relationship meant delving into the thick of it all, and he probably didn't want to.

Everything had been different since the photo shoot. Perhaps the forced connection reminded him she wasn't just any other woman, and his job had been a convenient excuse. Alexa was married to a bodyguard, as were Morgan, Sarah, and Hailey, and soon Wren would be too. Their husbands had handled their protection just fine.

Surely last night had been a mistake in Jerrod's eyes. He'd been too caught up in the excitement of the birth and vulnerable after he shared so much of himself with her. He'd forgotten where she came from for a moment and pushed her away when he remembered.

Her stomach sank lower as the truth became apparent. Jerrod couldn't handle who she was—and her experiences in the Baltimore stash house and strip clubs were part of that whether he liked it or not. She straightened her sagging shoulders, reminding herself that she would not be ashamed of what she'd lived through or what she'd done to survive. If Jerrod was, well, she couldn't help that, even if the possibility broke her heart.

She caught sight of her own devastated eyes in the mirror and looked away, trying desperately not to care as Shelby's smooth voice grew loud. Seconds later the door slammed, making Abby jump.

She looked to the sewing machine Mary was letting her borrow and her sketchpad—her solace. She made a beeline to the desk Jerrod had moved in from one of the other guest rooms. She opened the book to the next clean page and picked up a pencil, eager to escape. She didn't want this stress or need it, nor did she want to feel the misery she was drowning in as she sat among her things. She positioned her paper, ready to begin, finding comfort in the familiar, finding power and strength as she drew the first line.

~~~~

"Abby. Wait." Jerrod started after her, stopping on the first step, shoving a hand through his hair as she quickened her pace and disappeared down the hall. "Damn it!" He whirled. "What the hell was that, Shelby? What are you *doing*?"

"An experiment." She smiled coolly, crossing her arms, leaning against the counter.

He was still trying to catch up with the last two minutes. He and Shelby had been arguing, then out of nowhere she grabbed him, planting one on him seconds before Abby walked in. He narrowed his eyes as Shelby's intentions were suddenly clear. "You saw her coming."

She shrugged.

"Goddamn." He jammed his hands through his hair for the second time as Abby's stunned, pale face flashed through his mind. "Why did you *do* that?"

"Because I wanted to see what I just did for myself. You two have a thing." She rushed forward, giving him a shove. "Why did you come back here and throw her in my face?"
~~~~

"Throw her in your face?" He sidestepped her as she moved in again. "We hardly leave the farm. If you didn't come around all the damn time..." He clenched his jaw, turning away, staring out the window as he braced his hands on the frame, struggling to gather his patience. As much as he wanted to throw Shelby's ass out into the cold, he couldn't. She was as pissed as he was. Nothing good happened when Shelby was angry.

"Why are you doing this?" Her voice radiated with pain. "Why do you want to hurt me like this?"

He gripped the wood tighter, sighing. How many times had he heard the same tired line in the same wounded tone? "I don't want to hurt you, Shelby. I never have." He turned, facing her, hoping they could settle this once and for all. "I don't want to keep going round and round."

She reached up, touching his cheek as she looked in his eyes. "The night you left. You never let me explain. That thing you thought you saw with Rod was nothing. He didn't mean anything. We were fighting all the time, and I was lonely. It was just a hug. I still love you, Jerrod."

"I don't feel the same way." He grabbed her wrist, pulling her hand away, blowing out a breath. Shelby's embrace with her co-worker had been the perfect excuse to walk away from something he'd wanted out of almost from the beginning, especially when he was fairly certain she had staged the whole thing. "You and me, we're over. We tried to make things work. They didn't."

"Because you walked in when I was hugging Rod."

He shook his head. "Rod was the least of our problems."

"How can you say that? We were happy."

Did she not remember the constant arguments and days on end where neither of them spoke to the other? "No, Shelby, we weren't. We would've come to an end eventually. You standing in our living room in another man's arms just brought it around sooner. You need to move on."

Tears rolled down her cheeks as she laughed bitterly. "The way you have?"

"Abby's my friend."

"Give me a break. Friends don't look at each other the way you two do."

He squeezed the back of his neck as the truth hit the mark, realizing he was doing a crappy job of concealing his feelings. "We work together."

"Right. The dedicated son and his friendly office manager taking a much-needed break at the Quinn Family Farm. You're a hell of a team player."

He shoved his hands in his pockets as Shelby worked his last nerve, worrying that she wouldn't be letting this obsession with Abigail go. "I don't know what you think you're seeing between me and Abby, but there's nothing there. I'm not going to keep going over this with you."

She swiped at her cheeks. "When did you turn into such an asshole?"

"I don't know. Why don't you tell me?"

"The day you packed your things and walked away."

"I had to go. We both know it."

"You could've taken me with you. You could've gotten me the hell out of this town."

He crossed his arms at his chest. "You're more than capable of doing that yourself. You're a good journalist, Shelby. You can go anywhere you want and make it."

"Anywhere as long as it's not with you."

"That's right."

"Bastard," she hissed.

Enough was enough. Nothing was going to get solved this way; it probably never would. "Why don't you go home and cool off for awhile?"

She glared. "You've got nerve, I'll give you that. I hate you, Jerrod Quinn. I *hate* you!" She stormed to the door, slamming it behind her.

He rolled his eyes to the ceiling and closed them, weary to the bone. Shelby exhausted him. She always had, with her constant demands and vile tantrums. He was rid of her for now, but she would be back soon enough with her crocodile tears and empty apologies. God, he just wanted her to stay away, but he would have to put up with her mercurial moods and endless need for drama until he and Abby left for the trial. Hopefully she would go back to town and focus on her job instead of him or Abby, but he doubted it. He would give Timmy a call and have him distract her for a while. His brother could do his part to keep Abby safe. God knows he'd tried.

The floorboards creaked above his head as Abby walked around her room, pacing, he knew. She was a pacer when she was upset. Steaming out a long breath, he scrubbed at his face again, trying to figure out how the hell to fix this. Shelby left a mess with her selfish disregard, and he needed to clean it up. If he'd had any inkling as to what she'd been up to, he would've ended her game before it began.

Starting up the steps, he searched for the right words, especially since he and Abby had yet to talk about last night. She'd been out in the barn with Uncle Jimmy before he had a chance to pull her aside and explain. He stopped outside her door and knocked. "Abby."

She didn't answer.

He knocked again. "I'm coming in."

Silence.

He pushed open the door, stepping in, staring at Abby's back as she sat at the desk he'd dragged in from the other room, listening to staticky Top 40 hits playing from the small AM/FM radio with tinfoil on its antennae. She was the picture of serenity, except for the frantic strokes of her pencil on paper. "Abigail."

"This isn't a good time," she said quietly. "I'm busy."

He walked closer, standing over her, watching the dark lines turn into a long skirt and some sort of fancy shirt. Her ability to make the difficult appear simple always fascinated him. "I think we should talk about...downstairs."

"I don't."

They were going to anyway. "The whole thing was a mistake. That wasn't what it looked like."

"It looked like your lips were pressed against Shelby's, kind of the way they were pressed against mine last night."

He puffed out a breath. "Yeah." He crouched down at her side, hoping she would look at him. "Shelby's having a hard time accepting that we're through."

"I can only imagine." She picked up a dark brown colored pencil, adding a belt to her sketch. "Mixed signals are usually confusing."

He ran his tongue along his teeth. Abby's cool indifference slapped at him more effectively than Shelby's rants ever could. "There are no mixed signals where Shelby's concerned." He touched her hand.

"There are no mixed signals, Abigail."

She pulled away. "I'm not sure I agree."

"Abby—" He clenched his jaw. "Will you look at me?"

She stopped drawing and met his gaze with unreadable eyes.

"Shelby and I are over."

"I'm don't know why you're telling me this."

"Because last night..." He stopped himself before he told her that he'd ached for her, craving her as he lay in his own bed. "Because I want to be sure you understand."

"I understand everything just fine."

He narrowed his eyes, trying to decipher what that meant. "Abby, last night in the kitchen," he tried again. "You and me... My job... I got caught up." He scratched at his jaw as he fumbled. "I can't have a relationship."

She leaned in closer, dropping her voice. "This is pretty personal stuff. Close Protection Agents probably shouldn't discuss such private information with their principals."

Jackson warned him long ago that she had a spicy streak. "Damn it, Abigail."

She sat up straight, replacing the dark brown pencil with tan. "I really need to get back to work. We both have a job to do. You go ahead and be the bodyguard, and I'll be the sex-trafficked fashion designer in need of your services."

He snagged her wrist, holding firmly, preventing the next stroke to her paper. "I'm sorry."

"Apologies aren't necessary." She tugged out of his hold, her eyes heating for the first time. "Go away, Jerrod. We have nothing more to say."

He stood as she began adding depth to her creation, leaving as she'd asked, when he wanted nothing more than to stay.

Chapter Thirteen

Shelby stormed into her office, slamming the door, throwing her purse to her desk as she took her seat. "Damn it!" Her breath rushed in and out as she stared at the pile of paperwork littering her blotter and shoved the messy stacks to the floor. "*Damn* it!" Today was not going the way she'd planned. Her trip to the Quinn farm was supposed to have turned out entirely different. Jerrod was supposed to have accepted her dinner invitation instead of turning her down; he was supposed to have kissed her back instead of freaking the hell out when he realized *Abigail* saw the whole thing.

She collapsed back in her chair with a huff. Why couldn't she make Jerrod see that they belonged together? What did she have to do to make him *love* her? She wanted him and planned to have him, but he was too distracted by the blue-eyed city girl with her silky black hair and ultra trendy clothes. She chucked a pen across the room, ignoring the stirrings of envy.

What did he *see* in the little twit anyway? She was short and too damn perky. She'd watched Abigail grin and laugh on her way back from the hen house, spinning around like she was freaking Liesl Von Trapp from the *Sound of Music*. Huffing out another breath, Shelby stared at her wall of accolades, trying to think past her crushing disappointment. Why the hell did he bring the fashion plate to flipping Parker, Nebraska? He hated it here. If he wanted time away from the office with his luscious little package why didn't he whisk her off to Tahiti or Aruba—anywhere but here... unless the situation was something else entirely, as she'd suspected all along.

She sat up with a start, flipping open her laptop, typing *Ethan Cooke Security, Los Angeles* into her search engine. Within seconds she searched the site, studying the picture of Jerrod among several hot, muscled men all duded up in black shirts, looking broody and intimidating for the camera. Interesting but not what she wanted. She clicked again, perusing credentials, contact information, so on and so forth, then she tried *Images*, hoping for random shots of the office staff. Instead pictures of the occasional movie star with one of Ethan Cooke's guards popped up, along with more group shots.

She navigated back to the contact page and picked up her phone, dialing the number given.

"Good afternoon, Ethan Cooke Security, this is Amber. How can I help you?"

"Yes, good afternoon. Can I speak with Abigail please?"

"Abigail?"

"Yes, Abby."

"I'm sorry. I don't know an Abby, ma'am."

"I think I must have the wrong number. Sorry."

"That's okay."

Shelby disconnected, her eyes narrowing as she smiled. "Gottcha." Abigail didn't work for Ethan Cooke Security, so who the hell was she? And what the hell was her last name?

Her cell phone rang, interrupting her thoughts as she glanced at the readout. Timmy. The Chief of Police would have to wait. She was busy. She pushed her phone aside and wiggled in her seat, getting comfortable as her fingers flew over the keys. It was time to piece together the story behind Jerrod's mysterious Abigail.

~~~~

Margret clenched her teeth, biting back her whimpers as Aleksey's fingers dug into her bicep. She quickened her pace as they walked down the long hall, hoping he might let up on the pressure if she stayed by his side. She glanced in the empty old rooms of the abandoned hospital, shuddering as Aleksey yanked her along. This place was way scarier than the filthy strip clubs and stinky stash houses she'd been bounced around in since the raids in July. Surely it was haunted or something. For the first time since her kidnapping she wished to be in a brothel.

"Let's go!" He gripped her tighter, pulling her faster passed the endless rooms, opening the last creaky door on the left. "In." He shoved her into the dingy space, and she careened forward, slipping, catching herself before her knees connected with the scarred, cracked tiles.

Brushing off her stinging hands, she righted herself, her eyes going wide as she focused on Dimitri standing in the center of the room, smoking his cigarette. He flashed her his cruel smile, and her heart froze.

"Ah, Little Mouse, have you missed me?"

She swallowed as fear clogged her throat, glancing around, looking for some place to hide or a way to escape. He was evil. He always hurt her when he raped her.

"You look different, Little Mouse."

Her shoulders tensed as he tossed his cigarette to
~~~~

the floor and walked toward her, looking at her through narrowed eyes.

"Your hair is thin and dull." He slid his spidery fingers along the arms of her t-shirt, brushing her skin, making her cringe.

"You are too skinny now." He clucked his tongue, pulling on the waist of her ill-fitting jean skirt. "This life is getting to you." He squeezed her jaw with painful pressure and kissed her cheeks, as if they were long-lost friends. "It gets to all of you eventually." He moved his face closer to hers. "The drugs make this better. Do you like to take them?"

Her heart quickened as she stared at him, wondering whether or not she should answer.

He pinched her chin. "I asked you if you like to take the drugs?"

"No," she whispered. She'd promised Abby she wouldn't touch the pills and whatever else they liked to push on them. She couldn't get away if her mind wasn't clear.

"Why not I wonder?"

She jerked a bony shoulder.

Luka burst through the doorway, carrying a large bag of fast food. The scent of greasy fries and grilled meat immediately filled the room, making her mouth water and stomach growl. She couldn't remember the last time she'd had anything more than the stale peanuts and pretzels she pilfered from the bowls at the bars.

"I hear your stomach talking, Little Mouse. Do you want to have a meal?"

"Yes," she answered, careful to keep her voice steady and level. If he knew she wanted that burger more than her next breath, she wouldn't get it.

"Well, come on." He gestured to the card table in

the corner. "Let's have some of this delicious food."

She hesitated, then followed, trying to figure his angle.

"Go ahead. Take a burger. Enjoy."

She reached in the bag, grabbing the warm wrapper, salivating like a dog. Hurrying, she unfolded the paper, taking a huge bite, fearful they would rip it away before she had a taste. Biting in again with an over-full mouth, she savored the globs of mayo and ketchup, the salty pickle and pungent onion, melding with charbroiled meat. Heaven.

"Do you like it?"

She nodded, ready for another sample as Dimitri slapped her arm, knocking the sandwich to the table. She glanced from him to the burger, tempted to reach for it despite the consequences.

"Would you like to finish and have fries too?"

She nodded again, her sheer desperation for food making her careless.

"What will you do for the rest of your meal?"

The delicious flavors soured on her tongue as she met Dimitri's eyes.

"Take a seat, Little Mouse. I don't want to fuck you right now; later, but not now."

She stared at the chair.

"Sit." He shoved her to the folding chair and took a carton of fries from the bag, setting them in front of her. "Eat."

"No thank you."

"*Eat.*"

She picked up a soggy, cooling potato and put it in her mouth, then another and another, relishing the starchy taste, hating that fried food could sink her so low.

"While you eat you can tell me what you know

about The Bitch."

She stopped chewing, darting him a glance, and looked at the table, knowing that The Bitch was Abby.

"What do you know about her?"

She gripped her hands together in her lap, unsure of what to say.

"What do you *know*?" he shouted, making her jump.

"I—I don't know who you're talking about."

He yanked her face close to his. "The Bitch. Fawn. Abigail. You know who I mean."

"I don't remember her," she lied. She thought of Abby everyday, holding on to the comforting memories of her hugs and pretty smiles and the promise that she would find a way to set her free.

Dimitri's huge hand plowed into her face.

She cried out in pain, pressing her fingers to her split lip, whimpering as blood trickled into her mouth.

"Do you remember now?"

She shook her head. "No."

He took aim again, knocking the chair backwards with the force of his fist to her cheekbone.

She screamed as her head hit the unforgiving floor, and she moved her bloodied palm from her tender mouth to her throbbing cheek.

"Get her up!" Dimitri yelled, pounding his hand on the table.

Aleksey rushed forward, yanking her to her feet.

The room spun in dizzying circles. Dimitri's face blurred in front of her as she fought to keep her balance.

"Sit and tell me or I will make the pain intolerable."

The pain was bad enough, but she was certain he could make it worse.

Aleksey shoved her back in the chair.

"Where *is* she?"

"I don't know," she sniffled, forming her words carefully, trying to minimize the discomfort to her lip. "I'm not sure where she is."

"What did she tell you all those times she took you into her room?"

Abby had taken care of her, risking punishment by sneaking extra peanut butter and jelly sandwiches from the kitchen. Abby had entertained her, telling her stories of college and walking the runways, of the exciting career she would have when they finally got away. Not once had Abby ever let her believe that she wouldn't go home. Somewhere deep down, she still held out hope. "That she wanted to go home."

"Home to where?"

"To Maryland." She hated sharing any part of Abby with him; she hoped Abby would understand.

"She is not there. Where else would she go?"

Abby's career would take her to Los Angeles, but she would die before she told him so. "She never said anything else. She always said she wanted to go home to Maryland. That's all."

Dimitri made a grumble in his throat as his eyes turned fierce. "You lie!" He brought his elbow down on the back of her hand resting on the table, cracking something, making her moan in agony. "You lie, little cunt!" He pushed her off her chair as she cradled her swelling fingers, crying, wishing Abby were here to hold her close and sing songs next to her ear the way she used to when the girls were being beaten and raped in the next room.

"Stand up!"

She stayed where she was, in too much pain to do as Dimitri demanded.

"Stand up!" He dragged her up by her hair, pummeling his fist into her stomach, sending her sprawling as she coughed, gasping for her breath. "You want to lie to me? You want to keep her secrets while she leaves you behind to live her life?" He kicked her in the ribs, causing her to jerk with the radiating ache. "Now I will fuck you, bitch. Now you will pay." He pulled his pants down and got to his knees, tossing her to her back, yanking her skirt up, slamming himself into her.

She closed her eyes, blocking out his cruel, agonizing thrusts, letting her mind float as she always did when Dimitri or any of the others used her.

"You'll come visit me in LA. We'll go shopping, and you can be my special guest at the Lily Brand Fashion Shows." Abby wiggled her brows, making Margret smile after she'd been crying, missing her mother.

Margret flashed to another moment when Abby forced her to dance and sing quietly until they both collapsed to the bed, laughing, despite the life they lived. And to the one and only time she saw Abby sob in despair. *"I'm so sorry, Margret. I'm so sorry I had to send you to that man. I tried to go instead, but Renzo wouldn't let me. I tried," she repeated, and for once Margret got to be the comforter instead of the other way around as she hugged the woman who had become her big sister. "I know, Abby. I know. Tell me about the fashion shows. Tell me about the dresses you'll make me when we're free." Abby's crying quieted to jerky inhales and exhales as they huddled together in the corner of the room. I'll make you something strapless. Probably blue to play up your eyes. We'll do an A-line to accentuate your tiny waist...*

Dimitri finished himself off with a sickening laugh and pulled her up to sitting, her ribs screaming, her head throbbing, forcing her back to reality. "I will give you one more chance to tell me what you know, Mouse. What do you know about Abigail Harris?"

"I—I don't know anything." Her lips trembled as tears ran down her cheeks.

He glared, grabbing her hair, shoving her back to the broken tiles as he shouted something in Russian, slamming her skull against the floor.

She tried to protect her head but it was no use. He was too strong. He rapped her head again, and she saw stars. He punched her face relentlessly, until she no longer fought to shield herself from each unbearable blow.

Dimitri's hollering faded and the pain vanished as she thought of Abby's big blue eyes.

"I'm going to take you away from this, Margret. I don't know when or how, but I'm going to free us both. Promise me you believe me. Promise me you'll never give up hope that I'm going to take you home."

Abby's gentle words and sweet smile filled her mind as Dimitri's cruel hands stole her last breath.

Chapter Fourteen

Abby spread fresh wood shavings around the last of the stalls, breathing in the cedar scent as she hummed along with the country music Mary liked to listen to while they worked. She paused, glancing up when Mary and Caleb Conroy stepped inside with the paperwork Mary signed off on every other day before Caleb drove off with the milk supply.

"...sure would be nice to see you there, Mary." He took off his dingy cap, blotting at the sweat on his ruddy face despite the cool temperatures of the barn.

"It's doubtful, Caleb. I don't have time for such foolishness. I have a farm to run." She turned the page over, picked up a pen, and signed her name.

"Sure would be nice to see you," he repeated, setting his hat back on his balding head, squirming. "The O'Neils put on a nice party."

Nibbling her lip, Abby watched poor Caleb fumble about, struggling to ask Mary on a date.

"Chuck and his band are going to play." He cleared his throat as Mary handed him the sheet.

"I'm sure you'll have a fine time, Caleb."

Abby wrinkled her nose. He was blowing it with his forehead wiping and cap fiddling. Unable to stand in for another second, she leaned her rake against the wall and stepped out. "Did I hear something about a party?"

Mary turned, and Caleb stood up straight.

"Good afternoon, Abby."

She smiled at Caleb. “Good afternoon. I had no idea you were a party animal.”

He pinked up. “Oh, I’m not. I was just wondering if Mary here was planning to attend the O’Neil’s annual barn dance.”

“A barn dance? I love to dance. Mary, we should go.”

Caleb perked up. “It’s a fine time—a live band, refreshments, lots of square dancing and stuff.” He pulled off his hat again and set it back in place as he cleared his throat for the second time.

Abby beamed. “*Fun*. What do you say, Mary?” She gave her a gentle poke to the side with her elbow. “I’ve never been to a barn dance, and I’ve never square danced before. We can do-si-do the night away.” She wiggled her brows.

Mary folded the quality card Caleb had handed off. “I don’t know, Abby.”

“You work so hard. I think we’d have a good time.”

Mary stared at her in her jeans and plaid coat, her hair up in a tight ponytail. The no-nonsense woman was in desperate need of a night out on the town. “I don’t have anything to wear to a barn dance.”

She grinned, sensing Mary was on the fence. “We’ll go shopping. We can go to the department store.”

“Now don’t start thinking you’re going to be dressing me up like some slick fashion plate.” She shoved her hands in her pockets the same way Jerrod always did. “I’ll leave the fancy clothes to you.”

Abby shook her head soberly, even though she had every intention of ‘slicking’ Mary up. There were a few dresses she remembered seeing on her own trip into town a couple weeks ago that would work very well. “No, certainly not.”

“I’d rather just go to the thrift shop.”

Her brows furrowed as her plans to smooth-talk Mary into the blue number she had in mind disintegrated. “The thrift shop?”

“There’s nothing wrong with used clothes.”

She smiled, liking the idea after all. She would take a few tired items and make them into something new. “You’re absolutely right.”

“Okay, I’ll go. But just for a little while.”

She threw her arms around Mary and winked at Caleb. “We’re going to have such a good *time*.” She eased back. “So, when’s the dance?”

“Saturday,” Caleb chimed in.

“Saturday?” She had four days to make big things happen.

“If that’s too short notice—”

“It’s definitely not,” Abby reassured, understanding that Mary was already looking for a way to back out. “We’ll go to town today, if that works for you.”

“I think I can find some time.”

“Perfect.”

Mary glanced at her practical blue sports watch. “In fact, we should probably go pretty soon. I don’t want to fall behind with the house chores.”

“I’d like to change first, then I’ll be ready. And I’ll help with the house chores when we get home.”

“I’ll finish up in here with Caleb. I’ll meet you inside in about twenty minutes.”

She nodded. “See you Saturday, Caleb.”

“Bye now,” he said.

Abby turned, grinning her triumph as she made her way down the row of stalls to the exit. She rarely played matchmaker, but Mary and Caleb had the potential to be an incredibly cute couple. Mary needed someone with a gentle, sweet side to chip away at all of that serious, and Caleb fit the bill.

She closed the barn door behind her, doing a victory wiggle despite the harsh winds, pausing when she spotted Jerrod sending a nail into one of the upstairs shutters on the house. He shoved his hammer in the tool belt hanging on his hip and descended the ladder from heart-stopping heights as she moved along the short path. He jumped down, skipping the last four rungs as she reached the back steps.

"Hey."

"Hi." She took the stairs inside with Jerrod following.

"All finished up?"

"Until this evening." She toed off her boots and hung her jacket on the rung, turned, and almost slammed into him as he settled his coat next to hers. "Sorry."

"No problem." He moved to the left as she did.

They both moved to the right.

She stopped. "Go ahead."

"You first."

Her stomach growled loudly, reminding her she couldn't head upstairs and avoid an awkward encounter no matter how much she wanted to. "Thanks." She skirted around him, making her way to the refrigerator.

Jerrod followed, leaning against the counter, crossing his arms at his chest. "How'd it go this morning?"

They'd run into each other several times while he'd been in and out of the barn with his tools, bending over in his snug jeans, repairing loose boards for his mother. "Pretty well." She pulled out the plate of leftover chicken and bowl of salad.

"Uncle Jimmy says you're turning into a real pro with the milking."

She plucked up a decent-sized helping of Mary's fresh-from-the-greenhouse greens, plopping them into a bowl, and pulled a knife from the drawer for the chicken. "Your family's taught me well."

"Who knew there was a farm girl beneath those designer clothes?" He smiled.

"Pretty crazy." She grabbed the cutting board and sliced a breast in half, waiting for him to be on his way. She'd tried to avoid alone time with Jerrod since the Shelby incident on Saturday. They needed some space until she could figure out how she was supposed to look at him and not *want* him despite what he thought of her.

"Abigail." He slid closer to her side. "When are you going to talk to me?"

"I'm talking to you right now."

"Only because you're too polite not to."

"I'm trying to work everything out." She looked up, meeting his eyes, sliding the blade along her skin instead of the chicken. "Ow!" She dropped the knife with a clatter as blood oozed down the pad of her index finger.

Jerrod moved in, twisting on the sink, grabbing her wrist, shoving her hand under the cold stream.

She sucked in a sharp breath as water hit her throbbing wound. She tried to jerk away and rammed into his chest. "I'm okay."

He held her hand firm, stepping closer, pinning her between the counter and his solid, muscled body. "Rinse it out some."

She breathed in his soap as he bent closer, examining the gash, his breath heating the top of her ear as he turned her hand from side to side. She closed her eyes as sparks tingled along her skin, remembering the way his lips had trailed hot kisses along her neck, the way his hungry mouth had demanded she keep up with his frenzied pace.

"Looks like you got yourself pretty good." He twisted off the faucet and grabbed a paper towel, gripping her finger between the ripped paper, holding it above her heart. "Firm pressure."

"I was careless." She turned, desperate for space, and managed to wedge them face-to-face and chest-to-chest. "I'll be fine."

His gaze darted to her lips then held hers. "You need a bandage."

"I'll get one," she said breathily. Even after the whole Shelby thing, even after the way he'd made her doubt herself, she *still* wanted to yank that mouth of his to hers. What was *wrong* with her? "Excuse me."

"Abby." He rested his hands on her shoulders. "Can we clear the air?"

"I don't know what you want from me."

"I want you to talk to me." He moved his palms down her arms and back up. "I want us to be the way we were in LA—when we used to have fun together."

His casual touch was pleasure and pain. "Nothing's the same. Ever since the photo shoot..." she hesitated. *Screw it*. She was sick of dancing around the truth. "My feelings for you aren't simple, Jerrod. I didn't realize things had changed until the photo shoot. I understand that only makes this more awkward..."

His eyes filled with regret as he gripped her arms tighter. "My job—I can't offer you more, Abigail." He shook his head. "I can't."

"So you've said."

"Your safety comes first."

She sighed, tired of his lame justifications. "Don't."

"Don't what?"

"Use your job as an excuse. You're not interested. I understand 'no thank you' just fine."

"It's not an excuse, Abigail. It's the truth."

She tilted her head, her brows raised. "I'm perfectly safe here."

"For the most part you're right, but what about when we leave in a couple weeks? We'll be stepping right back into the line of fire. They want you dead, Abigail, and I won't let that happen. If keeping my distance *now* means you're alive in six weeks because my focus is where it needs to be, I'm willing to make a few sacrifices."

When he said it like that he made sense, but what about the rest? What about the way he'd kissed her? She almost asked, but couldn't bear to hear the real answer as to why he'd stopped. "What if you weren't my bodyguard?"

He slid his finger down a lock of her hair, skimming her cheek along the way. "You're a beautiful woman."

What kind of answer was that? "This is messed up—all of it." She pulled his hands away. "I don't want us to be like this, Jerrod. I don't."

He rested his hands on the lip of the counter, not budging an inch for her to move by. "I don't either. I miss you. I miss the fun we used to have when it was just the two of us."

"So do I," she admitted. But what now?

"Okay. Good. Let's make this easy. Do you want to catch a movie with me tonight? Lady's choice, of course."

She bit the inside of her cheek as she looked in his eyes, more confused than ever. How was *anything* about this entire situation easy? "Jerrod—"

"We could have dinner first."

She shook her head. They'd done the whole dinner and movie thing numerous times before, but a once simple evening out now felt too much like a date—a date he didn't want...or did he? She would compromise. "How about we rent something and watch a movie here?"

He shrugged. "Your call."

Supposedly it was her call, but she felt like she was along for the ride—wherever Jerrod chose to steer them. "I need to get a band aid." She pushed against him, assuming he would move, but he held his ground.

"Hold on."

She huffed out a breath. "What?"

"Friends." He held out his hand.

She hesitated, then took his, shaking it. "Friends." Even if that wasn't what she wanted. "I'm going to get that band aid." She moved around him, starting toward the stairs.

"Can I fix you a sandwich or finish making your salad? We can have lunch together."

The air was clearer, kind of, but she wasn't ready to dive into the way things used to be, if that was even possible. She stared into his steady blue eyes, realizing her world had officially turned upside down—again. A situation she once had some semblance of control over was now out of her hands. Jerrod had been the man she'd relied on for the last six months of her life. He'd soothed her during some of her worst moments and kept her safe. Now he left her unsettled as she struggled to figure out how to navigate their strange new "friendship."

"Uh, I'll get something after I clean up," she said. She took the stairs to the bathroom and grabbed a Band-Aid, covering her wound, then went to her room, pulling boot-cut jeans and a snug spaghetti strap black top from her drawer. Turning, she stopped, facing the window, staring out at the endless snowy fields and highway far in the distance as she took off her work clothes and put on her pants and top. Freedom. She dismissed the sudden yearning to be away from the house and Jerrod as she walked to the closet for her black button-down sweater and boots.

She slid soft cashmere up her arms and plunked her feet in buttery leather, glancing outside once again, looking to the horizon as her heart rate quickened and the stirrings of unease skittered along her spine. "No. No." She breathed in and out, clutching the edge of the bed as the familiar grips of panic came back to haunt her. "You're fine. You're fine," she assured herself as sweat popped along her forehead, and Jerrod's footsteps on the hard wood floors downstairs echoed like gunshots in her head.

Standing up straight, she grabbed her purse with a trembling hand. She had to go. She had to get out of here *now*—away from the farm, but more, away from Jerrod and all the confusion. She glanced down at her wrist and the watch she put on every morning before she started her day and unclasped it, leaving it on the side table. *I can find you anywhere with this.* The thought was typically a comfort, but today she didn't want to be found, not by Dimitri or Victor, not by Jerrod either. She looked back at the pretty twists of silver and gold and left the jewelry behind, pausing in the hallway, glancing to the stairwell to her right, leading to the kitchen and Jerrod, then the stairs to the left, and turned, walking quietly down the steps, desperately trying to avoid any squeaks that would give her away.

She inched her way forward, careful to keep her heels from connecting with the floor as she moved closer to the front door, snagging the keys to Mary's pickup when she made it. Closing her eyes tight, she twisted the doorknob slowly and stepped outside, breathing in the blessedly frigid air as she continued to sweat.

Mary came around the corner, and Abby jumped, pressing her hand to her chest. "You scared me."

"Sorry, honey."

"I'm ready," she schooled her voice and breathing. "I grabbed the keys unless you need to go inside." She prayed Mary didn't need to go in.

"No. No. I'm all set."

"Great," she said with a punch of desperation, glancing over her shoulder, full-well understanding she was breaking the rules, but for once she didn't care. She needed this break from Jerrod and the mess between them—from her life. She desperately wanted to be a normal woman for one afternoon.

They walked to the truck as Abby looked behind her once more and opened her door, hopping into the cab.

Mary buckled in and turned over the ignition. "I guess we should get this show on the road."

"I guess so." Abby wiggled her foot up and down, willing Mary to hurry before Jerrod figured out she was gone. He was going to be mad, but they were only going to the thrift store. He'd said himself she was safe here, and she planned to be careful.

Mary put the truck in drive, pressed on the gas,

and they bumped down the long lane.

Abby sat back, sighing her relief, relaxing her shoulders, releasing her death grip on her purse when they reached the highway. If she was going to be free for a few hours, she was going to enjoy herself. “So, what do you think you’d like to wear to the dance?”

“Honey, I have no clue.”

“Well, I can help you with that.” She smiled, a genuine smile as Mary accelerated and they headed toward town.

~~~~

Jerrod climbed the stairs with the veggie sandwich he made Abby, trying to figure out what he should say when he handed over this latest peace offering. She said she would eat later, but ‘later’ had been over an hour ago. He’d waited a good thirty minutes, dawdling over his plate of last night’s baked chicken and creamy mashed potatoes, hoping she would come down so they could talk away any remaining awkwardness and move on, but as he took his last bite, he realized she was still avoiding him despite their handshake and plans for an evening movie.

He didn’t know how to make their situation better. Everything was so damn messy. Biding his time and giving her space didn’t work. Cornering her in the kitchen and forcing her into strained conversation hadn’t gotten him anywhere either. Their situation had only grown more complicated when Abby confessed to not-so-simple feelings, and he’d kept his mouth shut, giving her the impression he didn’t have any of his own. What else was he supposed to do?

His explanations had been the absolute truth. They would head to trial in less than three weeks. The
~~~~

relative safety and relaxed precautions they were enjoying here in Parker would be a thing of the past. Her security would heighten; safeguards would increase. It was more vital than ever to concentrate on procedures and protocols and forget the rest. Mixed up emotions and this new discord in an otherwise smooth relationship were liabilities neither of them could afford. Close protection worked best when agent and principal were on the same page. That's why he never got involved with his clients—and had never been tempted to until Abby.

He reached the top step and walked to her room, slowing when he didn't hear the radio, frowning at her open door. Abby always shut herself in as far as she dared. Now that he thought of it, he hadn't heard a sound from upstairs since she went to get her Band-Aid. His concern vanished into a smile, and he relaxed, shaking his head. Maybe things *were* okay between them. She must've fallen asleep. Getting up at three-thirty every morning was finally getting to her. He proceeded forward, knocking on the doorframe and peeked in. "Abby?"

His brows furrowed for the second time as he glanced at the empty, undisturbed bed and her work clothes tossed over the armchair. Her dresser drawers were slightly ajar, and her watch lay on the side table. He stared at the pretty timepiece she always wore as the cloak of unease settled on his shoulders. "Abby," he called louder, heading toward the bathroom, but the door was open and the light off. He took the stairs in twos to the living room, glancing at the vacant couch and loveseat. Where the hell was she? "Abigail?"

Picking up his pace, he popped his head in each room, calling for her as he wandered through the house, stopping as he passed a window, realizing the pickup was gone. She didn't. She couldn't have. But the lead ball in his gut warned him she did. "Shit."

He dropped the plate, rushing out the door, running around the side of the house to the barn. She was in the barn. She had to be. Mom must have run errands, but Abby was still here. He yanked the door open. "Abigail," he shouted.

No one answered.

"Fuck. *Fuck*!" Dread turned into outright fear as he sprinted back to the house and into the kitchen, picking up the landline, dialing Mom's cell. Within seconds he could hear her ringtone echoing from her downstairs bedroom. "I can't believe this." He slammed down the phone, running trembling fingers through his hair. "I can't fucking *believe* this."

He picked up the cordless again and dialed Timmy's cell, barely able to hear the ringing over his pounding heart.

"Hello?"

"Have you talked to Abby?"

"Not recently. I'm having lunch with Shelby—monthly police log bullshit. We just sat down a couple minutes ago."

"She's gone."

"Who?"

"Abby, damn it," he snapped, gripping the corner of the wall, trying to keep his cool as fear consumed him. How long had she been gone? Where the hell did she go? "Mom and the pickup are missing too. I tried Mom's cell; it's in her room."

"I'm sure everything's fine. They probably went to the market."

"She knows not to go anywhere without me." He slammed the side of his fist on the granite countertop, making the cookie jar rattle. "She knows that, Tim. And she's not wearing her watch. She could be anywhere. They could have her." He scrubbed at his jaw, trying to quell his helpless anger.

"All right. I'll go check out some of mom's typical spots and see if I spot the truck, then I'll head out. If she doesn't show up in the next hour we'll call out a BOLO."

He wanted to demand the BOLO now, but Tim was right. Abby was probably fine. Calling unwanted attention, putting her name and description out over the radio was more detrimental than waiting the hour, if Timmy didn't find them first. "I'll stay here in case they come back." And make himself crazy. "Call me if anything turns up."

"You know I will."

Jerrod hung up, carefully, slowly, returning the phone to its base, certain he might crack the plastic into several pieces. How could she do this? Abby had known from the very beginning that she was never, ever to leave without him. Parker was probably safe, but her seekers could be anywhere.

CHAPTER FIFTEEN

ABBY DROVE UP THE LANE, AVOIDING THE WORST OF THE juts marring the dirt road as she sang along with Lady Antebellum, belting out *We Own The Night* with plenty of gusto. She grinned, thrilled when Mary joined in and eased off the gas as the house came into view, not wanting the afternoon to end. The last two hours had been *perfect*—shopping, laughing, lunch out. Girl time!

She slapped her hand against the steering wheel in time with the beat, high on sheer happiness. It had been *months* since she'd wandered through stores without a babysitter by her side or enjoyed a late-afternoon meal in public without watching her bodyguard watch everyone else around them. For the first time since her kidnapping she drove instead of taking the passenger's seat—just in case there was a tail and need for a quick getaway. She'd had her 'normal' and wanted plenty more. Just a few more weeks and she would have her life back.

She pulled up to the spot where Mary typically parked, threw the transmission into park, and twisted up the volume, jumping out of the cab. She hurried around to Mary's side, pulling Mary out of her seat.

"Abby, honey, what are you doing?"

She moved to the music, in full groove-mode, laughing. "Dancing. Dance with me, Mary." She shook her hips, tossing her hands over her head, laughing harder when Mary actually wiggled about. She wanted to bottle up this snapshot of pure joy for the next time she was stuck in some dark place, dealing with the consequences of a situation she'd never asked for.

"So you really think you'll be able to make me something with the pile of clothes we bought?" She took Abby's hand and turned in a stiff circle.

Abby grinned. "Absolutely. I already know what I'm going to—"

"Where the *hell* have you been?" Jerrod shouted, booking it around the corner of the house, his eyes smoldering as they met hers.

She froze, her shoulders automatically tensing as she braced against Jerrod's angry tone. She'd expected him to be upset, but this was several stratospheres into furious.

"You mind your tone, son." Mary stepped closer to Jerrod. "Abby helped me with some shopping for the barn dance."

Abby glanced at Tim and Shelby as they walked around the house. Tim reached in and turned off the truck.

Jerrod's ragged breathing filled the air as he seared her with another look. "What were you thinking?" He kicked a rock, sending it careening across frozen dirt. "What the hell were you thinking, Abigail?"

She would not apologize for taking what she needed. "That I'm suffocating."

"You know better, damn it! You *know* better." He shook his head, his jaw clenched.

"Jerrod Quinn," Mary scolded. "That's enough."

He turned away, shoving his hands in his pockets, and pulled them out, jamming a hand through his hair. "Goddammit!"

"Abby," Mary took her hand. "I'm so sorry, honey.

I don't know what's gotten into him."

She swallowed the lump of emotion, squeezing Mary's fingers as she stared into her questioning gaze. How could she tell Mary that Jerrod had every right to be angry without breaking her cover? "I'm sorry—"

"Don't be sorry." Mary wrapped her up in a firm hug. "It's been ages since I've had such a fine time. Thank you for lunch."

She squeezed her eyes shut, fighting back tears. "I just needed to be," she whispered, giving the woman who had become her friend the only explanation she could.

Mary drew away. "Everything's going to be okay, honey. Trust me on that." She tossed a nasty look her son's way.

She nodded, unable to speak as her lips trembled. Everything was *not* okay, nor would it be anytime soon. She grabbed the bagful of treasures they'd discovered at the thrift shop, looked at Tim, Shelby, and Jerrod's stiff stance as he still stood with his back to them, and walked toward the house.

Jerrod turned, following hot on her heels. "We need to talk about this."

She picked up her pace, her heart accelerating with the sensation of being chased. "Later."

"No. Now."

She dashed up the front steps, trying to gain distance.

He snagged her arm as they reached the porch. "Abigail—"

"Don't touch me!" she screamed, whirling, shoving at his chest.

He dropped his hands and immediately backed off. "Take it easy," his voice gentled.

Her body trembled and her breath tore in and out

as she glanced at everyone staring at her from the driveway. Humiliation stained her cheeks as tears began to fall. "I said later," she repeated on a shaky whisper, trying to find her composure.

"Okay." He studied her with measuring eyes. "I'm sorry I grabbed you. I shouldn't have."

She wasn't interested in his apologies as she met Shelby's smirking stare. Anger quickly replaced embarrassment as she looked at Jerrod again. "You might have a job to do, but I'm still trying to live my life. Somewhere along the way you forgot that."

"Abigail—"

She walked into the house and up the stairs, closing herself in her room, locking the door. She gripped the knob, her breath rushing out, and dropped her hand, then opened the door just as quickly. She laughed humorlessly as more tears fell, hating her weakness, but did it really matter if the lock was in place? A closed door symbolized choices and freedom she didn't have. She was a prisoner whether the door was opened or shut. Jerrod could walk in at anytime, just like Dimitri or Renzo or Victor had. She wasn't free anywhere she went—the stash house, the condo in LA, or the pretty farmhouse in Nebraska. There was no place she could go to escape the reality that her life was not her own.

The trial would come and go and hopefully her testimony would keep Renzo in jail, but what about Victor and Dimitri? They could stay under the radar for years. Was this *her* sentence? Would she live like this indefinitely?

Hopelessness consumed her as she walked to her sketch pad and grabbed her pencil like a lifeline. She sat at her table, frantically drawing her ideas for Mary's new dress, understanding for the first time that she might never have an opportunity at 'normal' again.

~~~~

Jerrod sat at the kitchen table with a full plate in front of him but didn't bother to pick up his fork. His stomach ached and his head throbbed. He didn't have an appetite for beef brisket and scalloped potatoes no matter how many times his mother eyed him across the table.

He pushed his meal away and rested his forehead in his hands, rubbing at his pounding temples. Abby was home and out of harm's way, but overall, today had sucked ass. From a security standpoint, everything turned out a-fucking-okay, but he couldn't ignore the fact that Abby had rushed to her room crying and his mother kept shaking her head in disapproval.

Sighing, he squeezed the back of his neck, regretting the way he'd handled the entire afternoon. Protocol had flown out the window when he heard the loud blast of music and Abby's laughter in the driveway. His relief had been huge when he'd rushed around the house and spotted her safe—so had his anger. He shouldn't have shouted; he definitely shouldn't have grabbed her arm when she told him to back off, but she shouldn't have left.

"You need to eat," Mom said quietly. "It will help with your headache."

"I'm not hungry."

Mom set down her fork, her mouth firm with displeasure. "I imagine not."

He barely suppressed a groan as he rubbed at his chin. He'd been waiting for her verbal ass kicking
~~~~

since she glared at him in the driveway. “Mom—”

“I’m disappointed, Jerrod. I didn’t raise my men to treat women the way you treated Abby today.”

“Mom—” he tried again.

“I know your father was hard. I know we don’t show much affection, but land sakes, Jerrod, what happened to my sweet son?”

He squirmed in his chair as he had when he’d been a boy. No one brought on a bought of guilt and shame they way his mother could. “I overreacted.”

“You had no right to come down on her the way you did.”

“I agree, but—”

“I don’t want excuses.” She pointed her finger as her voice grew even sterner. “I heard my son being a horse’s ass. I saw you grabbing that tiny little thing. You’re not too old for a firm hand to the butt, sir.”

He looked down at the table, trying not to smile despite the lecture. He was twenty-eight and outweighed his mother by a good hundred pounds, yet he had no doubt mom would make good on her threat. “No, ma’am.”

“So, what do you have to say for yourself?”

He met her gaze. “I acted like a jerk, and I’ll apologize to you and Abby for that, but this whole situation isn’t as simple as it seems.”

She crossed her arms. “I’ll take an explanation.”

He studied his mother’s strong, steady eyes, debating how much he should tell her. “Abby’s not Ethan’s office manager. She’s in hiding.”

Her eyes softened with concern as she folded her hands on the table. “What’s she hiding from?”

“I can’t give you all the details, but she’s in trouble.” He sat up further in his seat. “She was abducted a few months ago—went through hell.

Luckily a couple of my colleagues and the FBI were able to track her down. She's going to testify against her abductors."

"That poor, sweet thing." She cast a worried glance toward Abby's room. "Is she going to be okay?"

"I'm trying to keep her that way."

"I don't understand. I thought you weren't doing WITSEC anymore."

"I'm not. Abby refused to give up her identity. She has family she's close to. Ethan was aware of my background, so he assigned me to her protection."

"My word. That poor girl," she said again.

A vehicle rolled up in the driveway, honking twice. Mom frowned. "What on earth is Merl doing here? I don't have any deliveries coming until the end of the week."

Jerrod glanced toward the dark beyond the windows and stood as his mother did. "Are you sure that's Merl? It's a little late for the mail."

"As sure as I can be. Merl gets around to things in his own time. You know that."

The doorbell rang, and moments later, the vehicle drove away.

"Why don't I get it?" After today he wasn't taking any chances. He walked to the door, peeking out the side of the glass, noticing the large yellow envelope addressed to Jerrod. Not Jerrod Quinn, just Jerrod and the Los Angeles address in the left-hand corner. Ethan must have sent him something. He opened the door and grabbed the mysterious package, pressing his fingers around the outline of what felt like a book.

Frowning, he carefully opened the parcel, unsure of what to expect, and pulled a magazine free, staring at Abby grinning on the March cover of *Trendy*. She was so damn beautiful with her perfect smile and big blue eyes. Her dress fit like a glove, showcasing her flawless body. Curious, he turned through the pages, finding several shots of Abby in different outfits—the red dress, jeans and a fancy black top, a business-like skirt and blouse. Zenn was right; the camera loved her.

Flipping some more, he stopped on the picture of him and Abby on the swing. Barefoot, sleeves rolled, chest exposed, he grinned with his arm around her as she leaned back, laughing. He studied the happy couple enjoying a sunny spring day and continued his search until he found the two-page spread of him and Abby in bed. On the left page, she sat on top of him in her underwear, their fingers clasped while she smiled down at him. On the right, she lay mostly naked, his arm covering the majority of her breasts, his fingers in her hair, while they stared in each other's eyes, their connection and chemistry unmistakable.

His gaze trailed over her gorgeous body as he flashed back to their make-out session in the kitchen. He'd molded that soft warm skin beneath his palms. Throaty purrs had escaped that long, graceful neck as her pretty mouth answered his demands.

"What are you looking at?" Mom stepped up to his side.

He closed the magazine with a snap, clearing his throat as he turned and started back to the kitchen, trying to get his hormones under control. "Ethan sent along an advance copy of the magazine Abby's featured in."

"A model?"

"Actually she's a fashion designer, but she's spent plenty of time in front of the camera—or used to anyway." He leaned against the counter.

"Let me see." Mom pulled the thick copy closer,

smiling. "She's such a beautiful girl."

"Mmm." He stared at Abby in the barely there red dress.

"Do you mind if I take a look-see?"

"No." He handed over the proof copy.

The glossy pages slipped through mom's hands, landing open on the picture of him and Abigail lying among the sheets. She gasped, looking from him to the magazine and back. "Jerrod, what on earth? Since when are you a model?"

He rubbed at his chin, not loving the fact that his mother was staring at him and Abby in bed. It was too damn weird, especially after she'd just interrupted his thoughts. "I'm not."

She reached down, grabbing the magazine. "Looks like it to me."

"I was helping Abby out. The guy she was supposed to work with never showed up for the shoot, so I gave her a hand." He avoided eye contact, crossing his arms as he felt his mother staring at him.

"Jerrod, look at these pictures. Look at the two of you." She whistled through her teeth. "I'd wondered..."

He scratched his head, shifting uncomfortably. "It's nothing."

She glanced at him. "It's certainly something."

"It's not."

"I think you should take a closer look, son. Come talk to me." She walked to the table and sat.

He took the seat next to her, hating the thought of dissecting his feelings for Abby with his mother. He could deny whatever he wanted, but somehow she always knew the truth.

"Jerrod." She took his hand.

"Yeah." He steamed out a breath.

"You know I love you. I loved your father too. You

two were as opposite as can be, but honey, on this one point, you're exactly the same." She pointed to the picture of him and Abby.

He frowned, loathing being compared to dad in any way. "What's that supposed to mean?"

"It means you need to speak up. Women like to hear the words from time to time."

Dear god, this was as bad as he was afraid it was going to be. "I'm not in love with Abby."

She shrugged. "Maybe you are and maybe you aren't. It would be a shame to let such a sweet, beautiful person slip right through these fingers of yours because you're afraid."

He sunk in his chair. "I'm not afraid. I just can't. I have an obligation to keep her safe." He huffed out a breath. "We kissed a couple times." He shook his head, hardly believing he was having this conversation. "Everything's fucked up." He winced when she glared. "Sorry. Screwed up."

She nodded, letting his slip of the tongue slide. "And what about after she's safe?"

"It'll be awhile before Abby can get back to a normal life. Especially after that hits the shelves." He gestured toward the magazine. Once *Trendy*'s March issue hit the newsstands, Dimitri and Victor would have a good idea of where they could find her.

She squeezed his fingers. "Just think of all the time you'll have lost. And she's been right here the whole time."

He grunted as his mother's comment hit home. "I don't know. Sometimes I think she and Timmy—"

Mom shook her head. "Timmy's not for Abby, honey." She pushed her chair back and stood. "We have the barn dance coming up. Abby has her heart set on going. Bless that sweet little thing. Maybe you could bring her as your date."

Somehow the idea was tempting. "I think it's better to leave things alone."

She pressed her lips firm. "I guess that'll have to be up to you. I'm going to take this fancy magazine to my room, get in my pajamas, and give it a read. I'll hand it over to Abby in the morning. Hopefully you two can straighten today out a bit. And try to get her to eat something."

"I'll bring her something, but she doesn't have much of an appetite when she's upset."

She *tsked* her disapproval. "She's going to waste away as it is. She's so tiny."

He smiled. Abby had a small frame, but she wasn't a skeleton by any means. "She'll be all right."

She gave him a kiss on the cheek. "Night, son."

"Good night." He slung an arm around her waist, hugging her tight. "I love you."

"I love you too." She walked away, and he sighed, picking up his fork, sampling a bite of cold, cheesy potatoes. He forked up more as his cell phone rang. He glanced down, looking at the readout. Ethan. Ethan wasn't supposed to call unless there was a serious problem. Grabbing his phone, he pressed 'talk' and pushed back from the table, starting up the stairs. "Yeah?"

"Hey, I have some news."

His shoulders tensed as he quickened his pace, ready to grab Abby's hand and be gone.

"They found Margret Stowers."

He paused mid-step and veered toward his room instead of Abby's. "Where?"

"She's dead, man."

His heart sank as he closed the door behind him. "Are you sure?"

"Yeah. News has been traveling through the precincts out east. Jackson got a call from his friend, Doug, on the Pittsburgh PD. Margret's parents were notified this afternoon."

Jerrod sat on the edge of the bed, closing his eyes. "Damn." This was going to rip Abby apart. She'd been searching for the pretty blue-eyed girl since the night of her rescue.

"A homeless man found her in Houston Monday morning. It took the ME's a few days to identify her. She was in rough shape. They beat the fuck out of her—massive head and facial trauma. They raped her and left her naked and stuffed in a dumpster."

"Fucking bastards." Anger burned in his gut as he ached for the girl as much as the woman in the next room. Abby spoke of Margret often enough that somewhere along the way he'd lost the ability to distance himself from her case. Months ago, he'd stopped thinking of the fifteen year old as just another missing person waiting to be found. "She loves that kid."

"I'm sorry, man. This is tough."

"Yeah." He rubbed at his temple. "I'll talk to her. I don't know what the hell I'm going to say." No matter how he told her, he was going to break her heart.

"Shitty situation."

"Doesn't get much worse." He stood. "I should probably go."

"Good luck, man."

"Thanks." He hung up and tapped his phone against his chin as he expelled a deep breath, trying to figure out how to handle this. Telling Abby would've been hard if they were on good terms, but now? She had lived with the mantra that finding Margret was only a matter of time. She'd fully expected to bring

Margret home, safe and alive. How many times had she spoken of blue dresses, shopping trips, and the fashion shows she'd promised her young friend?

He ran his hand through his hair, shaking his head. "Damn it." Margret was finally going home, but not the way she should have. "Damn it," he said again, drowning in helplessness. What was this going to do to Abby? How was this going to set her back?

He walked to his door, stopping when a vehicle pulled up to the house. He moved to the window, glancing out as Timmy got out of his pickup. He turned and made his way across the hall, raising his hand to Abby's mostly closed door, and dropped it.

How the hell should he start the conversation? With an apology? He clenched his jaw, remembering his harsh words. If he could go back...he would probably handle the situation exactly the same way, minus the grab as he chased her up the front steps. Abby had been reckless, putting not only herself but his mother in danger.

You might have a job to do, but I'm still trying to live my life. Somewhere along the way you forgot that.

He hadn't forgotten. He'd done everything in his power to keep her security as low-key as possible, but the fact of the matter was she needed twenty-four-hour protection. *I'm suffocating*. Her eyes had pleaded with him for understanding. And he did, but keeping her alive came before everything else—even her happiness. He hated that for her. Abby deserved all the happiness in the world, but he was about to knock her back another step.

He raised his hand once more. It was time to get this over with, despite how his stomach sank. He knocked, hoping she would invite him in without having to invade her space. "Abby. We need to talk for a minute."

The staticky music grew louder.

"Abigail, please."

No answer.

"Abigail, I got a call from—" Screw this. He wasn't going to stand here and yell over her music. "I'm coming in." He opened the door and stepped in, stopping as he stared at the mess of denim and pale blue plaid scattered around the floor. "Wow, this is some project," he tried.

She didn't acknowledge him as she sat in the office chair, cutting along the seam of a very large pair of jeans, her foot tapping along with the beat of the catchy song. She'd taken off her sweater and twisted her hair into a loose bun, leaving her long graceful neck and smooth shoulders exposed in her black spaghetti strap top.

"We need to talk, Abigail."

"So talk." She set the long strip of the once-pant leg on the floor and got back to work, starting on the other leg.

"Can you set that down for a couple of minutes?"

"Nope." She continued with her task.

He rocked back on his heels, unsure of how to deal with this side of Abby. This was the second time he'd seen it, and the first time hadn't gone well. He blew out a deep breath and walked to the radio, switching it off.

She reached up and turned it back on.

He flipped it off.

She moved to turn it on, and he grabbed her hand. "Come on."

"I'm sorry, I thought this was my room." She tossed him a nasty look.

"It is."

"My door was closed—or mostly."

"Yeah, I know. We need to talk," he said for the third time.

"If you're expecting an apology, I can't give you one." She lifted her chin. "I had fun today. Your mother and I..." Her lip wobbled and she looked down. "I needed to go," she mumbled.

"Abby—" He crouched down in front of her. "You have to *talk* to me if you're feeling like you're suffocating." He took a chance and touched her knee. "We could've figured something out."

Her miserable eyes met his. "You would've let me go to town on my own?"

"No, but—"

"Then what's there to work out?" She huffed out a breath and stared at the floor.

"Today could've ended so differently. You know that as well as I do. You didn't have your watch. There was no way for me to find you."

"I was fine."

"*This* time. Thank god everything worked out." He touched her chin, wanting her to look at him. "We're a team. This doesn't work if we can't communicate."

She pulled away from his grip and stood, walking to the window. "I don't feel like a team. I feel like I arrived with my pal from Los Angeles, but somewhere along the way he vanished." She turned, facing him. "Where did he go, Jerrod?"

He got to his feet. "I'm right here."

She shook her head. "No, you're not. Everything's different. I don't know how to be around you anymore. I don't know how to pretend that our relationship is simple the way you can."

She wasn't telling him anything he wasn't struggling with himself. He jammed his hands in his pockets. "It isn't simple for me either. So how do we fix this?"

"I don't *know*." She sat on her bed, her face in her hands. "I don't know if we can," she said wearily.

He walked to her, standing over her, staring down at her slim, slumped shoulders. How could he tell her about Margret now? It was tempting to wait until tomorrow. One day wasn't going to change the facts. She looked up at him, lost, and he knew he couldn't keep the truth from her, even for a few hours. "Abigail." He crouched in front of her again, taking her hands. "Abigail, I have to tell you something."

She swallowed. "What?"

"Ethan called."

Her fingers tightened against his. "Alexa?" she whispered as the pulse pounded in her throat.

"Alexa's fine."

"Olivia?"

He shook his head. "Your family's fine. It's—it's Margret." Damn he didn't want to do this.

"They found her?" She stared at him with such cautious optimism, he almost looked away.

"Abigail, she's dead."

Her hands went limp in his. "No," she whispered as her eyes filled.

"They found her in Houston."

She shook her head. "No."

He gripped her fingers, willing her to take the strength he offered. "I'm so sorry, Abby."

Tears fell down her cheeks. "When?"

"A couple days ago."

"What did they do to her?"

He held her gaze, running his thumb along her knuckles, not wanting to say. "Abby—"

"I need to know." Her voice broke. "I need to

know what they did to my poor, sweet Margret."

"Abigail." He pressed her palm to his cheek, wishing he could vanish her pain.

"Please."

He sighed. "They beat her."

A moan escaped her throat as she closed her eyes and more tears fell.

"Abby." He moved to the bed, sitting next to her, wrapping his arm around her.

"I promised her I would save her. I promised." She sucked in several shaky breaths and rushed to her feet. "It's too hot. I have to—I have to get out of here." She hurried into the hall and down the stairs. The back door opened and closed.

Sighing, he stood, grabbed her jacket, and followed her down the stairs. They were at odds, but he wasn't going to let her deal with this on her own. He moved to the back door, stopping with his hand on the knob, tightening his grip as Timmy leaned against the fence, holding Abby close, his Parker PD jacket draped around her shoulders while she wrapped her arms around him. Her powerful sobs muffled through the glass as Timmy pressed Abby's face to his chest.

Jerrod dropped his hand and turned away, going back upstairs as he struggled to absorb the crushing blow. Mom said Abby wasn't for Timmy, but maybe she was wrong.

~~~~

Shelby sat curled up on her couch, her laptop resting on the plush arm of the sofa as she entered the monthly 'crime' report she and Timmy had been discussing before their lunch was so interestingly
~~~~

interrupted. She rolled her eyes as she typed the details of Mr. Hannigan's second drunk and disorderly and the Bohaken boys' brush with the law regarding a bat and Ms. Tilly's mailbox. Life in Parker was intense.

Pausing, she lifted her glass, savoring the pinot noir on her tongue, then stopped typing all together, settling back against cozy cushions, remembering the one-sided phone conversation she overheard Timmy having with his brother and the frantic way Jerrod had searched for his lady love...or client.

She'd had plenty of time to revaluate the whole Jerrod/Abigail situation. Maybe he *didn't* have feelings for her. But there was certainly something going on. Timmy had mentioned a BOLO, and Mr. Cool had been ruffled in a way she'd never seen before—not even when he walked into his own home to see the love of his life in another man's arms.

Shelby narrowed her eyes as she pursed her lips. What were they hiding? It had to be something big. Jerrod never yelled, and he'd shouted at his city princess plenty. Poor, defenseless Abby had been terrified. *Don't touch me!*

At first she thought Abby's quivering lips and waterworks had been an attempt to get out of the hot seat—she used the trick herself all the time—but the trembling and wild-eyed fear appeared to be genuine. And Jerrod sure as hell backed down quickly enough.

So what was up? Why was Abby so afraid? Shelby's instincts had hummed every time she was around the beauty queen. She'd smelled a story all along—once she was wise enough to put her insecurities aside and concentrate on a potential upswing in her career. But she needed Abigail's last name. Jerrod had been very guarded with it, and so had Timmy. Baby brother almost slipped at one point, but he caught himself, glancing her way, then at Jerrod, shutting his mouth as she followed them back from the barn.

Jerrod was going to get her out of this town after all. Eventually he would figure out that she was the best damn thing that ever happened to him and come running to wherever she decided to settle. She could wait him out for a little longer. While she waited she might as well add another plaque to her wall at the office, but in order to do that she needed to figure out who the mysterious Abigail really was. Everything would come together after that. She was going to have to find a way back into Jerrod's good graces and invite herself over for dinner. Clues to her big break were somewhere at the Quinn Family Farm.

CHAPTER SIXTEEN

ABBY HELD THE PISTOL IN BOTH HANDS AND TOOK AIM, firing at the cans Tim set up for today's lesson. The first piece of aluminum flew off the old tree stump, then the next one as she caught the side of it and smiled.

"Getting better," Tim encouraged, his voice slightly muffled through her ear protection. "Go ahead and try for the next three—rapid shot."

She nodded, licking her lips in the cold air and closed one eye, aiming again, pressing the trigger, once, twice, three times. Two of the three cans flew to the ground with a satisfying ping and thud.

"Nice," Tim held up his hand for a high five.

"Not bad for my third day." Smiling, her palm met his with a solid smack, pleased that her persistence was getting her somewhere. Thursday she shot numerous rounds and hit absolutely nothing without Tim's help. Yesterday wasn't much better, but today she was finally showing improvement.

"Not bad at all. I'll set them up once more, then I should head back to town." Tim walked to the old tree trunk, wearing blue jeans and his Parker Police jacket, his radio as always on his hip.

"Okay." Abby set the pistol on the makeshift table they'd created out of logs and a two-by-four and cupped her hands around her mouth, blowing warm air on her chilly fingers, thankful he'd been able to give her any time at all. Their practice sessions were a welcome distraction, filling her quiet afternoons. Tim had come out to help her everyday since Jerrod told her about Margret.

The wind blew a frigid gust, and she hunched, pausing as she pulled off her ear protection, certain she heard Margret's sobbing on the breeze. "Margret," she whispered, pressing a hand to her chest as she thought of her sweet, beautiful friend. Her heart literally ached with sorrow; her stomach roiled with the anger of injustice. Margret died unspeakably at the hands of their worst nightmare—surely Dimitri or Victor was responsible.

She bit her bottom lip, blinking rapidly as another wave of guilt devastated her. She didn't save Margret. She didn't protect her from the monsters who thrived on greed and misery. *I want to go home, Abby. I just want to go home.* She sucked in several deep breaths, fighting back another bought of tears, haunted by Margret's small, scared voice. How would she ever forgive herself for failing so miserably?

She wanted to be in Baltimore to lend support to the Stowers family as they prepared to lay their daughter to rest. She desperately needed to say goodbye to the young girl gone too soon, but she was stuck here, hiding on a farm, waiting for her day in court to bring down Lorenzo Cruz and the Mid-Atlantic Sex Ring. And she would take them down—for Margret, for herself, and the countless other lives they'd destroyed with their cruelty and lust for money.

Clenching her fist, willing her grief away, Abby picked up the gun, ready to continue with her practice, finding empowerment with each shot she mastered.

She was sick of feeling helpless, of depending on others to see to her safety. She understood the need for Jerrod's protection, but she also needed to know she could take care of herself. She was no longer a captive in the stash house, but Dimitri, Victor, and Renzo still owned a piece of her. She was taking it back. Before her abduction, she'd never questioned her abilities to stand on her own.

"Okay." Tim moved back to her side. "You're good to—"

"Ten-seventeen-A in progress," his radio belched. "Sixteen thirty-two Old Hamilton Road."

He sighed, shaking his head. "Abby, I have to go."

She lowered the weapon. "All right."

"We can pick this up tomorrow."

Footsteps crunched on the frozen dirt behind them. They both turned.

"Or you can finish up with Jerrod." He smiled as Jerrod came their way in his winter coat and hat, his black knit cap accentuating his blue eyes and the dark stubble along his jaw. "Hey, big brother."

"Hey." Steam puffed from his mouth with his greeting. He stopped next to Abby and Tim, slipping his hands in his pockets.

"I'm heading out. Sounds like something's heating up over at the Rutherfords'."

Jerrod's brow rose. "Shocking."

Tim smiled. "It keeps things consistent. Abby's finishing up her round if you want to give her a hand."

"Oh, that's all right." She didn't want Jerrod's help. He made her too damn nervous. They'd barely spoken since Wednesday night, except for when he cornered her in the barn yesterday and this morning to ask her if she was okay. "I can wait until tomorrow."

"Or you can give it a go and show Jerrod what you've got." Tim's radio squawked again. "I've gotta split. See you guys tonight."

"Bye. Thanks," she called as Tim jogged to the cruiser.

He stopped with his hand on the door, gesturing toward the cans with his head then got in and took off with a quick u-turn in the pasture. The air was uncomfortably silent as the police car whipped down the lane, lights blazing.

Abby shoved her free hand in her jacket, looking from the cans to Jerrod, trying to think of a way to end the awkward moment. "I can clean up if you'd rather go back inside. It's pretty cold..."

"Nah. Go ahead and practice." Jerrod crossed his arms at his chest, clearing his throat.

She shrugged, studying the sinful effect a day's growth of beard had on an already gorgeous face, trying to ignore the frenzy of nerves invading her stomach. How was she supposed to concentrate on her accuracy when he was standing here looking like that? "Okay." Licking her lips, she put her hearing protection back in place, took the stance Tim showed her and fired, missing her target each time she tried. She huffed in frustration, sliding him a glance, her cheeks heating despite the frigid air.

"You're a little stiff."

"I know. I'm..." She almost confessed to her jitters. "I did fine when Tim was here."

"Yeah, well now I'm here," he muttered as he stepped up behind her.

She locked her shoulders tighter as their bodies brushed, and he settled his hands on her waist.

"Relax, Abigail."

She breathed in his familiar pine scent and swallowed. "I'm trying."

"Stand up a little straighter." He adjusted her hips, correcting her form. "Put your left foot out a bit more in front of you."

She did as he instructed.

"Bend your arm here and position your hands a little more like this." He cupped warm hands over hers on the weapon. "Good." He stepped back. "Now aim and give it a go."

She pressed the trigger, hitting each can dead center. "I did it." Grinning, she looked at him.

He gave her a small smile. "Good job. I'll line them up again."

She nodded, glancing at his ass in dark wash denim as he walked ahead and set the cans right. He turned, starting back, and their eyes met, holding. She looked at the ground, hating that nothing was the way it used to be.

"Okay, go for it." He stood to her side.

She tried to stand as he showed her, fired, and missed.

"Close." He moved behind her, making slight corrections, his hands on her hips, then her arm. "Now try."

She fired and hit her targets. "How do you know?"

He shrugged. "I wouldn't be very good at my job if I didn't."

"Show me. I want to see you shoot."

"This is your lesson."

"I've been out here for a while. I'm getting cold." She handed over the pistol in the darkening skies and hurried to set up fresh cans. "Be a showoff for once," she said on her way back. "Tim definitely likes to." She moved well out of the way as he dropped the empty clip, shoved a full one home, and blew each can off the trunk, hitting the aluminum a second time before it fell to the ground. She stared in amazement. "Holy crap, Jerrod."

He shrugged again. "You don't make Marshal if you can't handle a gun."

She laughed incredulously. "You more than handled it."

They grinned at each other for the first time in too long, and for just a moment everything felt exactly right. Talking to Jerrod soothed her as nothing else could. Seeing him smile was even better. "Tim was going to show me a couple of basic defense moves after we finished with this," she said in a rush, taking a chance. Despite the rocky few days she wasn't ready for him to walk away.

"We can do that if you want."

Her shoulders relaxed as she nodded and pulled off her earpiece. "For a few minutes anyway." They picked up the cans, leaving them in the recycling receptacle and started toward the house. "I told Mary I would help her with her dress."

"I can't remember the last time I saw my mother in anything but blue jeans or her robe."

"Get ready to be amazed."

He smiled as they climbed the steps, and he opened the door for her.

Abby stepped in and moaned, treasuring the slap of warmth and scent of cinnamon and apples as Jerrod closed the door behind them. "It smells so *good* in here." She took off her jacket, hat, and boots.

Mary pulled a pie from the oven and hurried to the cooling rack. "Maybe I can actually get you to eat a healthy slab of this later."

She breathed deep again. "You can count on it."

"I'll hold you to it." Mary moved to the stove next, stirring the chili in a huge pot. "I'll serve you up a piece at the O'Neils' myself."

"I'll be ready. What can I do to help?"

"Nothing yet, honey, but I'll let you know when I need a hand."

"Call when you're ready." Jerrod secured the pistol in the lock box and set the metal above the cabinets. "We'll be in the exercise room." He looked at Abby. "Ready?"

"Yes."

They made their way down the hall to the small workout space equipped with weights, a bench, and an ancient treadmill. Jerrod opened the closet, pulling out a folded mat and set it on the floor. "So, I guess we'll focus on the stun and run, which is the goal." He peeled off his sweatshirt, exposing a dusty blue thermal top.

"Stun and run?"

"Surprise your attacker and get the hell out of there."

She nodded.

"You've got several key spots you can aim for and cause serious damage—the eyes, nose, ears, throat, the package, and the knees."

"Okay." She nodded again, taking everything in.

"The eyes are pretty easy—scratch, gouge, claw, whatever you can do. We won't demonstrate that one."

She smiled. "We probably shouldn't."

"Let's work on the nose. You'll want to use the heel of your palm and push up, right here." He put his hand above her top lip, showing her what he meant. "The more weight you put behind the action, the better." He stepped closer. "Go ahead and make the movement on me—slowly. I don't want anything broken before the dance."

"I'll try to control myself." She smiled again as she stood on her tiptoes mirroring the position he'd demonstrated.

He took her wrist, pushing up on her hand slightly, tickling her skin with the scruff of his unshaven face. "That's the motion you want but a hell of a lot harder. If you do this one right you should buy yourself enough time to get a good running start, or you could possibly disable your attacker all together."

"I think I've got it."

"Good. Now we'll try something different using your elbow. We're still focusing on the nose, but this is a tactic to use if someone grabs you from behind." He turned his back to her, bending at the knees, making their height a bit more even. "Grab me and I'll show you what I mean."

She wrapped her arms around his solid waist.

He pivoted slightly and brought his elbow up to her nose. "See that?" He glanced over his shoulder.

"Yes." She let go and he turned.

"Okay. I'll come after you now. Are you going to be okay with that?"

She didn't like anyone coming at her from behind, but she couldn't practice if she wasn't willing to try. "I think so."

"If it's too much, just say stop, and I'll let you go."

"All right." She turned and her palms grew sweaty as his powerful arms came around her, lifting her off her feet. *I've got you, Little Bitch.* She froze, her heart kicking into high gear as Dimitri's voice echoed in her head.

"Abby, bring your elbow up like I showed you."

She gripped Jerrod's forearms, wanting to break free, but she was powerless to move, paralyzed by her memories. *You want to run, then I teach you lessons in the closet. The door slammed and the bar scraped into place, trapping her in the dark.* Her breath rushed out, and she gasped for air.

Jerrod set her down, turning her to him, cupping her face in his hands. "Abigail, it's okay."

She clutched his wrists, struggling to keep her head from going light. "I almost got away. I snuck out of the basement and made it to the front door, but Dimitri caught me and shoved me in the closet."

"Okay." He stroked her cheek. "You're safe here with me."

She closed her eyes, swamped by utter defeat. "I hate this." She looked at him again, concentrating on his steady blue eyes staring into hers and the gentle, comfort of his thumb moving along her cheek. "I hate that I freeze when I'm supposed to fight."

"We'll work on it."

"Now."

He shook his head. "You've had enough for today."

She held his hands in place on her cheeks as he tried to pull away. "No. Right now. Grab me again."

"Abby."

"And again and again until I'm not afraid anymore."

He studied her. "Tomorrow."

It was her turn to shake her head. "Help me. *Please*." She pressed her hands on his, willing him to feel her urgency. "I don't want to be afraid anymore. I don't want to hear his voice mocking me every time someone comes up behind me. I don't want to think of that damn closet or how I could hardly breathe."

"Okay." He nodded. "But you tell me to stop if it gets to be too much."

"I will." But she was going to beat this tonight. She and Jerrod had their problems, but there was no one she trusted more to help her conquer her fears.

"Go ahead and turn. I'll tell you the first few times until you're more comfortable, then I'll just grab."

Nodding, she turned her back to him, slamming her eyes shut, preparing herself for the buckling fear.

"Here I come." He scooped her up gently.

She gasped, gripping his arms as *Little Bitch* echoed through her head like a nightmare.

"Give me some fight, Abigail," Jerrod said close to her ear.

"I—I can't."

He set her on her feet. "Let's do this tomorrow. We'll try again whenever you're ready."

Dimitri was winning. "No. Again."

"All right. Coming at you," he said before she could think and picked her up.

Her pulse pounded as she forced herself to keep her eyes open, but still she made no move to defend herself.

Jerrod dropped her to the mat.

She took several deep breaths and wiggled, shaking off the dredges of panic. "I think I'm ready. Try again, please."

"Go," he said as he moved in.

She sent her elbow back and gave aim to his nose.

"Whoa." He dodged her arm and set her down.

She whirled with a triumphant whoop, jumping into his arm. "I *did* it."

He held onto her, grinning. "You sure as hell did."

She eased her head back, still clinging. "Don't tell me this time."

He nodded and they moved apart.

She turned her back to him, waiting, bracing herself, and he came up, yanking her up with such force she fought to stifle her scream.

"Fight, Abigail. Forget the damn fear and *fight* me.

If someone's coming after you they aren't going to tell you first."

Her heart pounded as she trembled, but she used her terror to send her arm back in the motion he'd shown her.

"Awesome." He dropped her to her feet and clapped loudly twice. "Keep it coming."

His enthusiasm motivated her, bolstering her confidence. She blew out several deep breaths while seconds passed, anticipating his next move. "Are you going to—" Her breath whooshed out as he ripped her off the mat, and her elbow flew back, connecting with his face.

"Ow!" He dropped her. "Damn."

"Oh." She whipped around. "Oh, Jerrod. I'm so sorry."

He blinked, sending a tear coursing from his watering eyes as he pressed his hands to his face. "Bull's eye," he said, muffled and nasally.

"Let me see." She pulled on his wrist. "Let me see," she encouraged, examining his nose. "You're not bleeding."

"You've got that move down."

"She pressed tenderly at the bridge of his nose then hugged him. "I'm sorry. I didn't mean to hurt you."

He wrapped her in his arms, returning her embrace. "I'll make it."

She snuggled closer, pressing her head to his chest as his hand moved down her hair. She'd missed this simple comfort and the easy way they had with one another. She drew back enough to look at him, not ready to break their connection. "I'm sorry," she repeated. "And not just for hitting you."

Closing his eyes, he pressed his forehead to hers.

"We've both made a few mistakes."

She gripped her arms tighter around him. "Yeah," she whispered.

He cupped her face in his hands. "Are you okay, Abby?"

She knew he asked about Margret's death and she blinked back tears. "No."

He steamed out a breath. "I'm so damn sorry."

"I wanted to save her." A tear fell despite her best efforts. "I loved her so much." She sniffled.

"I know you did."

"I don't know how to forgive myself for letting her down."

"You tried." He gripped her closer. "You *tried*, Abigail."

"But it wasn't enough."

He shook his head. "No, it wasn't, but she knows, Abby. I can promise you she knows you never gave up."

Another tear fell as his words brought her a stirring of peace. "I hope so."

"Is there anything I can do?"

"This works pretty well."

He brought her against him again.

Tim had offered her kindness, but this was what she needed. "Thank you for helping me."

"You're welcome."

"Kids." Mary peeked in. "Oops, excuse me."

Abby pulled away. "It's okay. Do you need some help?"

"I do." Mary looked from Abby to Jerrod. "There are several dishes that need to be brought to the truck. And I have some flowers out in the greenhouse."

"Okay. Let's get things together, then I'll help you

with your dress and makeup."

Mary frowned. "No makeup."

"Just a little." She smiled at Jerrod, ready to put her sorrow away for a while and enjoy the people around her.

He winked.

Her smile widened as she grabbed his hand, following Mary down the hall, ready to brow beat the woman until she decided that a touch of makeup would be the perfect idea.

~~~~

Country music blasted through the O'Neils' barn as Chuck and the Nebraska Reds rolled into their next song. Portable heaters warmed the huge space while hundreds of fairy lights twinkled, twisting around the rafters. Orange and yellow mums from mom's greenhouse decorated tables loaded down with enough food to feed the hundred or so guests three times over. The banjo and fiddle, Stetson hats and bolo ties weren't exactly Jerrod's scene, but Abby was having fun.

She shuffled in her cowgirl boots, Tush Pushing along with the rest of the dancers in the center of the floor, turning with a sassy move of her hips in denim and plaid, smiling at Jerrod across the room. He gave her a subtle nod, pulling another long, cool sip of water from his bottle, certain she was trying to make him crazy in that outfit of hers.

Abby had managed to pull off country-girl sweet with a hint of city-girl sexy in her mid-thigh length skirt and plain white t-shirt she knotted at the waist and rolled at the sleeves. His gaze kept wandering from the two braids she'd twisted into her hair to the
~~~~

tiny tease of her stomach where denim and cotton separated, down her smooth, slim legs, but it was her gorgeous smiles she kept flashing his way that stoked the fires of this eye-crossing *want*.

He crossed his ankles as he leaned against a stack of hay bales, remembering the addicting flavor of her pretty, pouty mouth. He wanted another sample. He yearned to taste the rest of her...and what the *hell* was his problem? Clearing his throat, he drained the last of his drink, attempting to reign in his libido. He and Abby had finally cleared the air. She'd hugged him with abandon and confided in him the way she used to. He wasn't about to mess everything up again by thinking about things that couldn't happen. That's how the whole damn mess started in the first place.

Her laugh floated over the music as she and Timmy turned in unison, wiggling their butts. Jerrod smiled, shaking his head, relieved to hear that silky sound. He wished he was the one making her laugh, instead of Tim, but seeing her happy was more important. Abby had been through hell the last few days. She'd taken the news of Margret's death incredibly hard. Her sad, hollow eyes and quiet, late-night crying had ripped at him, and he'd been helpless to do more than stand back and watch while she suffered.

A night like this was just what she needed. Abby was in her element surrounded by music—whether it be country or her typical Top 40. She'd learned several new dances with Tim's instruction, catching on within minutes, having the time of her life. He wanted this for her—fun, laughter. No one deserved it more than Abby.

Mom's pretty blue dress caught his eye among the crowd. He could still hardly believe that was actually his mother. She was beautiful with the slight touch of makeup and her blond hair twisted into some fancy 'do. Abby had pulled off the impossible with stunning results. For the first time in his life he watched Mary Quinn glow as she moved about the dance floor, with Caleb Conroy at her side.

Crossing his arms, he studied her closely. Mom seemed different somehow—outside of cosmetics and the twist in her hair. He narrowed his eyes, trying to put his finger on what had changed. Then she grinned and a dozen years vanished from her face; the strain he'd never noticed around her mouth disappeared. In an instant she was young and carefree, like the pictures he remembered from her high school yearbooks. He blinked, realizing Mom looked happy in a way she hadn't...ever. He frowned, wondering if twenty-eight years of marriage to somber Donald Quinn put the usual serious look in her eyes. Mom and dad had rarely smiled when he was growing up; they'd laughed even less. They were always busy with the farm and dad's responsibilities to the town. *Women like to hear the words from time to time.* Did dad ever give Mom the words she'd wanted and needed or stop to hug his wife?

Looking at Abby, his frown deepened, as she and Timmy laughed, turning in a do-si-do, remembering his mother telling him that he and dad were alike when it came to showing emotion. He didn't want to be like his father in any way, especially when it came to his relationship with Abby. She was so kind and sweet; she deserved the touches and soft looks, the warm embraces, and not just behind closed doors.

He stood up straight, tossing his plastic bottle into the recycling bucket close by, and started toward the dance floor, then stopped just as quickly as the reality of Abby's situation overshadowed his desire to give Abby the dance she always asked for. The idea of throwing caution to the wind was tempting. As much as he hated dancing, he wanted her to wrap her arms around him and smile. But what about tomorrow? Hell, what about right now? The complications and risks were still the same whether they sashayed the night away at a barn dance in Nebraska or cohabitated in their Los Angeles condo. Dimitri and Victor were still waiting to end her, no matter where they were.

The song ended, and the band announced a ten-minute break as he made his way back to the hay bales. Canned country music filtered through speakers while thirsty dancers made their way to the refreshment tables.

Abby said something to Timmy and smiled, walking toward Jerrod, her cheeks rosy in the warm space. "I'm having so much *fun*."

"Looks like."

"You should join us."

He shook his head. "I'm more of an observer." He noted the flicker of disappointment, regretting that things couldn't be different. "I like watching you. I haven't seen you laugh for awhile."

Her smile dimmed. "Things haven't been very funny."

He nodded, not wanting to see the light vanish from her eyes. "How about a drink?"

"I could use one."

He scanned the choices among the tables. "Water, punch, iced tea, or it looks like coffee? I think there's beer too."

"Uh, water."

"I'll get it."

"I'll come with you."

"Okay." He offered his arm, giving her what little he could.

She smiled, slipping her arm through his, linking them as they made their way to the beverage station. "Do you see that?"

He glanced around. "What?"

She cupped her mouth, whispering something while people talked and laughed around them.

"Huh?"

"I don't want to speak too loudly." She stopped and tugged on his shoulder, bringing his ear to her height. "Your mother and Caleb."

He looked up, spotting Caleb handing his mother a cup of red punch as they smiled.

Abby bit her lip, smiling at him. "I knew this was a good idea. They're having a great time." Her smile dimmed. "You're frowning." She rubbed her finger between his brows. "No frowning. This is good. She's happy."

He liked seeing that carefree smile on his mother's face. "Yeah, of course."

Concern furrowed Abby's brows. "Are you weirded out?"

He pressed his finger between her eyebrows, rubbing at the worry line as she'd done to him. "Nope."

They grinned at each other.

She moved her face closer to his, examining his nose, touching the tender bridge. "How's it feeling?"

Their gazes locked. "Fine."

She moved her fingers to his jaw, stroking his chin. "You shaved off your scruff."

"Yeah." He grabbed her wrist, stopping her torturous movements, glancing at her mouth.

She licked her lips. "I like the scruff."

"I'll keep that in mind." He cleared his throat and stood up straight with a small smile. How the hell were they going to pretend everything was normal when the air snapped and hummed between them after a casual touch and basic conversation? "How about that water?"

"Yes, please."

He didn't offer his arm as they moved forward. They both needed to keep their hands to themselves for sanity's sake. "Excuse me," he said, skirting around Ms. Hazlerick, and reached into the bowl of ice. His hand landed on a bottled water just as Shelby grabbed the same one from the opposite side. *Great*. He and Abby were still fumbling a bit; the last thing he needed was Shelby messing things up.

"Sorry," she said with a flirtatious smile, swiping curled red locks behind her ear. Her tight jeans and low-cut, button-down plaid left little to the imagination.

"No problem." He moved his hand. "Go ahead and take it." He snagged another bottle and handed it to Abby.

"Thanks," Abby said with the slightest hint of tension. Her gaze left his as she searched the room. "I see Tim over by the table. I'm going to head over."

He took her hand before she could walk away. "I'll come with you." Tim got Abby on the dance floor. He sure as hell was going to take this time with her now.

"Jerrod, wait," Shelby called.

"I'll have to catch you later," he tossed over his shoulder, pulling Abby to his side as they wandered through the crowd.

Abby looked at him with surprise. "That was pretty rude."

He shrugged. "I don't always feel polite."

The band started up again, playing something slow as he and Abby met up with Timmy at the table. Abby pulled a huge drink from her water and set the bottle down.

Timmy stood. "Should we do it up?"

She looked at Jerrod. "I don't know. Do you want to dance?"

There was nothing he wanted more, but not in the barn surrounded by dozens of people. He wanted to take her home and circle her round until they lay in his bed, which was exactly why he needed to keep his distance. "I'll leave the twinkle toes to you two rock stars." He took the seat Timmy vacated.

"I guess it's you and me," she said to Timmy with a shrug. She and Tim took to the floor, moving to a country classic Jerrod had heard a time or two, whether he wanted to or not.

Shelby strolled over, pulling out the chair next to him, plunking herself down. "I was trying to talk to you."

He played with the bottle Abby left behind, suppressing a weary sigh. "I was busy." Shelby hadn't been out to the farm since Abby's disappearing act. He'd enjoyed the reprieve.

"You blew me off."

"I was talking to Abby."

"Jerrod." She took his hand. "I want us to be friends. The way you and Abigail are." Her eyes sharpened on his.

He pulled his hand away, trying to calculate her new game. "I don't know if you and I can ever be friends, Shelby."

Her eyes filled as she blinked rapidly. "Why do you like to hurt me?"

Here they were again. "We have a history, and

most of it's rocky. Most of the time I don't think you even really like me."

She grabbed his arm, clinging. "I *love* you."

He shook his head, ready to be finished with this. "You're used to me."

Her lip quivered. "How can you say that?"

"Because it's true." He looked Abby's way, catching her eye, giving her a small smile, hoping like hell she wasn't getting the wrong idea.

"Why does she get the best part of you?"

"No one get's the best part of me." His hand froze on the water bottle as the words left his mouth, stunned by his own truth.

Shelby scoffed. "Just the job, right? Whether it be Marshal or cop or bodyguard. No one gets to have all of you, except the badge or shield you're holding at the time."

He tuned Shelby out, staring at the white tablecloth, realizing that Mom was right. Dad had given himself to the farm and the town of Parker; his family had gotten what was left. For close to fifteen years Jerrod had worked his ass off to prove to his father and himself that he was different—maybe even better than the man who'd ridiculed him from his teen years on, only to realize he was exactly the same.

Rushing to his feet, he started toward Abby, ready to take what he wanted, what she wanted. One dance didn't have to alter the universe. The song would end. He would go back to the table, and she would continue on with Tim, but nothing else had to change, except they would both be happier. He would still be Abby's bodyguard. She would still be his principal. They were at a barn dance in Parker, Nebraska for Christ's sake. What the hell could happen? The risks to Abby's safety wouldn't increase because he held her in his arms for one rendition of whatever the hell Chuck and his band decided to play next.

A camera flashed to his right, mere feet from Abby and Tim as they talked, holding each other close, oblivious. Ms. Hammlin, *Parker Gazette*'s photojournalist, moved closer, capturing another picture of the couple directly to Abby's side. Jerrod rushed forward, yanking Abby against him, shielding her face with his chest as he shoved the camera out of the way. "No pictures."

Ms. Hammlin, stumbled back a step as Abby stared up at him, wide-eyed. The dancers around them did the same, and the music stopped.

"No pictures," he repeated, as if the fifty-something was any other paparazzo he'd dealt with when he pulled duty in LA. He brought Abby closer against him.

"Jesus, Jerrod. Take it easy," Timmy moved forward, taking Ms. Hammlin's arm. "Are you okay?"

"Yes. Yes I'm fine, Timmy." She swiped a hand down her dress, giving Jerrod another shocked look, and turned away.

Timmy whirled as the music started again. "What—"

"What the hell are you doing?" Jerrod fired off in a low, dangerous tone, stepping closer to his brother. "She was taking pictures right next to you. Are you trying to help them find her?"

"I wasn't—"

"You weren't paying attention," Jerrod said as his anger grew. He was supposed to be able to count on Timmy for backup.

"You're right, I wasn't."

"That's all you have to say?" He gripped his arm tighter around Abby's waist, realizing she was trembling.

"That's enough, Jerrod." She pulled away. "Tim and I, we were careless."

It pissed him off further that Abby was going to bat for Timmy when they were both in the wrong. He was sick of being the asshole when he was just trying to do his job. "You can't afford mistakes."

"People are still looking over here," she whispered, her eyes hot with misery and embarrassment as they darted about. "I want to go."

"We don't have to—"

She scoffed and walked toward the side door.

He shook his head in disgust. "You better make damn sure she doesn't make the paper." He hurried after Abby, catching Shelby's curious, calculating stare, and picked up his pace when Abby rushed out into the dark without him. "Abigail, wait."

She moved faster as he caught up to her side.

"Abby."

She got in on the passenger's side of Mom's truck, slammed the door and buckled up, staring straight ahead.

He opened her door. "Abby—"

"I don't want to do this anymore, Jerrod," she said, her voice quiet and weary. "Please, let's just go."

He stared at her, watching her lip tremble as she turned her head, understanding they were right back where they'd been hours ago. "Damn it." He slammed her door closed, making her jump, and swore again. Why couldn't *one* evening go right? Just one. He turned away, took two steps in a half-assed pace, and walked around to his side, getting in with another slam of the door.

Gripping the wheel, he closed his eyes in frustration and inhaled deeply, trying to shake the clutches of defeat. He glanced Abby's way once more and started the truck, driving the five miles home in silence, wanting nothing more than to rewind the last fifteen minutes. If he had accepted Abby's invitation to dance in the first place, none of this would've happened.

He pulled into the drive, parking in mom's usual spot, and killed the engine as Abby got out. "Abby, wait."

"Not right now. Please." She climbed the front steps and opened the door with the key mom had given her.

He huffed out a breath, following after her, ran up the stairs, and stopped outside the half-closed bathroom door as the shower turned on.

Abby peeled off her shirt, and he turned away, going to his room to wait. He'd be damned if they were going back another step tonight.

He sat on the edge of the bed and stood just as quickly, restless and tense, taking off his jeans and t-shirt, pulling on his shorts, biding his time. They were going to fix this. She'd asked for space, but tonight he couldn't give it to her. If they didn't find their way through the constant rough patches of late, they were going to ruin a perfectly good thing. An idea came to mind and he started downstairs, switching on the teakettle. A cup of green tea and easy conversation had helped smooth the way last time; it didn't hurt to try the same tactic again.

Jerrod added bags to steaming water as Abby's feet padded down the hall and into her room. The floorboards creaked above his head, and finally there was silence. It was now or never. He climbed the stairs, stopping outside her door, and peeked in. She sat by the fire in her plush white robe, staring down at the floor, her hair wavy from the braids. She was so damn gorgeous—and alone. And she didn't have to be. He was right here, exactly where he wanted to be. With a deep, nervous breath, he pushed open the door, leading with the mugs, hoping a silly cup of tea would work as well as it had the first time.

Chapter Seventeen

Abby sat on the rug absorbing the heat of the fire as she leafed through the copy of *Trendy* Ethan sent a few days ago. She studied herself sitting in Jerrod's lap on the swing, laughing in his arms while he grinned—one of his grins that even now sent a rush of tingles through her belly.

Pressing a hand to her stomach, she blew out a long sigh, touching Jerrod's smiling face, missing the couple in the picture. *That* man and woman understood each other. They were happy and got along. Why couldn't she and Jerrod find their way back to that symbiotic place?

She sighed again, leaning back against the frame of the cozy loveseat. They'd been heading in the right direction tonight with easier conversation and relaxed smiles, but then he reverted back to bodyguard mode, yanking her against him while he shoved the camera away. And he'd had every right to. She closed her eyes, shaking her head, wishing for a redo. She'd been enjoying her dance with Tim and their foolish debate over country music versus her preferred Top 40 instead of paying attention to her surroundings. She should have been more careful. Tim too. Jerrod was only doing his job—a job she was quickly learning to hate.

She focused on the magazine again, perusing articles, stopping on the sensual spread of her and Jerrod lying in bed. She'd stared at their sexy poses more than a few times, remembering jokes about brownies and meals for life, entranced by their natural chemistry oozing from the pages. She looked to the opposite page, studying the way they stared in each other's eyes—the official turning point in an otherwise good thing. How many times had she wished the photo shoot away? How often did she regret laying among the sheets with Jerrod, stirring up emotions better left undiscovered? For the rest of her life she would know what she was missing. For the rest of her life she would *want*. Her door creaked open, and her gaze shot up, locking with Jerrod's as he stood in the shadows of the hall.

"Do you mind if I come in?"

Sitting up straight, she closed the magazine. "No."

He walked in, bare-chested and in shorts despite the cool temperatures of the house, carrying two steaming mugs. "I brought you some tea."

She wrapped her robe tighter, glancing at the tattoo on his mouthwatering bicep, taking the hot cup. "Thanks."

"You're welcome." He settled himself on the rug next to her, leaning against the small couch the way she did.

Unsure of what to do or say, she wrapped her hands around the warm crockery, sipping at the slightly sweetened tea. "It's good," she tried.

"Good." He gave her a small smile.

"Jerrod." She moved awkwardly, trying not to spill her drink as she turned, fully facing him. "Tonight was my fault—"

"Abby—"

She shook her head, needing to finish. "I wasn't thinking. Tim and I were talking. It didn't register that the lady was taking pictures until you came over, but it should have. My safety is as much my responsibility as yours." She touched his wrist. "I'm sorry for getting angry with you when I'm the only one to blame."

"I'm sorry I was so rough." He took her hand, giving her fingers a squeeze. "I know this isn't easy on you."

"No, it's not, but it's not easy on you either." She eased her hand from his and put her mug down, wrapping her arms around her knees. "I hate this—all of it. I don't like the way things are between you and me. I miss Margret desperately. I keep wishing her home safe with her family or out on some silly date with a fifteen-year-old boy. I'm worried about my sister. I want to be able to pick up the phone and give her a call." She sighed. "I want my life back."

"I wish I could give you all of those things."

She blinked as her eyes filled, knowing he meant it. "I keep yearning for normal—to go to the store on my own, to walk down the street and feel like I don't have to look over my shoulder, to look at a man and not automatically wonder if he has ulterior motives, but then I realize those things might never happen. I find myself mourning for the Abby I was in early May, before everything changed." She shook her head, disgusted with herself. "And how selfish is that? Margret's parents just want their daughter back—alive—and I'm sitting here thinking about foolish things that don't even matter. I'm getting my second chance." She dashed at her cheeks, catching her tears.

"I don't think it's wrong to wish you had never been abducted."

"But I was."

He nodded. "And you're dealing with it. Your strength amazes me, Abigail. You're still kind and sweet despite everything you've been through."

Another tear fell as she reached for his hand, touched by his words. "I'm just me."

"You're an amazing woman."

"Aw, you're making me sloppy, big guy." Hesitating, she got to her knees and gave him a hug. "Thank you."

He set his mug down and returned her embrace. "I mean it."

She eased back. "I'm glad you do. What you think means a lot." She sat down, pulling the magazine out from under her, suddenly feeling awkward and unsure. They used to talk like this all the time, but something about tonight was different. Jerrod rarely spoke freely with his feelings, as he did now.

"What do you have there?"

She looked down at her smiling face on *Trendy*'s cover. "Oh, the proof copy. I was looking at a couple of the articles." She licked her lips, averting her gaze in an attempt to conceal her fib.

He slid the magazine between them. "There's some pretty good stuff in here if you're looking for makeup tips and 'sex positions that will drive your man wild,'" he said, making air quotes.

She laughed as he grinned. "There's more in here than that."

"I know." He winked. "Connie Withers did a nice job with the *Escape* article." He started turning through the pages.

"She really did." She swiped a lock of hair away from her cheek, relaxed again in Jerrod's presence. "The new line will be off to a great start if I ever get a chance to talk to Lily. I've come up with some really great stuff; it just needs to be sewn."

"You'll have to show me."

She smiled, thrilled that everything felt right

between them again. "Okay."

"Zenn might be crazy, but he took some nice pictures."

She looked down at the page with them on the swing, and a smile ghosted her mouth. "Zenn's demanding, but he get's what he wants."

Jerrod flipped again. "You look great—beautiful in all the shots."

She stared at him as he kept flipping, trying to figure out what was going on. Typically Jerrod's mind was a mystery. He rarely told her how or what he thought. The only time he'd let her in was the night they helped Mama birth her bull. "Thanks. You look good too."

He stopped on another page. "That's a powerful picture right there."

She glanced at herself straddling him. "Mmm." She had no clue what else to do or say as the image of them in bed and him currently sitting next to her shirtless and delicious stirred her up. In defense, she moved to shut the magazine.

He stopped her, placing his hand over hers.

She tried to pull away as sparks hummed along her skin. "Jerrod."

He gripped her tighter. "Do we look at each other like that all the time?"

"I—I don't know," she said quietly, swallowing as they both stared at the sexy couple lying among the sheets.

"I wanted you right there."

Her gaze flew to his, caught off guard and utterly shocked. "Jerrod—"

"I've tried to stop, but I can't. For two weeks," he shook his head. "Hell, from the first second I saw you I've been telling myself I can't be with you, that I don't want to be, but I'm lying to myself. And you. Why? For what reason?"

Her heart pounded as she pulled her sweaty hand from his grip. After the confusion of the last few weeks she'd finally convinced herself she and Jerrod would never be together. "I don't—" She rushed to stand and turned away from his steady blue eyes as her insecurities came flooding back. "I thought you didn't want me."

"I wish to hell I didn't. Our situation would be easier all the way around." He stood, turning her to face him.

"Why are you telling me this?"

"Because I don't want to be like my father."

She frowned. "I don't understand."

"He didn't treasure my mother the way he should have. He never gave her what she needed." He walked to the portable radio, switching it on, fiddling with the knob until he found anything playing music instead of commercials. Tim McGraw's voice crooned through the speaker as Jerrod came back, holding out his hand. "Will you dance with me?"

She hesitated, still trying to adjust to this surprising twist in the evening. "You don't dance."

"I do tonight."

She stared into his eyes, now intense. "Jerrod, what are you doing?"

He shook his head. "I don't know, but I'm sick of trying to figure it out."

She slowly extended her hand, taking his.

He held her gaze as he pulled her to him and started moving to the music.

She wrapped her arms around his waist and rested her head on his chest, breathing in the soap on his warm skin, closing her eyes as he snuggled her closer.

They turned slowly, and she relaxed, enjoying the moment for what it was. Jerrod was finally giving her the dance she'd been asking for for months. Minutes passed and the song ended, rolling into the next quiet melody. She looked up, smiling as they continued circling round. "Thanks for the dance."

"You're welcome." He slid her hair away from her temple.

Her heart stuttered, and she stepped back, unable to bear the idea of ruining a special moment with another kiss he would regret. "I should probably say goodnight."

He moved forward, closing the space between them, cupping her face. "Tell me to go and I will."

She slid her palms up his arms, pressing her hands to his. "I don't want you to go, but I can't let you stay."

He clenched his jaw, nodding.

She stepped away. "I can't keep letting you take what you want until you remember you don't want it after all."

"Is this about the kitchen?"

"Yes, and Shelby, and the way the whole thing made me feel. For the first time in a long time you made me doubt myself. I did a lot of things last summer that I'm not proud of, but I can't be ashamed, even if you are." She turned away.

"Whoa." He turned her back. "Abby, what are you talking about? I'm not ashamed of you. I never could be." He pulled her to him, wrapping her up. "Never." He held her tighter. "I'm so sorry I ever gave you that impression."

"I just thought maybe—"

He drew her away. "You just thought I couldn't

handle what you've been through, what you did to survive."

"Yeah," her voice shook.

"Abby," he looked at her with such regret she had to swallow against the ball of choking emotion. "Damn, I've screwed this up."

She shook her head, realizing she'd been completely wrong. "No, I misunderstood."

"The only reason I stopped us that night was because I was afraid I wouldn't be able to focus on your safety. I still am. That's it, Abby." He kissed her forehead. "That's absolutely all."

She nodded.

"Abby—"

"Stay," she whispered, hoping to soothe, wanting him as he wanted her. "Stay," she said again, pressing his hand to her cheek.

"I'm so sorry."

"It's over now. Stay with me, Jerrod."

He held her gaze, capturing her lips slowly, tenderly, rubbing and nibbling, deepening the kiss by torturous degrees.

Flutters rushed through her stomach, and a small hum escaped her throat as his tongue sought hers, his flavor filling her senses. She clasped her fingers with his as he brought her impossibly deeper, drawing out the pleasure of the endless embrace.

She savored his unhurried pace and open her eyes as his lips moved along her cheeks and jaw, then down her throat, inciting a quiet moan. "Jerrod," she whispered, easing her heavy head back, inviting him to take what he chose.

He slid her robe aside, bathing her collarbone with his tongue, nipping at her shoulder as her hands wandered along his waist and up his back, bumping over contours of muscle, reveling in the feel of him.

“I want to look at you,” he whispered next to her ear, his voice rough. She nodded and he tugged at the tie, groaning as his gaze traveled up her naked body. “God, you’re beautiful,” he murmured as he sent bulky cotton to the floor, taking her under with another gentle kiss, trailing rough palms down her waist. She shivered as goose bumps followed in their wake.

“Are you okay?” He eased her back, brushing his fingers through her hair. “Is this okay?”

How could it not be? “It’s perfect.”

“If I do anything that makes you uncomfortable—”

“You won’t.” She didn’t want to think about anything but the way he made her feel.

“Abigail, if I do—”

“I’ll tell you.” She pulled his mouth back to hers and guided his hand to her breast, wanting him to go on touching her the way he had in the kitchen. He brought his other hand up, molding her, sliding teasing fingertips over her nipples.

She closed her eyes as a firestorm of heat flooded her core, and she whimpered, ready for more. His mouth replaced his hands, lapping, circling, suckling, her legs buckling with each delicious sensation, her nails digging into his strong shoulders as the liquid pull started between her thighs. “Jerrod,” she shuddered out as he continued to shower her sensitive skin with endless attention. “Jerrod,” she said again, clutching at his hips, sliding her hands into his shorts and over his muscled butt, tugging at the elastic waist.

“Wait.” He pulled back. “I need to get—we need—just hold on.” He hurried from the room, crashed into something down the hall, swearing, and came back limping slightly with a package in his hand.

She couldn't help but grin. "Are you okay?"

"Yeah." He smiled. "Tim's old room is like a damn obstacle course, but I knew he would have what we needed." He held up the box of condoms. "He stays out here sometimes during haying season." He shrugged and closed the door, locking it, studying her. "Is that going to bother you?"

She shook her head, trying to ignore the troubling idea of being locked in her room.

He narrowed his eyes. "What's wrong?"

"Nothing." She covered her breasts with her arm, suddenly self-conscious.

He walked to her. "Abby, we don't have to do this if you've changed your mind."

"No, I want to." She was ready and eager for this next step, but small drudges of fear were there below the surface. "I'm nervous," she admitted, looking down. "But I want to be with you. It's my first time since—"

"I know."

"I was raped, Jerrod. I know you know that, but some men aren't comfortable with the aftermath." She averted her gaze for the second time. "I won't think less of you if you aren't." Or she would try not to anyway.

He picked up her robe, settling it around her shoulders, and tipped her chin until their eyes met. "Tonight is between you and me. Whatever comes of it is ours. We don't have to have sex."

"I want to have sex. I *liked* sex, but what if I have a flashback?"

He shrugged. "Then we'll work through it."

She nibbled her lip, worrying, wishing they'd just kept going instead of stopping and giving her time to think. "I want this to be good. I want you to be satisfied."

"I wouldn't worry about that."

"But I am. What if I can't...get there, and you think it's because of you, but really it's because of me?"

"Maybe you won't get there this time." He kissed her forehead. "Maybe I won't either."

She raised her brow.

He smiled. "Abby, I just want to be with you whether we lay together or decide to be together."

A thousand weights lifted off her shoulders, and she hugged him. "Okay."

"Would you like to dance again?"

"No, I want you to take me to bed."

His brows winged up. "And she gets straight to the point."

She laughed as she took his hand, and they walked to the bed. "I want you. I've wanted this for awhile."

He pulled her against him, running his hands down her arms. "I've wanted you since Jackson introduced us at the hospital. Everything about you fascinates me, Abby." He kissed her.

She shook her head in amazement. "I never had any idea."

He kissed her again, longer this time, and she wrapped her arms around his neck, her breast rubbing against his chest. She pulled herself closer, savoring the feel of their bodies touching.

He tossed the robe to the floor, sliding his hands along her waist and over her butt. She copied his movements, pulling at his shorts, freeing him of his clothing, standing naked with him, staring. He was magnificent—hugely so. She'd always called him big guy, having no idea—or not exactly.

He brushed kisses along her neck, pausing. "What's wrong?"

"Nothing." She shook her head, worrying some. "It's just that I've never had— you're pretty—" She swallowed, mortified. "It's nothing."

He smiled. "We'll go slow. Come here," he whispered next to her ear, walking her backwards. "Lay down with me." They sat on the bed and lay back, their mouths colliding as they faced each other on their sides. "How's this?" He slid his fingers through her hair. "Are you doing okay?"

"Yes, I'm fine. I don't want you to be afraid to touch me."

"I'm not afraid to touch you." He sent his finger on a journey from the valley of her breasts, down her stomach, circling her bellybutton, making her quiver. "There's nothing wrong with taking our time."

"I know." She traced his tattoo as she'd wanted to for months.

"I want to take my time with you, Abby." He pressed feathered kisses to her shoulder.

She closed her eyes as her body vibrated, aching, eager for Jerrod to make her feel and forget the rest. "Not too much time."

"Slow, Abby." His breath heated her skin as his mouth skimmed her breasts and his teeth grazed her ribs.

She quivered, arching, playing her fingers through his hair. "Not too slow."

"As long as it takes." He moved his hand between her legs. "Open your eyes, Abigail."

She did, looking into his as he slid his fingers over hot, sensitive skin.

"Mmm," she whimpered as he explored, pressing and rubbing, sliding. "Mmm, that feels good."

"Good," he said, smiling, his breath growing ragged as he continued his torturous teasing.

"I'm—I want—" She yanked his mouth to hers, giving up on her useless words, wrapping her arms around him, growing frantic as sensations built, layering. Then he dipped inside her and her legs tensed, her hips moving with his rhythm as the familiar twinges grew to throbbing.

"God, Abby, you're so wet," he groaned, panting against her neck.

"I think I might—"A log snapped in the grate like the sound of a huge hard hand cracking against skin. Her eyes flew open, and she stiffened as Margret's cries echoed in her head.

Jerrod froze, his breath heaving. "What's wrong?"

"I don't know." She sat up, pulling away, the moment lost. "I thought I could do this. I want to. I heard the log pop—it sounded like a slap. It made me think of Renzo hitting Margret." She rested her head in her hands consumed by hopeless memories. "I don't want to think of her right now. I definitely don't want to think of him. I want to think of you and me."

He sat up. "So we'll back up a couple steps."

She looked at him. "I don't think I can. Dr. Tate said I would know when it was right. It's *right*. I want you. I do."

He caressed her arm. "Maybe tonight's not the night."

"Yes it is. I like what you're doing. I love the way you make me feel. I want you inside of me."

"We'll get there." He gave her wrist a gentle squeeze.

"Okay." She lay back and spread her legs. "Let's do it."

He stared at her, his eyes unreadable, as he pulled

her up to sitting. "Abby, I'm not going to mount you like a bull."

Tears bloomed in her eyes, suddenly afraid she would never be able to have a healthy, intimate relationship with a man like Jerrod. "Why does it have to be like this? Why does everything have to be so damn hard?"

"Because you've been through hell."

"I want this, Jerrod." She touched his cheek. "Right now. I want this part of me back. They don't get to have it anymore."

"So let's take it back." He brushed his knuckles along her cheek.

She nodded.

"This is ours, Abby, just ours."

She nodded again as he brought his mouth down on hers and eased her to the bed, settling himself between her legs. He kissed her endlessly, taking her hands, clasping them at the sides of her head until it was impossible to think of anything but this tender moment with him.

"Are you ready, Abigail?"

She stared into Jerrod's steady blue eyes, his body pressing hers into the mattress. She'd never wanted anything more. "Yes."

He freed his hands from hers and tore open the condom package, protecting them both, and slowly eased his way inside her, holding her gaze. "God, Abigail," he grit out as she gasped, clutching at his waist, taking him in.

"God," he said again, dropping his head, blowing several steaming breaths against her neck as he lay still. "You feel so good."

She flexed her fingers against him, gulping in air as sparks of sensation exploded through her system.

She wiggled her hips, sliding her hands up his hot, damp back and into his hair, ready to ride the wave, eager to fly. "I'm ready. I'm ready," she said as their eyes locked, and he began to move slowly, staring down at her.

Their mouths met for a long, tender kiss, heating as he brought her higher with each lazy thrust. She purred, gripping his hips, moaning as wave after wave of heat built, then cried out in triumph as she erupted, her orgasm scorching her from the inside out.

His fingers moved into her hair as he pumped faster, letting himself go, groaning loudly as he jerked, arrowing himself deeper. He rested his forehead against hers as they lay still, the sounds of their heavy breathing mixing with the crackling of the fire.

"I got there." She slid her fingers down his sweaty back, her limbs heavy after a thoroughly amazing bought of loving. "I definitely got there."

He lifted his head. "Looks like we both did."

She smiled at him. "Right now I feel perfectly, fabulously normal."

He kissed her. "You *are* perfectly, fabulously normal." He kissed her again, stroking her cheek. "And beautiful." His mouth met hers for the third time. "You're so damn beautiful."

"You make me feel beautiful." She pressed her hands to his cheeks and snagged his lip, wrapping her legs around his waist, sliding her calves over his butt, certain she had one aspect of her life completely under control. "I like this—you and me, like this."

"It's not half bad." He grinned.

She squeezed her thighs tighter around him, pushing him deeper inside. "So, when do you think we can do that again?"

He chuckled. "Now works for me."

She walked her fingers down his hips and clutched his ass. "I think I can handle that."

They laughed, and he took her blissfully under.

~~~~

Jerrod opened his eyes, snuggling closer to Abby's warm body and berry-scented hair, nuzzling his face against the soft skin of her neck. He smiled, noting the sun on its way above the horizon, and glanced at the clock. Abby had missed the morning milking—a first since their arrival.

They'd had several firsts over the last few hours, and he didn't regret a single one. Sleeping with his principal was probably a bad idea. There was no going back to the way things used to be, but as he lay pressed against the woman he'd wanted for the last six months, he didn't care. Being together didn't have to complicate their situation—it did, but he would just have to find a way around that. He and Abby would have to adjust to the new changes in their relationship. And that's what worried him. So far that hadn't worked very well for them.

Blowing out a breath, he slid a finger along her shoulder. How did two people who spent day and night together separate intimacy from the job he still had to do? There were going to be times when he would have to draw the line for safety's sake, and she would have to roll with it. That concerned him too. What would that do to the personal side of what they had? He'd never been in a situation like this before, but there were a lot of things he'd never dealt with until Abby walked into his life.

She stirred, making a sleepy sound in her throat as she moved back, pressing her sexy ass against him.
~~~~

He paused, his finger halfway down her arm, tempted to reach around and play with her breasts, but he was still unsure of how she'd react. She said she wanted 'normal' in the bedroom, but he didn't want to trigger unwanted memories by catching her off guard.

She looked over her shoulder, her eyes still sleepy, and smiled.

He smiled back. "Good morning."

"It *is* a good morning." She wiggled, teasing his already raging erection.

He brought her closer, kissing her neck, nibbling at her ear, finally caressing the points of her breasts as she moved against him in a sinuous rhythm.

"Mmm."

"Is this okay?" he whispered.

"Absolutely." She pressed his hands more firmly to her as each breath came faster.

"I want you," he said next to her ear. He had to have her. Throwing caution to the wind, he lifted her leg and slid inside her, sucking in a breath as he pushed himself deeper into her tight, hot, wetness.

She stiffened on a gasp, pulsing around him, crying out as he moved and heightened her climax. "Oh, god." She reached behind, wrapping her arms around the back of his neck as she rode the wave, then sagged, coming down. "More. I want more."

So did he. He pulled himself free, wrapped himself in a rubber and plunged in again, groaning as she did.

"Jerrod."

He rolled, taking her with him so her back lay against his stomach, and thrust up.

She grabbed for his hand, rubbing his fingers against her. "Touch me. God, touch me, Jerrod."

He took over, pressing, circling, sliding, bringing

her up as she called his name. She moved her hips with his hurried pace, her moans feral and raspy until her throaty purrs turned into one long moan and she stiffened, bowing back against his chest. "More, Jerrod," she cried out, and he thought he might go mad.

He adjusted their positions with a quick move, laying Abby under him, ramming himself inside her, groaning as her head tipped back and she called out, begging him to take her higher. Her lack of inhibitions urged him on, driving him crazy, encouraging him to pump harder as she wrapped herself around him, pushing him deeper.

They rolled again, and Abby had her way, taking him in as she rode frantically, reaching back, caressing him.

"Abigail," he panted, wanting her to stop as much as continue. Her fingers teasing his hot, sensitive skin were going to end it. He clutched at her hips, anchoring her, thrusting up as they called out together, exploding at the same time.

She collapsed against his heaving chest, gasping. "Oh...my...god." Lifting her head, she looked into his eyes, her cheeks flushed, her face damp with sweat. "That was—" She shook her head. "I don't even know."

He stroked his hands down her back, pleasantly empty, content to lie like this for as long as she was. "So you liked it?"

She grinned, sliding her finger over his pecs. "You're definitely memorable, big guy."

He chuckled. "Oh yeah?"

She nibbled his lip. "Mmhm. You, my friend, are a stallion."

His smile turned into a wince. "Jesus."

She laughed as her finger wandered up his neck

and over his cheek. "And I'm looking forward to enjoying the ride often." She wiggled her brows.

He grinned. "That makes two of us."

The back door shut downstairs, and Abby looked toward the closed bedroom door. "I didn't help with the milking."

He wrapped his arms around her, recognizing the guilt in her voice, understanding their night together was quickly coming to an end. "So we'll handle the milking tonight."

She sat up. "I still have to get the eggs."

This was one more item he could add to his list of why he didn't love farm life. "We'll get the eggs and muck the stalls." He pulled her back to his chest and rolled, loving the way she felt under him. "After I get a taste of that mouth." He dove deep, relishing Abby's sweet flavor, enjoying the way her tongue eagerly sought his as she played her fingers through her hair.

The kiss heated to flashpoint and she clung, her small, firm breast pressing to his chest, revving the flames of want again.

"What do you say we go one more time?" He pressed his lips to the hammering pulse in her neck. "Then we'll get those eggs," he murmured, nibbling her shoulder, then greedily sampled her beautiful breasts.

"We can't," she said, her eyes closing as she bit her lip. "Your mother's right downstairs." A cupboard closed and the squeaks of her steps on the boards highlighted Abby's concerns. "She might hear."

He wandered down her body, a stroke along her ribs, a nip below the bellybutton, exploring as he didn't last night, kissing her hips, running his hands over her thighs, savoring the sounds of her whimpers and sharp expels of breath. "You do have a point." He stuck his fingers inside her, and her eyes flew open as her legs trembled.

"Jerrod, what are you doing?"

"Taking what I've been wanting." He scooted himself down, pulling her closer, his fingers never stopping their rhythm. "I want to taste you, Abigail. All of you. I never got around to it last night."

She shivered, and her eyes grew hot as his tongue darted over smooth, wet skin, finding her as sweet as the rest her sexy body. He groaned, never enjoying the pleasuring of a woman more as their eyes locked and he moved in again. He suckled and teased; her brows furrowed and her mouth formed an 'o' with each staggered breath.

He kept his pace steady, both fingers and tongue, as her stomach jumped and shuddered, as she clawed at the sheets, moaning, growing wetter with every plunge and plunder.

"Jerrod." Her hips rocked. "Jerrod." She froze, tensing, throbbing, contracting wildly as she tipped her head back, calling out quietly as she came. "Jerrod," she said again, looking at him as her climax subsided. "I've never—you make me—I've never been like this."

He crawled up, lying between her legs, brushing his fingers through her hair. "Good." The caveman in him wanted to be the best she'd had.

"It's kind of hard to believe that this has been here the whole time." She pulled his mouth to hers. "It's so *good*. I feel so happy."

He smiled even as he worried, wondering how everything would be once they left the farm. Their vacation from reality was almost over. "That's what we want."

Her smiled dimmed. "I want to make you happy

too."

"You do." He stared into her eyes, settled for the first time...ever. The contentment he'd always searched for was right here, flushed and beautiful, looking up at him. He brushed his lips along her forehead. "You make me happy. Trust me."

She smiled again. "I've never trusted anyone more." Her gaze wandered to the door. "We should probably go get those eggs and see to the stalls."

"Yeah, I guess we should." But he didn't want to. He moved to his side, reluctantly untangling himself from her soft, warm body, and they both climbed from the bed. She grabbed her clothes, sliding them on as he pulled on his shorts and gathered their trash, reaching for the doorknob.

"I'm going to get rid of this."

She nodded.

He walked across the hall.

"Jerrod."

He stopped, turning.

She moved next to him, wrapping her arms around him, standing on her tiptoes. "The last couple minutes, that was amazing."

"I'm not complaining."

She pulled him closer, snagging his ear. "I'm a big fan of reciprocation," she whispered. "Think about that today." She slid her fingers down his stomach and traced him through his shorts, smiling mischievously as she moved past him, hurrying down the stairs. "Good morning, Mary. Sorry I'm late."

Jerrod stood where Abby left him, swallowing as he thought of her returning the favor, and stepped in the room. He smothered his urge to call her back as he caught sight of his cell phone lying in the center of his bed. "Damn it." Lunging forward, he picked it up, checking for missed calls. He was already making careless mistakes. He'd been so caught up in Abby he never gave his phone a second thought. What if Ethan had needed to issue an evacuation? And he never checked in with Adam. "Son of a bitch."

He continued to admonish himself as he searched for some place to throw his garbage, not wanting to advertise to his mother that he and Abby had burned up the sheets. He spotted a plastic grocery bag in his closet, dumped the old belts and socks into a bin, and shoved the trash in, tying it off, tucking it to the middle of the trashcan until he could take it out later.

Grabbing his jeans, he pulled them on, then a sweatshirt, and hurried down the backstairs toward his mother's small office, booting up the desktop. Adam sent e-mails once a week, updating him on the Task Force's progress in apprehending Victor Bobco and Dimitri Dubov. So far the leads were slim. He signed into Ethan Cooke Security's system, then accessed his dummy account. Any activity he created using his mother's IP address would be scrambled. He clicked on Adam's latest message.

Finally something positive to share. We're closing in on Dubov. Location narrowed down to one of two spots. Briefing in the a.m. Will report ICE's findings.

Peace

Jerrod read Adam's simple reply three times and pounded his fist on the desk. "*Yes*. It's about damn time." This was huge. If Immigration and Customs Enforcement really had a bead on Dimitri it would only be a matter of time before they nabbed the bastard. Then they needed to find Victor, and Abby would be two huge steps closer to moving on with her life.

He glanced out the window, catching sight of her bundled in her hat and work coat, heading toward the henhouse with her basket in hand. He smiled and logged out, walking down the hall to grab his boots and jacket. *They* would be two steps closer to moving on with their lives together.

CHAPTER EIGHTEEN

SHELBY LEFT HER CAR IN THE COVER OF A THICK OF TREES and hurried up the lane in her heels, picking her way over the juts and rocks, wrapping her coat tighter around herself in the bitter winds. She quickened her pace as she came to the clearing, wincing when she spotted Jerrod pounding away at the dark red boards of the barn atop his ladder. If he turned and spotted her, her plan would fizzle before she had a chance to begin. The whole 'I want to be friends thing' she tried last night was a bust, getting her no closer to another invitation for dinner, so now it was on to strategy number two.

She rushed closer to the cover of the house and smiled, noting that Mary's truck was gone and Uncle Jimmy's was back at his house in the distance. This was going to be easier than she'd first thought, unless Abigail was inside. She scoffed, rolling her eyes at the idea of having to make nice and strike up some sort of conversation, but every reporter made sacrifices for the good of their story—and this was going to be one hell of a story.

Jerrod was definitely Abigail's bodyguard. That was the only reasonable explanation for the tight leash he kept her on in Nowheresville, Nebraska, and the aversion to pictures. *You might have a job to do, but I'm still trying to live my life. Somewhere along the way you forgot that.* Shelby grinned, remembering Abigail's wrenching words the day of the big blowup, loving how everything was coming together. Jerrod was *absolutely* on the job. Any lingering doubts she'd had vanished in the O'Neil's barn when he pushed Ms. Hammlin away with her camera.

Tiptoeing her way up the front steps, she walked into the warmth of the living room, making a beeline for the stairs, listening as she climbed. If all was right with the world, Abigail would be in the studio this afternoon instead of in her room doing whatever it was she did when she holed herself up in there for hours on end.

She crept down the hall, stopping in Jerrod's doorway, breathing deep, closing her eyes as she absorbed the familiar scent of his soap. She turned away, her heart aching, missing the man she'd planned to marry since high school, and knocked on Abigail's door, concentrating on the now. Jerrod would come back to her eventually; she just had to wait a while longer until he realized his mistake. She'd waited when he trotted off to Los Angeles and then Manhattan. "Abigail."

Stepping into Abigail's bedroom, she let loose a quiet, "*yes*!" when she found the space empty. She sniffed at the air and wrinkled her nose, detesting the subtle perfume scent, hating everything about Jerrod's across-the-hall roommate—her competition. She glanced over her shoulder and walked to the small desk in the corner of the room, picking up the sketchpad, leafing through dozens and dozens of excellent drawings of clothes she would love to wear. *Vocation or avocation*? she wondered as she set the pad back exactly the way she found it. Something told her it was both. She opened the drawers next, finding sketching pencils and fancy colored pencils, but nothing that told her anything other than Abigail enjoyed drawing and making Mary Quinn dresses because she was a first-rate kiss-ass.

She hurried to the dresser, opening each drawer, glaring as she glanced at Abigail's pant size. "Bitch." Maybe if she starved herself with vegetables and tiny spoonfuls of this and that the way the California chick did she'd look like a freaking goddess too. She shut the drawer with a slam and winced, peeking out the window, making certain Jerrod was still on his ladder.

Moving to the closet next, she found Abigail's purse. "Jackpot." She rifled through, passing over the tube of expensive lip-gloss, the package of tissues, grabbing hold of the small wallet. She unfastened the snap, studying Abby's ID and credit card, grinning at her triumph. "Abigail Monroe. Got you now, don't I?" She shoved the California license away and put the purse back, sliding the closet door closed, eager to be on her way.

Scanning the room one last time and pausing in the doorway, she made certain everything looked as it did before she came in. She stopped as she spotted the *Trendy* magazine on the floor by the loveseat. Her eyes popped wide as she stared at Abigail's striking face on the cover. "No *way*." She hurried forward, snatching up the copy, and walked down the hall to the bathroom, locking herself in as she sat on the toilet seat, studying the blue-eyed stunner with perfect skin grinning among the headlines.

Flipping through each page, she grit her teeth, teeming with envy, glaring at every awesome shot of Abigail. She turned to the next page and gasped, almost dropping the magazine as she gaped at Jerrod and Abigail *swinging*. "What the hell?" She rushed to her feet, pushing the picture closer to her face, still unable to believe what she was seeing. Jerrod was a bodyguard, not some fashion model.

She flipped some more, muttering, halting on the page of the little whore straddling Jerrod in a barely there black bra and panty set. She made a noise in her throat, her eyes filling as she studied the sexy couple smiling at each other, their fingers clasped. "Friends my ass." She struggled not to rip the page to shreds as she looked at the next. Jerrod cuddled the naked tramp close, his arm covering her breasts, his hand in her hair as they stared at each other. "How could you, Jerrod Quinn?"

She threw the magazine to the floor, wiping at the torrent of tears, trying to gain control of each ragged breath. Abigail wasn't Jerrod's client; she was his freaking hussy. They were definitely sleeping together.

She brushed at her cheeks again and picked up the thick magazine, yanking at each page, wandering back to the article she hadn't bothered to read, skimming the page discussing Abigail Harris's *Escape* line. Who the hell was Abigail Harris if her license identified her as Abigail Monroe? She'd never heard of either.

Shelby shoved the magazine in her bag and stepped from the bathroom, ready to get to the bottom of this. She would have to read the damn thing from cover to cover when she could actually see straight. She slowed as she passed the window, realizing Jerrod no longer stood on the ladder, no longer caring if he caught her. She had the truth now and planned to run with it—and more. She walked back to Abigail's sketches, lifting each page, taking pictures with her phone as an idea came to mind. This was going to be good. Her next stop was wherever she wanted to go, because this was going to take her places. Jerrod Quinn and his slut could go to hell.

~~~~

Snow Patrol blasted through the stereo speakers as Jerrod stepped into his mother's small studio, closing the door behind him. He pulled off his hat and jacket in the warm space, smiling as Abby sat at the potter's wheel, dipping her hand in the bucket of water at her side, laying dripping fingers back on the bowl she was forming. She sang along with the band, wiggling her hips in time with the beat as small spatters of gray landed on her dingy jeans. He winced as the spinning clay began to wobble.

"No. *No*!" She took her foot off the pedal as her creation folded in. "*Damn* it."

"How's it going in here?" he shouted over the music.

She screamed, whipping her head around. "You scared me."

"Sorry." He turned the stereo down to a dull roar. "What are you making?" He gestured toward the chunk on the wheel.

"A mess." She huffed. "It doesn't matter how much I practice. I can't get this right."

He hung his jacket on the hook. "I think you're pulling up too quickly on the sides."

She narrowed her eyes. "Are you an expert?"

He smiled. "No, but I can make a bowl."

"Will you show me?" Her big blue eyes pleaded with him. "I don't want to ask your mother again. It might send her over the edge. I want to get this *right*. I refuse to leave this farm until I've made one decent piece."

He'd come by hoping to steal a couple of kisses. He still had a dozen boards to get to on the front side
~~~~

of the barn alone, but he walked toward her anyway. "I'll see what I can do. Pull that up and we'll start again."

She took the clay from the wheel, handing it to him as the CD began to play Pearl Jam.

He nodded his approval as he kneaded the chunk back into a smooth ball. "Good tune."

"It's definitely slow and broody—right up your alley."

"Don't mess with 'The Jam,' Abigail."

They smiled at each other as he set the clay in the center of the wheel and pulled up a stool behind her. He sniffed at her damp ponytail and nuzzled her neck, smelling the body cream she rubbed on herself everyday. "Mmm, you took a shower."

"Yes I did." She laughed, squirming away. "Your scruff is scratchy."

He wrapped his arms around her waist, burrowing in again, loving that he could finally touch her the way he wanted to. "I thought you liked my scruff."

She tried to evade again, chuckling. "I do. It's incredibly sexy." She looked over her shoulder, grinning. "Now, let's make this bowl, big guy."

He leaned in close to her ear. "What do you say we forget the whole pottery thing and go take advantage of a quiet house?" He'd been craving her since they parted ways in the barn a couple hours ago.

She shuddered, leaning back against him. "Now *that's* tempting."

"Mmm. More than." He playfully sunk his teeth into her earlobe, ready to make good on his suggestion. He'd done little but think of the tenderness they shared last night and the way she went wild in his arms this morning.

"Jerrod," she said breathily. "Pottery first. I'll take

thorough advantage of you tonight."

He slid his tongue along her lobe, wanting her right this second. "Promise?"

"Cross my heart." She tilted her head back, her heated gaze staring into his.

He grinned. "I'll be counting down the hours."

"That makes two of us." She wiggled her brows. "Now back to the bowl."

"If we must." He tried out his puppy dog eyes and chuckled when she laughed.

"Nice try, big guy."

"It was worth a shot." He shrugged and scooted in, pressing himself closer to her body, dipping his fingers in the water as she did. "Palms against the clay. Pushing down hard," he instructed.

"I know how to do this part." She molded the wet clay, forming a smooth, rounded chunk.

"Looks good. Now stick your thumbs in the center and make a hole."

She did.

"You've got it."

"The next step is where everything falls apart." She looked behind her, giving him a quick kiss.

He dipped his hand in the water again. "You need to open it up, using your sponge for support, then press out with your hand. Like this." He created an upside down 'u.'

"I *do* that."

"Show me."

She set the wet circular sponge to the outside and put her hand in the small opening with her hand formed the way he showed her.

"Good. Just more gently." He wet his hand and stuck it in the widening hole, shaping the piece with Abby. The clay moved up perfectly.

"How do you *do* that? It must be in the genes."

"I've done this a time or two."

"I feel like *Unchained Melody* should be playing instead of *Come Back*."

He grimaced, sticking his hand in the bowl once more, flattening the bottom. "Let's stick with Pearl Jam."

She twisted at the waist, meeting his gaze. "You continue to surprise me, Mr. Quinn—an animal in bed and a skilled potter in the studio." She touched the tip of his nose with her dirty finger.

His brow shot up. "And we've only hit the tip of the iceberg."

"Oh, do tell."

He pressed his messy hands to her breasts, molding his palms to her white cotton shirt.

Her eyes went wide, gaping at him. "Jerrod, how am I supposed to explain this to your mother?"

He shook his head, smiling, sliding his thumbs over her perky nipples. "I'd just plead the fifth."

"Jerrod." She tried to turn further. "It's the middle of the day."

He snagged her around the waist, pushing her back against his chest, sending one hand to her crotch, rubbing through denim.

She froze.

"We can't do this here," she said with less conviction, resting her head in the crook of his shoulder as he kissed the back of her neck.

"I'm only sampling."

"I guess that's okay then." She looked up, turning her head slightly, and he captured her lips, diving deep, humming in his throat as he lost himself in her addictive flavor.

"My mother went to town." He said against her

mouth. "She'll be gone for hours."

She spun on her stool and crawled in his lap, wrapping her legs around his waist, attacking his neck with greedy nips. "Why didn't you say so?"

He clenched his jaw, closing his eyes as she pulled his shirt free from the waist of his jeans and sent her clay-streaked hands up his back, making him shiver. "My mistake."

She went after his ear next. "I'm sure it won't happen again."

"Never," he said as he stood, palming her ass, staring in her eyes. He walked with her to the table by the wall and set her on top of the dusty space. Her breasts brushed his chest with each heaving breath, and he wondered how he'd managed to keep his hands to himself over the last six months, because there was no way in hell he could now.

Their mouths met, wild and ravenous, and she went to work on his snap, tugging at his jeans as he changed the angle of the kiss, taking her deeper, groaning.

He unhooked her bra through her shirt and lifted her filthy top, exposing taught, pink nipples begging for his attention. He drew her in, tasting her perfumy flavor. "Right now."

"You don't have a condom," she said, arching up, angling herself so he took in more of her breast as she ran her fingers through his hair.

"I'll pull out." He ran frantic palms along her waist. "I'll pull out, Abigail."

"Okay," she panted.

"I just need to feel you for a minute."

"Yes." She snuck her hands into his boxers, clutching his butt, pulling them crotch to crotch as she rocked against him. "Just for a minute."

He yanked at her pants and the table creaked ominously. He tugged again, grabbing her around the waist as the tabletop collapsed, crashing to the floor, the dishes shattering in a pile to their right. They both stared, gasping, and came back together desperately. "We'll fix it later," he murmured as she nibbled his mouth.

"Later," she agreed, pulling at the elastic of his boxers, exposing him as he sent her jeans to her knees and she kicked off her sneaker, pulling one leg out. "I want to ride you."

He sat on the edge of the broken table, leaning his back against the wall. She followed and immediately took him deep, moaning as she gripped his shoulders.

"God, Abigail," he hissed through his teeth. She was so damn hot and tight.

She moved up and down, continuing the frenzied pace, and he clutched her hips, watching Abby bite her swollen lip and close her eyes as her whimpers grew longer with every rock of her body.

"Go, Abigail, go," he encouraged, out of breath, on the brink as Abby teetered on the edge, revving him impossibly higher.

She clawed at his shirt, throwing her head back on a stunned cry, freezing, then gyrated faster, working him harder as the orgasm consumed her.

"Abby," he gasped, "I'm close. I'm going to come." He wrapped an arm around her waist, but she continued to move her taut, sexy body, staring in his eyes, moaning, lost in pleasure as her throbbing center begged him to follow her.

"Abigail," his fingers bit into her hips and he exploded, filling her, shoving himself deeper in his ecstasy. He rested his head on her shoulder as she collapsed against him, still shuddering and shivering.

He brought his arms around her, stroking her back beneath her shirt as they caught their breath, closing his eyes as she pressed a tender kiss to his neck. “Abigail.” He drew her away, cupping her sweaty face. “That was a really bad idea.”

She nodded. “I know.”

He slid his thumb along damp skin, unable to stop touching her. He still filled her as she clung to him, but they weren’t close enough. “I should’ve pulled out.”

“Definitely.” She licked her dry lips, staring at him, her eyes still glazed with passion.

“This would be a really shitty time to end up pregnant.”

She nodded again. “I agree.”

“I can’t get enough of you, Abby. I absolutely can’t, but we can’t do this again.”

“I know. I’m sorry.”

“I’m pretty sure we both made the decision. Neither one of us stopped.”

“I like the way you feel inside of me.” She traced a finger down the buttons of his plaid worktop, glancing up from under her lashes. “I’ve never had unprotected sex before. Josh, my friend with benefits in college, we were safe every time. It was never like this.” She shrugged. “You feel good—different—perfect.”

He clenched his jaw as her confession kicked his hormones back into high gear. “I like it a hell of a lot better this way too, but—”

She pressed a finger to his lips. “I get it.”

He kissed the tip of her nose. “Condoms from now on.”

“Every time.” She hugged him and stood, pulling her pants back on.

He got to his feet, zipping himself up as the studio

door opened.

Shelby walked in, stopping, her eyes going huge as she stared at the mess on the floor. "What happened in here?"

Abby cleared her throat as she tied the shoe she'd kicked off. "The table broke."

Jerrod struggled to suppress a smile as Abby glanced at him. "You should clean up while I fix this."

She nodded, smiling at him as she reached for her jacket with handprints on her breasts and ass, her ponytail a mess, her cheeks rosy and her lips still swollen. "I'll make us some lunch."

He sent her a wink. "Sounds good."

She walked out, ignoring Shelby altogether.

Shelby slammed the door shut, her cheeks going pink with temper. "What are you doing?"

He bent down to examine the bent joint on the table leg, already knowing this wasn't going to go well. "Fixing the table."

"You have clay in your hair, on your face, on your button snap. And her... You were making out in your mother's *studio*."

"I'm not having this conversation." He stood, figuring the table was a loss. He'd have to build mom a new one.

"You *are* sleeping with her."

His eyes flew to hers. "That's none of your business."

"What happened to 'Abby's my friend'? How could you do this to me?" She sniffled as tears poured down her cheeks.

He rubbed at his forehead, trying to figure out how to proceed from here. He hadn't expected Shelby to walk in seconds after he pulled himself free of Abby. "Shelby, you and I aren't together." He grabbed a broom and swept up Abby's dried attempts at...whatever that had been.

"Do you love her?"

He stopped the broom, not willing to go there with his ex. He didn't know exactly what he felt for Abby, or maybe he did, but he sure as hell wasn't going to discuss it with Shelby. "Shelby—"

"Jerrod, I love you." She rushed to him and grabbed his arm. "Come back to me. Please come back to me. We'll make it work this time. I can move to Los Angeles."

He could smell Abigail on his skin and taste her on his tongue. She was the only woman he wanted. He peeled Shelby's hand from him. "Shelby, you need to move on. You can't keep doing this."

"Bastard!" She shoved him, her green eyes flashing. "You're going to pay for this, and so is she." She whirled.

He grabbed her, turning her back. He'd had more than enough of her threats. "Leave Abby alone."

"Jerrod." She collapsed against him. "I love you," she sobbed.

He moved away, attempting to find a stirring of compassion as he looked into her genuinely hurt eyes. "Shelby." He took both of her arms gently. "We didn't work. You know that."

"No." She shook her head vehemently.

"Shelby, come on. Come on," he said again, staring at the woman he'd traded peanut butter and jelly sandwiches with in grade school and lost his virginity to in the back of dad's old Chevy his sophomore year. He couldn't help but hug the pretty journalist he'd tried to build a life with. "You're holding on to the past. You deserve so much more than what we had. We both do."

"I've never wanted anyone else."

He closed his eyes. "I can't be with you anymore."

"You're in love with her."

He sighed.

She yanked away from him. "I *hate* you. God, do I *hate* you." She ran to the door, slamming it behind her, and hurried away.

He clenched his jaw, watching through the window, making certain she didn't detour to the house to mess with Abby. He unclenched his jaw and shook his head, wishing somehow he and Shelby could've ended as friends. They had a long history, and not all of it was bad, but somewhere along the way she'd grown vengeful and bitter.

He steamed out a breath, rubbing at his jaw. There was little doubt Shelby would be hot for revenge. Tim was going to have to help him put out this fire. Tim had a way with her; he always had.

He swept up the mess and grabbed his phone from his hip, dialing, glancing at the house through the window again, eager to put Shelby behind him. He wanted Abby and their quiet lunch. More, he wanted the trial over with so they could get back to their own home. He'd been exactly right when he said he and Shelby both deserved better, and he finally had it.

~~~~

Shelby typed the last word, added a period, and sat back, smiling. Her self-satisfied grin quickly dissolved into hopeless tears. "Damn it." She stared at the bright screen in her dark living room, her breath rushing in and out in her misery as she thought of the way Jerrod and Abigail smiled at each other in Mary's studio. Never once had he looked at her the way he
~~~~

did Abigail. Never ever did he want her so ferociously that they broke tables and crockery in their haste to be together, nor had he been playful the way he was with *her*.

Jerrod and Abigail were different; *he* was different. He'd never been unkind during the months they lived together, but he wasn't attentive and sweet the way he was with her. She closed her eyes, dropping her face in her hands, giving into another bought of tears as she finally understood Jerrod wasn't coming back. He was in love with his fashion-designing supermodel.

She'd been right all along. Something about Jerrod's 'friends visiting the farm' story had been off from the beginning. The advanced copy of *Trendy* confirmed her suspicions. She'd read the March issue cover-to-cover after she raced home from the Quinn's, surprised by the tidbits Abigail shared of her harrowing story and her dedication to the *Escape* line's mission, with the enthusiastic backing of Lily Brand Designs. She'd searched the internet for hours, finding plenty of information on Abigail's show-stopping designs at numerous college fashion fairs, her abduction and rescue, and rumors that she was the prosecution's star witness against the Mid-Atlantic Sex Ring. Then there was nothing. Abigail Harris ceased to exist until Toni Torrell's article outed her as Lily's hot new designer three weeks ago—the day before Jerrod and Abigail made their surprise appearance in Parker.

Google Images had several photos of Abby pre-graduation, walking the runway in Washington D.C., London, Paris, and Milan, wearing fellow designers' clothes. She posed with some of fashion's biggest names, flashing her stellar grin, but the picture Shelby came back to time and again was dated two days after her rescue. Abigail wore dark shades and a black cap hiding her hair while she looked down, gripping her arm around Jerrod's waist, clinging as he hugged her close on their walk through the airport. He wore his own shades and black cap tugged low, holding up his hand to block any further pictures from the crowd of photographers.

Abigail and Jerrod had been together since July—*months*. He'd moved on quickly enough after he dumped her and headed back to Los Angeles as if what they'd had was nothing. Shelby looked at the picture of Abby smiling with her famous fashion friends, then back at her and Jerrod snuggled up on their jaunt through Reagan International, detesting the bitch for her beauty, talent, and success, but mostly for stealing Jerrod Quinn.

She exed out of the pictures and pulled her laptop closer, ready for payback. Abby had the spotlight for now, but Shelby Haggerty was about to try it out for a while. Toni Torrell had promised her a feature page in *The Times* along with a position if the article was everything she'd promised. Her feature story was going to kick *ass*. Parker Nebraska would be a thing of the past once her exposé broke in the morning. Abigail and Jerrod were in for a surprise.

Shelby reread the piece she'd painstakingly written and attached Abby's spring sketches she'd downloaded from her phone. LA's Fashion Princess was going to have to start her *Escape* line from scratch. The poor thing wouldn't want to launch her new product with ideas the world had already seen. She pressed 'send' with a flourish and closed her laptop, eagerly anticipating her big break and the opportunity to knock Jerrod and his hussy down a few pegs.

Chapter Nineteen

"Jerrod," mom whispered.

"Hmm?" He wrapped his arms tighter around Abby's warm, naked body, pulling her closer, nuzzling her neck, content to lay just like this and surrender to another hour or two of sleep.

"Jerrod," she hissed louder, and his eyes flew open in the dark.

"Mom?" He blinked away his sleep-induced confusion and shoved himself up to sitting, already tense. "What's wrong?" Mom rarely came upstairs, and she sure as hell wouldn't have walked into his room once she figured out he was in bed with Abby.

"I think you might want to see this." She held up the *Parker Gazette*.

He took the paper, holding it close to his face, reading the headline: LA's FASHION PRINCESS GONE COUNTRY. There was an old picture of Abby filling the front page.

"Son of a *bitch*." He glanced at the byline and rubbed at his eyes as he started reading.

From skyscrapers to corn fields, LA's Fashion Princess and former sex trafficking survivor Abigail Harris...

"You've got to be fucking kidding me." He flipped to the next page, noting that the extensive article continued, showcasing several of Abby's latest designs among the print. "Goddammit."

Abby rolled over. "Jerrod?"

"Mom, call Timmy and tell him to get here."

She nodded and hurried from the room as he got out of bed, searching for the pants and shirt Abby had peeled off him hours before.

Abby sat up, covering her breasts with the sheet. "What's going on?"

"Get dressed." He found his jeans, yanking them on, then the long sleeve t-shirt. "Pack your bag. We have to go."

Her face paled in the dim light. "They're here."

"Not yet." But they would be.

She crawled across the bed, gloriously naked, her hand shaking as she reached for her robe. "What are we going to do? Where are we going to go?" She stood, her jaw tense, fighting her chattering teeth as she wrapped herself tight in the white cotton.

His mind raced with the steps he needed to take, but he couldn't stand seeing Abby trembling in terror. "Hey," he said, speaking with a calm he didn't feel as he framed her face, stroking his thumb along her cheek as her whole body shook. "It's okay. We're going to be okay." He kissed her forehead. "Stay away from the windows. Grab what will fit in the suitcase we came with. Don't forget your cap and jacket."

"All right." She nodded and hurried from the room.

He dialed Ethan, waiting impatiently through two rings.

"Cooke," he said groggily.

"It's Quinn. We're evacuating."

"What? Why? Where?"

"Abby's been discovered. She's in the local paper. We're heading to Cheyenne. We'll take off from there. I don't think it's a good idea to go back to Denver." He grabbed jeans from his drawers and a few simple, nondescript tops, shoving them in a small carryon, then took his black cap and the jacket he arrived in from the closet. "I can have us there in a little over three hours. Book us anything leaving around the ten-thirty/eleven o' clock range."

"I'll call you back in less than twenty. Be careful."

"Thanks." He hung up, glancing at his watch. They'd only been up for ten minutes, but it felt like hours. "Abby, come on." They needed to get the hell out of here.

Abby rushed in with her bag and purse, dressed in jeans and a gray hoodie, her eyes clouded with worry for the first time in weeks. "I'm ready."

"Good." He slid his holster over his shirt, checked his weapon, and shoved the Glock in its place against his ribs. He pulled the pistol out just as quickly when a truck came barreling down the lane. "Stay here. Mom," he shouted as he took the stairs in twos.

"I'm here, son." She carried Grandpa Quinn's old shotgun—the first gun he'd ever fired.

"Go upstairs."

"It's just Timmy."

"Go on until I make sure. Keep Abby close." Mom could handle a weapon as well as the rest of them.

The porch light shined on Timmy as he booked it up the steps and came inside.

Jerrod put his gun away, not bothering to greet his sleepy-eyed brother. "Mom and Uncle Jimmy can't stay here."

"I know." Timmy scrubbed at his face.

"Wait a minute, boys," Mom said with a hand on her hip. "I'm not going anywhere."

Jerrod glanced at his mother, then his watch again. Fifteen minutes had ticked by. "Mom, I don't have time for this. I have to go. You're going to do whatever Timmy tells you until this blows over."

"What about the farm?" She asked with her brows raised.

"Screw the farm. This is your life. These people will kill you just because they can."

"Jerrod—"

"I'm sorry," Abby's voice trembled as she walked down the stairs carrying their two small bags. "I'm sorry, Mary. You've been so kind to welcome me, and I've put you in danger."

"This isn't your fault," Jerrod said as he looked into her eyes brimming with tears, trying to ignore the urge to wrap her up in a hug. He needed to keep her safe, not soothe her. He'd given her all the gentleness he could upstairs; now it was time to work.

"Now honey, you listen to Jerrod. This isn't your fault." Mom pulled Abby into a hug. "You two need to be on your way."

"Please do what Jerrod and Tim ask." Abby eased back, looking Mom in the eyes. "*Please*. They're monsters," she said, gripping mom's hand.

"Okay, honey. I'll pack a few things and leave with Timmy." She gave Abby's cheek a gentle pat and broke their connection, moving in to give Jerrod a hug. "You be careful. Watch your back and keep Abby safe."

He hugged her hard, always hating when he had to say goodbye to his mother. She was the one person he regretted leaving behind. "I will. You need to be careful for a while too." He kissed her cheek and let her go.

"I will, but Shelby didn't mention you or any of us by name in the article."

"At least that's something." His blood boiled as he thought of the unnecessary danger Shelby had caused everyone in this room. "I still don't want you out here by yourself for a while. You or Uncle Jimmy. Make sure you have a couple of Timmy's men with you until you get the all-clear."

"All right, son."

"We need to go. Timmy, I'm going dark. Contact Ethan at the number I gave you. He'll keep you filled in." He gave his brother a quick hug.

"Got it." Timmy gave his back a solid smack. "Be careful."

"You too."

A car sped down the drive, stopping with a screech of brakes. Jerrod went instantly on alert, blocking Abby behind him, pushing her toward the stairs as he and Timmy pulled their weapons. Someone's footsteps crunched toward the front steps. Jerrod clenched his jaw as he caught sight of long red hair in the front window. Shelby. He had absolutely nothing to say to her. "Come on, Abigail."

She nodded, stopping in front of Timmy. "Goodbye, Tim. Thank you for all the fun." She kissed his cheek. "Tell Uncle Jimmy thank you and goodbye for me."

He nodded. "I will. Listen to Jerrod and come back and see us when things are better."

She gave him a small smile. "I would like to."

Jerrod took her hand and opened the door as Shelby raised a hand to knock in yoga pants and a sweatshirt. "You've got some fucking nerve coming out here."

"I got a strange phone call—two of them. It creeped me out."

He pulled Abby with him to the rental car. "I'd plan on several more, or worse." He didn't care that her eyes bloomed with fear. She'd made this mess. "You have no idea what you've done, Shelby. No fucking idea. I hope it was worth it." He got in as Abby took her seat, reversed, and drove off, not bothering to look back in his rearview mirror. If he ever saw Shelby again, it would be too soon.

Abby stared out the window, gripping her hands tight in her lap as they drove down Commerce Way toward the onramp. "Where are we going?" she asked quietly.

"To Cheyene." He merged on Eighty West, checking for a nonexistent tail, and kicked his speed up to eighty-five—ten over the speed limit, eager to put distance between Abby and Parker, Nebraska. "Ethan's booking us a flight."

"Then what?"

"I'm not sure until he calls me back." His cell rang as if on cue, and he checked the readout. "This is him right now." He pressed 'talk.' "Quinn."

"First available flight out is 10:35. United flight 2233 to Indianapolis. Tickets are waiting at the counter."

"Thanks, man."

"Abby made *The Times* again. Toni Torrell and Shelby Haggerty are sharing the byline."

He huffed out a breath, absorbing the latest wave of anger. "Yeah."

"I'm taking it you know Shelby."

"Yeah," he said again. "My ex decided to pay me back. She likes to make it count." He grit his teeth in frustration, glancing at Abby as she turned her head his way.

"She doesn't mess around."

"No." He shook his head, still trying to believe she'd actually done this. Shelby was capable of a lot, but this was a new low.

"Give me a call when you land, and we'll figure

out the next step."

"Will do."

"Later."

"Later." He hung up and gripped the wheel tight. Abby's face was in the news again, and not just here in Parker. Shelby had already received 'creepy' phone calls, which meant the bastards were on to them. They were more than likely already on their way to Nebraska. He needed to talk to Adam and figure out what the taskforce had on Dimitri. Hesitating, he dialed, understanding the risks he took by calling anyone other than Ethan.

"Hello?"

"It's Quinn. What's the word on Dimitri?"

"We've got him narrowed down to two locations. Surveillance is running now."

"Good." His shoulders relaxed a fraction, knowing the men he used to work with and trusted had a bead on one of their problems. He wanted to ask where they thought Dimitri was, but Adam wouldn't and couldn't tell him over the phone. "Good," he said again.

"Are you in trouble, man?"

"Nope. Everything's fine. Just checking in."

There was a long pause. Adam knew as well as he did that everything was *not* fucking fine. "Okay."

"I'll talk to you later." He hung up, rolled down his window, and tossed the phone out, watching it crack into pieces on the pavement in his rearview mirror.

Abby stared at him. "Why did you do that?"

"New place, new phone. No risks."

"Why did you tell that person everything's fine?"

"Because you never know who's listening."

She let loose a trembling sigh. "I hate this."

He took her hand, running his thumb along her

knuckles. "We'll be okay." He wanted them settled somewhere hundreds of miles from here. "We're going to make this work, just like we've done all along."

She nodded, pressing a kiss to his knuckles, and set their joined hands in her lap as they passed a mileage sign. Cheyenne Wyoming was 200 miles away. He glanced at the odometer, tempted to punch the gas, eager to hurry them along, but he kept his speed at eighty-five, more than ready to leave Nebraska behind.

~~~~

The plane touched down with a bump and rush of breaks, slowing as the jet approached United's terminal. Jerrod leaned closer to Abby's side, glancing at the snowy mix falling outside the window, then at his watch. They'd lost an hour with the time change—not that it mattered much. He and Abby still had problems, whether it was three-thirty in the afternoon or midnight.

He reached for his cell, muttering a swear as he remembered that his phone lay in pieces somewhere on Interstate 80. Now that they were on the ground he needed to talk to Ethan and find a place for them to lay low until more secure arrangements could be made. Their unexpected departure from Nebraska meant a safe house scenario was more than likely in the cards. As much as he hated the idea of locking Abby behind shaded windows and closed doors, her days of wandering free were over. They should've had another week and a half on the farm, but this morning's articles changed that.

He looked at Abby's pale cheeks and tensed shoulders, struggling to ignore another rush of anger,
~~~~

understanding that the useless emotions did him little good. Shelby made her choice; now he and Abby were dealing with the consequences. He sent her another glance, brushing his fingers along her hand, winking as the plane rolled to a stop and the flight attendant's voice filled the cabin.

"Are you ready?" he asked.

She gave him a small smile as she grabbed her carryon and purse from below the seat in front of her. "Yeah." She'd said little during the four and a half hour flight, spending most of her time staring out the window. She was trying to stay strong, but he knew she was struggling to hold on.

He took both their bags and stood, wedging his body into the aisle, making certain he and Abby weren't the first or the last passengers to deplane. "Come on." He snagged her hand, pulling her in front of him. "Right by my side. Just like always," he murmured close to her ear.

She nodded, moving forward, following the line out as they walked the jetway.

He stepped to her right side, slipping an arm around her waist as they moved closer to the gates, his eyes scanning the groupings of passengers waiting to board and the hoards of people lounging around or walking by on their way to catch another flight. "You okay?"

"Yes."

"We'll grab a phone and a bite to eat. I'll call Ethan and figure out what's next."

"I'm not hungry."

She'd nibbled two or three bites of a banana nut muffin in Cheyenne and handed off her peanuts and pretzels to him mid-flight.

"Abby, you need to eat something."

She pressed a hand to her stomach. "I don't feel very well."

Without fail, her appetite had vanished. "We'll get you some crackers and a ginger ale."

"Ginger ale actually sounds really good."

"One ginger ale, coming up." He smiled and kissed the top of her head as he continued his scrutiny of Indianapolis International's other patrons, pausing when he spotted the small shop selling novelties, snacks, and magazines. "This looks like a good spot."

"Sure. When we're finished here I want to hit the bathrooms."

"You've got it."

Abby broke free of his hold, heading toward the cooler of drinks mere feet to his left.

He struggled not to pull her back and keep her at his side as he looked around at strangers perusing magazines or purchasing packs of gum. He'd grown accustomed to the quiet and safety he and Abby experienced over the last three weeks in Parker. For the first time in years, he actually missed the farm.

"Do you want something?" she asked as she grabbed a soda.

"Uh, just a water, thanks."

She pulled a bottled water from the cooler and studied the small selection of crackers, pretzels, chips, and cookies, choosing a bag of pretzel rods. "Do you want a snack?"

"I need a real meal." He took a pay-as-you-go phone from the shelf, noting the thirty-minute card included. "Are you all set?"

"Yes."

"Let's pay for this and get out of here."

Jerrod paid the bored-eyed woman at the register, using cash. "You can keep the bag," he said as he and

Abby walked out, stopping next to the women's restroom close by. "Go ahead, and I'll get this taken care of." He gestured to the phone he battled to pull from the thick plastic.

"You don't have to tell me twice." Abby set her snacks on top of their carryons and hurried to the bathroom.

Several moments later, Jerrod finally freed the throwaway phone and entered the information from the card quickly, knowing he only had a fifteen-minute charge before he would have to plug in. The screen beeped, alerting him to a successful activation, and he dialed Ethan.

"Cooke."

"It's Quinn."

"You're secure?"

"Not yet. We'll find a hotel until you can send someone to give me a hand. He glanced around, waiting for Abby's return.

"I don't have anyone until Saturday—Friday at the earliest."

"That's a long damn time." He'd handled solo situations like this numerous times in the three years he worked WITSEC. Four days had never been a big deal. Hell, he'd been on his own for weeks at a time, relocating participants on the fly, but they had never been Abby. Of the thousands of witnesses he'd helped transfer, she was the one who mattered most. When they reached their final destination, he wouldn't be handing her off to another Marshal. When all of this was over, he wouldn't wave and walk away. He blinked as he realized he had no intention of letting her go.

"We weren't exactly planning on your ex's little exposé."

"Yeah, I know." He rubbed at the back of his neck, trying to concentrate on his conversation with Ethan instead of his epiphany.

"I'll do my best to finagle coverage and get someone out there sooner. I know what's at stake here, man."

"We'll be fine, but I'll take the help as soon as you can send it. I'll check in tomorrow."

"I'll have a better idea of who's coming and when."

"Thanks."

"Take care."

"Will do." He ended the call, checking the time he had remaining until the battery went dead.

"I feel much better," Abigail said as she came out of the restroom. Her cheeks still lacked color, but her eyes seemed brighter.

"Good. Let's take a seat while I make one more call, then we'll get food and find a place to stay."

They picked up their bags and seated themselves against the wall, facing the crowds as he dialed Adam's number.

"Hello?"

"It's Jerrod. Have you heard anything more?"

"Not yet."

"What the hell's taking so long?" It wasn't uncommon for surveillance to take days or even a couple of weeks, but he needed answers now.

"I'm sorry, man. You know how this shakes down. We can't afford mistakes."

He rubbed at his forehead as he steamed out a breath. "I know."

"What the hell's up? Are you in trouble?"

"You could say that."

"Where are you?"

He stayed silent.

"I know. You're not going to tell me. Fucking protocol." Adam sighed. "Come to New York. Shane and I can help you out."

The idea of giving Abby a secure location with men he trusted was appealing. "I don't know." They both knew he wouldn't confirm or deny his plans over an unsecure line.

"Look. Maybe we'll see you and maybe we won't, but you know where we are if you want a couple extra sets of eyes."

"I appreciate it." The phone beeped, alerting him to his dwindling time limit. "I've gotta go."

"Keep in touch."

"I will." He hung up as Abby swallowed her bite of pretzel, washing it down with a sip of soda. "Let's walk." Staying idle was never a good idea.

She shouldered her bag and purse and stood, walking with her snacks in hand. "What did you find out?"

"Well, we have a couple of options." He slid his arm around her waist, keeping her close, talking next to her ear like any cozy couple would. "We can lay low here in Indianapolis until Ethan gets someone out to help, or we can head to some friends of mine. My old roommates."

She slowed, her weary eyes meeting his. "The taskforce guys?"

He nodded, understanding Abby's nonexistent trust for law enforcement and their agendas. He couldn't blame her. The Baltimore Taskforce would have left her twisting in the wind if it hadn't been for her sister. "This would be off the radar—just a couple of my friends giving us a hand for a couple of days."

She shrugged. "What do you think?"

"I wouldn't hate having the backup. And the

anonymity of where we would be going is a big plus."

She nibbled her lip. "You want to go."

"I want you safe."

"I trust you, Jerrod. If you think this is right."

"These are good guys. I lived with them for two years."

She sighed. "I guess we should book another flight."

"I think this is the right move." He gave her a kiss. "I'll call Ethan." He dialed Ethan with his remaining four minutes.

"Cooke."

"I need flights." He glanced behind him, making certain no one stood too close as they continued down the concourse. "LaGuardia. My service time is running out."

"I'll set it up right now." Ethan's fingers flew over the keys. "I can get you guys out of there at five-twenty on American. Flight 1727. It's direct."

"Set it up."

"I'm halfway done."

The phone beeped again. "I'll check in tomorrow. We'll be staying with some friends."

"Got it."

"Thanks." Ending the call, he pulled the memory card from the phone as he and Abby stepped out of the busy path. He dropped the chip on the floor, crushing it under his heel as she stared into his eyes. He picked up the mangled pieces, tossing them in the trash as they walked by. "Looks like we're changing carriers. Let's go." He wrapped his arm around Abby again as much for safety as comfort while they made their way to the American Airlines ticket desk.

~~~~
~~~~

Abby snuggled her head on Jerrod's chest as the cab drove toward the address in West Manhattan. She'd been to The Big Apple on several occasions, typically loving the edgy energy the city emanated, but not this time. Tonight the bumper-to-bumper traffic and noise was a shock after the quiet of the farm. Everything was crowded, and the buildings were so tall, closing them in, accentuating the frantic bustle everywhere they turned.

She closed her eyes, struggling to ignore the honking horns and bright lights. The familiar flutters of unease were back, turning into waves of panic as she yearned to be anywhere but here. Burrowing herself closer to Jerrod, she concentrated on the scent of his clothes and the steady beat of his heart, willing the worst of her fear away.

He wrapped his arms tighter around her, stroking a soothing hand down her back. "You okay?" he murmured next to her ear.

Not even a little, but she nodded. From the moment they'd landed she'd wanted to run. Something about being here felt *wrong*. She'd almost grabbed hold of Jerrod a dozen times while they made their way through the airport, insisting that they leave, but he had enough to deal with without her hysterics. He was under enough pressure; he didn't need her making things worse. The best thing she could do was keep her mouth shut and let him do his job.

He kissed the top of her head and rested his cheek on her hair. "We're just about there."

"Okay." She breathed him in, clenching her thighs, fighting off the trembling that wanted its way.

"This is good right here," Jerrod said to the cabbie,

freeing himself from her death grip to reach for his wallet.

The man pulled to the curb, taking the cash Jerrod handed him.

"Thanks." Jerrod looked at her. "Are you ready to meet the guys?"

Her head was light with fatigue; her body ached with pent-up tension. The last thing she wanted to do was make small talk with a bunch of strangers. "Sure."

He opened the door and got out, grabbing his bag and her hand, pulling her to his side as she shouldered her purse and carryon. He closed the door, and they joined the crowds as the frigid winds slapped at her face.

"Damn it's cold," he said, hunching his shoulders against the next nasty gust.

"Where are we going?" Her teeth chattered—and not just because she was freezing.

"Two buildings up."

Thank goodness they were close. She needed to lock herself in the room they would borrow for the next week and shake and shiver away the worst of the dread settled in the pit of her stomach.

Jerrod slowed as they came to the dark green awning covering the 'Riverside' entrance. "Here we are." He opened the glass door, letting her into the warmth of the lobby, smiling as they stepped into the elevator seconds before it closed. Jerrod pressed the button for the twelfth floor and took her hand, clasping their fingers, holding her gaze as he leaned against the glossy metal. "This is a good place, Abby. These are great guys."

For the first time since he rushed out of bed this morning he seemed relaxed. Jerrod needed this time with his friends and the extra backup. If he said this was a good place, it was. "I'm looking forward to meeting everyone." She smiled, knowing he would relax further if she did. "I hope they don't mind that we're coming."

"Adam invited us. We can have Gavin's old room, which isn't much bigger than your bathroom back home, but you'll be safe here—as safe as you were at the farm."

Then why didn't she *feel* like it? She nodded, giving him another smile anyway.

The elevator dinged as the door slid open, and they walked down the hall, stopping at apartment 12-3. Jerrod knocked loudly, competing with the football game blaring on the other side. The door opened, and a handsome, well-built man with black hair and brown eyes appeared in the doorframe, grinning. "Well, if it isn't trouble," he said in a heavy New York accent, reaching out, grabbing Jerrod up in a 'bro' hug.

Jerrod smiled, hugging him back. "Hey, man."

"Good to see you." The guy gave Jerrod a solid smack to the back.

"It's been awhile."

"Come in. Come in." He opened the door wider, letting them in.

Abby stepped inside, glancing around at empty white walls, dark wood furnishings, and leather couches, admiring the excellent view of the city through tall windows.

"Adam, this is Abby. Abby, Adam."

Adam's hand swallowed hers as they shook. "Welcome to our castle. Make yourself comfortable."

She smiled, staring at the white Immigration and Customs Enforcement insignia on the black t-shirt he wore, wishing she felt as relaxed as she did when Jerrod introduced her to Tim. "Thank you."

"You guys want a beer or something?"

"Nah, I think we'll pass." Jerrod looked at Abby for confirmation as they took off their caps and jackets.

She shook her head.

Jerrod laid their stuff on the nearest chair and shoved his hands in his pockets, peering down the hall. "Where's Shane?"

"Florida. Or he's on his way. His team got a hot lead on some asshole who likes to traffic narcotics." He looked at Abby. "You want something to eat? There's not much in the fridge, but we can order in anything you want."

"We grabbed something at the airport." Jerrod held her gaze, studying. "Abby might want to hit the hay. It's been a long one."

"I am pretty tired." She gripped the strap of her purse, desperately craving quiet.

"Like I said, *mi casa es su casa*." Adam took a seat on the huge leather couch, grabbing his already opened beer. "Go catch some Zs, Abby. We'll see you in the morning."

"Gavin's old room?" Jerrod confirmed.

"You know where it is." Adam crossed his ankles on the coffee table.

"Come on." Jerrod gestured with his head. "I'll show you."

"Thank you for your hospitality," Abby said, following.

"Brothers take care of brothers. Isn't that right, Quinn?"

"You've got it." Jerrod started down a short hall, turning into a closet-sized room with just enough square-footage for a queen-sized bed and a dresser, which was jammed into the corner.

She stopped before she entered, staring at the

single window in the small space—her saving grace.

"It's pretty tight in here." He set his bag on the floor. "Is this going to be okay?"

"Yeah. It's fine." She set down her carryon by the dresser and wedged her way around to the window, looking out at the buildings across the street, trying her best to ignore their drab, cramped quarters that reminded her too much of her room at the stash house.

"Abby."

She turned, meeting his eyes.

"What's going on?"

"Nothing." She crossed her arms at her chest. "We've had a long day. I'm ready to rest."

"Does Adam bother you?"

She shook her head, still trying to figure out what it was exactly that made her uncomfortable with this entire situation. "He seems very nice." And he did. She just needed to adjust to their new space and the idea of being surrounded by men she didn't know.

"He's a loud son of a bitch, but he's one of my best friends."

The affection in his voice was unmistakable. She tried hard to relax her shoulders, hoping to convince him as much as herself that this was okay. "Really, Jerrod, I'm fine, just tired. I look forward to getting to know him better after I've caught up on my sleep."

He glanced toward the hall as Adam shouted at the television. "Let me talk to Adam for a couple of minutes, then I'll come in."

She wanted to be alone. "Go ahead and catch up." She schooled her voice to keep the desperation at bay. "There's no point in you coming back to watch me sleep."

"Are you sure?"

"Yes." She tried her best to smile as she squeezed her hands against her arms, ready for him to leave her be. "Go see your friend."

"Call me if you need anything."

"I will."

"Light on or off?"

"Off." She waited for him to flip the switch and shut the door most of the way then whipped up the window, breathing in the frigid air, gasping, closing her eyes against the refreshing whips of wind. Traffic rushed by far below as pedestrians hurried to their destinations. Buildings towered in every direction, and she wanted to be gone, terrified that a night of decent shut-eye wouldn't solve her need to flee. Eight hours of sleep couldn't erase her craving for the familiar surroundings of their condo or the quiet of the farm.

Another gust rushed along her face and arms, chilling her already cool skin. Shivering, taking as much as she could, she shut herself back in the cramped space and crawled to the center of the bed. Wrapping her arms tight around her legs, she rested her forehead against her knees, shutting her eyes, letting the terror wash through her. She was sick of fighting the dread that had consumed her since Jerrod told her they had to leave Nebraska early this morning. Dr. Tate said it was often better to experience the panic, live through it, and move on. She was ready to move on.

Her breath shuddered in and out as her arms shook and her legs trembled. Tears coursed down her cheeks as she purged herself of the fear. She was safe here with Jerrod's friends. His former co-workers were no different than the guys he worked with at Ethan Cooke Security, except they were Federal Agents instead of Bodyguards. Adam and Shane weren't the problem; the real issue stemmed from her phobias and inability to trust. She no longer knew if she disliked most men because there was an actual reason or if she just assumed there was.

Lifting her head, she listened to the strange voice down the hall mixing with Jerrod's as they laughed, clearly comfortable in each other's presence. She gripped herself tighter, looking out the window, imagining snow-covered fields and the comforting low of cows, stiffening when footsteps started down the hall. Her heart flew to her throat as a shadow blocked the hall light shinning into the room. The door opened slowly with an ominous creak, and she whirled off the bed, rushing to the corner, fighting to bring air in and out of her lungs as Jerrod stepped in.

"Abigail?"

She collapsed against the wall as her knees buckled, her relief huge.

He flipped on the light. "Abby, what are you doing?"

She fought to stand upright on jellied legs as fresh tears streamed down her cheeks. What *was* she doing? Why was she behaving this way? How could she tell him that she hated being in this place, in this city? How could she tell him that she wanted to run away? "I don't—I don't know."

He closed himself in the room and skirted around the bed. "It's okay." He wrapped her up in a hug. "It's okay," he murmured against her hair.

She hugged him back, even though it wasn't okay. Being in New York and in this apartment was definitely not all right.

"Come lay down with me."

"I'll be fine in a minute." She sniffled, easing out

of his embrace. "Really. I'm just having a hard time settling in."

"Come lay down with me," he said again as he pulled back the covers and sat on the edge of the bed. "Let's get comfortable." He tugged at her snap and unzipped her jeans, easing snug denim down her legs. "Snuggle up with me."

"Okay." She toed off her sneakers and slid her pants off the rest of the way, then crawled in next to him, hating that she relied on Jerrod to help her feel better.

He wrapped his arms around her and tossed his leg over her hips, cocooning her from the world. "Abigail," he murmured against her neck. "Do you want to go?"

She shook her head, sliding her hands along his back, more relaxed as they held each other close. "We don't need to do that. I need to be able to function in new places with new people. This is an opportunity to show myself that I can."

He adjusted his head on the pillow, staring into her eyes, sliding the hair back from her forehead. "You did fine in Nebraska."

The farm had been as much home as Los Angeles. She shrugged. "I guess this is just different."

"If you change your mind all you have to do is say the word and we'll figure something else out."

She wouldn't have that option if they moved to a safe house. She needed to take this change in their plans as an opportunity to grow. "I don't need to."

He leaned in, pressing his lips to hers.

She clung, absorbing the tenderness he offered, and smiled, kissing his chin, then his cheek. "You can visit with Adam. I'm okay now. Promise." And if that wasn't quite true, it damn well would be.

"In a few minutes." He pulled her closer. "I'm not ready to let you go."

"I can handle that." She closed her eyes, warm, content, safe, and drifted off to sleep in his arms.

Chapter Twenty

Shelby glanced over her shoulder as she unlocked her front door and stepped inside. *Finally* she was home. She set her purse and cell phone on the arm of the couch and flipped on the living room light, letting loose a huge sigh of relief. She'd spent two *days* trying to slip away from Timmy's cool, watchful eye, biding her time, waiting for him to step into the restroom and Mary to head to bed. As soon as Timmy shut the bathroom door and Mary wandered to the small guest bedroom, she tiptoed out the back door and booked it to her car.

Now that she was here she could take a bath and change her clothes. She'd been in her pajamas since she rushed out to the Quinn farm early yesterday morning. Timmy's insistence that she stay with him and his one-hundred-and-one precautions were ridiculous. She was *not* about to spend another night on his lumpy couch while he slept on the recliner next to her. Jerrod had infected everyone with his paranoia, totally screwing everything up—not that anything had gone as planned. They'd waited for something bad to happen since sunrise yesterday, which it didn't. Of course it didn't. This was Parker freaking Nebraska. *Nothing* happened here.

She rolled her eyes, slipping off her sweatshirt on the way to the bedroom. That's why she was leaving. Toni Torrell and *The Times* had come through with their job offer, but the excitement of finally getting out of this tiny town was strangely absent. And the dredges of guilt that stirred in her conscience for writing the article in the first place took her completely by surprise. She'd done her job. The residents of Parker had a right to know that Abigail Harris, Lily Brand's next big thing, had walked among the community.

She turned into her room, switching on the lamp as she kicked off her sneakers and pulled off her pants, pausing as she stared at herself in the mirror. Maybe the murmurs she'd heard about poor, sweet Abby had twisted her stomach some. Perhaps the fact that Mary was pissed and Jerrod drove off in a huff didn't exactly sit well. And no matter how she'd tried to charm her way out of trouble with Timmy, he hadn't taken the bait. She frowned. Why did Timmy's curt words and disappointing stares bug her the most? Why the hell did she care what Jerrod's baby brother thought one way or the other? She didn't, absolutely didn't.

Shaking off her sudden attack of guilt, she moved toward the master bath, reaching for the light when her cell phone rang in the living room. She ignored it, hoping Timmy would get the hint. She stepped in the pretty space, catching a movement out of the corner of her eye as a huge, rough hand covered her mouth, slamming her back against a solid chest. Her eyes went huge as she gasped, trying to scream.

"Stay quiet," a deep voice hissed in a thick Russian accent next to her ear.

Her breath heaved in and out with the surge of adrenaline flooding her body. She automatically kicked her leg back and tried to bite at his palm.

"Stop!" The stranger whirled her around, shoving her toward the bed, the power of his push knocking her to the floor.

"Help!" She scrambled up in her bra and panties, trying to find a way around the muscled hulk advancing her way. "Help me!"

"I said shut *up*!"

She opened her mouth to scream again despite his demands and took a fist to the cheek. She groaned, seeing stars as the painful blow knocked her back to the bed.

"Perhaps now you will listen." He crawled on top of her, leaning close, breathing stale, smoky breath in her face. "When I say shut *up*, you will shut up."

She pressed her hand to the terrible, radiating ache, trembling, staring at the jagged scar along his right cheekbone, trying to think over the fear.

"Where is she?" He glared at her through mean brown eyes.

"Who?"

"Don't be stupid." He cracked her across her injured cheek and squeezed her jaw. "Abigail. Where is Abigail Harris?"

She whimpered, afraid he would break her bones as Jerrod's angry voice echoed through her head. *You have no idea what you've done, Shelby. No fucking idea.* She understood now, perfectly, as the man gripped her harder. "She left. She left town yesterday morning."

"Where did she go?"

"I don't know."

He slapped her again, yanking at her hair, bringing her face close to his. "Don't play these games with me."

"I don't *know*," she sobbed. "They left in a hurry."

"They?" He loosened his grip. "Who's they?"

"Abigail and some guy."

He narrowed his evil eyes. "What's his name?"

"I'm not sure."

He shook his head and took her hand, wrenching her fingers back until bones popped.

She screamed in agony, afraid she might pass out.

"Who is the man?"

"Jerrod," she whispered, cradling broken, dislocated fingers on her chest.

"Jerrod who?"

"I don't know his last name."

He muttered something in Russian, landing a blow to her temple, then her eye. "You are making this painful for yourself, stupid cunt. Tell me what you know, or the punishment will get worse."

"I think—I think it's Quinn." She squirmed under his heavy body, wanting to escape from his brutality, but it was no use. He was too big and strong.

"You think or you know?" He bunched his fist, threatening.

"I know." Her cell phone rang again in the next room, and she prayed Timmy would come.

"What else do you know?"

"That the person calling my phone is a cop, and he'll be here soon if I don't answer."

He smiled, his grin ferocious. "Hopefully he will think you are worth dying for."

A new wave of dread consumed her as she thought of what this monster might do to Timmy. "No."

"I want information, and you have it. Now tell me where she *is*."

"I really don't know. Jerrod took her away."

"He said nothing?"

"No, he was mad at me for writing the article."

He grabbed her hair in both hands, hollering

something she didn't understand as he rammed her head against the mattress over and over again. "Who is Jerrod Quinn?"

"He's a bodyguard," she confessed, crying, wanting this man to go away before Timmy came. Jerrod was long gone. She needed to protect Timmy.

He stopped, his breath heaving. "Where would he go?"

"I don't know Jerrod very well anymore. Maybe back to Los Angeles or New York City. He was a US Marshal there."

Another slow smile bloomed across his face. "It is a small, small world, Shelby Haggerty."

Her cell phone rang for the third time. Taking a chance, she brought her knee up as hard as she could, tagging her captive in the balls.

He crumpled forward, and she scrambled out from under him, sprinting toward the phone. She pressed 'talk' with her uninjured hand as the monster came running down the hall.

"Help me, Timmy! Help me!"

The stranger whirled her around, knocking her to the floor. She struggled to deflect his punches, tasting blood, feeling her skin swell with each agonizing blow. He hit her again and again until the world faded to a hazy gray, then went black.

~~~~

Adam smacked at his alarm, attempting to silence the ringing, and groaned, realizing his cell phone was making the incessant noise, not the damn clock. "Fuck," he muttered as he reluctantly reached for his phone, wondering what Donnelly wanted at four-fucking-thirty in the morning. He was *supposed* to be
~~~~

off duty until noon. "Yeah, hello?"

"I need information."

Adam's eyes flew open as he sat up, recognizing the dreaded Russian accent. "You're not supposed to call this number—ever."

"My situation doesn't give me much choice. It has taken me two days of dodging the police to find this phone to use."

He threw his covers back and got out of bed, pacing the small space in his room, regretting that he'd been desperate enough to make a deal with the devil. "What do you want?" But he already knew.

"Jerrod Quinn. He protects Abigail Harris."

Sweat beaded on his forehead as he glanced toward the bedroom door left ajar down the hall. "How do you know?"

"The reporter told me before I killed her. Find me Jerrod Quinn."

He swallowed, lowering his voice as he heard Jerrod's murmurs mixing with Abby's. "I'll see what I can do."

"You'll do better than that. I want the information today. I need to find that *bitch* before she ruins me."

He brought the hem of his t-shirt up to his face, wiping at the drops running down his temples. "It might take a day or two."

"A day would not be good for your sister's health. Two days would be deadly. Her baby is due very soon, yes?"

Dread iced his veins as he collapsed to the edge of his mattress, certain he was going to puke. If Dimitri touched Samantha... He sent trembling fingers through his hair as he struggled to even out his breathing. He never should have gone to that casino. Why the *fuck* did he sit his ass down at the Black Jack table? He knew better. Standing, he walked to the wall, leaning against the cold, white paint as his mind raced. He needed to end this. "I know Jerrod. I know where he is." He clenched his fist at his side.

"You know him?"

He grit his teeth, disgusted with himself. "Yes."

"This better be the truth. I'm sure I don't need to tell you your sister will die with pain if it is not."

"He's here in Manhattan. He came after the article broke in the Nebraska paper a couple days ago."

"Where?"

"I'm not exactly sure, but he calls every day asking for updates on your whereabouts."

Dimitri laughed. "The hunted hunts, I see." He chuckled again. "I am in Chicago. I will come as soon as I can. Find him quickly." The line went dead.

Adam stared at his phone, his breath rushing in and out, fighting not to throw it as he dropped to his knees with the crushing weight of despair. What the hell had he done? Would it really come down to Samantha's life for Jerrod and Abby's? Jerrod was as much family as Samantha. This wasn't supposed to have gotten so out of hand.

Gaining his feet, he dialed Samantha's number as he got dressed.

"Hello?" His sister's sleepy voice filled his ear.

"Sammy, it's Adam. You and Greg need to pack a few things and head out of town for awhile." He wiped at the tears on his cheeks.

"What?"

"We've had a case go sour. People know who you are. You need to go right now. Don't use your credit cards, just cash."

"Adam."

He squeezed his eyes shut as fear trembled in

Sammy's voice. "Please. *Please*, Sammy. This is dangerous shit."

"Okay. How long?"

As long as it would take for him to send a bullet through Dimitri's brain. "I don't know. A few days."

"Okay."

"Hurry and go."

"I will."

"I've gotta go." He wiped at his cheeks for the second time.

"Be careful."

"I will. You too." He hung up and walked down the hall, stopping next to Gavin's old room, peeking in as Jerrod wrapped a blanket around Abby's shoulders while she stood by the open window in her underwear. He rested his forehead against the doorframe, hating himself for putting one of his best friends—and the woman he clearly loved—on the line just because he couldn't kick his need to gamble.

Stepping back, he walked to the front door, desperate to walk and *think*. He would fix this. He had to make all of this go away before anything happened to anyone except for the bastard who deserved it. His stomach pitched for the second time. He was desperately afraid he might not be able to take Dimitri down.

~~~~

Abby shot up, gasping, searching frantically for Margret as her friend's wrenching cries echoed in the dark. She closed her eyes, opening them just as quickly, desperate to shake herself loose of the horrifying grips of her latest nightmare. Pressing a hand to her racing heart, she stumbled out of bed on
~~~~

weakened legs, making her way to the window, yanking it open, greedily breathing in the bracing air.

"Abby." The mattress squeaked as Jerrod stood, walking up behind her, wrapping a blanket around her trembling shoulders. "You're okay," he whispered.

"No, I'm not," she struggled to say over chattering teeth. "I'm not." She'd woken countless times over the last two nights, sweaty and terrified. Despite her own pep talks and efforts to settle in, she hadn't been able to shake the need to run away. "I don't know why this is happening. I can't figure it out." She shook her head, swiping her hair back from her sweaty brow, certain a nervous breakdown was right around the corner.

She'd fought to cope for the last forty-eight hours, but the strategies Dr. Tate taught her were little defense against the constant flashbacks. "I can't stop thinking about Margret. She's in every dream, calling for me." She wiped at the hot tears streaming down her chilled cheeks. "I keep waking up thinking I'm in that damn closet."

He turned her to him, hugging her tight. "Maybe our room is too small."

"I don't know." She pulled away from him, needing her space, wanting more fresh air.

"I'll get you a glass of water."

She nodded. "Okay."

Jerrod closed the door most of the way as he stepped out, and she sat on the bed, pressing her hands to her face, giving into her despair. If she couldn't get a grip she would be little more than the pathetic mess Alexa found at Zachary Hartwell's home months ago. Heck, she was pretty much there already. Eating had become a dreaded chore; sleeping wasn't any better. And she had no clue *why*.

Adam was loud but kind. Shane was a bit more reserved but had been nothing but sweet and welcoming since his return last night. Neither of Jerrod's friends wanted to hurt her, yet she couldn't relax her guard. She'd tried distracting her busy brain with movies and sketches to replace the designs she could no longer use—thanks to Shelby, but the need to look over her shoulder was constantly there.

The door opened, and she stiffened, preparing herself for...*what*? What was it about this place that made her so darn jumpy?

Jerrod stepped in, handing over the water. "Here you go."

"Thanks." She took the glass, drinking deep.

He closed the window and sat next to her. "Abby, what can I do to help you?"

"I don't know. I don't know what I can do to help myself." She set down the glass and rested her forehead in her hands. "I have no idea what's going on with me. I haven't had flashbacks like this since the beginning."

"Maybe we should try the living room tonight. I think the couch is a pullout." He slung his arm around her shoulders. "Just a couple more days and Ethan will have someone here." He kissed her temple. "We'll get a place of our own after that."

"Staying here is fine." She looked at him, wondering if he bought her fib.

He raised his brow.

"Okay, I *want* it to be fine." She touched his cheek. "I'm so sorry, Jerrod. I'm so sorry I'm like this." Her lips trembled in her misery.

"Hey." He grabbed hold of her chin, pulling her closer. "There's nothing wrong with you." He kissed the tip of her nose.

"There *used* to be nothing wrong with me."

"Abby, you don't give yourself enough credit."

"I don't deserve any right now." She shrugged, shaking her head, truly ashamed. "What if—what if I'm like my mother?" There were few things she feared more than the idea of following her mother down the path she'd taken.

"You always come back to that."

"I know, and I'm not exactly sure why. I don't really even remember her." She stood, huffing out a breath, needing to move. "The State took us away when I was pretty little, but I remember flashes—impressions, I guess." She grabbed the blanket, wrapping it around herself. "She used to be beautiful. I've seen pictures. Apparently she was a good mom until my dad walked out." Abby shrugged. "I remember the nasty motel she kept us in, and being hungry. She had long, black hair and awful whiskey breath. She cried and laughed and *yelled*. My mother scared the crap out of me." She swallowed as she looked to the window, then at Jerrod again. "She called me Abby Dabby. I remember that distinctly. Then she shut herself in the bathroom and slit her wrists, with her little girls in the next room. The coroners brought her out zipped in a black bag. I wasn't supposed to see that, but I did."

"Abigail." Jerrod stood, walking to her, sliding gentle hands down her arms. "Your mother was mentally ill, and an alcoholic on top of that. You absolutely aren't either of those things." He brushed tender fingers over her cheeks.

"But how did it start? How did she get that way?" That's what scared her most—her lack of knowing or understanding.

"I'm not sure, but you're not like your mother."

"Sometimes I think I might be," she murmured, looking down. "It terrifies me."

He lifted her chin until their eyes met. "I wish you could see what I see. I wish you saw the strong, beautiful woman I do. This is a rough patch, Abby—another tough spot you're going to make it through."

She stared into Jerrod's steady blue eyes, loving him as she loved no other. "Do you know how lucky I am?" She stood on her tiptoes, pressing her lips to his. "What would I do without you?" She brought his mouth back to hers, clinging when he deepened the kiss.

She drew away, giving him the first sincere smile she'd had since they left the farm. "Come on," she whispered, pulling him the two steps to the bed. "Let's go back to sleep. There's a fifty-fifty shot I'll make it until the sun comes up without a nightmare."

He lay down, snuggling her to him. "If you don't, I'll be right here."

She kissed him again, savoring the comfort only he could bring. "I know." She laid her head on his chest, listening to his heartbeat as they held each other close. She made it until sunrise before the next wave of terror woke her.

Chapter Twenty-One

JERROD RELAXED IN HIS OLD RECLINER, SOCKS ON, ANKLES crossed in jeans and a long-sleeved t-shirt while he and Shane watched an action flick on TV. The noisy commotion of a skyscraper blowing up echoed through the room in surround sound, as Bruce Willis found himself trapped in the crosshairs of danger. Seconds later the movie cut to a commercial break.

"Damn it. I hate when that happens," Shane complained, dropping his long, muscular legs from the coffee table as he bit the chicken from the last meaty hot wing.

"Some bastard down at the broadcast studio did that just to piss you off," Jerrod said, snagging his bottled water on the floor at his side.

Shane wiped his mouth on a paper towel, his bold green eyes full of fun as he grinned at Jerrod. "Probably."

"Why don't you just stream the movie? Then Bruce can kick ass without interruption."

"Quinn." Shane shook his head. "Always so practical."

He chuckled, glancing at Abby while she sat hovered over the tiny kitchen table in her gray hoodie and snug jeans, drawing with frantic, jerky sweeps of pencil to paper. His smile vanished as the overhead light accentuated her pale cheeks and dark under eye circles. She paused, swiping at loose strands falling from her ponytail, then got back to sketching as if her life depended on it.

He exhaled a long, helpless breath. She hadn't moved from her spot all day, even when he'd invited her to sit with him and relax for a while. She'd insisted on working; her deadlines were approaching quickly. He knew as well as Abby that her designs were no longer about Fashion Week and the *Escape* line. Each dress, shirt, or outfit she created was a desperate attempt to distract herself from the constant flood of flashbacks.

They'd been in the city less than forty-eight hours, and Abby was a mess. He couldn't remember the last time she'd laughed, and each smile was strained. The slightest sounds made her jump. He'd caught her glancing over her shoulder more than once. And the endless nightmares. She'd awoken again at dawn, screaming, drenched in sweat, her eyes glazed with terror. She was suffering, and he didn't know how to help.

He'd toyed with the idea of taking her back to LA while he hugged her close in bed, soothing her as she sobbed hopelessly curled against his chest. Staying here clearly wasn't working, but leaving posed too many risks. Until Task Force brought in Dimitri or Ethan sent backup, he and Abby were better off here in the apartment.

"Can you pass me the chips?" Shane held out his hand.

Jerrod reached forward, snagging the bag of Fritos, tossing them over. "So, how are things going with the Dubov case? Any more progress?"

Abby's head whipped up, her gaze locking with Jerrod's as he said Dimitri's name. She swiped at her hair again and got back to work.

"We haven't heard jack shit in weeks."

Jerrod paused with the bottle of water to his lips, frowning. "On Dimitri Dubov?"

Shane shook his head. "Nothing. Task Force was hot on him down in Houston and Miami, I think back in October, maybe early November, then everything fizzled." He scooped up more hot chili dip and bit in, talking with his mouth full. "They missed him by fifteen or twenty minutes on both attempts. Someone tipped him off; they had to. He's been off the radar ever since." Shane went after the dip again, scooping, stuffing his face.

He knew about October and November. Adam had told him, just like he told him about the surveillance Task Force started earlier this week. "Are you sure we're talking about the same Dimitri Dubov?"

"Mid-Atlantic Sex Ring," Shane confirmed, grabbing his beer as the commercial ended and the movie came back on, picking up where the action left off. A spray of bullets filled the room as the building tumbled and cars exploded on impact.

Jerrod no longer paid attention to the carnage on the television as he played through his conversation with Shane and the information Adam had shared over the last few days. Someone had bad information; it had to be Shane. He was US Marshal. Adam was Immigration and Customs Enforcement. ICE typically got their hands on the details first when it came to cases like Dubov's. He wanted to shrug his shoulders and chalk up the last five minutes to a miscommunication between the two agencies. Crap like that happened all the time, but the sudden weight settling on his chest urged him to make sure. Righting himself in the chair, he stood, starting down the hall.

"You all right, man?"

"Yeah. I just need to use the john." He closed himself in the small room and pulled from his pocket another pay-as-you-go phone he'd purchased at La Guardia, dialing Ethan.

"Cooke."

"I need you to access a couple of files for me—ICE. Fugitive Task Force. Dimitri Dubov. What do they have on him?"

"I thought your pal was keeping you in the loop."

He rubbed at the back of his neck, attempting to banish the stirrings of unease. "I thought so too, but I've heard a couple of things; now I'm not so sure."

"This is going to take me a couple of minutes." Ethan tapped at the keys as two minutes ticked into three. "I'm almost through the first firewall." He continued typing as time ticked away. "Okay, I'm in. Dubov. Dimitri. Active file."

"Are there any recent traces on him?"

"Looks like they almost had him in Houston—mid-October, then again in Miami in early November. An informant called in a tip to Miami PD on November third. Fugitive Task Force put a team together and moved on it right away. The guy who snitched was found full of bullets on November fourth."

Jerrod ran a hand through his hair. Ethan's information matched Shane's. "Are you sure, man?"

"I'm reading the file."

"There's nothing else? What about a trace earlier this week and surveillance?"

"I don't see anything."

He jammed his hand in his pocket. This didn't make any damn sense. "Who was in on the attempted apprehensions? Who made up the teams?"

"Local PD—"

"Give me the ICE agents."

"I'm seeing Gabe Lorimar in on Houston and Gerry Groves in Miami. Adam Merriwhether flew down from Manhattan. He was in on both."

Someone tipped him off. They had to. Shane's words echoed in Jerrod's head as the hair stood up on the back of his neck. Adam was the common denominator in both failed attempts to apprehend Dimitri, and he'd been feeding him bullshit for the last week. "I need to call you back."

"What's up?"

"I'm not sure." He glanced around, looking in the corners of the room, feeling around on top of the cabinets, under the towels and sink, wondering if the house was bugged. The fact that he was checking made him nauseous. "I'll call you later."

"Okay."

He stepped from the bathroom, moving across the hall into Gavin's old room, yanking open drawers, peering inside as he patted around the tops of wood. He searched the small closet and tipped the lamp for cameras or listening devices, finding nothing, but that didn't mean there wasn't something here. He put on his shoes and snagged his holster, sliding it over his shoulders, then checked his weapon, shoving the pistol into the leather holder.

He slid on his coat, taking Abby's from the hanger, and grabbed her purse, pausing. Was this really happening? He scrubbed his hands over his face as the idea of Adam being dirty shook him to the core. As much as he didn't want to believe it, the possibility was definitely there. He needed to get Abby out of here until he could think everything through and figure out what the hell was going on.

Stepping from the room, he walked down the hall

toward Abby, studying Shane still stuffing his face, his shocking green eyes glued to the movie and his short brown hair standing in messy spikes. He wasn't sure if his former roommate was friend or foe. If Adam was dirty, was Shane too? He stopped next to Abby's seat at the table and brushed his fingers down her arm.

She stopped drawing, looking up.

He gave her a small smile. "Come on."

She closed her sketchpad and stood like a shot. "What's wrong?"

"Nothing. I thought you might like to get some fresh air."

She held his eyes, nodding. "Okay."

"You heading out, Quinn?"

He looked at Shane lounging on the couch, his sturdy boxer's build filling out his ratty Marshals t-shirt. They'd been friends for three years. Or maybe they hadn't. "I'm taking Abby out for a bite to eat and a walk."

"You want company?"

"Nah, we're just going up to the Thai place on West 68th." He took Abby's hand and started toward the door. "We might grab a movie after."

"Call if you change your mind."

"You know I will."

Abby zipped up and pulled the bright red hat mom knitted her from her pocket.

He gave her a barely perceptible shake of his head, and she shoved it back. "We'll be back in a couple hours."

"See ya later."

Jerrod closed the door behind them, wanting to hurry to the elevator, but kept his pace slow and easy. There were cameras all over the building. If someone was keeping an eye on them, he wasn't about to let them know he was on to them.

"What are we—"

"It's been a while since we've eaten out. You'll like this place," he interrupted as they stepped in the elevator, checking his watch. He wanted them long gone before Adam came home.

Abby clutched his hand tighter in hers, knowing him too well not to understand that something was up.

He pulled her into a hug, sensing her tension, brushing his thumb along her skin, reassuring her the only way he could.

The doors slid open after the endless decent, and they stepped out, heading directly into the bitter cold as the sun sank in the sky. He wrapped his arm around her shoulders, protecting her from the winds as much as from the unknown, his eyes scanning as they joined the hundreds of pedestrians on their way home for the evening.

"What's going on, Jerrod?" She asked quietly.

"I'm not sure, but we're going to walk until I figure it out."

"Did they find me?"

He was starting to wonder if he'd brought her right to the men they'd been trying to avoid all along, but he wasn't about to tell her that. "No."

"Then—"

"Take your hair down," he said as he picked up his pace, moving into a large grouping of people, intentionally pushing them to the center of the pack.

"What?"

"Pull the elastic from your hair." If they had a tail, they would loose them easier without a visual point to follow. Red hats and ponytails were easy to spot.

She did as he asked.

Steering her right, they crossed at West 68th as he'd told Shane they would, but they passed the Thai restaurant and kept going, heading up another block, then one more before Jerrod pulled the phone from his pocket and let it fall to the sidewalk among the crowds. "Let's grab a cab." Instead of holding up his hand, he walked them into standstill traffic, weaving around cars, searching for a vacant taxi as pedestrians crossed at the crosswalk. Spotting an empty cab, he opened the door, letting Abby in before him. "Rockefeller Center," he instructed the driver as he glanced out the windows, satisfied they were lost among the sea of yellow taxis.

"What's at Rockefeller Center?" Abby asked, her eyes full of questions and worry as she stared at him.

"Distance."

"Distance," she repeated, nodding, and gripped her hands together in her lap.

"We're okay, Abby." He slid an arm around her, tugging her closer to his side, wanting her to relax. She laid her head on his shoulder and hooked her arms around him, clinging as she had the night they arrived in the city.

He wedged his body in the corner, changing their positions so she stretched out and rested her cheek against his chest while he cradled her. "We'll find another place to stay," he murmured, running his fingers through her soft hair, looking out the window as the car inched its way through the stop-and-go traffic. His mind raced through the events of the last five days, trying to make sense of it all. Adam told him the Task Force was running surveillance on Dimitri, which was a bunch of bullshit. Adam had more or less lured him to the city with his false information and offers to help out with Abby.

He shifted in his spot, glancing down, realizing Abby's grip had relaxed. He stared down at her beautiful face as she slept, struggling to keep still in his restlessness. No matter how he tried to convince himself that there had to be a reasonable explanation or he was missing some vital piece of information, he couldn't shake the sickening dread that Adam and possibly Shane were mixed up with Dimitri Dobov, Victor Bobco, and what was left of the Mid-Atlantic Sex Ring.

He'd never flat-out told anyone that Abby was the Abigail Harris due to testify against Lorenzo Cruz, but his former roommates were smart enough to put the pieces together when he started asking for the whereabouts of the ring's missing men. He'd been in contact with Adam for months, never sharing vital information, but still... If Adam was playing for the wrong side...

He looked out as the cabbie slowed, frowning, then glanced at his watch as they approached the bustle of Rockefeller Center. Forty-five minutes had passed in a blink. "Abby." He kissed her forehead. "Abby, we're here."

Her eyes flew open and she sat up, looking around. "Where are we?"

"Rockefeller Center, remember?"

She yawned hugely, then gave him a smile. "I do now." She turned her wrist, looking at her watch. "I guess I fell asleep."

"The snoring was embarrassing, and the drooling..." He wiped at his shirt in mock disgust.

She rewarded him with a grin, the first one he'd seen in days, as the cab pulled up to the curb.

"Thank you," Jerrod said, paying their fare as they stepped out into the bitter cold, walking two blocks north. He hailed another taxi as Abby's teeth chattered and she shivered at his side. "Nine-Eleven Memorial," he said as they took their place in the backseat and headed south.

"Why are we doing this?"

"I don't want to be found."

She shook her head. "You don't want Adam and Shane to find us?"

"I don't know." He met the driver's eyes in the rearview mirror. "I have some stuff to figure out."

"Like what?"

"We'll talk about it later." He gestured toward the cabbie.

"Fine." She sat further back against the seat, staring out the window.

Another hour passed in silence as Jerrod periodically glanced out the back window, searching for anything resembling a tail, though it would be almost impossible to tell in the chaotic city traffic.

They got out at the memorial, walked four blocks east, bought another phone, and took their last cab. "The Ritz."

Abby's eyes widened as she looked at him.

He shrugged. "Might as well do this right." Adam wouldn't be searching for him in a luxury hotel—if he were searching for him at all. And if Abby relaxed even a fraction and ate a real meal, tonight would be worth it.

Moments later the cab pulled up in front of the majestic building. They got out, walking quickly to the entrance in their hustle to escape the chill rolling off the Hudson Bay a couple hundred yards away. The doorman pushed open the glass door.

"Good evening, ma'am, sir."

"Good evening." They stepped inside, instantly

cloaked by elegant warmth. Dark wood, marble floors, candles, and pretty white flowers arranged in crystal vases added to the ambiance of comfort and luxury.

"This is beautiful." Abby beamed.

"Not bad," he said as they walked to the black granite desk.

"Good evening, sir." The suit-clad gentleman smiled politely as he looked them up and down in their jeans and casual jackets.

"Hi. We need a room." He pulled out his Ethan Cooke Security credit card.

"Do you have reservations?"

"No."

"Okay." The attendant tapped at his keyboard. "It looks like we have a couple of expanded one-bedroom suites available tonight. Last-minute cancellations."

"Does a suite sound good to you, honey?" Jerrod winked at Abby.

"Uh, yes." She smiled at him.

"We'll take it."

"I need to see an ID, Sir."

Jerrod handed over his license and bodyguard identification. "We'll need to keep the registration out of the system."

The man looked from him to Abby and back. "Let me call my supervisor." He picked up the phone.

"Sure." He should have had Ethan set this up, but that hadn't been an option. The Ritz was used to dealing with high-profile discretion—another reason he'd brought Abby here. No one would know they checked in except for the man standing in front of them and the woman stepping out of the office down the hall. And in moments only the woman in her navy blue power suit would know where they were located in the building.

"Good evening, Sir." The pretty blond smiled at him, then looked from his license to his bodyguard identification. She tapped several buttons on the computer and smiled again. "It looks like you're all set." She slid a card over without revealing a room number, and also passed back his identification and credit card. He and Abigail were officially invisible patrons. "If you'll follow me, please."

He took Abby's hand as they followed the manager through a door and down a long hall to a private elevator. She used a key to access the door. "If you need anything at all, please let us know. Room service will know you as Mr. Smith."

"Thank you." They stepped inside, and he pressed the button, taking them to the sixteenth floor. The doors slid open, and they walked to their room. He stepped in, turning on the light, scanning the posh space decorated in dark wood and different shades of blue. "Come on in."

Abby grinned as she closed the door behind her. "This is *beautiful*. And look at our view." She hurried over to the windows with her usual enthusiasm. "The Statue of Liberty." She turned and rushed into his arms. "This is amazing, Jerrod. Thank you for this."

"You're welcome." He eased her back, stroking his fingers along her cheeks. "Tonight it's just you and me. I want you to relax." He kissed her forehead. "I want you to go in and take a bath. We're going to order in some damn fine food and enjoy the hell out of this." Or he would try to.

"It's a date."

He smiled, relieved to see Abby's eyes bright and her shoulders relaxed. "I'm going to make some calls while you soak in that monster tub."

"I'm willing to accept this mission, Captain." She

saluted and closed the door most of the way.

Seconds later, he heard water splash against marble as he pulled the new phone from the plastic, grabbed the card, punched in the information, and dialed Ethan.

"Cooke."

"We're secure for now at the Ritz."

"What the hell's going on?"

"I don't know." He shook his head. "Adam told me the Task Force was on Dimitri's tail. Supposedly they were running surveillance on two suspected locations they thought he might be at. This afternoon Shane told me they haven't heard anything on Dubov or Bobco since November. After talking to you it turns out Shane's right and Adam's not."

"Sounds sketchy."

"That's why Abby and I left." He sighed, rubbing at his jaw. I'm trying to figure out Adam's angle. Why would he make shit up?"

"I hate to say it, man, but it sounds like he's playing both sides."

"It sure as hell does, doesn't it?" He sat on the couch, closing his eyes, as Ethan confirmed what he already knew.

"What do you want to do?"

"Hang here until you can get me someone."

"I can have Stone there tomorrow night."

"I'll take him." The phone beeped in his ear, alerting him to his low balance and battery power. "I need you to add minutes to the phone. I'll text you the serial number."

"Do you think you're safe until tomorrow?"

"I don't see why we wouldn't be. We changed cabs three times, and we're here unlisted. I don't plan on leaving this room until Stone knocks on the door." He walked to the bathroom, peaking in at Abby lying in a sea of bubbles, her eyes closed, her cheeks pink, smiling, humming. “Abby needs this. Being at the apartment wasn’t working for her.” He battled his guilt. Somehow she had known something was off, and he’d ignored it. “I thought bringing her to Manhattan would be a good idea. I thought my friends help and the anonymity would be the best thing. I was wrong.”

“There’s no way you could’ve known. No one expects their bothers to be dirty bastards.”

“Yeah.” He pressed a hand to his stomach, struggling with the sharp twist of betrayal.

“I’ll get you those minutes. Stone’s flight is already booked for nine tomorrow morning.”

“Thanks.” He hung up, expelling a deep breath, part relief, part disbelief. Help was on the way, but some sixty blocks north Adam probably waited for him and Abby to walk back into his trap.

CHAPTER TWENTY-TWO

ABBY RELEASED THE STOPPER, RIDDING THE TUB OF MOST of the bubbles. She turned on the faucet, rinsing the remaining suds from her body, and stood. She wrapped the huge towel around herself as she looked out at the New Jersey lights across the Hudson Bay. Closing her eyes, she sighed, savoring the sense of peace she hadn't felt since her last night on the farm.

For the first time in two days her head didn't throb, and her stomach didn't ache. Now that she was relaxed, she craved food. She'd done her best to gag down little bits of cereal or a sandwich at the apartment, but she needed something more substantial. With her nausea gone, she had every intention of stuffing herself full of fabulous five-star cuisine.

Jerrod had yet to share why he'd brought her to the Ritz in the first place, but as she glanced around at fresh-cut flowers and sniffed at the soothing tropical scent lingering from her bath, she didn't care. Pretending everything was perfectly fine for a few hours wasn't going to hurt anyone. Their problems would still be daunting when they woke tomorrow. Tonight she wanted a nice meal with the man she adored. Tonight she and Jerrod had a date.

She stepped closer to the door, peeking into the sitting area, smiling as Jerrod lay sprawled on the couch, shoes off, arm behind his head, asleep with the television murmuring in the background. The poor guy was exhausted. He needed a quiet evening as much as she did. The last couple of days had been draining for both of them. Adam and Shane's hospitality was appreciated, but this was definitely better. It was almost as if they were finally home in their condo, but here someone else was in charge of the cooking and cleaning up.

Smiling, she turned away, glancing at her jeans and the oversized sweatshirt she'd folded and set on the chair, then at the matching "his" and "her" robes. This was totally an eat-in-your-robe kind of night. She pulled the soft terrycloth from the hanger, groaning as she enfolded herself in sheer pleasure, pulling the belt tight, rolling the huge sleeves to her wrists.

Satisfied and ready for tonight to begin, she opened the door wider, tiptoeing to the phone and room service menu by the table at Jerrod's side. She flipped to the entrées, perusing her options as she settled herself on the arm of the couch.

Jerrod's eyes flew open, and he sat up. "What's wrong? Are you okay?"

She studied his sleepy blue eyes and smiled. "I'm perfect. And hungry." She held up the menu, wiggling it.

He scrubbed at his face and reached for her hand. "Let's see what they have."

She slid onto the cushion next to him, her arm brushing his as she opened the thin book in her lap. "I saw a spinach and gnocchi dish that sounds amazing."

He wrinkled his nose. "Rabbit food."

"The best stuff around."

"I need a *steak*."

"I think I'll start with a shrimp cocktail." Her eyes stopped on the desserts. "Oh, my. They have a triple chocolate pyramid."

"You should probably get it." He bumped her with his elbow.

She nibbled her lip, contemplating. "Will you share it with me?"

"Try and stop me." He stood, picked up the phone, and dialed room service. "We'll make the call before you change your mind." He winked. "Yes. I'd like to place an order. I'll take two shrimp cocktails, the spinach and gnocchi deal, the NY Strip—medium—and the triple chocolate pyramid." He turned toward the window, rubbing at the back of his neck. "No, I think that'll do it. Thanks." He hung up, stretching his shoulders, letting loose a barely perceptible sigh as he turned back, meeting her stare, smiling again.

She narrowed her eyes a fraction, noting the strain behind his gestures as she glanced toward the coffee table, looking at his weapon. As much as she wanted to ignore reality and pretend tonight was theirs, she needed to know what was going on. Patting the cushion next to her, she gestured with her head. "Come on back."

He sat down.

She snuggled up against his side and kissed his cheek. "How are you?

"Good." He hooked his arm around her waist, pulling her closer.

"You don't seem fine." She played with his fingers as she peeked up from under her lashes.

"I'm just a little tired."

He held his body rigid, and his typically easy gaze was sharp and alert despite the quiet of their extravagant sixteenth-floor surroundings. There was more going on than sleep deprivation, but she nodded anyway. "The last couple of nights haven't been very restful."

"No." He pressed his lips to her forehead.

She eased back, smiling, looking into his eyes. "Is there anything you wanna talk about, big guy?"

He shrugged. "Can't think of anything."

She traced his ear with the pad of her finger. "You seem tense."

He shook his head. "Nope. I just need to catch a solid stretch of Zs." He settled himself more comfortably against the cushion.

She moved her fingers to his clenched jaw. Jerrod wasn't ready to talk, so they would move on—for now. "How about a shoulder rub?"

"This right here works pretty well for me." He lifted his head, sniffing at her neck. "You smell good."

"Thanks. She moved out of his grip. "Take off your shirt."

He raised his brow. "Dinner will be here in twenty minutes."

She chuckled. "Just do it."

He tugged his t-shirt free of his jeans and pulled it off.

A rush of sexy tingles swarmed her belly as she tracked her gaze over the bumps and ridges of his mouthwatering torso. No matter how many times she touched and tasted his gorgeous body, she wanted more. Crawling behind him, she sat on the back of the couch, ready to rub her hands all over his skin. "Prepare to enjoy," she said, squeezing his tight, solid shoulders.

He groaned. "God, that feels *amazing*."

"Good." She concentrated on the knots along his shoulder blades, then slid her fingers up and down his neck.

He moaned, letting his head fall forward.

She smiled as the muscles in his back unclenched by degrees.

"You have magic hands, Abigail." He looked back at her.

"Better?"

"Much."

"That's what I was hoping for."

"Mission accomplished."

She moved from her perch on the couch and crawled into his lap, hooking her legs around his waist. "I like this." She settled her arms around his neck. "Just the two of us again."

"Me too." He kissed her.

She drew back. "Why is it just the two of us? Why are we here instead of with your friends?"

He held her gaze, sliding fingers through her hair, sighing. "I wanted us to have a night away. You don't seem very relaxed at the apartment."

"I'm not, but I was managing."

He arched his brow. "Barely."

She shrugged. There was no use denying what they both knew. "There's something about being there that makes me uncomfortable. I don't know what it is."

"So tonight we're taking a break." He traced the lapel of her robe, pulling her in for another kiss. "I talked to Ethan while you were in the bath. Stone's coming tomorrow."

"Stone?"

"He's a little rough around the edges, but he knows what he's doing."

She'd met Jerrod's co-worker a handful of times. He was handsome and gritty—like a dark prince—yet he didn't make her uneasy the way Adam did. "Stone doesn't bother me."

"Good." He nipped at her jaw with playful bites.

She glanced out the window, staring at Lady Liberty lit up in the dark as he skimmed his fingers along her jaw and down her neck. "We have a great view."

"It's pretty," he murmured, snagging her earlobe. "We'll have to take advantage of the telescope when the sun comes up."

She closed her eyes, shivering, her skin humming beneath his heated breath and wandering hands. "Definitely."

He gripped her chin between his thumb and finger, bringing her mouth to his, kissing her slowly, his tongue seeking hers, coaxing hers to dance at his unhurried pace.

She slid her palms along his shoulders, letting loose a purr as he took her deeper, pulling her closer as each dive of his tongue grew more urgent. She captured his bottom lip, tugging, suckling as her hands continued their journey down his pecs and over his stomach, enjoying the way his muscles jumped and tensed. She moved lower to the edge of his jeans.

"Abby," he whispered, going still.

"Hmm." She unfastened the snap and dipped her fingers into his boxers, brushing the tip of him, liking the idea of taking charge.

"Abigail, dinner will be here in a few minutes."

She held his heated stare, biting her lip, smiling. "I guess I should probably get started then." She untangled herself from his lap and got to her knees, settling herself between his thighs as she rained kisses over his chest, sliding her tongue down the line of his six pack, nibbling at the skin just above the elastic of his underwear. Tugging on his clothes, she pulled jeans and boxers past his hips, stopping mid-thigh.

She traced him with her finger, then rubbed gently with her palm as she looked into his eyes. "I like touching you. I love the way you taste."

He clenched his jaw, swallowing.

She sent him another slow smile and went to work, taking him deep, reveling in the heady satisfaction of his fingers curling in her hair and his sharp intake of breath.

"Abby," he grit out.

She glanced up as she continued, gripping him in a tight hand.

"God, Abigail," he hissed, closing his eyes, letting his head fall back as his thighs flexed with her steady up and down movements.

She changed her pace, slow, then fast, her reward his sharp, unsteady exhales.

"Abby," he moaned, his hips rocking. "Abby, I'm going to come."

She kept her pace steady as his frantic fingers clutched at her hair, urging her to hurry.

"God. Mmm," he gasped, jerking as he let himself go.

She slowed, staring at him as he looked at her. "Did that work for you, big guy?"

"I'll let you know when my eyes uncross."

She smiled.

"I should—" Someone knocked at the door, cutting him off. He stiffened, automatically grabbing his gun, instantly on alert.

The easy moment was lost as she moved to the side and he stood, pulling up his pants, zipping his jeans closed. "Go ahead and wait in the bedroom for a minute." He peered through the security hole, waiting for her to do as he asked.

She got to her feet and walked to the bedroom,

shutting herself in slightly, watching through the crack as Jerrod secured his weapon in the back waist of his pants and opened the door. He made polite conversation while the waiter set up their plates and lit a candle in the center of the small table. Smiling, Jerrod signed the bill, his eyes cool and guarded the entire time. Something new was definitely up. She planned to have the whole story after their meal.

Jerrod let the man out, locking up after him as she stepped from the bedroom, breathing in the delicious scent of grilled meat and savory herbs, trying to ignore the sinking feeling settling in her stomach. She still longed for one normal night.

"Dinner smells amazing," she said, wanting desperately to hang on to her illusions.

"It looks great too." He shoved his wallet away.

She took his hand, walking with him to the table. "Should we eat?"

He tossed her a bland look, and she laughed.

"I'll take that as a yes."

They pushed in, picked up their forks, and she dug in, savoring plump shrimp and every sinful bite of spinach-stuffed gnocchi in a rich cream sauce, despite the silence in the room. She glanced Jerrod's way several times, hoping to catch his eye as he cut bite after bite, but he was too distracted.

"Is it good?" he finally asked over a mouthful of steak and baked potato as she forked up the last dumpling.

"Definitely."

"Good."

She swallowed, wiping her mouth.

"Don't forget your dessert."

She pressed a hand to her bloated stomach. "I'm so *full*."

"One bite?"

She nodded. "Okay."

He slid his fork through layers of smooth ganache, thick mousse, and the solid dark-chocolate bottom. "Open up."

She took the piece, closed her eyes and let it melt on her tongue. "I think I could easily eat every bite."

The dish touched her hand as Jerrod slid it her way.

"But then I'd be sick as a dog, so I'll let you go after it, champ."

"I'm always willing to help out." He pulled the plate back and sampled. "Wow. This is amazing."

"Everything was."

Jerrod ate the last of the dessert and sat back in his chair. "I'm stuffed."

"I didn't know that was possible."

He smiled. "It's rare, but it happens." Holding her gaze, he touched her hand. "This was nice."

"Yeah." Sort of. The food was delicious and their view amazing, but Jerrod was somewhere else, rolling through the motions of their 'special night.'

"I'm going to hop in the shower. Why don't you pick us out a movie?"

"I don't want a movie." She wanted to feel connected.

"I thought we could at least pretend." He smiled again and stood. "I'll shower up while your food settles. We don't want any cramping in the bedroom."

She grinned, hoping they were back on track. "Sounds serious."

"Extremely." He leaned over the table and kissed her. "Door stays locked. Don't let anyone in. No one."

She rolled her eyes. "I know the drill."

"I'm just reminding you."

"Check." She made an exaggerated checkmark in the air.

He went to the bathroom, and she stood, walking to the bedroom, moving the shams to the foot of the bed, then pulled back the pretty navy toned comforter, sighing, struggling with her frustration. This *sucked*. She wanted one simple evening without guns and safety reminders. They couldn't even be intimate without rehashing the rules keeping her alive. No matter where they were or how fancy their surroundings, she was still Lorenzo Cruz's prisoner.

Picking up a pillow, she tossed it down with a huff and wandered back to the sitting area as the shower shut off. As she walked toward the bathroom, Jerrod's cell phone rang. She stopped outside the door, listening, knowing she shouldn't.

"...expect him around five-thirty. Just tell him to give this number a call. I'll let the manager know to let him up. Great. No. I've been thinking about it though. I can't think of much else. Adam likes to gamble. He's gotten himself into some trouble in the past. I'm wondering if he got in over his head again. That's the only thing that makes sense—if he actually has anything to do with this at all."

Frowning, she inched closer. Adam? Was Jerrod's best friend after her? And what about Shane? Had she and Jerrod been staying with the people who wanted her dead? She gripped the doorframe as her knees buckled and her stomach churned with the possibilities.

"...yeah. Later." Jerrod opened the door, slamming into her, a long towel wrapped at his waist. "Whoa." He gripped her arms, preventing her from falling over.

The scent of soap filled her nose as he held her close. "Is Adam part of the ring?"

He blew out a deep breath as he looked into her eyes. "I don't know."

"But he could be."

"I don't want to think so, but yes, he could be."

"Why? What makes you say that?"

He took her hand, walking with her to the couch, pulling her to the cushion next to him. "Adam's stories aren't adding up. He told me the Task Force was actively running surveillance on Dimitri. This afternoon Shane told me they haven't heard anything since November. I double-checked with Ethan. Task Force has no idea where he is."

"You think Adam's protecting Dimitri?"

"The idea crossed my mind. The Task Force almost had him twice, and they lost him at the last minute. Shane thinks he was tipped off. So do I. Adam was part of both attempted apprehensions."

She pressed her fingers to her temple, trying to take it all in. "What about Shane?"

He shook his head. "I don't think so, but I can't be sure."

She stood and walked to the window, unable to fully believe that this was actually happening. Was there no one they could trust? "What are we going to do?"

"Sit tight and wait for Stone to get here."

"What about the trial? Adam knows who I am. He knows I'm the Prosecution's star witness."

He walked to her, laying his hands on her shoulders. "We're going to get this figured out."

"Before or after I'm dead?"

He turned her to him. "Nothing's going to happen to you, Abby. Nothing."

"No?" Tears filled her eyes as hopelessness consumed her. "I used to tell myself that, and for a long time I believed it. Now I'm not so sure."

"I won't let anything happen." He pulled her into a hug. "I won't."

She wrapped her arms around him and held on. "I hate this for both of us. I want a normal life. I want to be here in the city with you because we both love it. I want to be in this hotel for a romantic evening because that's what we've chosen, not because we're hiding from men who want me dead and will happily take you out as well."

He eased her back. "We can still enjoy the city. It's all around us. We can still have a romantic evening. Tonight's for you, for us." He kissed her lips. "Just for us, Abigail. Like the night at the farm."

She stared into his eyes, wondering how many more nights they would have. Despite Jerrod's assurances that everything would work out fine, she was beginning to wonder if either of them would make it out of this situation alive. The men they were supposed to trust—his *friends*—were potentially involved with the wrong side. They had tonight, but nothing else was guaranteed. "Take me to bed."

He kissed her forehead, her nose, her cheeks and chin.

"Take me to bed," she repeated as she pulled his mouth to hers as tears fell down her cheeks.

"Hey." He cupped her face in his hands. "Don't give up on me."

"I'm trying not to."

"You aren't going anywhere, Abby. In six months from now your *Escape* line will be running full throttle. You'll be walking in and out of stores on your own. You're just getting started."

She rested her forehead on his chest, gripping her fingers against his towel, too afraid to hope.

"Abby."

She couldn't stem the flood of emotion.

"Come here." He picked her up, carrying her to the bed, laying her down. He crawled next to her, settling himself at her side, stroking his fingers through her hair. "I thought you weren't giving up on me."

"Do you want children?" She blurted out of nowhere.

His hand paused, then kept moving. "Yes. Someday."

"Alexa's having a boy." She sniffled as she thought of her sister, wondering where this was coming from. "She and Jackson are going to have the family she's always wanted. Olivia and Owen. Their little girl and little boy." Tears spilled again. "What if I don't get the chance to have my own Olivia and Owen?"

"You might not. You might have two Olivias or two Owens. You never know what you're going to get."

She gave him a small smile. "I want a family, Jerrod. I want to have that chance."

"You'll get it."

"You seem so sure."

"I can't let myself believe anything else. I can't let you either." He gripped her chin between his fingers, giving her a gentle shake.

"There's a lot at stake." She grabbed his wrist, holding on. "I want us both to be okay."

"I've never lost anyone I've protected." He wiped her tears away. "And I wasn't in love with them, Abigail."

Her heart stuttered as her eyes widened. "You're—you're in love with me?"

He nodded. "Oh, yeah."

She sniffled and smiled as he gave her the words she'd longed to hear but wasn't sure she ever would. "Well, I guess that's a good thing, because I love you too."

He grinned, kissing her. "That is pretty handy."

She took his cheeks in her hands, peppering him with more playful kisses. "Jerrod Quinn loves me."

"Damn right I do." He pulled her on top of him and rolled, smooshing her into the mattress, brushing the hair back from her temple. "What do you say we pick up where we left off?"

"I'm okay with that."

"Good," he murmured, nibbling at her bottom lip, then traced with his tongue.

She closed her eyes, relishing the weight of his powerful body covering hers, his taste, everything about this magical moment that belonged to them as she caressed the solid muscles of his back.

He parted her robe, circling her nipples with the pads of his thumbs, sampling one breast, then the other.

"That feels good," she whispered, freeing him of the soft cotton, craving the feel of his skin pressed to hers as her limbs grew weighty with each ripple of arousal.

Mouths met again, and she played her fingers through his hair as he slid his hand down, dipping inside her.

She tipped her head back with a gasp, gripping his shoulders as the ache built with the languid coaxing of each skilled sweep, each movement taking her higher until she crested sweetly on a quiet moan. "Be with me," she whispered, still breathless, staring into his eyes. "Be inside me." Despite their promises to protect themselves she wanted this.

He captured her mouth and pushed himself forward.

Whimpering, she took him in, clasping their fingers as he moved slowly, each gentle thrust drawing out their pleasure as she ached for release. "Come with me. Come with me," she shuddered out, teetering on the edge.

He pressed his forehead to hers, clenching his jaw, groaning, filling her as
they rode out the staggering wave together.

They breathed each other's breath, holding their gaze. "I love you, Abby."

She smiled. "I love you too." She kissed his cheek. "Do you know what I want?"

"Uh, I need a minute."

Grinning, she shook her head, content, relaxed. "I want you to wrap your arms around me so we can go to sleep."

"I can get behind that."

"I thought you might."

He kissed her, pulling himself free, and tugged her back against him. "See you in the morning."

"Mmm." She wanted to stare out at Lady Liberty and savor this perfect night, but as she blinked in the dim light from the sitting room, she fell dreamlessly asleep wrapped up with Jerrod.

Chapter Twenty-Three

Jerrod opened his eyes to the sun's blinding rays, squinting as he glanced at the bright reflection bouncing off the clock, raising his brows in surprise. They'd slept past eight, which actually wasn't all that shocking after the last few days and their impromptu romp in the dark. Abby had woken him in the middle of the night, straddling him while she pressed hot, wet kisses to his neck and chest. She'd taken him in before he'd fully realized he wasn't in the middle of some erotic dream.

Looking down, he grinned at the sweet sexy vixen still asleep in his arms. Abby was every man's fantasy. There wasn't an inhibited bone in that siren's body of hers. She was as enthusiastic between the sheets as she was with everything else she had a passion for. He thanked his lucky stars she was his. He was even more grateful their night away made a difference. The Abby he'd fallen for was back in full force. Taking her away from the apartment had been the right thing, regardless of their possible issues with Adam. If only he'd done so sooner.

She stirred, blinking her eyes open, and smiled. "Good morning, Mr. Quinn."

He winked. "Morning."

She moved, laying on top of him, resting her arms on his chest. "Did you sleep as well as I did?"

He rolled, pushing her into the mattress. "Like a rock."

She traced his lips with her index finger. "I think we both rest better when we're naked."

He smiled, snagging her finger, giving her a gentle bite. "So that's the key to a good night's sleep?"

Her palms slid up and down his back, sending a wave of goose bumps along his skin. "It must be."

He pulled her nipple into his mouth, teasing the aroused point until her breathing quickened. "It doesn't have anything to do with good sex and the fact that we completely wore each other out."

"Mmm, nope." She pinched his butt. "We should probably just plan on a new dress code."

"You won't have much of a career if naked is the new trend."

She shrugged. "I guess I'll just have to sell bracelets. Accessories are always in."

He laughed, enjoying the Abby he'd missed over the last couple days. "Bracelets, huh?"

"Sure."

He teased her other breast with the pad of his thumb. "I'm glad you slept well."

"I'm glad we both did. No nightmares makes all the difference."

"It certainly helps." He went after the sensitive skin of her neck, enjoying her breathy moan next to his ear immensely. "We should probably have breakfast."

"After we work up an appetite." She wiggled herself against his erection.

He closed his eyes, as ready for another round as she was. "We really need to think about birth control. We're not being very smart." He nipped at her chin. Their "condoms from now on pledge" had been forgotten—more like ignored last night.

"Pull out." She grabbed hold of him. "But actually

do it this time." She guided him in, gasping.

He sucked in a sharp breath as he pushed himself deeper, gritting his teeth with the rush of pleasure. He'd never taken these kinds of risks before Abby. It was too easy to forget the rules and consequences while they stared in each other's eyes. Not only had he taken his principal to bed and fallen completely in love, he was also being unbelievably irresponsible. They were both too smart to be this stupid, but he just didn't care.

"I can't get enough of you. You feel so good." She rocked her hips and gripped his butt cheeks encouraging him to move.

He slid back and forth.

She arched up. "Mmm. *So* good."

"This definitely doesn't suck." He arrowed deeper, moving in slow thrusts.

"Oh," she gasped as her fingernails dug into his waist. "Oh, keep *doing* that." Her breath came in rapid pants as each whimper grew longer and her muscles clenched. "Yes, just like that. Oh god. Oh *god*."

He shuddered, trying desperately to concentrate on his rhythm as she pulsed and throbbed around him. "Abby." He had no choice but to hold himself perfectly still, struggling to stay in control as she continued to contract, bucking in the throws of ecstasy. "Abby." He yanked up the towel he'd worn around his waist last night and pulled out. She grabbed hold of him, gripping. He pressed his forehead to hers, groaning loudly as she sent him over the edge. "Damn," he whispered, out of breath.

"That good, huh?"

Grinning, he lifted his head. "Not bad."

"I like you better inside." She kissed him, wiggling her brows.

"A temporary solution to our situation."

"Oh, the sacrifices."

They smiled at each other as her stomach growled, and her eyes widened. "I guess I'm hungry for more than just you. What do you say we have some breakfast?"

He chuckled. "I could eat."

"I saw a banana-raspberry smoothie and bran muffin on the menu that sound good."

He frowned. "Our ideas of breakfast are two different things."

"Don't think I won't steal a bite of your eggs, but first I have to shower." She nudged at his shoulder. "Orgasms are sweaty business."

He laughed, letting her up. Abby was definitely back. "I'll order up our food."

"Sounds good." She walked from the room, beautifully naked, completely easy in her own amazing skin. He wanted her again as she slipped into the bathroom. He wanted everything with her—the children they weren't ready for, marriage. The whole package. They just had to make it through the next few months, then he would happily take his chances in the baby department. He would be different than his father had been with him. But that was for later. He got out of bed and picked up the phone, dialing room service.

"Good morning, room service."

"Yes, good morning. Can I get the banana raspberry smoothie and a bran muffin?" He winced. "Can I also get the eggs benedict with a cup of coffee."

"Certainly. We'll deliver that in just a few minutes."

"Thanks." He hung up and made his way to the bathroom, stepping into the steamy space. He picked up his boxers and pulled them on, then his jeans as he watched Abby suds herself up behind the wall of glass. "You're absolutely stunning, Ms. Harris."

"Thank you, sir." She sent him a slow smile, biting her bottom lip as she rubbed the bar of soap over her breasts.

He swallowed the ball of lust as he followed the trail of bubbles down her wet skin. "And cruel, incredibly cruel."

She laughed as he left her to her shower and grabbed his shirt from the floor where he tossed it before last night's dinner. He wandered to the window, staring out at the Statue of Liberty in the distance and the traffic rushing by on the street sixteen stories below.

Eventually he and Abby would have to venture back out into the real world. Luckily he would have another pair of eyes, a man he knew he could trust. He'd only worked with Stone once at Tatiana Livingston's *End Famine Now* event back in October. Ethan had hired the newest addition to their team after he'd taken over Abby's coverage, but he heard good things—for the most part. Stone McCabe was quiet and from all accounts somewhat moody, but he did his job, and that's what mattered. Stone didn't have to say a damn word as long as he helped keep Abby alive.

There was a knock at the door, and he tensed, immediately on alert. He grabbed his gun from the side table by the bed and pushed the weapon into the back of his jeans as he moved to answer, peeking out the security hole. Twisting the knob, he opened cautiously, ready to slam the door closed.

"Good morning, sir."

"Good morning."

He rolled the cart to the center of the room. "Let me set this up for you."

"Actually, this is good." He handed off a twenty and the tray of dirty dishes from their dinner.

"Are you sure?"

"Yes, thanks."

The shower shut off.

"Enjoy your day, sir."

"You too." He let the man out, locking up. Moments later, Abigail came out with damp hair, wearing the clothes from yesterday. "No naked breakfast?"

She grinned. "Maybe we'll do a naked lunch."

"I can live with that." He smiled as she chuckled, thrilled that she seemed completely relaxed.

He picked up the glass of her dark pink concoction, handing it over. "Your brew."

"It's a smoothie." She sipped. "Mmm. And really good. Try." She held the glass to his lips.

He pulled his head back. "I'd rather not."

"*Try*," she said in a tone much like his mother's as she tipped the cup.

He slammed his eyes shut, preparing for the worst, and looked at her when he found the drink sweet and delicious. "Hey, that's not bad."

"Told you." She gave him a knowing smirk and drank deep.

He eyed her muffin wearily. "I'm not trying that thing."

She shook her head mournfully. "You don't know what you're missing."

"I'll have to live my life wondering."

She bit in, rolling her eyes on an exaggerated moan. "You sure you don't want some?"

"Positive." He pulled the lid from his own plate

and breathed deep. "*Now* we're talking. He cut himself a big bite of egg, English muffin, and hollandaise, and chewed, enjoying the melding of flavors. "Now this is moan worthy."

"Enjoy, big guy."

He took another exaggerated bite, staring at her. "You better believe it," he said over his mouthful.

She sat at their table. "What should we do today besides look through the telescope and watch TV?"

"Well, we need to stay here until Stone gets in." His cell phone rang. "Hold on." He picked up. "Yeah?"

"It's Ethan."

He set his fork down, alerted by Ethan's tone. "What's up?"

"We've got a problem—a couple actually."

"Great." He stood, no longer interested in his breakfast. "What?"

"Your brother called me on my way to the office."

He fisted his hand at his side, instantly consumed by dread. "My mother—"

"Your family's fine."

"Okay." He relaxed his hand. "Good."

"It's your ex."

His relief was short lived. What had Shelby done now?

"She's in critical condition at Lincoln General."

He closed his eyes, shaking his head. "Son of a bitch."

"Someone—more than likely Dimitri or Victor—found a way into town and just about beat her to death."

"Goddamn." He moved toward the window and back, too restless to be still. "I thought she was with Timmy."

"She gave him the slip Tuesday night—"

He froze. “Tuesday night? And he’s just getting around to sharing this information?”

“He’s been kind of busy with roadblocks and canvases. He’s had his hands full with the whole damn thing. He sounded like hell.”

Jerrod grunted, hating that Tim had to deal with everything on his own.

“He’s in Lincoln now with Shelby and her family. They still don’t know if she’s going to make it. He said she’s touch and go.”

He clenched his jaw, remembering the pretty redhead with pigtails chasing him around the schoolyard at recess. “What the hell happened?”

“She left his place and went home. I guess someone was there waiting for her.” He sighed into Jerrod’s ear. “She was able to answer her cell phone and scream for help. By the time Tim got there, whoever beat the shit out of her had left through the back door. They life-flighted her to the trauma center in Lincoln, barely alive.”

“Damn it.” Why the hell did she have to write the damn story? Why couldn’t she have just left it alone?

“Tim sent your mother and Uncle away as a precaution. A couple of his men are staying out at the farm taking care of the animals.”

“Okay. Fine.” He rubbed at his forehead, wishing there was some way he could head back to Nebraska and help. Turning, he met Abby’s concerned stare. He had enough problems of his own right here.

“I hate to do this to you, but are you ready for the rest?

He sighed. “Yeah, lay it on me.” Their situation fucking sucked whether, he was ready for more or not.

“Someone tried to breech my system at two-thirteen a.m.”

"Did they?"

"No, but they gave it one hell of a try. I traced the IP address back to a residence in Manhattan right before I called."

Adam. The coincidence was too huge not to immediately suspect him.

"Someone's sloppy and desperate to find you, if that's what this is. They did a shitty job of covering their tracks."

If Adam was sharing information with Dimitri, he would definitely be desperate. Adam probably hadn't expected them to vanish last night. "Sounds like it." He rubbed at his jaw, weary already.

"The good news in all of this is Stone's on his way. He left on a redeye after he got off duty last night. He changed planes in DC at eight. He'll be in New York in about and hour tops."

Well thank god something was going right. "Excellent. We'll meet him there."

"I figured as much. I booked the three of you a flight back to LA at eleven. American flight 1723. Tickets are at the kiosk. We'll get you home and figure things out from there."

He was ready to be back with a team of men he could trust. "We'll head out now. Have Stone meet us at our gate. I'll give you a call when we get through security."

"We'll see you this evening. It'll be good to have you here."

"Thanks." He hung up, sighing, looking at Abby.

She stood, any traces of the fun they'd had this morning gone. "What now?"

He rubbed at the back of his neck, his mind racing with Ethan's news and the need to get them the hell out of Manhattan. "We've had a change of plans.

We're going to meet Stone at LaGuardia and head to LA."

"Why?" She asked with the slightest tremble in her voice. "Jerrod, what's going on?"

"Shelby's in the hospital in critical condition."

She closed her eyes, pressing her hands to the side of her face. "They hurt her."

"Yeah."

She looked at him. "What else?"

He didn't want her worrying about the details, but she had a right to the truth. "Someone tried to breech Ethan's system early this morning."

"They're trying to find me." She swallowed, folding her arms at her waist. "Adam's trying to find me."

"We aren't one hundred percent sure it's him, but I think so."

"God." She stared up at the ceiling. "When is this going to end?"

"Soon." At least, that's what he hoped.

She tossed him a humorless laugh.

"Abby, this is going to work out." He needed her to believe it. "I'll handle Adam once we get home, and you'll take care of Lorenzo in court."

"And what about Dimitri and Victor?"

"They'll get them. Eventually they'll make a mistake."

"There's always *another* one." Her eyes filled as her voice tightened with tears. "There's always someone else lurking in the background."

Abby was falling apart, and he didn't have time to deal with it. "We're going to take care of it. As soon as we're back in LA, I'm going to take care of it."

"Who are you going to call? Another trustworthy fed?" She turned, heading toward the bathroom.

"Hey." He grabbed her arm, turning her to him. "Hey."

"What?" Tears fell down her cheeks. "This is never going to end. You can give me all of the promises and reassurances you want, but we both know it."

"Yes it is." He wrapped his arms around her. He had to believe that eventually they would live a normal life. "Yes it is, Abby."

"I just want to go home. To *our* home."

He shook his head. "We can't."

Her lips trembled as she nodded, her defeated, hopeless eyes staring into his. "I know."

"Soon." He gave her chin a gentle squeeze. "Very soon." He kissed her. "I love you. We're going to have all the things you want. All of them."

She nodded as she sniffed. "I love you too." She hugged him. "I'm sorry. I know this doesn't help." She stepped back, wiping her cheeks. "My pity party's officially over."

He kissed her again. "It's not a pity party."

"A little bit." She held up her thumb and finger an inch apart.

He smiled. "Grab your purse and we'll get out of here."

She sniffled again. "Okay."

He put on his holster, checked his weapon, and slid it in the leather holster. His jacket came next. He held Abby's out as she walked back from the bathroom, helping her put it on. "Ready?"

"Let's do this." She squeezed his hand.

"Same precautions as always."

"They're the best." She gave him a small smile.

He nodded, glancing out the peephole and opened the door, stepping into the hall, ready to grab his pistol as he looked both ways, moving to the elevator with Abby at his side. They descended sixteen floors in silence, walking out of the building, his arm around her waist as he held up his hand, flagging down a taxi. They just had to make it into the cab and he could... He froze, catching a movement out of the corner of his eye as something cold and heavy cracked against his temple before he had a chance to pivot. Sharp pains radiated through his skull as he fell to his knees, his vision hazy and gray as Abby screamed. He glanced up, struggling to gather his bearings as two men grabbed her around the waist, each gripping one of her legs.

"Jerrod! Jerrod!" She bucked and clawed as they carried her to the van that screeched to a halt at the curb.

"Abigail!" He sprinted forward, lightheaded, the world spinning as they lifted her in, closing the door, peeling out as quickly as they arrived. "Abigail!" He followed, drawing his weapon, firing at the tires. He took aim for the second time but didn't shoot as he lost his balance, falling in the middle of the street. Righting himself, he shoved his gun away, running after the van as it accelerated into traffic. "Abigail!" The blue work vehicle disappeared around the next block. "Fuck!" He grabbed his phone with a trembling hand, dialing Ethan as he continued to follow on foot.

"Coo—"

"Put a trace on her watch. They have her. They fucking have her, man." He wiped at the blood dripping down his face, trying desperately to think over the gripping terror he'd never known before as he lost sight of the vehicle once and for all.

"Goddamn. I'm calling the information up now. Okay. Okay. Here she is. I've got her right here. They're heading on Battery, taking a right onto State

Street."

Jerrod ran over to the cab, shoving the couple about to get in out of the way, slamming the door. "Get me to State Street."

The cabbie twisted in his seat. "That was fucking rude, pal."

"State Street. Now." He was loosing precious seconds arguing.

"Look, buddy—"

He pulled his gun from the holster, pointing it at the man. "Fucking drive."

"Jesus." The driver turned and punched the gas, skirting his way around cars, nosing his way into the gridlock.

"Where is she now?" Jerrod asked, jamming a hand through his hair, struggling to concentrate on the fact that Ethan knew exactly where she was rather than the sound of her screams echoing in his head.

"Still on State, which has turned into Water Street. I'm alerting the police.

"I got the first three numbers of the plate. New York. 3-5-5. Navy Blue work van."

"Got it. Good. Austin just walked in. Contact NYPD," he muttered to Austin. "Give them this. Send a text to Stone. Tell him to stand by. They have Abby. Jerrod," Ethan gave his attention back to Jerrod, "they've gained some speed. It looks like they're heading toward the FDR."

He huffed out a helpless breath, bopping his leg up and down. Clenching his fist, he shook his head in hopeless frustration as the cab inched its way down State Street among the sea of bumpers. "Come *on*, man."

"There's nowhere for me to go. The traffic will thin out in a couple hundred yards, or it should, anyway."

He stared ahead at thousands of taillights. He wasn't going to get to Abby like this. "Fuck this. Where's the nearest subway station?"

"South Ferry's a block south. I can't get you there any faster, buddy."

"Shit," Ethan said.

"What?" Jerrod froze at the alarm in Ethan's tone.

"I lost her."

His heart plunged as his stomach clutched with dread. "What do you *mean* you lost her?"

"The transmission stopped."

"Goddamn. Here." He grabbed a twenty from his wallet, throwing it at the cabbie and got out, sprinting for the subway station.

"I don't know where she is, man."

But Jerrod knew who did. "I've gotta go." He moved faster as the stairs to the station came into view. "I'm going to hop the subway. When I call you back I'll have answers."

~~~~

Abby sat huddled on the floor, clutching her arms around her legs, resting her forehead on her knees, struggling to concentrate on each rapid, shuddering breath instead of the small, dim space her captors had forced her into. She peeked at the huge, black-soled boots inches in front of her and slammed her eyes shut, trying to ignore Aleksey's heavily accented voice filling the van.

She shook her head, certain this couldn't possibly be real. Any second now she would wake from her nightmare and be snuggled in Jerrod's arms. She squeezed her hands into balls, purposely digging her
~~~~

nails into her palms, hoping for relief from this terrible dream. Glancing up, she expected to be surrounded by comfort and warmth, ready to take in the amazing view from their sixteenth-story window. Instead she stared at the glaring stranger across from her as he held a bloodied wad of paper towel to his nose. She'd made him bleed like a fountain when she rammed her elbow into his face, just the way Jerrod had showed her, but her desperate efforts to escape had been fruitless as the well-muscled man and Aleksey forced her into the van.

She swallowed, fighting back tears as the reality of her situation sunk in. This was as real as the first time she'd been taken, but today would be so much worse than the brothels and strip clubs of last summer. She had no doubt Luka, Aleksey, and the stranger were driving her to where Dimitri waited. Their boss would be eager for revenge.

She wiped at her sweaty brow as her breakfast roiled in her stomach. If she planned to survive, she had to calm down and *think*. Her captors certainly had the advantage, but she wasn't without her own. She knew Aleksey and Luka from Baltimore. Neither was nice, but they weren't as cruel as some of the other guards. She looked at both men sitting in the cabin, noting the guns strapped to their belts, trying hard to remember the time in the stash house she'd fought so hard to forget.

She glanced at Aleksey, recalling that he liked to sleep. He often dozed off in the afternoons. And Luka wanted her. He'd made that clear months ago at the stash house when he pawed her after Renzo left for the evening.

She looked at the weapons again, bolstered by the fact that she knew how to use them. Perhaps she could seduce Luka and steal his gun while Aleksey caught his nap. A nasty kiss or two was an option very much on the table if it meant she could shoot him and walk away—whatever it took to get home to Jerrod and Alexa.

"Yes, Little Bitch is right here," Aleksey said, interrupting her thoughts as he spoke on his cell phone. He looked over his shoulder from the passenger's seat, grinning as their eyes met. "Dimitri tells me he's waiting for you." All three men laughed.

A wave of fear rushed through her, and she shuddered, glancing from Aleksey to the stranger, her conviction to stay as calm as possible wavering as the trembling overtook her body.

"Little Bitch is scared." Aleksey chuckled. "She should be."

Her lips quivered as she rested her forehead against her knees once again, trying her best to rebuild her composure, knowing they'd win if she let them see her terror. She thought of Jerrod's soothing embraces, and a tear tracked down her cheek despite her best efforts. He'd been bleeding when they ripped her away from him. The pole the stranger hit him with had knocked him to the sidewalk, but he'd gotten back up, running after her. He had to be okay.

She sniffled. But what if she didn't see him again? What if last night *was* their last night together? *I've never lost anyone I've protected. And I wasn't in love with them, Abigail.* Another tear fell as she yearned to be with him, pulling her arms tighter around herself, blinking as her watch pressing against her leg registered. Lifting her head, she studied the pretty piece of jewelry he had given her all those weeks ago. *I can find you anywhere with this.*

She sat up straighter with new hope,

remembering she wasn't alone. Jerrod would find her, but she had to do her part and stay alive. One of the first tools he taught her was to always pay attention to her surroundings. She glanced out the windshield, attempting to gather her bearings in a city vaguely familiar as it rushed by. There were landmarks all around—none that she recognized, but she would if she kept looking. And she wasn't paying close enough attention to Aleksey's conversation, even though he spoke in Russian. She'd learned several words while they'd held her against her will. As she tuned in, she caught Dimitri's name twice, and something about 'the building.'

"What do you look at?" the man sitting across from her asked.

"Nothing," she murmured, staring straight ahead, concentrating on the skyscrapers.

He kicked his leg out, landing a blow against her ankle. "I ask you what you look at?"

She clutched at the throbbing along her foot as he dropped his paper towel and crawled closer, blocking her vision with his ugly face. She fought back another wave of unease as she breathed in his putrid breath.

"I ask you questions, so you answer."

"I did answer," she said quietly, looking down. "I said nothing. I'm not looking at anything."

He gripped her chin, pulling her face forward, glaring, saying something in Russian as he held her gaze.

She cringed, instantly going into panic mode when she recognized the word 'hood.'

He took the long stocking hat Aleksey tapped against the back of his shoulder, tossing it her way. "Put this on."

She stared down at the retched black knit cap,

gasping for air. It was just like the one she wore the first time Dimitri and Victor took her. She scurried back like a crab, horrified by the idea of sitting in the dark. She couldn't save herself in the dark. She couldn't *breathe* in the dark.

He grabbed her by the tender ankle, yanking her to him. "Now!" he screamed in her face.

"No!" she shouted back, more terrified by the confines of the hot, rough fabric than his retaliation.

"Listen to me." He snatched her up by the jacket. "Put it *on*."

"Don't touch me!" She shoved him, the edge of her palm connecting with his nose.

He rushed her, slamming her back against the floor of the van.

She gasped, losing her breath from the violent force, barely having a chance to recover from the first shock before he wrenched her up by the hair, sending hot, sharp pains through her neck as he shoved the hat over her head and pressed his palms over her nose and mouth.

Her eyes popped wide in the black hell as she smothered, her hands beating at him, her legs kicking as Aleksey shouted, "Dostatochno!" The weight lifted from her face, and something crashed behind her.

"She needs to be alive, idiot! Dimitri will kill her when he's ready."

Abby lay still, gulping in breath after breath, her arms and legs weak and heavy after the fight for her life. She kept her eyes closed in an attempt to cope with the stifling darkness, waiting for the endless ride to be over. As much as she hated the idea of seeing Dimitri, the confines of her airless space was worse. She pressed her wrist to the hard metal floor, reassured by her watch. As long as she had it, everything was okay. Jerrod would come for her. He would take her to Baltimore to testify, and all of this would finally be over.

The van slowed, went over a bump, and stopped with a slight squeak of brakes.

"Get her," Aleksey demanded.

Someone—probably the vile man—pulled her up by the arm and tossed her over his shoulder. The back doors opened, and she gasped as he jumped down, his feet crunching as if they walked on a dirt path. Yet the men's voices echoed as if they were in a building.

Goose bumps covered her skin in the cool space—wherever they were—as she strained to listen over the talking, catching the faint honks and constant rumble of traffic somewhere in the distance.

The man stopped, opening a door, the hinges squeaking with a wretched, rusty protest. "You will wait here." He grabbed her by the wrist, pulling her from his shoulder, letting her fall.

She landed with a bone-jarring thud, crying out as rocks bit into her hands and ripped at her jeans. The door squeaked again, slamming closed, and she immediately pulled off the hood, blinking in the dim light shining through the edges of the boarded-up windows high above her head.

Something scurried behind her, and she rushed to her feet, grimacing from the throbbing pain in her knees. She looked around at the chunks of concrete and graffiti in the filthy space, spotting a rusty chair in the rays of sunshine. She walked to it, giving the dingy metal a testing wiggle, and stopped dead, gasping as she noticed the cracks in the glass of the pretty watch. "No. Oh, god, no." Her heart thudded in her chest as she pulled the piece closer, examining the second hand, which stayed frozen in the center of the clock face. "Please work. *Please.*" She slid a shaky hand through her hair and paced, caught in the clutching grips of outright panic.

When did it break? How would Jerrod find her? How would she go home? Frantic, she rushed closer to the filthy, broken windows, noting the rusted bars. She hurried to the solid door, pulling at the deteriorated knob, falling back as the piece gave way but the door held firm. "No. No. This isn't happening."

She spotted the old table by the wall, pushing it toward the grouping of windows, and climbed on, jumping, gauging the distance to her only chance at escape. They were too high.

Tears rained down her cheeks as she collapsed, sitting, sobbing away the worst of her terror. *Don't give up on me.* Jerrod's words echoed through her head as she attempted to shore herself up, trying to stay positive, but as she looked around at her no-win situation, she quickly lost hope.

CHAPTER TWENTY-FOUR

TWENTY-FIVE AGONIZING MINUTES LATER, JERROD hustled up the subway steps two blocks east of the Riverside Apartments. The train ride had stretched on endlessly while he made his way to the Upper West Side, sick with helpless worry, praying desperately that somehow he was going to find Abby before it was too late. He jogged west, each step pure misery as the impact echoed in his throbbing head.

Grabbing his phone, he weaved his way through the crowds clogging the sidewalks, dialing Shane's number. He'd wrestled with the risks of calling his old roommate, unsure of Shane's allegiances. But he needed answers; he needed to know what side Shane was playing for once and for all.

"Hello?"

"Shane. It's Jerrod."

"Jesus, man. Where the hell are you? We've been looking for you. Adam's been frantic."

"I bet." Adam probably shit his pants after he came home last night and found them gone. He clenched is jaw. "Where is he?"

"At the apartment. He looked like hell when I left."

Jerrod grunted his response, glancing behind him, still uneasy, wondering if he had a tail. "Where are you?"

"On my way to work."

"When did you leave?"

Silence hung on the line. "About fifteen minutes ago. Why? What's up, Jerrod?"

He debated how much to tell Shane, but he had to say something. He needed information. "Has Adam been acting different lately?"

"Yeah. Some I guess."

"How?"

"He's been edgy. What's up, Jerrod?"

"Is he gambling again?"

Shane sighed in Jerrod's ear. "I was wondering the same thing. He got pissed when I asked. He says no, but he could be."

Looking both ways, Jerrod crossed the street with dozens of other pedestrians. "How much do you know about Dimitri, and don't fuck with me."

"Dimitri who? Dubov?"

"Yeah."

"I told you what I know yesterday. He hasn't surfaced since November."

"He has Abby."

"*What*?"

The utter shock in Shane's voice went a long way to convincing him he had nothing to do with any of this. "Dubov has Abby, and Adam knows where."

"What the fuck are you talking about, Quinn? I thought Abby was with you."

"She was until some bastard bashed me in the temple forty minutes ago." He absently brushed at the raw wound, trying his best to ignore the pounding ache radiating through his skull. Getting Abby back was all that mattered right now. "Adam's dirty."

"Bullshit," Shane fired back.

A week ago he never would've believed it either. "It's the truth, man. I wish to hell it wasn't." He picked up his pace, as the dark green awning came into view.

"I'm trying to figure out if you are too."

"Fuck you. Are you *on* something, Quinn?"

"Look, Adam e-mailed me Saturday night telling me Task Force was running surveillance on Dimitri. They had him pinned to two possible locations. He found out I was having some trouble and encouraged me to bring Abby to New York. He assured me we could hang low here and you guys would give me a hand. We come and you tell me the team hasn't had anything on Dubov in months. I check with my boss. Turns out you're right."

"There's gotta be some—"

"Six months," Jerrod interrupted, not wanting to listen to Shane defend Adam. "Six months in Los Angeles and Abby's fine until some bitch reporter messes it up. Three days in Manhattan and she's gone." He slid a hand through his hair, barely able to stand the thought of Abby out there somewhere alone.

"I don't know what to say, Quinn."

He pulled open the glass door of the building. "There's not much to say. I'm here at the apartment." This right here would tell him whose side Shane was on. If he tipped Adam off that he was in the building, he would have his answer. "If I don't get her back, I promise he won't live to see another day."

"Don't do anything stupid, Jerrod."

"I'll do whatever it takes." He hung up, stopping next to the elevator, punching the 'up' button repeatedly, impatiently waiting. The door finally slid open, and he stepped in, pushing the button for the twelfth floor. He dialed his phone again, pacing away his restlessness during his twelve-story ride.

"Cooke."

"Did you pick up Abby's signal again?" He kept

hoping there had been a momentary glitch.

"No."

He rubbed at the back of his neck. "What about the police? Do they have anything?"

"Not yet. They've issued a city-wide BOLO."

He fisted his hand, tempted to punch his helpless frustration away, which would solve absolutely nothing. "Goddamn." The elevator stopped with a jolt and ding, and the door slid open.

"I just got off the phone with Stone. He's on the ground. Where do you want him?"

"I'll let you know in about five minutes." He stopped in front of apartment 12-3. "I'll call you right back." He hung up and pulled his gun from his holster, settling it in the back of his jeans as another wave of adrenaline surged through his veins. This was it. Abby would live or die based on what Adam had to say. Adam was going to spill one way or another. He desperately wanted to pound on the door, but instead he knocked three times.

Adam opened the door dressed casually in jeans and a t-shirt for a day at headquarters, his eyes widening a fraction before he smoothed himself out and smiled. "Hey, Qui—"

Jerrod rushed him with a hand to Adam's throat. He let his rage flow free as he slammed him against the wall, pulling Adam's gun from the holster at his hip, pressing the weapon under Adam's chin. "Where are they taking her?"

"What the fuck are you doing?" Adam's breathing quickened as he stared at Jerrod. "I—"

"*Where*?" He jammed the barrel up harder.

"I don't know what you're talking about." Sweat beaded along his forehead as his eyes darted about. Adam had never been a good liar.

"They have her, goddamn it." He rapped Adam's head back, growing angrier by the second. "You fucker, they *have* her."

"Jerrod—"

Shaking his head, Jerrod held his gaze, planting his heel down on Adam's bare foot.

Adam hollered in pain. "Goddamn. You just broke my fucking *toes*."

Jerrod smacked Adam's head against the wall for the second time. "You're lucky it wasn't a bullet."

"I don't—"

He brought, his elbow up into his 'friend's' nose. "Wrong fucking answer."

"Son of a bitch," Adam groaned, pressing a hand to his nostrils as blood poured. "I don't know where they took her. I don't."

The front door burst open. Jerrod pointed the gun at Shane as he pressed his arm into Adam's windpipe.

Shane stared, his eyes huge. "Quinn, have you lost your mind?"

"Drop your gun and kick it over here." He pressed harder on Adam's throat, making him gasp and choke for each breath. "Now!"

The gun fell with a clatter. Shane kicked it in Jerrod's direction.

"Shane—" Adam choked out.

"Shut up," he said to Adam as he looked at Shane. "Come sit down where I can see you. Adam's about to tell us where Abby is." He loosened the pressure on Adam's windpipe.

He coughed violently. "I don't *know*."

Jerrod plowed his fist into Adam's stomach, growing more impatient with each denial. "Tell me *now*, you fucker!" He yanked him up, shouting in his face. "Next it'll be your balls!"

"Jerrod." Shane got to his feet.

"Sit *down*," he said through clenched teeth.

Shane sat.

"They're going to kill her if they haven't already." Jerrod shoved Adam to the floor, grabbing him by his sweat-soaked hair, yanking his face up to his.

"They'll hurt Samantha." Tears raced down Adam's cheeks.

"You son of a bitch." Shane rushed to his feet. "You fucking son of a bitch."

Adam shook his head. "I didn't want to do this. I didn't." Adam's eyes pleaded with Jerrod's. "I got in some trouble. I was supposed to help them elude capture; that's it. This wasn't supposed to have gotten so out of hand."

He didn't care about the whys. He just wanted Abby back. "Where *is* she, Adam?"

"They said something about a warehouse or an abandoned building." He wiped at his eyes.

"Be more specific."

"In Harlem."

He grit his teeth. "It's a big fucking place. East Harlem? West? Central Harlem? Where?"

"They said something about the abandoned row houses on 140th where they had the riots a few months back. They also said something about an empty warehouse on 142nd by the river. They don't tell me much. They just threaten. God." Tears poured again. "I didn't want to do this, man."

Jerrod shook his head. "But you did."

"For Sam. She's going to have the baby."

"Innocent people have died because of you. The Stowers girl is dead because you're an asshole."

"I got in over my head at the tables. There were some guys that were going to do me in."

"I guess it sucks to be you."

"I didn't have a choice."

Jerrod seared him with a disgusted look.

"Roll him over," Shane said as he pulled out a pair of cuffs.

"You don't have to cuff me."

Ignoring him, Jerrod tossed Adam over to his chest and slid the cuffs in place. "How did they find us today? Is someone following me?"

"No. Surveillance. They traced the cabs using the cameras around the city. It took them all night..."

"They definitely had to work harder than just coming here for a quick pick up." He'd heard enough. He took the piece of duct tape Shane tore from the roll and slapped it over his mouth harder than he needed to.

"Get his legs, Quinn." Shane gave him the roll.

He wrapped his legs at the ankles. Adam wouldn't be going anywhere or saying anything any time soon.

"She better be there, Adam," Shane warned. "If she's not they'll never find you."

Adam mumbled, nodding his head.

Jerrod stood, shoving Adam's gun in his own holster.

"Here, man." Shane handed him a damp towel and two Tylenol. "Wipe your face. That's one hell of a gash."

He impatiently swiped at the throbbing along his temple and tossed the towel down, dry-swallowing the pills. "Let's go."

They hurried out the door leaving Adam where he lay. "I'll take the warehouse," Jerrod said as he hustled to the elevator.

"I'll give the row houses a look."

He nodded, looking at the man he was relieved to

still call his friend. The door dinged, and they stepped inside as he pulled his phone from his pocket. "One of my co-workers is here from LA. He's waiting for instructions. I don't want any backup—just you, me, and Stone. I don't know who the hell to trust anymore. We're looking for a blue work van if they haven't moved it already, New York plates, first three numbers 3-5-5, one bullet hole in the right corner of the bumper." He dialed Stone's number.

"MacCabe."

"Stone, it's Jerrod. I need you to meet me up in Harlem at the 145th Street subway stop."

"I'm on my way." The phone disconnected.

The door slid open, and they booked it two blocks back to the tunnels, hopping the train seconds before the doors closed.

"I'll get off at 135th Street and grab a cab."

"Sounds good."

"I'm sorry, Quinn." Shane huffed with a shake of his head. "I had no idea."

"Neither did I until yesterday. I apologize for questioning you."

He shrugged. "Can't blame you. We're going to find her."

His heart ached with the possibilities that it was already too late. Abby disappeared almost an hour and a half ago. "I hope to god you're right."

"We'll find her," he said again.

Eventually the train slowed, and Shane moved toward the exit as they stopped at 135th Street.

"Call as soon as you know. She's more than my principal."

"I know, Quinn." The doors opened and Shane stepped out, hurrying through the crowds as he made his way to the stairs.

Eight excruciating minutes passed before the train finally slowed. Jerrod got off, running up the steps, looking around for Stone's dark brown hair and tough build. He wasn't here yet. "Screw it." He took off, gaining speed, knowing he was mere blocks from where Abby might be. His phone rang as he moved closer to the grouping of old, abandoned buildings. "Quinn," he said out of breath.

"I'm pulling up to the row houses now," Shane said. "I don't see anything. These places are burnt up rubble. There's no one here."

"Are you sure?"

"Yeah, man. No one's hiding in the bricks and trash."

"Then she's here." He glanced from one old mill building to the next—three in all, each a mess of broken glass and graffiti. "If Adam was telling the truth."

"I think he was being straight with us. He knows it's over."

"I hope to Christ so." He needed to hold Abby in his arms again and see those big blue eyes. He shook the thought away, knowing he had to concentrate on finding her, as he ducked among old mattresses and abandoned tractor-trailer beds decorated in gang signs. He inched his way closer to the first building as he assessed his surroundings in the bold daylight. The lack of cover in the winter sun was a major disadvantage. If Abby was here and her captors were keeping watch—which they would be—they would see him before he did them.

"I'll be there in ten minutes."

"I'll see you soon." Jerrod hung up and dialed Stone.

"McCabe."

"It's Jerrod. Come to the warehouses by the river on 142nd Street. You can't miss them." He moved toward a set of windows, glancing in at the uninhabitable space. The roof had long since caved in. No one was here.

Stone muttered something to the cabbie. "We're almost over the bridge. I should be there in about five minutes."

"I'm heading to the second building now. There's hardly any cover." He used the gutted Oldsmobile to his advantage, ducking behind the stripped vehicle, keeping his eyes open, straining to hear over the honks and traffic rushing by a block away. He inched his way toward one of the rusty barred windows, glancing in through layers of dust and grime. The place was disgusting but in better shape than the last one. He scanned the area, his heart accelerating as he caught sight of the bumper of the van he'd put a bullet through. "I see the van. She has to be in there somewhere."

"Wait for me, Quinn, and we'll get her."

He wanted to storm into the dingy space now and take Abby away, but he had no idea how many men stood guard or if she was in fact there herself. She had to be. "Hurry." He hung up as a car pulled around the building. He rushed back among the ancient litter, crouching as the man who'd hit him with the metal pipe opened a massive, garage-sized door. The Lincoln pulled in and the door closed behind them.

Jerrod made his way back to the window, watching as Victor Bobco stepped from the back seat of the vehicle, then Dimitri Dubov, both of the men smiling. "Son of a bitch," he muttered as his stomach clenched with dread. Abby was definitely here, and she was running out of time.

~~~~

Abby shoved up her sleeves, took another deep breath, and pushed at the filthy oil barrel, grunting with her effort. She'd been trying to move the thing for more minutes than she wanted to count, but it wouldn't budge. The drum was half full with ash, more than likely from the homeless trying to stay warm, but starting a fire wasn't on her agenda. Her focus was on escape. If she could just knock the barrel to its side and roll it to the windows, she had a real chance. There had to be a bar or two loose in the decrepit frames, but she couldn't find out if she couldn't reach them.

Backing up several feet, she ran forward, pushing at the stubborn metal with no effect. "Damn it." Her meager height and weight weren't helping a mostly hopeless situation. She looked at her watch and the frozen hands stuck at nine forty-five, closing her eyes. She'd been here long enough to understand that her transmitting signal was damaged, along with the rest of the jewelry on her wrist. Jerrod wasn't coming to save her—he would have no idea where to look. She would either find a way out of this situation on her own or die.

She cast an uneasy glance toward the huge rusted door. It was only a matter of time before Dimitri came for her. Shuddering, she turned back and shook her head. Escape—that's what she needed to focus on. Licking her lips, she got back to it, pushing and shoving until sweat dampened her skin despite the deep chill. "Come on. Come *on*," she whispered as she gave the barrel a frustrated kick.

She ran a hand through her hair, trying her best
~~~~

to keep her lips from quivering. *Don't give up on me.* Jerrod's words echoed through her mind as they had each time she'd been ready to sit down and accept her fate, but his steady blue eyes and her desperate desire to see him again gave her the strength to keep trying despite the odds.

"Okay." She gave her shoulders a shake to loosen them up. "Okay," she said again, backing up, running forward as she'd tried before, but this time she rammed the metal with the right side of her body, losing her balance as the heavy barrel fell forward with a huge crash. She coughed as ash spewed about the space, covering her clothing in soot. "*Yes.*" She rushed to her feet, brushing herself off with a renewed sense of hope, and began rolling the huge can toward the wall, stopping to push chunks of concrete and bricks out of her way.

Winded, she swiped her arm over her forehead, continuing on with her mission, smiling as she reached the wall. She grabbed the edge of the metal and pushed up in her attempt to right the barrel she'd fought so hard to topple, her arms trembling with the effort. Finally it moved and she gained leverage, righting the heavy drum, bottom end up. "Ha!"

The door opened behind her, and she whirled.

Luka stepped in. "What are you doing?"

She looked from him to the drum and back. "Uh, I want to start a fire. It's cold in here."

"You don't need a fire." He smiled, opening the door wider.

Dimitri walked in wearing black slacks and a gray long-sleeve shirt that accentuated his muscular frame.

She clutched the edge of the barrel as her legs turned to water, and her heart stuttered with the rush of outright terror.

"Little Bitch," he clasped his hands together, smiling, the cruel, hateful gleam in his eyes burning bright. "You're back." His gaze traveled down her body. "And filthy. But soon you will be dead, so this doesn't matter."

Victor and Aleksey walked in, flanking Dimitri's side.

She swallowed, glancing around at the heavy pieces of concrete, searching for a weapon as her breathing turned ragged. She could throw all the bricks and stone she wanted, but there were five men to stop her. There was no way out.

"Come to me." Dimitri pointed to the floor in front of his feet.

She stayed where she was, still gripping the barrel, too terrified to move.

"I said come. Now!"

"No," she shuddered out, still trying to think of a way to save herself.

"She has forgotten how to obey." He crossed his arms, shaking his head with a mocking *tsk*. "Victor, bring her to me."

"Don't!" Abby bent down, picking up concrete chunks, chucking them and backing up as Victor advanced. "Stay away!" A piece the size of her fist connected with his temple.

"You *bitch*!" He froze, turning away as blood gushed from his wound.

"Aleksey, grab her," Dimitri demanded.

Aleksey rushed forward, dodging pieces, grabbing hold of her arm.

"No!" She fought a useless battle, kicking about, twisting desperately as Aleksey carried her to his boss. "No!"

Aleksey kicked the back of her knees, sending her

to the floor at Dimitri's feet.

Dimtri bent down, slapping her across the face. "You will *listen*!"

Gasping, she fell back from the force and stinging pain, pressing her palm to her throbbing cheek.

"You don't remember how to behave, so I will help you." He slapped her again, and she cringed, bracing for the next blow as he raised his hand for the third time. "Next I will use my fist—the way I did with the little mouse."

Her eyes widened, staring into his as she recognized his nickname for Margret. "You bastard!" She rushed to her feet, shoving him back a step with the strength of her heartbreak and anger.

His fist flew forward, connecting with her already sore jaw, knocking her to the floor with a thud. "Who do you think you are?" He crouched down, grabbing a handful of her hair, and jerked her face to his. "I should kill you right now the way I did her. She cried and begged as I punched her again and again. She bled well." He smiled. "No matter how many times I told her to tell me where you were she wouldn't."

She blinked in horror, realizing Margret died trying to protect her. They'd shared their hopes and dreams more than once while they hid themselves away in her tiny bedroom. Margret had known she would go to Los Angeles and work for Lily Brand. From the beginning Abby had tried to save her young friend, and Margret lost her life trying to do the same for her. Bursting into tears, Abby covered her tender face with her hands, her depths of sorrow more than she could bear.

"Aw, she cries for the Little Mouse." He gave her a shove. "So touching."

Someday I'm going to look him in the eye and spit

in his face, Abby. I swear I'm going to do it. Margret's bruised and battered face and fierce whisper raced through her mind. Abby looked up as Dimitri's loomed close, and she let a wad of saliva fly.

He grabbed her by the neck, squeezing as the amusement left his eyes, turning deadly as he wiped at his cheekbone. "You will die," he said through clenched teeth, gripping her harder.

She gasped, grabbing at his wrist, fighting for air.

"I should break your neck." He increased the pressure of his cruel grip.

She closed her eyes, clawing, accepting that she would die.

"But you will wait." He let her go. "I will give you more time to think of your last breath." He stood, glaring. "Bitch." He wiped at his face for the second time.

She sucked in deep breaths as the room spun from her lack of oxygen. Trembling, she listened as Dimitri shouted in Russian.

Luka and the stranger who'd nearly killed her in the van hurried through the open doorway. Tension hung thick in the silence, and Abby scooted back, bracing herself, waiting for Dimitri to order her beaten or raped for his enjoyment.

"Borris, Luka, I want to thank you for your part in bringing Little Bitch to me."

Luka and the stranger—Borris—nodded, their smiles disappearing when Dimtri pulled a gun from his pants. Two loud pops echoed through the room, and both men lost most of their faces.

Abby screamed as she got to her feet and ran across the room in an attempt to escape the horror.

Dimitri laughed, walking to the dead men. "Unfortunately your services are no longer needed."

He kicked them, turned, laughing harder as he looked at Abby. “Aleksey, bring her to me. It’s time for Little Bitch to die.”

She backed into the corner as Aleksey walked toward her, realizing that this was it. He grabbed her, taking her back to the man who would end her. She stared into Dimitri’s evil brown eyes, understanding that he and The Mid-Atlantic Sex Ring had won. The prosecution’s lead witness would die, and Lorenzo Cruz would more than likely go free. She would never meet her nephew or say goodbye to Alexa. She and Jerrod wouldn’t get their chance to have everything they’d wanted with each other.

Dimitri gripped her chin, holding the gun to her temple. “You will die with pain.”

She closed her eyes and tears poured down her cheeks. She thought of Jerrod, shaking uncontrollably, waiting. Seconds passed, and she opened them.

“A bullet is too quick. Your agony will be much worse, but not here.” Smiling, he cracked the pistol along the side of her face.

The pain of the sharp blow barely registered as the black hole of unconsciousness reached up and swallowed her whole.

~~~~

Jerrod moved back to the window, his gaze passing over the bastard who’d hit him across the temple while the ass leaned against the Lincoln, reading a newspaper. Clenching his jaw, Jerrod crept closer to the jagged shards of broken glass, looking in from a different angle, trying to see down the long hall which Dimitri and Victor, along with two other men, had disappeared. In the twenty minutes he, Stone,
~~~~

and Shane had been here, he'd counted five men altogether.

He stepped back, crouching in his hiding spot, glancing at his watch, growing impatient as he waited for Shane and Stone to work their way back from their quick survey of the rest of the four-story building. They'd been gone mere minutes, but every second ticking by passed in what felt like centuries. Reconnaissance was a vital part of the extraction process, but this wasn't happening fast enough.

He rubbed at the back of his neck, huffing in utter frustration, trying to ignore the sick ache in his heart, understanding that the frantic desire to rush did no one any good. Every time he thought of the way Abby had screamed for him or the way her eyes had pleaded with his as they closed her into the van, he fought to turn it off. He needed to concentrate on the team's goal: bringing Abby out safely and taking her home.

He glanced toward the window again, knowing she waited somewhere among the dingy maze of rooms. But what shape was she in? What had they done to her, or what were they doing while he waited here helplessly, doing nothing?

Rocks crunched against the cement behind him, and he whirled, gun pointed.

"Easy, Quinn." Stone stopped short, bringing his hands up to his chest.

Jerrod dropped his weapon, catching sight of Shane hustling back from the opposite corner of the building. "What did you see?"

"There are several points of possible exit along the east side of the building," Shane said, still slightly breathless from his jog back. "Most windows are second story and up, so we don't have to worry about that as an escape route, but the doors are an obvious problem."

"I didn't notice any vehicles hanging around the area," Stone added with his arms crossed at his chest. "I don't think anyone else was invited to the party."

"If Dubov and Bobco are inside, we've got the last of the ring right here," Shane added.

"It's them. I'm positive." Jerrod had memorized Dimitri and Victor's faces months ago, when Ethan handed him Abby's case file and told him to board a plane to Maryland.

"Then it looks like it's time to finish this. We'll be bringing them out in cuffs or body bags." Stone shrugged. "Either way works for me."

Jerrod nodded, staring into Stone's unwavering brown eyes. Those options worked for him as well. "Let's do this."

"I'm ready," Shane said.

"Okay." Jerrod nodded again, ready to end Abby's nightmare. "We've got one man directly inside—armed. That leaves us with four more from what I've seen—whereabouts unknown. Our entry point," he gestured to the door thirty yards away, "is locked. I think this will handle whatever they're using to secure it." He pointed to the rusty remains of a beam among the debris. "Stone, I'll have you cover me and Shane. Shane, we'll do this up the way we used to." He and Shane had knocked down more than one door together in their years on Fugitive Task Force.

Shane nodded.

"We get in," Jerrod continued, "then take down whoever this asshole is." He glanced back in the window, catching sight of the man moving in the direction Dimitri and the others had gone. "Wait. He just left." He focused on his team again. "At some point we'll have to contend with him, maybe at the door when all is said and done but—"

Two loud pops cut him off, and his gaze flew to the door, his heart stopping as he recognized the sound of gunfire. "Abigail," he whispered, his voice thick with agony.

"Let's go," Stone said with a jarring pound of his fist to Jerrod's shoulder. "Let's go now."

The jolting punch was just what he needed. "Come on." He picked up the heavy beam with Shane, refusing to believe that the gunshots had been Abby's end. They moved quickly, struggling with the weight of their makeshift door rammer as Stone followed, pointing his weapon toward the warehouse, ready to fire on anyone who spotted them.

"Now!" Jerrod shouted, using his anger and fear to slam the heavy piece against the thick metal, denting it with their first effort, busting it open with the second. Dropping the beam, he and Shane drew their weapons, entering the eerily quiet building, covering each other, moving in the formation they all knew well—Shane first, gun pointing forward, Jerrod watching left and right, Stone heading up the back, waiting for their man to reappear.

They cleared four rooms, stopping at the next open door. "Hold up," Shane whispered, pointing to the bodies lying on the floor in pools of blood. One was the guard from out front.

"Two down," Stone muttered.

Two gunshots, two bodies. Jerrod prayed this meant Abby was still alive.

They moved from the space, pausing, pointing their guns down the shadowy east hall, when a clatter from above caught their attention. Jerrod glanced at both of his men, nodding. They kept going, moving faster, skirting the filthy debris silently as they climbed the flight of stairs and continued down another long hall. They stopped when they came to an intersection.

"There," Shane whispered.

Jerrod caught the same movement out the corner of his eye, his relief huge when he spotted Abby's dangling sneakers, her hair streaming down the side of Dimitri's arm as Dimitri carried her down the darkened hall toward another stairwell.

"We must hurry before we are found," Dimitri's voice echoed in a hissing whisper as he spoke to Victor and the other man who had been in the van, turning his body in a quick circle as he looked behind him.

Jerrod's momentary relief vanished as Abby lay limp, her eyes closed, her head bleeding, her left jaw and cheekbone swollen with bruises. His finger danced on the trigger as a red haze filled his vision with a primal fury he'd never felt before.

"Keep it cool, Quinn," Shane muttered. "No mistakes."

He fought to pull himself together, taking several steadying breaths, knowing Shane was absolutely right.

"Someone is here. Let's go," Dimitri said, moving closer to the stairs, awkwardly tossing his weapon to Victor. "Aleksey, get the car. We'll meet you out front."

Stone gestured toward the grouping of old offices with inner connecting doors, signaling that he would head that way.

Jerrod and Shane nodded.

Stone wasted no time, disappearing around the corner. Moments later there was a clatter from the direction he headed, and Victor and the man named

Aleksey stopped on the top step, pointing their guns.

"Who's there?" Victor shouted.

"Keep going, Dimitri. Take her out. We will see to this," Aleksey whispered.

"Help!" Abby opened her eyes, calling groggily. "Help—"

"Shut *up*!" Dimitri slapped at her, his big hand assaulting her bruised skin.

Jerrod steamed a breath out his nose, struggling to stay put when she cringed, whimpering. Dimitri would not hit her again, so help him.

The clatter of footsteps came again from further away.

Aleksey started forward. "I'll go see—"

A shot rang out from Stone's position, and blood bloomed along Aleksey's lower pant leg as he screamed, losing his balance, falling down the first few steps of the stairwell before he caught himself.

Within seconds all hell broke loose as Victor and the injured man started firing toward Stone.

Shane took off in Stone's direction, and Dimitri ran Jerrod's way with Abby while she covered her head and slammed her eyes shut.

Jerrod pressed his back to the wall, waiting for Dimitri to turn the corner. He pointed his gun as Dimitri came into view. "Freeze!" Jerrod yelled, his eyes locking with Abby's.

Dimtri stopped dead and took a step back.

"I said don't move."

"Jerrod," Abby whispered from trembling lips among the madness of gunfire.

Jerrod looked at Dimitri as she struggled not to cry, needing to keep his concentration. "Let her go."

Dimitri shook his head, smiling, backing closer to the huge grouping of windows behind him. "She will die first."

"The only one who's going to die is you, fucker. Now put her down."

Dimtri dropped Abby to her feet, dragging her within inches of the broken glass, and grabbed for her chin.

Jerrod aimed, firing, skimming Dimitri's right hip, full well knowing the bastard was planning to snap her neck.

Dimitri hollered, releasing Abby as he stumbled back.

Abby screamed, taking two steps before Dimitri grabbed her arm, pulling her body to his chest, using her as a shield.

"Now we will both die!" He yanked her off her feet, ready to dive out the second story window.

"Let me *go*!" Abby sent her elbow back, connecting with Dimitri's face.

Dimtri's grip loosened as he hollered, and blood fountained from his nose.

"Run, Abigail!" Jerrod shouted, knowing if Dimitri grabbed hold this time she would end up on the pavement far below.

Out of nowhere Stone appeared in the silence Jerrod hadn't noticed until now, sprinting forward, yanking Abby out of the way as Dimitri attempted to take hold of her for the second time. Stone pressed Abby into the wall with his body, shielding her as Jerrod opened fire. Shane's shot followed almost simultaneously, the shocking jolts sending Dimitri crashing back through the window.

Abby's ragged breathing filled the room as she broke out of Stone's arms and rushed forward. "Jerrod. Oh god, Jerrod."

He wrapped her up, holding her tight, breathing

in shampoo and soot from her filthy clothing as she clung to him, shaking, sobbing. "It's okay, Abby. It's okay. They're dead." He looked from Stone to Shane as he slid down the wall on weak legs, pulling her into his lap.

They nodded their confirmation.

"You found me," she muffled against his chest.

"I wasn't leaving without you." He murmured next to her ear and eased her back, needing to look at her, assessing her battered, tear-streaked face, kissing her forehead, her cheeks, her mouth, running trembling fingers over dark purple bruising. "It's over," he said as much to her as himself.

"You found me," she said again, kissing him, pulling herself close, wrapping her arms around his neck.

"Come on." He stood minutes later when he was certain his legs would hold him, picking her up, holding her tight, sure he might never let her go. "Let's get out of here."

She looked toward the window. "He's dead?"

He nodded, catching sight of Victor and Aleksey sprawled on the stairs and in the hall.

"I want to go home." She rested her head against his shoulder. "Let's go home, Jerrod."

He pressed his cheek to her hair. "Let's go."

Chapter Twenty-five

Abby checked her makeup in the mirror, scrutinizing her jaw and cheek, satisfied that the remains of her purplish-yellow bruising were well hidden. She touched the healing gash on her temple, examining the line of ugly scabs left from the butt of Dimitri's gun. Unfortunately there wasn't much she could do about that. Shrugging, she combed trembling fingers through the loose curls she'd twisted into the ends of her hair, trying her best to ignore the clutch of nerves sickening her stomach.

She glanced at the breakfast Jackson's mother brought up to the guestroom, shuddering at the idea of eating the homemade cinnamon roll—her and Lex's favorite, but not today. She didn't have an appetite for cinnamony dough and warm gooey glaze, no matter how sweet the gesture. Carol had attempted to feed her from the moment they walked through the Matthews' front door, but Abby's appetite had been on the fritz since they boarded the plane from LA three days ago, heading back to Maryland.

Thank God they were staying on Kent Island surrounded by the gorgeous Chesapeake Bay and warm, friendly extended family. Being here with Jackson's parents instead of in some sterile hotel had gone a long way to making her more at ease, but nothing could make today better. This was it. In less than two hours she would walk into Federal Court and face Lorenzo Cruz.

Jerrod knocked on the doorframe.

She gave his reflection a small smile. "Hey."

He smiled back, walking into the bedroom. "Ready to go?"

Turning, she faced him, letting loose a shuddering breath as she smoothed down her fitted white blouse and tailored above-the-knee navy blue skirt. "As I'll ever be."

He stopped in front of her, resting his hands on her hips, pulling her closer, locking his arms around her waist. "You're going to do great." He kissed her lips.

"I hope so." She adjusted his charcoal gray tie and fiddled with the collar of his button-down shirt. "There's so much on the line. I need to get this right for Margret. Today is for her."

"And for you." He tapped his finger to her nose.

"And me and the others, even Shelby, but mostly for Margret. She should be here." She looked down, still trying to cope with Margret's sacrifice.

"Hey." He lifted her chin, staring into her eyes. "She loved you too."

She nodded, overwhelmed by the guilt that had only compounded after Dimitri's gloating rant. "And paid for it."

"You would have done the same for her."

A tear fell down her cheek. "Yes, but—"

"He never planned to let her walk away alive, Abigail." He dried her cheek with his thumb.

Somewhere deep down she knew that. Jerrod had reminded her of the fact several times over the last week and a half, but her sorrow was no less. "I promised to save her. I didn't." She took a deep breath. "This—today—is the only way I can make that even a little bit right.

He pressed a firm kiss to her forehead and hugged her tight. "I'm sorry, Abby."

She held on. "Me too."

"Shane and Stone are ready whenever we are."

"Just one more second." She closed her eyes, resting her cheek against his chest, savoring the comfort of being in his arms. "Okay." She stepped back, bolstered by the embrace. "I'm ready."

"I'll be right there with you." He took her hand, giving a gentle squeeze. "Right in the front seat of that courtroom. You don't have to look at him while you testify."

"Yes, I do." This was her chance to finally put this chapter of her life away. "I'm going to look him right in the eyes while I twist the lock on his cell door."

He smiled. "Have I mentioned how much I love you?"

He'd told her at least a dozen times a day while they were home in California. The feds as well as Ethan and Jackson had assured them both that risks were minimal now that all of the major known players in the ring were dead or behind bars, but neither she nor Jerrod had let the other out of their sight since he carried her out of the warehouse. "I think I remember you saying that."

"Let's go toss away that key."

She nodded. "The sooner the better." Despite the flutters of apprehension for the day ahead, she was craving the small slice of normal she'd sampled while they stayed at the farm. Eventually she and Jerrod would be comfortable with her being out on her own. Finally they would have their chance to move on. "Wait." She pulled on his hand.

"What?"

She cupped his face in her hands, pressing her lips

to his, then the healing wounds on his temple, taking the comfort he was always willing to give and giving her fare share in return. Her testimony wouldn't be easy on either of them. "I love you too."

"Quinn." Shane stopped in the doorway, decked out in a dark suit and tie similar to Jerrod's. "We should go."

"We're ready." He took her hand, holding it while they walked downstairs to the kitchen.

"There you are, honey." Carol stood in her jeans and sweater, pulling Abby into a hug.

Abby returned her warm embrace. "Here I am." Jackson's mother—Mom to everyone who knew her—had always been so kind. She'd loved coming to the island when Lex and Jackson brought her during their college breaks all those years ago. The house was as beautiful and soothing as Carol and George Matthews were themselves.

"Did you have any luck with your breakfast?"

Abby eased away, shaking her head guiltily. "I'm sorry, Mom. I'm just not hungry."

"Of course you're not, sweetheart," she cooed as she pressed a kiss to Abby's injured cheek and stepped back to grab the small thermos and paper sack. "Here's some honeyed tea and a few graham crackers for the road. I want you to nibble and sip. A little bit of sweet will help settle your stomach."

Abby took the items handed to her. "Thank you."

"Promise you'll try."

"I will."

"Today will be difficult, but you'll do just fine. You're my spitfire, Abby Harris. You remember that."

"I will."

"All right. Go on now, and kick some butt the way I know you can."

Abby smiled, loving Carol even more.

Carol hugged her again quickly. "George and Stone are waiting in the garage. Here you go, Jerrod." She handed over another bag. "Rolls and lots of napkins for you boys for the ride."

He smiled. "Thanks, Car—Mom."

She winked. "You're welcome."

Shane opened the door leading to the garage. Abby walked out to the Escalade with Jerrod at her side, sliding into the backseat next to Stone. Shane took the passenger's seat while George pulled out of the garage—her team for the last three days, minus George—men she and Jerrod both trusted, men Jerrod would be working with on a regular basis now that her security would lessen and Shane would join Ethan Cooke Security.

She pulled her sunglasses from her purse, putting them on as the mid-morning sun shone bright, glistening on the choppy waters of the bay too brackish to freeze in the cool February temperatures.

"Looks like a good day to get this done," Jerrod said, squeezing her hand.

She smiled and opened the bag Carol had given her, nibbling at the cracker as she'd promised she would.

The SUV remained quiet while they drove over the Bay Bridge and several more miles to the United States District Courthouse in Baltimore. Abby leaned against Jerrod, staring out at the city she called home during her not-so-long-ago college days. It felt like years since she'd been carefree and on her own, but really it had only been months. The Escalade passed the fabric store she'd practically lived in and the café she'd stopped at regularly for tea, then she spotted the restaurant she and Renzo had eaten at on more than one occasion and sat up, looking away, understanding that she could never live here again.

Los Angeles was where she wanted to be. Jerrod would be there with her, and Alexa and her career. Despite the complications of the past several weeks, the *Escape* line was still ready to roll. She and Lily had gone over the designs she'd drawn while in Manhattan, picking and choosing what they would use for Fashion Week, tirelessly sewing, fitting, and resewing into the wee hours of the morning for much of the eight days she and Jerrod had been home. There was too much to look forward to to dwell on the now. Today would officially mark the first day of her new beginning.

She came to attention, swallowing as George slowed and pulled up to the curb by the courthouse. Dozens of reporters waited with their microphones and news cameras.

"Great," she murmured, remembering the similar swarms as she and Jerrod made their jaunt through Regan International back in July.

"Just look down and walk," Jerrod said. "We'll take care of the rest."

Stone got out first, wasting little time, then Shane, who opened Jerrod's door. Jerrod stepped out, giving her a nod to come forward as Shane stepped closer in front of her. Jerrod wrapped an arm around her waist and Stone flanked them from the back, touching a quick hand to both their shoulders, signaling for them to move through the pandemonium as the press swooped in.

"Ms. Harris, is this the first time you've seen your kidnapper since your rescue?"

"What do you plan to say to the man who held you captive?"

"Back up," Shane said as they pushed their way up the steps into the courthouse, leaving the reporters and their questions behind.

"Whew," Abby said, loosening her death grip around Jerrod's waist as she pulled off her sunglasses, trying to relax her shoulders.

"How are you holding up?" Jerrod asked.

"I'm okay." But, as she stepped through the metal detector and the inevitable drew near, she worried what her reaction to Renzo would be.

"Come on." He took her hand as they started up the stairs.

Her heart began to hammer, and the cold sweat started with each step closer to the courtroom and her captor. "Jerrod." She jerked on his hand as they reached the second floor and moved into the small room where they would wait for her to be called.

He stopped. "I'm right here with you."

"I know." She stepped closer to him, leaning against his solid body. "What if—what if I can't do this?" she asked on a trembling whisper. "What if we've come all this way and I can't?"

He slid a lock of hair behind her ear. "I have no doubt that you *can*. You're tossing away those keys, remember?"

And that's what she needed to remember. If she didn't do this, Lorenzo might go free. *I just want to go home, Abby.* She couldn't let down Margret, herself, or the hundreds of others deserving justice. Licking her dry lips, she nodded. "I remember."

Someone knocked on the door to the small room.

Stone stepped forward, his hand on his weapon, opening an inch. "Yeah."

"We're ready for Ms. Harris."

"Thank you."

She held Jerrod's gaze as her hands grew clammy. "God. Okay. God," she repeated, smoothing down her skirt as her pulse throbbed in her throat. "I need to go. Right now. I need to do this while I can."

"Let's go." Jerrod walked out by her side, with Stone following. Shane stayed behind, keeping an eye on who entered the room after them. They made their way through the next door, and Lorenzo turned in his chair at the defense's table, his eyes locking with hers.

She paused mid-step, burying her repulsion, studying him as he did the same with a smirk on his face. He seemed different. His smooth good looks had turned chubby. He appeared older, as if his time locked away had been a strain. Good.

She moved further into the room as Blondie stepped down from the stand to the bailiff waiting with handcuffs, ready to lead her away. She too looked awful in her ill-fitting skirt and gray roots showing. She glanced Abby's way, glared, and looked away. Blondie would get out of prison eventually with her last-minute plea bargain, but she would spend the next fifteen to twenty in the penitentiary, which wasn't long enough.

She glanced up, meeting Renzo's stare for the second time. Even with the distance between them and his not-so-fit appearance, he evoked a primal fear that made her want to run.

"Abigail," Jerrod whispered next to her ear.

She turned her head, looking into Jerrod's calm, steady eyes.

"He can't hurt you anymore. Never again."

She nodded.

"The prosecution calls Abigail Harris to the stand."

She swallowed as her crackers threatened to make

a second appearance and focused on the silent support of Jerrod's squeeze against her fingers, ready to do what needed to be done.

Prosecutor Bitner gave her a nod as she walked to the stand.

"Place your hand on the Bible," the bailiff said.

She did as she was told, glancing at Jerrod.

"Do you swear to tell the truth, the whole truth, and nothing but the truth, so help you God?"

She looked into Renzo's eyes. "Yes I do."

~~~~

"What happened next, Ms. Harris?" Prosecutor Bitner asked.

"He threw me to the bed."

Jerrod fisted his hands at his side as Abby's voice trembled. She'd been to hell and back over the last two and a half hours, answering question after question, reliving her worst moments in the stash house and strip clubs for dozens of strangers packed into the courtroom to hear. She'd shared—in minute detail—the horrors of her 'bookkeeping' requirements, strip routines in seedy bars, and lap dances in filthy backrooms, holding herself together through it all.

Over the months they'd lived together, he thought Abby had confided the majority of her ordeal, but as he sat on the uncomfortable wooden bench, listening, waiting for the grilling to end, he realized there was so much more to her horrible story. The fact that she woke everyday determined to not only function but thrive was a testament to her admirable inner strength.

He reached up to rub at the back of his aching
~~~~

neck, stopping as she looked in his direction. The last thing she needed was to sense his tension; right now she needed his strength. He gave her a barely perceptible nod, and she continued with her explanation for the jury. His gaze traveled to the bastard sitting smugly in the defendant's chair. Even though bailiffs stood within arm's reach and Stone sat inches behind Lorenzo on the opposite bench, the slime bag was still too close to Abby. The fucker deserved to rot in his cell for the rest of his life. After Abby's testimony, he would. She was kicking ass.

Taking a deep breath, he exhaled slowly, ready for all of this to be over. He and Abby were officially in the clear now that the Task Force had closed their files on The Mid-Atlantic Sex Ring, deeming the organization dismantled with the key players dead or behind bars. Even Adam sat in a cell waiting for his day in court. Dimitri's computer had been chock full of information the feds used to raid dozens more brothels over the last several days.

Bringing Abby back to Maryland had been a necessary evil, but this would finally be the end. After this, he and Abby were free to move on. During their eight days in LA they'd given it their best try, settling back into their condo with his clothing and bathroom supplies making their way to her bedroom and bath instead of his. They'd both worked, him in his old room via e-mail and conference call and Abby in the dining area, frantically sewing and fitting her models, with Lily at her side. For the first time in almost seven months, he'd been able to leave her home alone or let her walk the streets on her own, but neither of them had been ready for that.

"Did Lorenzo Cruz then rape you, Ms. Harris?"

"Yes."

"Just to clarify, Ms. Harris, in no way was your sexual encounter consensual."

"Mr. Cruz strangled me while he forced me to open a condom. He then violated me while the fifteen-year old girl he'd just beaten sat huddled on the floor. Neither me nor Margret Stowers consented to being assaulted that day—physically or sexually."

"Mr. Cruz raped you, then went after Margret Stowers?"

"Objection." Lorenzo's Defense attorney stood. "This is hearsay."

Judge Marris adjusted her horn-rims resting on her nose as she looked at Abby. "I'll allow it."

"Your Honor," the defense attorney started in, "I—"

"Attorney Stronger, I'll allow it."

"Yes, Your Honor." He took his seat.

"I'll repeat the question," Prosecutor Bitner said. "Mr. Cruz then raped Ms. Stowers after raping you?"

Abby nodded. "Yes. Lorenzo beat her for a second time after he raped me, then he raped Margret."

"No further questions."

Defense Attorney Stronger stood, adjusting his black tie as he walked toward the witness stand. "Ms. Harris, how many times did you say you were sexually assaulted while at the DC residence?"

"You mean *brothel*? I was held against my will in a stash house, Attorney Stronger. I was raped once."

"Once?" Attorney stronger raised his brows as he looked at the jury then back at Abby.

"Yes."

"I'm confused then, Ms. Harris. In your statement you shared that other victims were raped continuously."

"Yes. That's right—daily, hourly."

"Were you attracted to Mr. Cruz?"

She shook her head. "Lorenzo and I were friends—or I thought we were."

"Didn't you and Mr. Cruz have dinner on occasion?"

"Yes. We ate out a few times and met for coffee once or twice after fashion shows. As I said, I thought we were friends."

"Were you in charge of keeping track of the 'rapes'?

"Yes."

"And you were responsible for the rotation of each girl?"

"Unfortunately yes. I was forced to keep documentation of how many times young women were prostituted and how much money was made by the day, weeks, and months for all brothels in the Baltimore and DC area."

"Your Honor." Prosecutor Bitner stood, "where is this questioning going?"

"Attorney Stronger," Judge Marris said, "move this along."

"Your Honor, I'm trying to establish Ms. Harris's roll in The Mid-Atlantic Sex Ring."

"Proceed."

Attorney Stronger nodded. "Ms. Harris, you're a fashion designer, correct?"

"Yes."

"Didn't you make clothes to showcase the allegedly prostituted women for their clients?"

"By force."

"But you *did* make them outfits and then dole the girls out to paying customers."

"By force," she repeated.

"So isn't it safe to say that you prostituted these

'victims' as much as the accused man sitting here on trial, the man you had dinner with on several occasions, whom you claim was your friend? I'm wondering why you're not facing charges similar to my client's."

Murmurs filled the courtroom while Jerrod gritted his teeth, struggling to remain seated instead of rush forward and punch the shit out of the asshole for his implications as the prosecution stood to object.

"That'll be enough, Attorney Stronger," the judge warned. "Strike that from the record."

Abby looked at Jerrod, then the judge. "Your Honor, if I may, I'd like to respond."

Judge Marris looked from Lorenzo to Attorney Stronger, then at Abby. "Go ahead, Ms. Harris, but this will be off the record."

She nodded. "Could I please have a tissue and a glass of water?"

"Do you need a break, Ms. Harris?"

"No, Your Honor."

The bailiff brought over the requested items.

"Thank you." Abby dipped her tissue into the water and wiped at her battered cheek and jaw with an unsteady hand, exposing the purple and yellow mess she'd hidden with makeup. "Attorney Stronger, these are bruises I received a week and a half ago while I sat in a cold, rundown warehouse waiting to die at the hands of Mr. Cruz's colleagues.

"Their plan was to murder me before I could testify today. I was beaten and knocked unconscious with the handle of a gun, but my injuries aren't nearly as bad as what many of the other young women faced on a daily basis. I did not *choose* what happened to me. I never asked for my *friend* to organize my abduction. I did not ask to be shoved into the back of a van. I never once gave off some sort of signal that suggested I wanted to be raped, intimidated, and abused, nor did the other survivors. When everywhere you turn there's a man blocking the door to freedom, reminding you you're not allowed to leave, there are no choices. So no, Attorney Stronger, I did not prostitute the young women held against their will, but your client certainly did."

Silence filled the courtroom as several jurors wiped at their eyes. Abby swallowed, fighting back tears.

"No further questions," Attorney Stronger muttered as he took his seat.

"You may step down, Ms. Harris," the judge said.

Abby stood and walked from the stand, moving toward the door as Jerrod followed her into the hall.

"Abigail."

She dashed to the women's room down the hall.

"Abby." Jerrod picked up his pace, pushing his way into the bathroom, caring little that he didn't belong. He steamed out a breath as Abby vomited into the sink, trembling, tears tracking down her cheeks as she gripped the counter, heaving.

He pulled paper towels from the holder and ran them under cold water in the next sink over, damning Lorenzo Cruz and his attorney to hell.

She rinsed her mouth and stood up straight, pale and sweaty, holding his gaze with devastated eyes.

"Here," he said gently, wiping at her forehead with the damp towel.

"Thanks," she choked out.

"Damn, Abby. Come here." He pulled her into his arms, aching for her. "Come here," he repeated, pressing her cheek to his chest, holding on as her shoulders shook with her quiet sobbing.

"I can't do this anymore. I can't go back in there."

"You don't have to." He ran a hand through her hair. "It's all over. You more than threw away that key."

"I don't want to be here anymore."

He drew her away, staring into her eyes. "So let's go."

"I need to see Margret."

He opened his mouth to object. She'd had more than enough, but he nodded anyway.

"I need to say goodbye." She sniffled.

She wouldn't have peace until she did. "We'll get some flowers."

"She liked daisies."

"We'll take the guys back to the island and find some daisies."

She took his hand, kissing his knuckles. "Thank you."

He winked. "You're welcome."

"I love you."

"I love you too. Let's go say goodbye."

She nodded, wiping her cheeks.

~~~~

Abby kept her speed to a crawl as she drove Carol's sedan along the scarred roads of Severna Hills Cemetery, searching for the angel statue Agent Terron remembered from Margret's funeral two and a half weeks ago. She slowed further, spotting the tall, weathered landmark casting shadows over several plots in the distance. She hesitated, then stopped, gripping the steering wheel tighter as her gaze traveled over dull, leafless trees, gray headstones, and brown grass peeking through patches of snow.
~~~~

She glanced to the bright blue sky, waiting for the wash of peace she always felt when she brought flowers to Gran's gravesite in Hagerstown, but the warm sense of tranquility remained wretchedly absent. Today she was as sick at heart as she was to her stomach. "This is wrong," she murmured, frowning, hating that she was here among these sacred grounds.

Jerrod leaned in close, his chin brushing her hair as he looked out the driver's side window from the passenger's seat. "I think this is it. Terron said her plot's close to the praying angel."

She shook her head. "No, this entire situation. Look at this place. It's so...lifeless and horrible." She scoffed at herself, turning in her seat, rolling her eyes as they met his. "Of course it's lifeless. I mean Margret was so young. She shouldn't be here."

He slid his thumb along her jaw. "No she shouldn't."

She looked down at the pretty bouquet of friendly daisies Jerrod held in his lap. "I should've brought different flowers. I should've picked something with more color." She scoffed for the second time and closed her eyes, full well knowing she was focusing on the trivial instead of the overwhelming reality that this was a fifteen-year-old girl's final resting place.

"We can go get something different."

She shook her head, meeting his gaze, treasuring his patient understanding. "It doesn't matter. Pink flowers, red or purple won't bring her back. They won't make this any less awful."

"No," he said gently.

"I don't want—" She swallowed as her throat tightened with a choking ball of emotion. "I don't want to say goodbye."

He took her hand, pressing a long, firm kiss to her knuckles. "I wish you didn't have to. I wish I could change this." He kissed her again.

"Thank you." She blinked away her tears and glanced toward the gravestones, nibbling her lip, knowing she needed to get out and do what she'd come to do. "I need to find her." She took the bouquet of cheerful daisies from Jerrod and opened her door.

"Do you want me to come?"

The offer was tempting, but she shook her head, giving him a small smile. "I think I should do this myself."

"Sure. I'll be right here if you need me."

"I love you." She leaned over and kissed his cheek. "I love you so much, Jerrod."

"I love you too."

Bolstered by his unending support, she straightened her shoulders. "Okay. Here I go." She got out of the warm car, bracing herself against the cold as she clutched the flowers and started up the path, picking her way over the clumps of snow in her sneakers and jeans, looking for the black marble headstone Agent Terron said would be Margret's.

Veering off the concrete, she walked among the graves, moving closer to the angel, stopping when the pretty young face etched in stone caught her eye. Tears instantly flooded her cheeks and a keening moan escaped her throat as she crouched down, studying Margret's bright eyes and beautiful smile in the eternal picture. "Oh, Margret." She slid her finger down the image of the long brown hair she'd brushed and braided numerous times. "You smiled at me like that sometimes when we forgot, for just a second, that life outside my bedroom door wasn't what either of us wanted." She sniffled. "I'm glad we had each other.

You were my best friend during the worst time of my life."

The plastic protecting the flowers crinkled in the wind, and she looked down, setting the bouquet among the dead blooms still piled high from the funeral.

"I brought you daisies. I remember you said they're your favorite. I—" Her voice broke. "I'm so sorry, Margret. I'm so sorry I didn't save you." She sucked in several deep breaths. "I looked for you. We tried *so* hard to find you every single day." She took the tissue from her pocket, blew her nose, and shoved it back. "This should've ended differently. You should be here going out on dates and enjoying high school. You and your mom should be getting ready to be my guests at Fashion Week." She sniffled again. "I made your blue dress, the one you were going to wear when you came to visit. I'm going to show it off myself when I walk the runway in a couple weeks. Hundreds of people will see your dress, and you and I will know it's just for you." She pressed her lips firm as they trembled. "I know it's not enough—not even close. I know what you did for me, and I'm so grateful."

The car door slammed in the silence. Abby looked toward the road as Jerrod got out and leaned against the hood in his knit cap and jeans, his hands shoved in his pockets. "I met someone, Margret." She smiled his way, despite the deep ache. "He's amazing—the one bright spot in all the bad. He's so patient and kind." She looked back at the grave, knowing it was time to go. "I—I have to say goodbye, my sweet, beautiful Margret." She kissed her fingers and pressed them to Margret's cheek. "I'll never forget you. You'll always be a part of my heart. I love you."

Standing, she looked at the pretty girl one last

time and turned, walking toward Jerrod, meeting him halfway down the path.

He opened his arms and she stepped into his embrace, holding on, resting her head against his chest as he ran his hand down her back.

"You okay?" he murmured.

"No." She drew back enough to look at him. "I'm sick and sad, and my heart hurts, but this was right. Coming here today, saying what I needed to say."

He nodded, sliding loose strands of hair behind her ear. "I got a call a couple minutes ago. Lorenzo's been found guilty."

She blinked at the sudden shock of news. "What?"

"You did it, Abigail." He cupped her face in his hands, smiling. "Lorenzo won't be stepping outside a penitentiary anytime soon."

"But that was so quick." She laughed incredulously. "He's really going to stay in prison?"

"Damn right. It's looking like life without parole. You more than threw away those keys. The jury deliberated for less than three hours."

She glanced over her shoulder, looking at the black marble. "I'm glad we found out while we're here. It feels right, sharing this with Margret."

"I thought so too."

The wind blew, sending her hair dancing, and Margret's laughter echoed on the gusty breeze. Smiling, Abby looked at Jerrod, staring into his steady blue eyes. "I'm ready. I'm ready to go home and live my life."

Kissing her lips, he took her hand, and they started toward the car. "I'm looking forward to sleeping in our own bed tonight."

“Me too.” She clasped their fingers, grinning, welcoming the first true feelings of peace she’d felt in almost seven months.

CHAPTER TWENTY-SIX

"CAN WE HAVE ANOTHER BITE, AUNTIE AB?"

Abby stood along the edge of the dance floor among dozens of other guests, pausing with the forkful of dark chocolate cake and buttercream frosting at her lips. She looked down at Livy and Kylee blinking up at her, smiling in their matching flower girl dresses and curls twisted into pretty blond hair. "I just gave you both a bite."

"It was small." Livy looked at Kylee, who nodded her agreement.

"Big girls need big bites," Kylee added, turning up the wattage on her grin.

Abby laughed, glancing toward Olivia and Kylee's empty plates at the head table, unable to resist. "I guess I can't argue with you there." She sampled the taste she still held on her fork, then slivered off more for her niece and her friend. "There. That's it, my adorable little scavengers." She tapped both of their noses as Wren and Tucker finished their first dance as husband and wife. "Now go dance yourselves silly."

The girls clasped hands and ran off laughing.

Chuckling, she turned her attention to the gorgeous bride and groom kissing for the crowd, quieting the latest round of forks tinkling against glass. Sighing, she smiled, happy for her friends. Wren glowed in her strapless, beaded A-line gown, looking very much like a princess with the jeweled clip nestled among the riot of shiny black curls trailing down her back. And Tucker had yet to stop grinning. He'd been smiling since Wren walked down the aisle with Patrick at her side.

She backed up a step, letting a couple pass as she cut herself another bite of cake, gasping as strong arms wrapped around her waist in her off-the-shoulder fitted black dress.

"Got any cake for me?" Jerrod said next to her ear.

Her heart settled and she smiled. "Maybe." She turned in his embrace, stood on her tiptoes, and planted a kiss on his lips.

He arched his brows. "Maybe?"

"Maybe," she repeated, biting her lip as she looked him up and down in his black suit and tie. "For a dance."

He gave her a pained look. "Aw, Abby."

She struggled not to laugh. "Have you had a piece yet?"

"No. I went to grab a slice and they were gone. Damn phone call," he muttered.

She scooped up a bite for herself, rolling her eyes on a quiet moan as flavors melded on her tongue. "It's *so* good. It kind of reminds me of that dessert we had at Lily's dinner party." She forked up more, brought it to his mouth, and as he opened brought it to her own. "Mmm. Did I mention this is delicious?" She grinned as he narrowed his eyes.

"Kylee and Olivia just had to smile and look cute."

She laughed. "Aw, you're cute too, big guy." She scooped up the last huge bite, waving it in front of his face. "But I want to dance. All this can be yours for one measly twirl around the floor." She batted her lashes.

"A slow dance."

"A slow dance," she agreed, bringing the luscious

piece to his lips.

He took the bite and groaned. "Good," he said over the mouthful, and swallowed.

"Yes it was." She set her plate down on the tray close by.

"I guess a deal's a deal." He took her hand, walking with her to the middle of the Campbell's massive ballroom, pulling her more truly against him.

She locked her hands behind his neck, staring in his eyes as they moved in a slow circle. "See? Not so bad."

He shook his head. "No, not so bad." He leaned down, pressing his forehead to hers. "I would've danced with you for nothing."

"I would've shared...eventually."

They smiled at each other.

"Are you having fun?" He asked as his thumbs slid along the waist of her dress.

"Definitely. This place is stunning." The sheer number of creamy calla lilies and candles decorating the elegant space still amazed her. The Campbell's Monterey estate was massive—very much a California-style castle. "This is the perfect evening for a wedding."

"It's really nice."

"And I love that all of our friends are here." She glanced around at Morgan and Hunter also on the dance floor, at Hailey sitting on Austin's lap while they both rested their hands on her belly. She spotted Sarah sipping water as she, Ethan, Jackson, and Alexa talked to their girls. "Sarah's pregnant. She told us this afternoon while Wren was getting ready."

He smiled. "I guess you were right."

"Of course." She winked then frowned as she noted the slight hint of worry in his eyes. "What's wrong?"

"Nothing."

There was definitely something bothering him. "Are you thinking about the business trip?"

He shrugged.

"It's only two days in Kentucky, big guy." She wrapped her arms tighter around him, wanting to put him at ease. "Then you'll meet me in New York, and we'll have some fun."

"I guess I'm not ready to leave you yet."

She kissed his cheek, wondering if she could possibly love him more. "We've been doing okay so far." For the last week and a half they'd given 'normal' their best shot. She'd gone to the Lily Brand offices on her own while he went to work at Ethan Cooke Security. For ten blessed days they'd lived as she'd yearned to for months—eating late-night dinners after he pulled duty or she came in after a meeting, snuggle sessions on the couch in front of the TV, sweaty bouts of sex in their bedroom or wherever else they wanted in their condo before falling deeply asleep without having to worry about who hunted her.

The transition hadn't been easy for either of them. For several days she hadn't been able to walk down the street without glancing over her shoulder or break her habit of constantly checking to see that her repaired watch actually worked.

And Jerrod had finally managed to cut back on his welfare calls and texts. As they rolled into their second week of spending their workdays apart, he'd managed to check in once an hour instead of every thirty minutes. "Besides, I always have this." She gestured to the timepiece still fitted with a transmitter on her wrist. "And I'll have Stone with me at night and on the flight." Both their gazes traveled to the dark, sexy man leaning against the wall in the corner, pulling a sip from his beer. "I'm sure he'll boggle my mind with all kinds of stimulating conversation."

Jerrod chuckled. "He's definitely a man of few words, but we'll both feel better knowing he's there."

"Yes we will." She studied his deep tan, dark brown chin-length hair, and broad shoulders, looking forward to spending time with the enigma that was Stone McCabe. Surely there was more to him than muscles, good looks, and one-word answers. Two evenings at home and an endless plane ride to New York would be just enough time to dissect the inner workings of her temporary bodyguard—maybe. "So, how's Shane liking Europe? That was him that called?"

"It was. He's got another month and he'll be back and ready to roll."

"I'm glad we'll be seeing more of him."

"I have a feeling Ethan will be shipping him off to the Appalachia Project."

"You'll have a full report for both of them by Wednesday."

"Yes, I will."

The song rolled into the next slow tune, and she hummed along quietly, then sang along. "Rumor has it there might be karaoke later. How about a duet?"

"Hell no."

She laughed, well aware that Jerrod wouldn't be picking up a microphone any time soon. "I'll wear you down eventually.

"I don't think so."

"You underestimate my power, Mr. Quinn." She stroked her fingers along the back of his neck. "Someday I'll get you to sing. We'll do show tunes right in our own kitchen."

He looked at her with such horror she tossed her

head back on a laugh. "God do I love you."

He grinned. "I love you too, but show tunes will never, *ever* happen." His cell phone rang, and he glanced down at the readout with a frown. "It's Timmy."

"Go ahead and answer."

He pulled the phone free. "Hello? Timmy?" He blocked his other ear with his hand and gestured toward the hallway. "Hold on."

She nodded, following him toward one of the numerous balconies where the music finally faded.

"Yeah, I can hear you. That's good. Great. I'm glad she's doing better." His eyes widened as they met Abby's. "What? Are you sure? Wow. I guess congratulations then. Yeah. Yeah. Definitely. Okay. Bye." He hung up and shook his head as he shoved his phone away.

"What? What is it?"

"Nothing, I guess."

It was something, and it was big. "Jerrod—"

"Shelby's coming home from the hospital today."

She smiled. Shelby certainly wasn't her favorite person, but it was good to hear she was going to be okay. "That's great."

"Yeah."

"What else?"

He blew out a breath. "They're moving in together—Timmy and Shelby. Today."

Her eyes popped as wide as his had. "*What*?"

He shook his head again. "Apparently things have been changing between them for awhile. Her brush with death gave them both the shove they needed to take the next step." He shrugged. "She decided she doesn't want to work in LA anymore. She wants to stay on at the paper in Parker and be with him."

"Huh," she said, still in the throes of disbelief. "Are you okay with that?"

"As long as Tim's happy. He *sounded* happy—thrilled, actually."

"Well congratulations, Timmy."

He grinned. "I guess so."

"Do you wanna take a walk?"

"Yeah, I think I do."

"Let's go." She took his hand, and they wandered outside, down the balcony steps to the seashell paths leading toward the cliffs outlined by tiki torches. She smiled, looking from the twinkling lights of Monterey up to the stars as the wind tossed her hair around her shoulders and the waves crashed far below. Jerrod hooked an arm around her waist as they kept their pace unhurried in the abnormally warm temperatures. "This is amazingly beautiful."

He grabbed his tie flying in the ceaseless breeze. "I definitely can't complain."

They stopped at the cliff's edge, still able to hear the music pouring from the doors and windows of the enormous house, melding with the crash of the Pacific as she wrapped her arms around his waist, easy and relaxed. "It's kind of like a tropical paradise."

"Mmm." He nodded his agreement.

"But even as wonderful as this is, I still love our condo more. I love that even though the next few weeks are going to be a little crazy, I still get to meet you on the nineteenth floor at the end of each day."

He kissed the top of her head. "There's no place I'd rather be."

She smiled. "I didn't know I could be this happy."

He moved so that they stood torso to torso and settled his arms around her waist, surprising her when he started moving with her in a dance. "I'm glad, because you make me happy too, Abby." He slid his hand through her hair, uselessly tucking loose strands behind her ear only for the wind to catch them again. "For a long time I wasn't sure I would ever find someone who makes me feel the way you do." He kissed her lips as her heart simply melted with his sweet words. "You've been through so much. I wish I could change that, but I can't be sorry that it brought me to you."

"Jerrod." Her eyes filled. He always told her he loved her, but he'd never shared this. "You're going to get me going."

He held her gaze, moving in again, kissing her slowly, tenderly as they continued to dance. He drew back, and she rested her head against his chest, at ease in a way she didn't know she could be. "I thought our night in New York was perfect, but this right here..."

He bent close to her ear and sang along with Taylor Swift and Ed Sheeran as they spoke of everything changing.

She stopped, looking up, staring into his gaze as he told her in his smooth baritone voice that her eyes looked like coming home.

"Jerrod," she whispered, resting her hand on his cheek as he continued and she smiled.

The song ended, and she heard nothing but the surf as she continued to hold his stare in the flames of a dozen torches. "All this time." She sniffled. "You can sing."

"I love you, Abby."

"I love you too. So much."

"I'm not much of a romantic. I don't have any fancy words. I just want you to be with me forever. Will you marry me?"

Tears tracked down her cheeks. How could he think he wasn't romantic? "Yes, I'll marry you."

"I don't have your ring with me."

"That's okay."

"I have it back at the condo. I've had it for a while. I bought it when I got your watch."

She blinked, hardly able to keep up. "You did?"

He nodded. "I didn't know we were going to end up here—not then at least, but I knew it was perfect for you, and I didn't want anyone else to have it."

Another tear fell. "Do you know how lucky I am to have you? You can't possibly understand how much I love you."

"I have a pretty good idea."

She pulled his mouth to hers for a long kiss and eased back, grinning. "I can't wait to tell Lex. And Lily's going to want to design my dress."

"Maybe someday after *Escape* gets established you and Lily could think about a maternity line."

She smiled again as he did. "I already have a few ideas in the back of my mind."

"Do you want to go back in and find your sister?"

"Mmm, not yet." She spotted the bench in the shadows down the seashell path. "I think I'd rather go sit over there and make out with my fiancé for a while."

He grinned. "I don't hate that idea."

"I didn't think you would." She tugged on his tie, leading the way. "Come on, big guy. I'm going to knock your socks off."

He took her hand and pulled her against his side. "I don't hate that idea either."

They laughed, staring in each other's eyes as they hurried to the bench.

ABOUT THE AUTHOR

Cate Beauman is the author of the best selling series, The Bodyguards of L.A. County. She currently lives in Tennessee with her husband, two boys, and their St. Bernards, Bear and Jack.

www.catebeauman.com
www.facebook.com/CateBeauman
www.goodreads.com/catebeauman
Follow Cate on Twitter: @CateBeauman

THE BODYGUARDS OF L.A. COUNTY

Morgan's Hunter
Book One: The story of Morgan and Hunter
ISBN: 978-0989569606

Falling For Sarah
Book Two: The story of Sarah and Ethan
ISBN: 978-0989569613

Hailey's Truth

Book Three: The story of Hailey and Austin

ISBN: 978-0989569620

Forever Alexa

Book Four: The story of Alexa and Jackson

ISBN: 978-0989569637

Waiting For Wren

Book Five: The story of Wren and Tucker

ISBN: 978-0989569644

Justice For Abby

Book Six: The story of Abby and Jared

ISBN: 978-0989569651

Coming Fall of 2014

Saving Sophie

Book Seven: The story of Sophie and Stone

ISBN: 978-0989569668

31543625R00263

Made in the USA
Lexington, KY
15 April 2014